The Forgotten Midwife

ALSO BY LAURA ANTHONY

The Women on Platform Two

The Forgotten Midwife

LAURA ANTHONY

GALLERY BOOKS

New York Amsterdam/Antwerp London
Toronto Sydney/Melbourne New Delhi

Gallery Books
An Imprint of Simon & Schuster, LLC
1230 Avenue of the Americas
New York, NY 10020

First Gallery Books hardcover edition May 2026

GALLERY BOOKS and colophon are registered trademarks of Simon & Schuster, LLC

INTERIOR DESIGN BY KARLA SCHWEER

Manufactured in the United States of America

3 5 7 9 10 8 6 4 2

Library of Congress Control Number: 2026932119

ISBN 978-1-6680-4741-5
ISBN 978-1-6682-4193-6 (Int/Can Exp)
ISBN 978-1-6680-4743-9 (ebook)

To Sophie, my precious girl—
with all my love, Mam x

One for sorrow,
Two for joy,
Three for a girl,
Four for a boy,
Five for sorrow,
Six for gold,
Seven for a secret never to be told.

1

NOW

New York City

Riley

Manhattan is sweltering. It's one of those painfully hot summer days when the subway smells of old metal, perspiration, and a communal desperation to step aboveground. The train doors open and I am spat out on the platform with all the other sticky bodies.

Life on the pavement isn't much fresher. The air is heavy and exhaust fumes fill my lungs. The scent of cooking meat and spices wafts from a halal cart. I check my watch: 8:54 a.m. I can never understand how anyone stomachs meat in the morning, but still, someone is in line. I walk on, speeding up my pace. I need to be at the bridal store by nine, and I still have a few blocks to go. I try not to let the slow-walking tourists irritate me. I zigzag around them. A construction worker wolf whistles, and I pull a face. His friends laugh and pat his back, and my cheeks sting as I blush. And yet, as I turn onto West Twentieth Street, I can't imagine a single place in the world I would rather be.

My future mother-in-law, Janelle, and her eldest daughter, Misty, come into view, waiting outside the store. Janelle raises her arm above her head and waves. I run the last few yards.

"I'm late," I announce, bending in the middle to catch my breath.

"You're the bride. You're allowed to be late," Misty says. She's dressed casually, wearing a black leather jacket and jeans despite the heat. "And it's only five minutes, Riley. Don't sweat it."

"I'm sorry," I add, catching Janelle's eye. Her clothes are more appropriate for the weather: a flowy floral dress that buttons from her chest to her ankles, but she is nonetheless just as fashionable as her daughter. I straighten up and tuck my oversize T-shirt into my linen shorts, feeling self-conscious.

Janelle winks. "Even Jesus is late sometimes, honey."

I take in the exterior of the exclusive store. It's larger than I expected. And no doubt expensive. Ivory canopies perch above bay windows, like summer umbrellas shielding the mannequins inside from the sun. It's even swankier in real life than on Instagram and Google.

"Ready?" Janelle asks, flicking her long salt-and-pepper dreads over her shoulder. "You'll love this place."

I nod, trusting her more than I ever trust Google. She presses the buzzer on the intercom, leans forward until her lips are inches away from the small box, and says, "Hi. We're your nine a.m. The Jeffersons."

"Welcome," a muffled voice replies.

There's a buzz and a click.

Janelle smiles over her shoulder at me before she pushes on the glass door and opens it. Misty's hand reaches back for mine and I hold on tight.

"You're not going to make me wear anything floral, are you?" she whispers as we step inside.

We're transported to a world made almost entirely of white—the walls, the carpet, the furniture, and the staff. Three women with blonde hair of various lengths and tailored white pantsuits await us.

"Or blue," Misty adds, scrunching her nose. "I hate blue."

"No blue."

The eldest sales assistant glides toward us, and I'm relieved when she begins chatting to Janelle first.

"Actually, I don't love red either," Misty continues to me. "Or green. No one wants to look like a St. Paddy's Day ornament."

"Got it," I say. "No blue, red, or St. Paddy's Day memorabilia bridesmaids. Tell you what, how about you choose?"

Misty's eyes sparkle. "Okay. Great. Cool. Thanks."

She tilts her head toward a rail of dresses suffocating in plastic nearby.

"Don't let her bully you," Janelle says, breaking off her conversation with the sales assistant to shake her head at her daughter. "Misty, it's Riley and Samuel Junior's wedding. Not yours. Remember."

Misty tuts. "I know, I know. Jeez. Can't a girl get excited about a wedding?"

We're all excited. It's as if the air is made of glitter and happiness in here.

"Ugh, just wait until you're a Jefferson, Riley. Then you'll see how bossy Mom really is." Misty points an accusatory finger at her mother but can't keep a straight face.

Janelle smiles, taking the teasing in her stride. "Oh, hell yes," she says. "I *am* the boss."

Misty's face glows when Janelle winks at her. My happiness falters for a moment as I envy their mother-daughter relationship. Their teasing and jabbing and unbreakable bond. I wonder what it's like to be a grown woman with a loving mother ever present in your life. I lost my mom when I was twelve. My parents went out to dinner one night and never came home. A drunk driver. My grammy took care of me after that. She filled me to the brim with love as best she could, and I love her just as much in return. But sometimes, just for a fleeting moment, like right now, I wish my mom were still here.

"You all right, honey?" Janelle asks.

I glance at my soon-to-be mother-in-law as her dark chocolate eyes search my face. My lips part but no sound comes out. And when my eyes glisten, I feel foolish.

Without another word, she slides her arm around my waist and pulls me close, tucking my hip against hers as she kisses the top of my head.

"It's okay," she whispers. "Weddings bring out all the feelings. Gosh, when I married my Samuel, ooh-wee, did I cry like a baby. And not just because we had to live with his momma for the first six months, Lord rest her soul."

I smile. Sam and I have our own place in Hoboken, but I wouldn't mind living with the Jeffersons for a little while.

"Happy tears only," Misty says, beckoning to a younger sales assistant. "Here, this should help."

The girl is carrying a silver tray carefully with both hands. Three very full glasses of fizzing champagne wobble on top. Misty passes each of us a glass, and we raise our arms and clink.

"To family," she says.

"To family," Janelle and I echo.

Misty places her glass to her lips, but she pauses before she drinks to add, "And remember, family don't make each other wear horrible dresses."

"My gosh, girl, do you ever hush up?" Janelle says, smirking.

We all laugh, but my heart isn't quite in it as I start to think about the remainder of my day, and where I'm headed to next.

2

New Jersey

Riley

Loving Care Nursing Home always looks better on a sunny day, as if the warm rays shining down bring a brightness out in the otherwise tired redbrick walls. The potted flowers around the entrance stand a little straighter and more vibrant, and the sound of laughter carries around the grounds as children visit grandparents. The downside to summer visiting is a crowded parking lot. I circle three times before I find a spot. Parked up, I take some grocery store flowers and a box of chocolate from the back seat and walk inside.

I'm delighted to find Dustin, Grammy's favorite security guard, at the door.

"Well, hello, Miss Riley," he says, in the same gentle way he greets the children. "I wasn't expecting you until tomorrow."

"I know," I say. "But today was a big day. I want to tell Grammy all about it."

A brief sadness flashes across his face before he catches it, smiles, and says, "Ah, that's nice."

Dustin has seen me every Sunday for years. I was seventeen when Grammy's dementia became too difficult to manage at home and she moved here for support. It's only in the past two years that she has forgotten who Dustin is. And who I am.

"Are they for me?" he jokes, gesturing at the chocolates tucked under my arm as I sign in.

"You know she'll save you one."

"The one with the nut." He nods. "She always saves me the one with the nut."

I pull my shoulders toward my ears. "That's because she doesn't like nuts."

Dustin chuckles. "I like to pretend it's because she remembers. And not because hazelnuts are disgusting."

"I like hazelnuts, actually."

"Not me. They give me gas."

He rubs his stomach, and I laugh. Dustin has eaten Grammy's hazelnut delight for sixteen years.

"Go on through," he says, flicking his eyes to my signature in the visitors' book. "She'll be delighted to see you."

I wish so badly that that were true. Nonetheless, I'll be delighted to see her. I always am.

I walk through the double doors behind reception, and the familiar smells of antibacterial cleaner and overcooked mashed potato fill the waiting corridor.

Noticing me, Lucinda, the cleaner, stomps her foot on the vacuum to pause it. "Hey, Riley."

"How's Mr. Pickles?" I ask.

"Vet said he'll be as good as new in a week or so."

"So great to hear."

"Give your grammy a hug from me," she says, smiling as the machine rumbles to life once more.

"See you next week," I call out above the noise and walk on.

I'm disappointed when I bump into Dr. Green emerging from Grammy's room. Last time I was here, he'd just given her a sedative and she'd slept through my visit.

"Well, this is a nice surprise," he says. "Your grandma tells me she wasn't expecting you until tomorrow."

"Yes, I normally visit—" I cut myself off when I grasp the gravity of what he's telling me. "She said that? She actually knows what day it is?"

A confident grin tugs at his lips. "She'll be so happy to see you."

I place my hand on my chest and try to manage my expectations, but it's too late. I can feel my hope soar. I close my eyes. *Please. Please,* I think. *Just give me five minutes. Five minutes with Grammy remembering me.*

"Betty tells me congratulations are in order," Dr. Green goes on.

My heart is racing. I can't believe Grammy told him about the wedding. I tell her about Sam all the time—and sometimes he comes here with me—but I wasn't sure she ever really took any of it in.

Dr. Green lowers his voice to a whisper. "I hope you're keeping well. The first trimester is always the hardest."

"I'm not . . . er, I mean."

"Oh, I got the impression . . ." He flinches and rolls his shoulders back. "Betty said she wanted to talk about the baby because in nine months your life will change. I guess I put two and two together and got five. Please accept my apologies."

I shake my head, instantly downcast that Grammy isn't having such a good day after all. "I'm getting married in nine months. She's confused."

Dr. Green's brows knit. "I'm the confused one, Riley. Betty is lucid. I promise. For now, at least."

"Oh my God. Oh my God."

I turn toward the door, ready to race time.

"Hey," Dr. Green calls.

I whip my attention back to him, almost dropping the flowers and chocolates in my haste.

"Just take it slow, huh? She's excited to see you, but it's a lot for her, you know? We don't want to spook her."

"No. No. Of course not. I'll be calm. I promise."

My heart is trying to beat out of my chest. I can't remember the last time I was this excited.

He tilts his head toward the door. "Well, go. Go on. Get in there."

3

Riley

Grammy is dressed. Someone has changed her out of her nightie and into a pale blue long-sleeved blouse and navy pants. She's sitting in an armchair with her back to me, facing out the window. But even from this angle, I can tell she's different. Straighter, content, present. *Grammy.*

I place the flowers and chocolates on the table at the end of her bed and tiptoe forward.

"Hi," I say, so gently that hardly any sound comes out. I clear my throat and try again. "Hi, Grammy. It's Riley."

I hear a shift in the seat but she doesn't turn around.

"Grammy," I try again, taking a tentative step.

"Riley?"

The sound of my name passing her lips turns my tiptoeing to racing. I'm on my knees on the floor beside her in an instant.

"There you are, sweetheart," she says, in the singsong voice she's always used to soothe me.

Suddenly I'm a little girl again and my grandmother is the world.

"Grammy. Hi. Hey."

"Up, up, my flower," she says, cupping my chin in her hand as she encourages me to stand. "You'll get your lovely shorts all dirty down there."

I'm wobbly as I get to my feet and pull the nearby plastic chair over to sit as close to her as I can. I place both my hands on her arm—gently, overly aware of how fragile her frame is. She seems to shrink a little more every time I see her.

"Oh, Grammy. It is so, so good to see you." I choose my words carefully, as Dr. Green's advice rings in my ears. *Don't spook her.* "I brought your favorites." I turn my head over my shoulder and glance at the table behind us. "The tulips were half off in the grocery store 'cause they're a little droopy. So don't worry, I'm not wasting my money."

"Flowers." Grammy smiles. "Oh, how nice. I used to grow tulips in the garden."

"Yes. Yes. I remember." I'm so full of joy that for a moment I think I might burst. "Mom said you had green fingers. And I remember looking at your hands and being so disappointed when your fingers were white."

"How is your mom?" Grammy looks around, as if Mom might come through the door after me. "Is she coming in to visit?"

Grammy asks for Mom every time she's lucid. And each time my heart aches, but I manage to push out an "mm-hmm."

Her face lights up. "Tomorrow. Maybe she will come to see me tomorrow."

I shift in my chair. The plastic squeaks beneath me and the silly noise makes Grammy laugh, as if she's a schoolgirl. It's beyond wonderful to hear her laugh. I'd almost forgotten what it sounds like.

"Would you like some chocolate?" I ask, standing up, but before I'm fully upright, Grammy's hand reaches for me and I sit back down.

"What is it, sweetie? What's wrong?" she asks.

I put on a brave face. "Nothing, Grammy. Nothing at all. I'm just so happy to see you. And you know how much I love chocolate. I thought we could share."

She shakes her head. "But you don't look happy."

"I am, I really am," I protest too quickly. "Being here with you is making me so incredibly happy, honest it is."

Grammy eyes me skeptically as I suck my bottom lip between my teeth. She tuts and sighs. She can see through me as if I am made of glass. I am a terrible liar. When I was five years old and broke her favorite vase playing ball in the house, she wasn't disappointed about the shattered heirloom—she was disappointed because I blamed the cat. We didn't have a cat. But Grammy promised that if I told the truth we could get one.

"Everything is okay, Grammy. I promise," I try again, and this time there is truth in my words as I slide my phone out of my pocket. "I went to the bridal store this morning. Would you like to see some pictures? Maybe you could help me choose a favorite?"

Grammy cups her face with her hands. "Oh, Riley. When did you get so grown up?"

I open the photo gallery on my screen and she oohs and aahs over the pictures. We've flicked through several dresses when she taps the screen and says, "This one. Oh, this one is lovely."

She's chosen a silky, figure-hugging white dress with diamanté spaghetti straps. A lacy veil sweeps past my shoulders and bare arms all the way to the floor. I was indifferent toward this dress earlier, but suddenly I like it a whole lot more.

"You're going to be the most beautiful bride," she says, the rattle of age in her voice more pronounced than I remember. "You look just like your mom, you know."

I see the resemblance too. The veil frames my face and accentuates the high cheekbones my mom also had. Although my auburn hair is a shade or two darker than her strawberry blonde, it falls in loose waves down my back the way hers always did.

"I know you miss her," Grammy whispers, and I pull my eyes away from the screen to meet hers. "I know she's not coming to visit tomorrow. I remember now. I know my Stacey is gone."

When I was younger, I always loved how Grammy's blue eyes sparkled like the sea on a summer's day. But they're cloudy and duller now. Like the ocean after a storm. Sometimes I comfort myself that the only bright side to Grammy's illness is that she mostly forgets Mom is gone.

"You are excited, sweetie, aren't you? About the wedding?"

"I am. Of course I am."

"Then what is it? And please don't tell me that you are fine. I may be old, but I am not stupid."

"You really want to hear this?" I say, already feeling guilty that I am considering burdening her with my problems. But I am desperate to feel her scoop me into her arms and tell me it will be all right, as only the person who raised you can.

I lock my phone and set it aside. Then I take a deep breath. "I love Sam and his family. They're so kind to me. They have been since day one. But there are so many of them. Not just Sam's brothers and sisters. All his aunts and uncles and cousins and stuff. And they're always having family get-togethers. Thanksgiving. Christmas. Anniversaries. They just love each other so much."

"Isn't that nice," Grammy says, and I see her trying to imagine a crowded Thanksgiving table or a house full of guests raising a glass of champagne to ring in the new year.

Sam was surprised at first when he discovered it was just Grammy and me.

"No parents and no siblings. I save a fortune on Christmas gifts," I'd joked.

"Is it ever lonely?" he asked one evening over too much wine. He backpedaled quickly when he saw my face fall. "I mean, who needs five shaving gift sets anyway? I have a beard, guys, c'mon."

I wasn't lonely growing up. And I'm not lonely now. I loved my life with Grammy. I missed my parents, of course, but I was still a very happy child. I'm a happy adult. I have Sam. His huge family. A great bunch of friends—both his and mine. And I have Grammy. Even if she doesn't always remember me, I have my memories with her, and they are precious. But something about the wedding is making me feel emotions that I haven't felt in years. Not since my parents died.

"You wish you had family," Grammy says.

"I have you."

"Oh, Riley, you're a sweet girl. It's okay to want more. It won't hurt my feelings."

I sigh. I'm not so sure.

"I have you," I reiterate, desperate for her to hear me, desperate for her to know that she is enough for me.

"I wanted a family." Grammy licks her dry lips, and I hop up to pour her some water from the jug on the bedside table.

I help her hands—speckled with age spots, like cinnamon, from years of gardening in the sun—to cup the glass.

"Sorry. I think it might be a little warm," I say as we raise the glass to her lips together.

Grammy's squint tells me the water is definitely room temperature. I make a mental note to fetch some fresh water with ice before I leave.

"Anyway, where was I?" she asks, as I set the glass aside for her and sit back down. "Oh yes. Family. Your poppy loved me so much he used to say that he never needed anyone except me."

I'm warm inside as I fondly remember their romantic bond. I remember how his silver comb-over would lift in the wind and Grammy would slap her hand on it and say, "Derek, you're flappin' again!" I miss him. He passed away not long after my parents did. Grammy said it was a broken heart. I think so too.

"But as much as his love filled me up—and it did, Riley, just as Sam's love for you is wonderful—I always knew I needed more."

I suspect I've found the cause of Dr. Green's confusion. I think Grammy is going to tell me that I should have a baby.

"I needed your mom," she continues.

"Oh, Grammy. Sam and I want to take things slow. We only just bought a house. A fixer-upper, do you remember me telling you about it?"

I reach for my phone, ready to show her some photos of our rickety porch and kitchen that need replacing.

She places her hand over mine. "Riley, please. I must get this out."

I know she means to add, *before I run out of time*, and my heart pinches. I let my phone settle back onto my lap.

"Our Stacey. What joy she brought us." Grammy gulps, as if rewinding back over the years takes her breath away. "And then she had you. It was all just so perfect. And I don't regret a moment of it. Not a single moment."

Grammy's choice of phrase startles me, and I sit a fraction straighter with my head tilted to the side. I wonder if she's slipping away again—getting her words muddled. Surely regret is wrong in this context.

"Hmm," she says, observing me. "You're thinking I'm a doddery old fool."

"No," I gasp, a little too loudly for the compact space of the bedroom. "I love your stories. I just . . ." I trail off, not too sure what to say.

"You're wondering what I could possibly have to regret with a family I loved so dearly."

"Well, erm, yeah. I suppose I am."

"Could you do something for me?"

It suddenly feels oddly stuffy in here, and I want to open the window.

"There's something in the closet. Can you fetch it, please?"

Grammy is wearing white Crocs instead of her usual fluffy green slippers. It's too warm for a blanket or jacket, even if she hopes to go outside.

Stumped, I ask, "What is it, Grammy? What can I get for you?"

"The brown shoebox, please. The one that says 'Dr. Martens' on the side."

I have never seen my grandmother in any shoe other than a smart patent strap over a sensible block heel. A smile bursts across my face at the idea of her in trendy boots.

I stand up, drop my phone onto the seat, and open the closet. The bare space inside catches my breath. It's not the first time I've slid back the pine doors and peeked inside Grammy's closet, but each time, the lack of personal items hurts my heart no less. There are a couple of coats. One for rain and one for the cold. Both purple, her favorite color, and mine too, because it's bright like her. There's a pair of patent shoes that I haven't seen her wear in more than a year, and some blouses and pants that are wasted, as she spends most of her days in bed. And that's it. When Grammy first came to Loving Care, she brought plenty of her home comforts with her: framed photos of my parents and Poppy, her record player with the slightly wonky needle that you had to fiddle with just right so it didn't scrape the records, vases for flowers that she would pick from the grounds outside. But over the years, the doctors asked me to take more and more of her things away. She cut her wrist on a broken picture frame and it needed a stitch. She pricked her finger with the turntable needle. The flowers withered and died and started to smell. Dementia has stripped away so much of who Grammy once was that something as simple as helping her slip on a pair of old Dr. Martens fills me with joy.

I fetch the box. The dust on the lid makes me sneeze, and I brush it away with my sleeve. Then I return to her side and crouch on my haunches, ready to slip off her Crocs. She shakes her head.

"Don't you want to try them on?"

"Sit down, sweetheart. Open it."

There is an all-consuming sadness in her eyes. It makes me want to look away. The last time Grammy looked at me like this was when she told me about her diagnosis.

"Open it," she repeats anxiously.

I sit down in my chair and do as I'm told. I find shoes inside, but they are not the chunky black boots advertised on the side of the box. They are baby booties, dainty and small. Pale green and hand knitted or crocheted.

A wave of emotion crashes over me as I ask, "Were these my mom's?"

Grammy offers me a single nod. It's so subtle that if I blinked, I might have missed it.

"They're beautiful," I say, afraid to touch them, as if they might crumble to dust in my hands. "Did you knit these?"

"No." There's a wobble in her voice that stretches further than her age.

Dr. Green's words are in my head again. *Don't spook her.* I'm wearing her out. I panic slightly and reach for the lid, ready to put the booties away.

Grammy grips my hand and stops me. Her skin is clammy and I want to open the window more than ever, but I'm afraid to budge.

"They were your mother's, but I didn't make them." She sighs.

"Who did?"

"An Irish girl."

"I didn't know you knew anyone from Ireland."

My mind rewinds to the painting that hung behind the sofa in Grammy and Poppy's living room when I was growing up. A landscape painting. Green fields, green hills, and green trees. The vibrancy of the colors faded over the years, but I was always struck by the greenness of it. Poppy painted it in the sixties after a visit to Ireland.

"Hand-knitted stuff is pretty cool," I say, trying to imagine the artisan market where Poppy might have picked them up.

Grammy's eyes glisten and she is smiling, no doubt lost in a memory of a time when she and Poppy were young and in love. We are still and silent for a while until finally I ask, "Grammy, are you okay?"

There is no reply.

I touch her arm gently and she doesn't flinch. "Grammy," I whisper once more with a heavy heart.

Grammy sits like a statue. I hold my breath and listen for hers as I have become accustomed to doing over the years. When I hear her shallow intakes, the relief is instant.

"Oh, Grammy," I say, wishing hard that we had longer. "It was wonderful to see you."

I pick up the lid of the box once more and I'm about to pop it on top when I notice a piece of paper, or a letter, under the booties. I gently push the booties to one side and fish it out. It's folded into quarters, yellowed and distinctively old, but it's completely intact. No dog-eared corners or missing edges. I unfold it and read.

The first line is printed in a bold black font, but I can't make out a word of a language I don't recognize.

Deimhniú breithe arna h-éisiúint de bhun nahAchta um Chláru Breitheanna agus Básanna

I try rounding my mouth around the sounds, but it comes out as gibberish. Thankfully, there is an English translation printed below.

Birth certificate issued in pursuance of Births and Deaths Registration Acts

My eyes scan the remainder of the paper. Every line is printed in what I think might be the Irish language first, and a translation into English is provided directly below.

DATE AND PLACE OF BIRTH: *First August 1959. Thurles. Tipperary.*
NAME (IF ANY): *Mary-Kate O'Rourke*
SEX: *Female*
NAME AND SURNAME AND DWELLING PLACE OF FATHER: *Unknown*

NAME AND SURNAME AND MAIDEN NAME OF MOTHER: *Delia O'Rourke*

RANK OR PROFESSION OF FATHER: *Unknown*

I drop the paper and it falls onto the booties. The date of birth jumps out at me. My mom's birthday. I reread the words several times before the letters start to blur. I shift my attention back to Grammy. I kneel on the floor in front of her and place my hands on her knees, shaking them a little.

"Grammy," I say in a firm voice. "Grammy, come back."

I move my hands onto hers, shaking her more. I'm not quite as gentle as usual as I try to rouse her.

"Grammy, what does this mean? Please explain. Why do you have this? Are you trying to tell me Mom was adopted?"

Grammy's eyes peer straight ahead as if she's staring out the window. I wish she could see the birds flying in the clear sky or the little boy gliding a colorful kite with an old man. Simplicities like this brought her so much joy before.

"We'll never keep lies and secrets from each other, Riley, sure we won't?" she asked often as I grew up, while my cat, Oreo, circled her ankles and purred at her feet.

"Never," I replied, indignant, usually bending to stroke Oreo—our feline representative of truth telling. The furry mascot of our wholesome relationship built on honesty and openness.

Hiding a foreign birth certificate in an old shoebox for over sixty years seems like a pretty darn big secret, and I wish Oreo were still here to pet and hold. I wish I could rewind the years. I wish I were still a little girl playing in Grammy's house. I wish my biggest worry was a broken vase. Not a sickly grandmother. Not lost parents. Not an upcoming wedding without family. And now, a random birth certificate without any context.

"Grammy, you have to come back. You have to explain. Why did you give me this box? I don't understand. What are you trying to tell me?"

I'm startled by knocking. I look up to find Dr. Green standing in the gap of the door. I realize that my voice has become too big and too strong for the small bedroom.

"I'm sorry," I say, my face flushed and stinging.

Dr. Green's expression is full of sympathy.

"She slipped back," I add. "She's gone."

The doctor nods.

"That was shorter than last time. Last time we had time to go out in the garden," I tell him.

"Dementia is degenerative, Riley. She's done remarkably well to get this far."

I glare at him, not sure why I'm so full of anger. It's not his fault that my grandmother is slipping away from me, and has been for almost half my life.

"I know how hard this is," he continues, walking toward Grammy. "I wish there was more we could do. But we try our best to keep her well cared for."

"She needs fresh water," I blurt, placing the lid on the shoebox and tucking it under my arm. I leave before he can ask me about it.

"Bye-bye, Miss Riley," Dustin the security guard calls after me as I pass through reception and out the main doors with my head down. "See you next week."

4

Riley

The porch step creaks as soon as it feels the weight of my feet.

Inside, I can just about make out a hammer tapping above the loud bass of Sam's dance-hits playlist blaring from the kitchen. I find my fiancé on all fours, pulling up the worn-out tan linoleum that must have been there since the early eighties.

I place Grammy's Dr. Martens shoebox on the countertop and stare out the window that overlooks our tiny yard. The sky is still beautifully cloudless, and I hope Grammy is sitting in her bedroom armchair gazing up at it.

Sam jumps when he feels my hand on his shoulder.

"Sorry. Sorry," I say as he narrowly misses catching his finger with a blade.

He says something, but I don't hear him over the beat of the music. "Alexa, stop," I command firmly, and the music is gone.

"You're home," he says, smiling.

I try to smile back.

He places his tools down and gets to his feet. "Rough day?"

I nod. He sighs and slouches. I can tell he's tired. We moved in over a month ago, and we've spent every evening after work since DIYing.

"I'm sorry if Misty was annoying today." His face scrunches. "She can be a lot, I know."

"Misty is great."

"She is. She is. But Mom said she was pretty opinionated at the store. Dictating colors and stuff. She's just excited. She's never been a maid of honor before and—"

"And I love how excited she is. It makes *me* excited."

"Are you excited?" he asks cautiously, as if he's slightly afraid of the answer.

"Yes. Oh my God. Yes. Yes, I absolutely am."

"It's just . . ." He pauses and brushes the dust from his knees. "It's just Mom said you were very quiet earlier."

"Was I?"

He offers me a look that seems to repeat my question silently back to me.

"Look"—he steps closer and cups my shoulders with his hands—"I know we can be a lot. Too much sometimes. Jeffersons can be a lot to handle. I get that. And I know you're not used to a big, loud family and—"

"I love your family. I just wish I had one too, you know?"

"You do. You *are* family. Always have been, but it'll be official soon."

"I visited Grammy today," I blurt. "I just wanted to see her, you know, after trying on the dresses and all."

He nods and softly asks, "How did it go?"

"Good. Yeah. Good. She was lucid for a while."

"Oh, Riley, that's great. I'm so happy you had some quality time with her. How long has it been?" He pulls me into a hug, and I turn my head and press my cheek into his chest.

"Just before Christmas. She had that good afternoon when the carol singers were in."

"Oh yes. And she was embarrassed because she hadn't bought us gifts."

"Yes. Yes. Gosh. It's been eight months. She's here less and less." My voice cracks as I pull my head back to look up at him.

"Did you get a chance to talk to her about your dress?" he asks.

"I did. I showed her some photos."

A goofy grin ripples across his face, and I know what he's going to say next.

"Can I see?"

"No." I shoot him down quickly and giggle.

"Please. Just a quick peek. I can't wait. It's killing me to wait."

I break away from him to fold my arms. "You can so wait."

"Worth a shot," he says with a cheeky wink. We both laugh, but the respite is short-lived when he dips his head toward the countertop.

"New shoes?" he asks.

"Grammy's," I say.

His expression grows even more wide-eyed. I've no doubt he's imagining my elderly grandmother wearing black leather boots with yellow stitching, laced up around her ankles. "Cool. Go, Betty. Who'd have thought."

I lift the lid on the box, and he cranes his neck to peer inside from where he's standing. He jerks back when he spots the baby booties.

"Whoa! Riley. I thought we were going to wait a while. Until we have the house fixed up at least. These are sweet, but—"

"They're not for us."

The relief that washes over him would make me laugh on any other day.

"Who are they for?"

"That's just it. I don't know. Before I could ask Grammy about them . . ."

"She was gone again," he finishes.

I puff out, making myself lightheaded. "She said some Irish girl hand-knitted them. Years ago. Like in the fifties."

Sam's brow furrows with confusion.

"There's more."

I reach inside the box and pull out the birth certificate. It's slightly crumpled now, and I'm annoyed with myself for not taking better care of it. I'm overly careful with it as I unfold it and pass it to him.

I watch him try to make out the Irish words first. "What is this?" He reads on, finding the English translation. "Who is Mary-Kate O'Rourke?"

"I don't know."

"Is this real?" He turns it front to back, and back again.

"I think so." I point to the official-looking stamp in the bottom corner.

Sam runs his finger over it. "It's embossed."

"I know. I noticed that too, so I googled it. Here, look . . ." I take my phone out of my pocket and share the screenshot of my image search.

He compares the handwritten paper in his hand with the image of a present-day official Irish birth certificate on my phone and shakes his head. "They're not the same."

"They probably stopped handwriting them years ago. But look." I edge my phone closer to him. "The stamp in the corner is still the same."

"You think it's legit?"

"Think so."

His eyes drop back to the yellowish paper. "The date would make her . . . eh . . . um." He squints as he does the math in his head.

"The same age as my mom," I say. "Like, the exact same age. August 1, 1959, was her date of birth."

Sam inhales. "Wait. Hang on. Was your mom adopted?"

"I dunno," I snap.

Sam doesn't react.

"Sorry. I'm sorry," I say quickly. "I just . . . I'm so confused, but I shouldn't be taking this out on you. I'm sorry."

"I'm exactly who you should be taking this out on. We're a team, aren't we?"

My frustration melts a little, and I am so grateful for this man.

A moment of silence passes before Sam says, "Do you think your mom knew?"

I shrug. "She never said anything."

"Wow, Riley," Sam says with a tentative smile. "This is exciting."

"Is it, though?"

His shoulders round. "Hey, c'mon. You know it is. There's a reason Betty gave this to you. This could mean you have family out there."

I puff out, overwhelmed. I've known since I was a child that both my parents were only children. No siblings means no aunts or uncles or cousins. It's just the way it is.

Sam takes my hand and kisses the back of it. He needs to shave, but somehow his prickly skin against mine grounds me and I let out a sigh, noticing I've been holding my breath.

"I think we really need to follow up on this," he says.

"How?" I say, and it comes out snappy as I pull my hand back. "It's not as if I can pop into Loving Care and be all like, 'Hey, Grammy, any chance you've been lying to me for my whole life and hiding a huge secret, quite literally in the closet?'"

He sighs. "No. And we don't know when we can ask her. Or even if."

His *if* stings. My fists start to throb and I realize I'm clenching them.

"You're freaked out. I get that," Sam says.

"I'm not," I snap again, louder this time.

He cocks his head in a way that asks, *Really?*

I'm not freaked out. I'm angry. Angry at Grammy for slipping back. Angry at Mom for dying and leaving me. Angry at them both because

I can't sit down with them and ask the questions swirling in my brain. Questions that just this morning I didn't have.

"Don't blame Betty," Sam whispers.

I stare at the ground, grappling with my racing thoughts.

"When was she supposed to tell you?" he goes on, keeping his voice soft. "You were just a kid when your mom died. And then you were grieving. By the time you were in your late teens, Betty was already in care."

Sam's words press on my shoulders like a weight as I'm reminded how hard things have been over the years. I look up. "Why do you think she's telling me now?"

"The wedding," he says with a confident nod. "You want family at our wedding. . . ." He trails off, and I can tell he's treading lightly, trying not to upset me.

I don't speak. I am confused, hurt, shocked, tired, and emotional. But more than that, I am curious. I am so curious it hurts. The need to know if I have unknown relatives out there sits in my belly like a knot.

Sam takes my hand. "Let's just see what we can find, eh?"

I glance at the birth certificate again. I doubt googling *Who the hell is Mary-Kate O'Rourke?* is going to help much, but I humor him with a smile. "Sure."

"We can call whatever government office deals with this sort of thing in Ireland on Monday and take it from there. We still have nine months until the wedding. Who knows, by then you might have found out you're actually fifty percent Irish."

"Top o' the morning to ya," I say whimsically.

Sam makes a face before letting himself laugh. "We'll figure this out, Riley. It's going to be great."

5

1956

Thurles, County Tipperary, Ireland

Margaret

Joseph's pale blue Morris Minor is pulled over at the side of the winding road. I'm pacing around it like a clucking hen. Every so often I stop to observe him crouched on his hunkers as he attempts to change the rear tire.

"This thing. This bloody thing," he grunts occasionally. "I can't see what I'm doing."

I glance overhead, searching for light, but the moon and stars are tucked away behind a blanket of cloud.

Joseph has his grandfather's pocket watch with him, but I don't ask him the time. I don't think about it. The town hall dance ended almost an hour ago. It's usually twenty minutes home down the back roads, with Joseph driving steady. But we must be an hour pulled over, easy, as we battle a flat. If I'm not home by eleven, my pa will hit the roof. There'll be no excuse good enough. I'm wondering if we should cut our losses and start walking when Joseph stands up, punches the air, and announces, "I got it."

"Oh, I could kiss you," I cheer.

"Please. Be my guest," he says, puckering.

I press my lips against his and, as always, the touch of him makes my belly fizz. He steps closer, pushing his chest against mine until he banishes the air between us. For a shameful moment I imagine his bare chest under his tartan shirt, a hand-me-down from his brother that looks ever so smart. I dare to imagine more—his body and mine united as one. My desire for him almost makes me burst.

"Oh, Joseph," I groan, reluctantly pulling my lips away from his. "Do you really think my pa will agree?"

"We're courting two years, Margaret. I'd say your ma and pa are expecting wedding bells."

"The cost of a wedding, though," I say, slightly panicked as I attempt to tot the maths in my head. "I've heard folks say weddings cost an arm and a leg."

"And with my new job, can't we well afford it?"

Joseph's upcoming job in Dublin is a dream. For us both. Soon, I'll be a railroad engineer's wife and he'll be a husband and father. Six children, I think. I'd like three girls and three boys, but I know we'll both be grateful for however the Lord blesses us.

"I'm going to take you to every dance in Dublin," he tells me, taking my hand and spinning me around. "We're going to dance until our feet hurt."

I dance some jig steps on the spot, and Joseph throws his head back and laughs.

"Every weekend," I say.

"Every single weekend. And musicals too. Not just town hall ones, not anymore, we'll visit the Gaiety and the Olympia. I've heard the seats are made of red velvet and they're as comfortable as any fine armchair."

I close my eyes and try to imagine the grandeur of the city center theaters. The wide stages, the lighting, the velvet seats and plush carpet. The excitement of it feels too good to be true, and I could pinch myself.

"We'll walk in the Phoenix Park every Sunday," Joseph continues, almost breathless with anticipation. "And we'll visit the beach in summer. You name it, Margaret, my love, we are going to do it."

"Margaret Maloney," I say, trying his surname on as if it's a hat or a cardigan, and I slip into it as comfortably as though it was tailor-made for me.

"Margaret Maloney," he echoes softly.

I'm desperate to kiss him more, and I can feel him share the ache, but we should be on our way. Pa's lecture will grow longer and louder with every extra minute we're late.

"C'mon, we best get you home quick smart," Joseph says, stroking my cheek before he pulls away and separates us completely.

We whizz along winding roads, and I'm holding my breath as Joseph steers into the driveway of my family's farmhouse. Pebblestones crunch under the car, telling tales of our arrival, and it's no surprise when Pa is waiting by the door.

He taps his watch, and I will the car to come to a stop faster. Pa's face is a storm cloud as Josephs walks me to the door, although I insist I'm not in need of it.

"What time do you call this?" Pa says, and I think the question is for Joseph and not me.

Darkness hangs under Pa's eyes like indigo half-moons, and I wish he didn't have to work so hard. He'll be up at dawn with the cattle, and here I am keeping him awake hours past his bedtime.

I hang my head as I say, "I'm sorry, Pa. It won't happen again."

"I'm sorry we're late," Joseph says, stepping forward to take the heat. I understand why he insisted on guiding me the couple of steps to the door now. "It's all my fault, Mr. Lannigan. A flat tire of all things. And what mind, I checked all four before I set out. I won't have Margaret late ever again. You have my honest word."

Pa looks at Joseph with bleary eyes as he blinks sleep away. "All right, son. See that you don't."

I take my cue to say good night and get myself off to bed, leaving Pa and Joseph making small talk on the doorstep as usual.

Upstairs, I find my older sister, Sheila, neatly tucked up in bed in the room we've shared all my life. Her eyes open as soon as she hears me tiptoe into the room.

"You're late."

"Flat tire."

She props herself up on her elbow and makes a face. "Ha. I'm not falling for that. I'd say you were caught up by that Joseph Maloney's romancing."

I kick off my shoes and bound toward Sheila's bed. I throw the covers back and dive in beside her. She squeals as my icy toes touch her warm legs. But she shuffles over and makes room for me to lie beside her, just as I used to when we were kids.

I reach under the bed for the tatty copy of *Little Women* that we keep hidden.

"You didn't read any without me, did you?" I ask.

Sheila rolls her eyes. "No. But I had a good mind to. What time do you call this to arrive home?"

I stifle a giggle. I wonder if Sheila realizes how very alike she and our pa are.

"We're on chapter forty-five," she whispers.

Sheila and I started reading a few weeks ago, devouring a chapter or two a night after prayers. Ma and Pa wouldn't approve, of course. Whose parents would? Jo March is not a good role model, I understand that. And yet, I admire her so much it almost hurts.

I finish up the chapter where Amy and Laurie marry, and my heart sinks. Jo loved Laurie and he loved her. And yet because of the times and circumstance, Laurie married her sister. I find myself frustrated with the story, relieved it's only fiction.

"I don't like her," I say, snapping the book shut with a force that sends a tiny puff of dust into the air. "I don't like that Amy March one bit."

Sheila shrugs. "That's just life, Margaret. We don't always get what we want."

I'm about to argue the complexities of fictional characters with my sister when a tapping on the window jolts me. I get to my feet and hurry to draw back the curtain, knowing whom to expect outside. Joseph comes into view, his arm raised to throw pebbles carefully up at the window. The clouds have parted somewhat, and moonlight allows me to take in his huge grin.

"He said yes," Joseph says, and I'm lip-reading more than hearing him, but it doesn't hinder how much my heart soars.

"Your pa gave his blessing. We're getting married."

My head is light, and for a moment the room is spinning.

"See, and you thought my pa didn't like you," I tell Joseph, although I suspect he can't hear my whispers.

He doesn't reply, but his outstretched arms and cheesy smile tell me to pack my bags. Dublin is waiting for Mr. and Mrs. Maloney. I blow him a kiss and he reluctantly waves goodbye. I turn around to find Sheila on her knees on her bed, her arms raised above her head. She's waving them about as if she's cheering for Tipperary in the all-Ireland hurling final.

"Oh, Margaret," she says, and I find myself placing my finger against my lips so her excitement for me doesn't wake the whole house.

We share her single bed tonight, but we're too busy whispering and giggling to get much sleep as we take turns saying *Margaret Maloney* over and over and finding them the two most wonderful words in the world.

6

Margaret

Sheila wakes up feeling poorly the following week. She is hot and sticky, and Ma sends me cycling into town to fetch milk. Ma takes a thistle from the garden and boils it with the milk and a little sugar.

"That'll have your throat good as new in no time," she says, but Sheila struggles to drink it down. My three younger brothers play hurling in the garden, and Ma opens the kitchen window and shouts at them every so often.

"Pipe down, lads," she says, wagging a finger at them. "Our Sheila has a headache."

Sheila sits in the fireside chair in the sitting room. It's usually Pa's spot for reading the paper, but he's given it up today so Sheila can be near the fire that Ma has lit even in summer just for her. I fetch some blankets from the trunk at the end of my bed and drape them over her knees.

The milk and blankets do little to help, and Sheila is worse still by evening.

"I'm so cold," she says with chattering teeth, but the arch of perspiration dotted around her forehead and temples contradicts her. No sooner has she wiped it away than it returns. Ma says she needs to take to the bed for a day or two, but Pa says she can't miss Sunday Mass.

Sure enough, the following morning, Sheila is first up and dressed. It's three miles to the church and the boys race ahead, full of youth and lack of cares. Ma and Pa walk hand in hand as Sheila falls behind. I slow up and walk with her.

Pa is in his usual spot just inside the church door when we arrive. A foldaway timber table is in place in front of him, and a rectangular ledger is open on top. Hat off, he's poised and ready to collect the parish dues. Pa has volunteered as accounts keeper for the church for as long as I can remember. He took over from my grandfather after his passing, and Grandad took the job from his father before that. I couldn't have been more than four or five at the time, and I'm confident Pa hasn't missed a single Sunday collection since. The Lannigans and the church have lived in each other's pockets for generations, and Pa proudly identifies as a pillar of the community. Ma sometimes worries that he loves his holy family more than his biological one. She's never admitted that to me, but I hear it in the things she doesn't say. A slammed pot on the countertop when Pa is late home for dinner after hours of counting church funds.

This morning the line of parishioners queuing in front of Pa is particularly long, and I don't hear the familiar clink of coins being tossed into an old biscuit tin or the scrawl of Pa's pen in the ledger as he diligently records each family's contribution. Rather, I hear gentle sobbing. I make my way to the top of the queue and find one of our elderly neighbors talking to my father. Mrs. Keogh's headscarf is pulled so far forward it's hard to see her face, but nonetheless I can tell there are tears in her eyes.

"Please, Donny," she says, her voice cracking. "Don't write our shortcomings down. I'll find two pounds from somewhere. I'll have it by next week, I swear."

"Father Michaels wouldn't take kindly to any error in the bookkeeping," Pa explains. "He's a stickler for perfection. You know that as well as I do."

"But he'll read it from the pulpit, won't he? He'll tell the whole town that the Keoghs can't pay their dues."

Pa reaches across the flimsy table and places his hand on hers. "Yours won't be the only name called out, don't worry."

"But we'll be the only ones called out three weeks in a row. We're struggling a bit right now, you see." She pulls a hanky from her cardigan pocket and sniffles. I notice there are holes forming around the elbows where the wool is threadbare. "Two of the lambs died and Martin's bad hip is acting up."

Someone at the back of the queue grumbles and asks if we can hurry things along.

"I'm sorry to hear that. Really, I am," Pa says. "But Father Michaels—"

"Please don't write it down," she pleads once more. "We'll have it by next week. Martin's taking his watch to the pawnshop first thing tomorrow."

Pa sighs and shoves his hand into his pocket. He pulls out some money and it clinks when he tosses it into the biscuit tin. "There now," he says. "You're all paid up for this week."

Mrs. Keogh stands straight for the first time and lifts her head. "Thank you, Donny. You're a good man. We'll pay you back, of course."

Pa nods at her, and she shuffles out of line and into the church. Then, the *clink*, *clink*, *clink* of coins hitting tin begins.

In the pew Sheila sits with her head bowed. She doesn't even raise it for the hymns. Sheila loves singing, but I suspect her throat hurts too badly today. I sing loud enough for us both. Father Michaels, our parish priest with a full head of gray hair and a round belly, stands at the altar wearing a green vestment with a gold cross embroidered on the front. He smiles at the congregation as his sermon drags on and on, as usual, and I tell Sheila to rest her head on my shoulder. When Pa catches a glimpse of us cuddled together, he clicks his fingers and Sheila lifts her head.

After Mass, we shake Father Michaels's hand and Pa praises the *wise* sermon.

"How was the collection this week?" Father Michaels asks.

"Good. Yes. Very good."

Father Michaels makes a face that says he doesn't quite believe my pa. "And Mr. and Mrs. Keogh? How are they doing?"

"Ah, poor Martin's hip is giving him trouble. But the man is eighty-three, so—"

"I meant financially."

Pa's eyes narrow and I suspect he knew what the priest meant. "All paid up."

Father Michaels tilts his head to one side and his lips part into an O shape. "Well, that's a pleasant surprise indeed. Glad to hear it."

When Ma can't listen anymore, she shoos the boys on ahead and turns toward me. "Mind your sister. I need to hurry home to put the lamb in the oven. Your father will be here for another hour at least going over that ledger." She inhales sharply as if mustering the patience not to swear. "And you know he likes the dinner on the table when he gets in."

It takes Sheila and me twice as long as usual to walk home, and I find myself checking my watch every so often. The Sunday dance starts at half past three, and it's a solid hour's drive from the house to Limerick. Back home, the smell of roasting lamb greets us at the door. Pa has beaten us there, and we find him in the fireside armchair with the *Sunday Independent* open across his lap. The boys are out in the back kicking a ball. At seventeen and thirteen, Colm and Matthew are tall and lanky, and their long legs hog the ball. Much shorter, at not long ten, Finbar rarely gets a kick in, and I know grumbling and arguing are imminent.

Pa lowers the paper when he hears us come in. "G'wan up to bed now, Sheila, you're as pale as a ghost."

Sheila's face is the color of dishwater as she drags herself up the stairs, and Ma calls me into the kitchen. Without instruction I roll up my sleeves and set about peeling spuds.

"How is she?" Ma asks.

"Hot."

Ma tuts and rolls her eyes. "I spend so much time worrying about you getting sick with all those dances you insist on going to, I didn't think I had to worry about your sister. The only place she goes is the church."

"You can get sick at Mass, Ma," I say, making a conscious effort not to roll my eyes too.

Ma shoots me a pointed look that warns me she doesn't appreciate my tone or the implication that there are germs in the house of God. Pa saunters into the kitchen with the Sunday paper rolled under his arm.

"Sit down, Donny," Ma says. "I'll make you a cup of tea. The dinner will be ready soon."

I know I should hold my tongue and stick to peeling potatoes, but I can't help myself. I open my mouth and my frustration spills out. "Illness is illness, Ma. It doesn't differentiate where it spreads. Churches or dance halls. It's all the same. Sure, Mr. and Mrs. Keogh are always poorly. They were coughing and spluttering all over the church today. They should have stayed at home."

"Don't judge folks," Ma scolds. "They've fallen on hard times. I heard they haven't eaten meat in months, and I'm willing to bet they've no coal to heat their water neither. It's awful sad."

"Well, then, they can't afford Mass," I say. "They should save their money and buy coal. A warm bath would do wonders for Mr. Keogh's hip and it would help with the smell too. It's hard to sit beside them in the church."

Pa's nostrils widen and he puffs air out his nose. I expect a telling off, or to be sent to my room for blasphemy, but instead he says, "Let us count our blessings that we can pay our way. I'm telling you, I'd die of shame if I was in debt with our Lord."

"I don't think you have to worry about that, Pa," I say as I drag the knife against a large spud.

Ma and Pa would go hungry before they'd miss a penny to the church. My sister and my brothers and I could go hungry too, because everyone knows there is nothing more important than keeping Father Michaels, Jesus, and our Lord happy. Or so Pa thinks, anyway.

Ma and Pa's conversation shifts to the story on the front page of today's paper as they wait for water to boil. Some politician in Dublin had his bicycle stolen outside the post office, and it's the talk of the country.

"It makes you wonder about folks in that neck of the woods, doesn't it?" Pa says, as Ma places a cup with steam swirling out the top on the table in front of him. "Why anyone would want to live in Dublin is beyond me."

I imagine the cobblestone streets of narrow alleyways, buses and trains, and noisy, busy streets. I want to be a city girl. I fancy high heels and I might even try wearing trousers; it certainly makes cycling a lot easier. Maybe I won't even need my bicycle. I could drive. My heart skips a beat at the thought of sitting in a car of my own wearing a smart pair of trousers. Soon that will be the life Joseph and I share—a life without your neighbor's nose stuck in your business. A life away from Father Michaels's long, boring sermons. A life full of dancing.

7

Margaret

I gobble dinner so quickly I give myself the hiccups. I help Ma with the washup, all the while with one eye on the grandfather clock in the corner. Two p.m. Joseph will be here in half an hour and I'm still in my church dress. I dry the last cup and saucer, place them on the dresser, and spin on my heels to hurry upstairs.

"Are you going to sit with Sheila, love?" Pa asks. He's sitting at the head of the table, giving his best effort to the crossword in the paper.

I'm about to mention the dance. Joseph, his car, and running late are all on the tip of my tongue when Pa stands up and shoves his hand in his pocket to fish out rosary beads. He presses them into my palm and my fingers instinctively curl around them.

"Say a couple of decades of the rosary while you're up there, eh?"

My hands open and I stare at the polished mahogany beads. Pa's good beads. The ones that John-Joe Lynch from Lynch's Pub in the village brought back from a pilgrimage to Lourdes last year. Pa rarely lets these beads out of his sight. I nod, deciding I can pray and get dressed at the same time.

Upstairs, the curtains in the room I share with my sister are pulled, and I find Finbar on his knees at the side of Sheila's bed. His arms are folded and his head is resting against them as gentle snores shake him slightly. I take the woolly gray blanket from the end of the bed and drape it over him. Sheila hates this blanket. She says it's scratchy and uncomfortable. I've spent the last few weeks knitting her a new one with every spare moment I have. It's her birthday soon. She turns twenty-one next month, a whole eleven months before I do. And I hope she loves the pale blue blanket I've worked so hard on. Blue is her favorite color. I bought the soft, fragile wool in Dublin, when Joseph and I were last that way for a dance. It's delicate and fiddly and cost me extra knitting hours, but it will be worth it all if Sheila loves it. I'll have to lie about the wool, of course. Pa would burst a gasket if he knew Joseph and I went to Dublin for dances. But it wasn't the first time, and it won't be the last.

Suddenly, Sheila groans and a throaty gargle shakes her body. I dash toward her and place the back of my hand against her forehead the way Ma used to when we were little. She's burning, and her usually shiny sandy-blonde hair is dark and matted. Another gargle rattles through her, and the fine hairs on the back of my neck stand on end. I call out for Ma at the top of my lungs. Finbar wakes and, seeing Sheila, begins to cry. Suddenly, changing my clothes for a dance is of little importance. I pull my brother to his feet and tuck him close to my hip. Maybe Joseph appears at the window. Maybe he does not. All I know is that I clutch Pa's rosary beads tightly and chant, "Hail Mary full of grace. The Lord is with thee. Holy Mary mother of—"

8

Margaret

Ma has the wherewithal to send Finbar downstairs to his brothers before she panics. Pa comes thundering up the stairs and says we should call Father Michaels. "He'll know what to do."

"She doesn't need God, Donny, she needs a doctor," Ma shouts.

In all my twenty years I have never heard my mother raise her voice to my father, but for once, Pa listens. He grabs his coat and hat and sets off into town on his bicycle.

Pa returns with Doctor Henry. Father Michaels comes too. And some neighbors. Nosy bloody neighbors. I sit downstairs with the boys. We chat by firelight and I cook up a supper. I fry leftover lamb on the stove and shove it between slices of brown bread that Ma made fresh this morning. No one takes a single bite. Neighbors leave, one by one. They tut and shake their heads. They say it's awful to see a young woman so sick and agree on their way out to collectively pray. Some acknowledge my brothers and me, huddled in the kitchen. They tell us to call on them anytime day or night. Others see themselves out without a word our way. Hours tick by and the boys drop off to sleep. Ma, Pa, Doctor Henry, and Father Michaels do not come downstairs.

Before first light on Monday, Sheila is gone. No one comes to tell me and the boys. Not at first, but I know. Ma screams, and I could swear I feel the house shake. The older boys turn away and drop their heads into their hands. Finbar jumps into my arms, desperate to be held.

"What's wrong? What's happened?" he asks.

"I think Sheila . . ." I heave out, feeling I might be sick.

"She's dead. Can't you hear Ma wailing?" Matthew, my middle brother, huffs through angry tears.

"Is she really?" my eldest brother, Colm, asks, looking up from his hands to find my eyes.

He is a soft and gentle soul with a kind heart, and I watch as it breaks.

"Ma," I puff out as our mother comes into view in the doorway.

"We'll have to make sandwiches," she says, dazed and staring into the garden. She doesn't seem to see us gather around her. "The neighbors. They'll need feeding when they come. And Father Michaels, of course. He'll have a hunger on him when he's finished saying prayers." She shakes her head. The boys cry, but I do not. It hurts too much to cry.

"Pa?" I ask, wondering if he will join us. Wondering if he will come down to this shattered family.

"Your pa is with Father Michaels," Ma hisses through gritted teeth. "My little girl is cold five minutes and already they're planning a funeral."

I throw my arms around her and she flops against me, heavy as she breaks. "Oh, Margaret. What will we do without her? What will we do?"

9

Margaret

The graveyard sits on the edge of town, perched on a lonely hilltop overlooking the living. On the periphery grow tall trees with thick bark and knobbly branches that droop toward the ground like tired arms. Evergreen throughout the seasons, they guard the graves like smartly dressed soldiers. Sheila and I climbed these trees many times, usually on our way home from school. We'd go right to the top, swaying in the wind where the branches are thinnest, marveling at the view of rooftops and tiny people out walking.

The memory is bending me in the middle when I feel a hand on my back—Joseph. I haven't seen him since the night he asked Pa if he could marry me. He takes my hand without a word. Neighbors and locals begin to file into the graveyard around us, and Joseph holds my hand a little tighter. I spot Linda O'Rourke among the crowd. Her eyes are red and puffy from crying as she walks toward us. Linda, Sheila, and I are best friends. Linda is six months younger than Sheila and six months older than me. As kids we pretended we were triplets. We even have matching scars on our knees from a day when Sheila made us all laugh so hard that we fell out of these very graveyard trees. Linda tore her best Mass dress and her ma reddened all our backsides for misbehaving. We swore we'd stay out of the trees after that—which, of course, we did not. I try to remember the last day we climbed them, and I'm sadder than ever when I cannot.

Linda drags the sleeve of her blouse under her eyes as she reaches me, but the tears are falling faster than she can wipe them away.

"There's a good turnout," she whispers, sounding like the old ladies stopping to shake Ma's and Pa's hands.

"Yes, indeed. And no rain."

"Warm too."

"Very. I don't need this," I say, tugging at the edges of one of Ma's long black cardigans draped over my shoulders. It's at least two sizes too big for me, and much too heavy for the humid weather, but Ma said our family have to wear black today. Since I don't have any black clothes of my own, I have to make do. Linda is wearing a dress I can tell belongs to her ma too, a green polka-dot thing that despite being too long and too big complements her porcelain skin and fiery red hair. Even with blotchy cheeks and teary eyes, Linda O'Rourke is a standout beauty.

"The boys look smart," Linda says, nodding toward my brothers, all mini-replicas of Pa in black suits and crisp white shirts. Last night, Ma sat with the iron and ironing board for hours, and Pa told us to leave her as long as she needed. It took her three hours to iron three shirts.

"I will miss her," Linda admits at last, before stifling another sob.

Joseph hurries to catch her before she wilts. He reaches back for me, and soon all three of us are huddled together, crying and swaying on the spot. In an instant, I feel the pinch of a firm grip on my shoulder. I break away from Joseph and Linda to find Pa beside me. His eyes are round and red-rimmed as he shakes his head.

"Not now, Margaret." He coughs. "We can't fall apart now. Not with everyone watching."

I pull myself to stand up straight, and he nods and offers a weak smile as he returns to my mother.

Soon, every able-bodied person in Thurles town must be here. They're scattered around the graveyard like spectators at a sporting event. Their collective whispering carries on the wind, humming like bees.

"Isn't it just terrible," someone mumbles.

"So young. Was she twenty or twenty-one?" someone else whispers.

"Twenty-one, I think."

"No, no. Not yet. She was in my Teresa's class in school," someone else says, joining the quiet conversation.

"Diphtheria, was it?"

"So they say."

"Nasty. Nasty virus. Targeting the young, the damn thing."

"Not anymore. Sure, aren't the children vaccinated these days?"

"That they are. My Teresa wasn't, but her brother is just a year younger and he's got the vaccination. And the rest of my lot too. One less worry, thank the heavens."

"Ah, poor Sheila. If she'd just been a year younger. You know, Mary and Donny will never be the same now their eldest is gone."

"At least they have another girl."

"Aye, that. Small mercies."

I want to scream. I want to drown out their hushed gossip. I want to tell them that my parents can't simply replace one daughter with another. I cannot fill my sister's shoes. And I would never want to. Sheila is gone and our family will never be the same again.

10

Margaret

I can't watch as they lower the coffin. I know it's over only when I hear Father Michaels announce, "There's a bite to eat waiting at the Lannigans', and Donny and Mary would be delighted if you could join them."

"Delighted," I snort as I finally open my eyes. "Why in the name of God would Ma and Pa be delighted?"

"It's just a turn of phrase," Joseph says, and I have to squash a flash of temper that his politeness stirs in me.

The house is cramped, with neighbors squeezed into every corner of the kitchen and sitting room. They spill into the hall and out the scullery door into the garden. Their voices take up much too much space in our home. Children run around the garden shouting and laughing and enjoying the sun sinking in a summer sky. Their parents stand chatting and eating the sandwiches Ma and I buttered up last night. My hand aches from old men shaking it and telling me they are sorry for my family's troubles. Ma has barely budged from the kitchen sink since we got back to the house. She washes cups and saucers and plates and passes them to me to dry. She stops only to butter more bread, saying things like, "John-Joe Lynch looks hungry. Take him some ham and cheese. And has your Joseph eaten? I don't want his mother thinking I wouldn't feed the boy."

I haven't seen Joseph put a bite in his mouth. I doubt he has the stomach for food today.

I say, "He said the soup is lovely, Ma. Everyone likes the food. You've done Sheila proud."

Ma smiles, and a silent tear trickles down her pale cheek. I swallow the lump in my throat and place my hand on her back. "Won't you sit down, eh?"

But Ma shakes her head and searches for more delft to be washed. She can't sit still, I understand. And part of me worries that she may never be able to sit still again. I stay by her side and dry every cup and plate she passes my way.

Later, when most of the locals have left and only a few of Pa's drunk friends remain out back drinking homemade poitín and talking about the good old days, Ma finally flops into the fireside chair. At some point she falls asleep. It's a relief to see her finally close her eyes. Joseph offers to drive Linda home.

Linda shakes her head. "You're needed here. I'll walk."

"It's dark and those roads are no place for a woman to be out walking alone," I say, taking her hand so she understands how much her support has meant to me today. She nods, and I'm relieved that she will get home safely with Joseph driving.

"I'll come back," Joseph says, bleary-eyed.

I breathe out. "Go home. Get some sleep. It's been a long day."

"But I don't want to leave you."

"I need to check on the boys. And get Finbar to bed."

"And your pa?" he says, gesturing his head toward the door where the sound of Pa, John-Joe Lynch, and Father Michaels's conversation carries in from the garden.

"He's drunk. I'll need to get him to bed too."

Joseph's face pinches with concern.

"Please," I say, too tired to find more words. "Just take care of Linda. I will see you soon."

He nods, kisses me, and says, "Tomorrow," and then I watch as he walks Linda outside to his waiting car.

Upstairs, I find Finbar asleep on Sheila's bed. He's curled into a petite ball and his breathing is rough and heaving, and I can tell he cried himself to sleep. The pain in my heart is so great that for a moment I can't bear it and I think I might die too. A tiny part of me wishes to close my eyes and never have to open them again in a world without my big sister. I scold myself instantly for the selfish thought. How could I leave Ma with three sons and no daughters?

Moonlight shines through the open curtains and onto Colm sleeping in the chair by the window. Matthew is sitting on the floor next to him. His arms hug his knees into his chest and his head rests on top. Pa's rosary beads dangle from his fingers and I slide them out of his hands, taking care not to wake him. I slip into bed still wearing Ma's cardigan and pull the covers over my head. I begin to pray. I beg God for strength for all of us. A gentle snore sounds from one of the boys, reminding me of their presence. My sister is gone, but my brothers are here and there is a gentle comfort in that. I rock myself to sleep, grateful not to be alone.

11

Margaret

My eyes sting when I feel someone shaking me awake. It takes some time to adjust to the subtle light of dawn streaming in the window. Pa is leaning over me and his breath smells of alcohol.

"Up you get, love," he whispers.

I rub my eyes and sit up. My brothers are still sleeping in the same spots, and I don't think long has passed since I dozed off. Pa clearly hasn't been to bed yet, and if I concentrate, I can hear the sound of male voices downstairs. I suspect that John-Joe Lynch and Father Michaels are still here. A sting of fury wakes me fully. *Have those men no homes of their own to go to? Can't they leave my family in peace instead of pouring drink into my grieving father?*

"Come on. Up you get. That's my girl," Pa says, backing away to give me space to get out of bed. "Your mother is waiting downstairs."

"Waiting for what?"

Pa shakes his head. "Not here. We'll wake the boys. We'll talk downstairs. That's a girl. Hurry on up now."

He clicks his fingers and leaves the room, and I understand that's my cue to follow. Unsteady with sleep, I slide my feet over the edge of the bed and stand up. The cold timber floor nips at my stocking feet, and I cover each of my brothers with a blanket before I leave the room. On the landing, I am certain that John-Joe Lynch and Father Michaels are still here. I tuck one side of Ma's large cardigan over the other and make my way down the stairs.

The kitchen is bright as day breaks outside the window. Ma is sitting at the square table with her hands curled around a cup of something. Pa, John-Joe, and Father Michaels occupy a side of the table each. I spy a plate of biscuits in the center of the table. Ma says biscuits are daylight robbery and that they are only for Christmas or special occasions. My blood boils at the sight of them because there is absolutely nothing special about this occasion.

"Have a seat, love," Pa says, pulling out the empty chair next to him.

The squeak of the legs against the tiled floor is amplified by the stillness of early morning, and all eyes are on me except for those of Father Michaels, who goggles the plate of biscuits. He reaches for a Garibaldi and dips it in his cup before stuffing the whole thing into his mouth.

"Sit down," Pa says again.

I look at Ma, and she nods as she pulls her cup closer to her.

"I'm fine standing, thank you."

Father Michaels takes another biscuit. Ma eyes him with disgust but doesn't utter a word.

"Sit," Pa says once more, his tone sharpening.

I exhale, making it obvious I would rather not, but nonetheless I do as I am told.

"Tea?" Ma asks, readying herself to stand.

"Something a little stronger might be better, Mary," John-Joe says, offering me a swig of something at the bottom of the glass he has been drinking from all night.

My stomach heaves. "No, thank you."

Ma stands, pours tea from her favorite pot into a cup, and places it in front of me. "There's biscuits there too," she says, pointing lamely.

"They're mighty nice," Father Michaels says, dusting some crumbs off his shirt.

Sheila loved Garibaldi biscuits. She used to say they were the best part of Christmas, even better than presents and cake. I reach for one but can't bring myself to bite it.

"What's going on?" I ask, setting the biscuit down to rub my sleepy eyes. "Why am I down here?"

Ma's shoulders tremble, and I'm about to stand and make my way around the table to comfort her when I feel Pa's hand press firmly on my knee.

"It's a big day, Margaret," he says. "It's the day our Lord calls on you."

"Hasn't our Lord called on our home enough this week?" I say as I glance across the table at my shattered mother. "What more does he want?"

Father Michaels gets to his feet and looks at me with disapproving eyes. I want to ask him to leave. And I want him to take God and John-Joe with him, and then I want to hold my ma and let her cry on my shoulder.

"As you know, the eldest daughter of the Lannigan family has joined the Sisters of Penance for generations," Father Michaels says, with his hands clasped under his round belly. "Your Pa's sister Rita, and their aunt Beatrice before that, and so on and so on. Now it's your turn."

A noise bleeds out of Ma, and I watch as she struggles to gather herself.

"I'm not the eldest girl," I tell him.

"No. But with Sheila gone, you are the eldest *living* girl now. The duty to our Lord is falling on your shoulders."

I snort. "I don't want to be a nun."

I wonder, not for the first time, if Sheila wanted that life, a life of solitude and dedication in the convent. I never asked, of course—we simply didn't discuss such things. But from the time we were children, Ma and Pa made sure we knew our place in this family. Sheila's future was in the convent, serving God, and mine was in the home—serving a husband and children.

"I don't want to be a nun," I repeat.

Father Michaels's eyes narrow. A redness creeps in from his temples and spreads across his cheeks as he raises his voice. "It. Is. Your. *Duty*, Margaret."

"No." I fold my arms on the table.

"Donny," he says, looking to my father to step in and instruct me, but before Pa opens his mouth, I go on.

"This is ridiculous. Everyone has had too much to drink and no one is thinking straight. I'm going back to bed."

Father Michaels slams his fist down on the table and crushes a biscuit beside his cup. "You are a Lannigan."

"Not for long," I say. I can't take my eyes off the smashed biscuit. Crumbs are stuck to his hand and I wait for him to dust them off but he does not. "I'll be a Maloney soon. I'm getting married."

Father Michaels sits back down, clasping his hands on his belly to observe me.

"Joseph Maloney has asked for my hand. Tell him, Pa." I turn toward my father, but he doesn't make eye contact. "Tell him," I say again, louder.

Father Michaels finally wipes his hand and clears his throat. "But you are a Lannigan still, sweet Margaret. And as such, you are promised to God. And to God you must be true."

"Pa, please! Tell him. Tell him I'm marrying Joseph."

My father doesn't lift his head.

"Pa!" I say, my voice ferocious and determined.

"Donny," Father Michaels says again.

My father exhales and finally allows his gaze to meet mine. I see a broken man as he says, "Lannigan women have an obligation, love. There is nothing more to be said."

Ma growls something under her breath that I can't make out. Father Michaels casts her a look that suggests she's testing his patience as much as I am. I stand up and, with wobbly legs, hurry over to the safety of my mother's side. She stands and drapes her arm over my shoulder.

"Don't make me go, Ma. You won't make me, sure you won't?"

Pa replies for her. "You should pack."

I clutch my mother and wait for her to speak up. There is silence except for the sound of slurping as John-Joe drains his glass.

"It's time to leave," Pa says with slurred speech, the drink getting the better of him. "John-Joe will drive and Father Michaels will see that you get settled in all right."

"John-Joe is drunk," I snap.

No one bats an eye at my observation, but I feel Ma grow heavier, and I think without me to lean on she would topple to the floor.

"You should pack," Pa repeats, and once again he will not look me in the eye.

"You're all mad. This is madness. I can't run off to a convent in the middle of the night. Besides, I'm only twenty. Sheila wasn't to join the Sisters of Penance until after her twenty-first birthday. That's ages away for me yet."

Father Michaels groans. "Your sister wasn't running off to dances every weekend and planning to marry the first fella that asked. She was at home praying. She was preparing for our Lord's calling. You have a lot to learn and it's best we get started now."

"Joseph and I are courting two years, Father. It's not some fling. We are in love. We were hoping you'd marry us." I place my hand on my racing heart, trying to steady myself. "Next spring."

"Ah, sweet child," he says, softening. "He will find a new girl. Sure, aren't those town halls full of them. Your heart belongs to the Holy Spirit now. Not many girls are as lucky."

"I will not go! Not one of you can make me."

Pa's cheeks flush, and the flash of temper that ripples across his face scares me. "You will do what is asked of you, Margaret, or you are no longer a Lannigan. I will not have you bring shame on the good name of this family. Is that clear?"

Ma rocks beside me. She seems shorter than usual, as if grief has chiseled inches off her.

"Pack!" Pa says, with a finger aimed toward the door. "John-Joe will start the car. Don't keep him waiting. Do not embarrass us."

I break away from Ma and charge up the stairs, taking two steps at a time. My mind is racing, and at the same time I cannot seem to think. I eye up the window and wonder if I could climb out and down the drainpipe. I could, I decide. But where would I go? My first thought is to run to Joseph's house, into the safe embrace of his arms. His parents have little to no relationship with Father Michaels—Pa makes no secret of his disapproval that the Maloneys skip Mass more often than they attend—but, nonetheless, no family will interfere between a man and his daughter. They'd pass me back to my father as if I was a prize heifer at the county fair.

Linda can't help me either. Her pa doles out communion at three Masses a week. If possible, her family are even closer with Father Michaels than mine. Two of Mr. O'Rourke's brothers are priests, and a cousin too. It's enough to get Linda off the convent hook even though she's the elder daughter. Her brothers' fates, however, are not quite so free. When we were children, eleven or twelve, or thereabouts, Linda overheard Father Michaels tell her pa that with eight sons, the least he should offer to the church was three.

"The reward in heaven will be greater than you can imagine," Linda mimicked the priest as she repeated his words verbatim. "He's right," she'd added, switching back to her own voice. "Everyone knows a priest in the family is worth at least two nuns."

"Horseshit," I'd snapped back, and Linda made me put fivepence in the swear jar. I still think about the sweets we could have bought with that.

A gentle knock sounds on the door behind me and Ma peers through the gap.

"Let me help you pack," she whispers, taking care not to wake my brothers.

"Ma, is there nothing to be done?"

"Not tonight," she says, resigned. "Your pa is full of grief and Father Michaels is in his ear about damn duty and responsibility. In time, your father will get his mind back. I will pray for it every day, my love. But for now, you must be brave. Can you be brave, my sweet girl?"

I pull out a suitcase from under Sheila's bed. A layer of dust sits on top, gathered over years of non-use. I blow it away, coughing as it swirls into the air. I lift the case onto the bed and pop it open as Ma gathers clothes from the wardrobe. She folds my best dresses and places them in the suitcase, and then she reaches for Sheila's favorites and folds those too.

"They'll help you remember her," she says as she places them next to mine.

I shake my head as tears fall. I don't need floral dresses to remember my sister. I reach under the bed once more and pull out *Little Women*. Ma's eyes sweep over the cover and she allows herself a crooked smile.

"We weren't finished," I say, gulping in air as sobbing shakes me. "We had a few more chapters. But I can't read them alone."

"Take it with you," Ma says. "When you miss her the most, you might just find reading helps."

"I doubt Father Michaels would approve."

Ma's smile widens. "Father Michaels doesn't have to know."

I add the book to the case and, finally, I open the bottom drawer of my bedside table. I take the half-knitted blue blanket, wool, and knitting needles and place them on top of all my clothes, and then I close the case.

"What about Joseph?" I ask, closing my eyes so I can imagine his face. "Will you explain? Will you make sure he understands this is short-term? Just until Pa comes to his senses."

Ma strokes her hand over my hair. "I'll talk to his mother. Sunday, after Mass. The Maloneys are good people, love; they'll understand our predicament."

Sunday? I can't bear the thought of being parted from Joseph for so long. Not when my heart bleeds for Sheila and I need his arms around me.

"I love him, Ma."

"I know. I know you do."

"Margaret Mary Lannigan, what's keeping you? We can't keep these men waiting all night," Pa shouts up the stairs.

"What's happening?" Finbar wakes, his voice muffled with sleep.

"Our Margaret is off to the nuns for a little while," Ma says.

"No. No." Finbar begins to cry. Ma opens her arms and he jumps out of Sheila's bed and clambers into them. "I don't want anyone else to go away. Please, Ma."

"Come on, now, let's get you into your own bed." She bends and kisses the top of his head, then turns him away and guides him toward the boys' room.

I drag the suitcase off the bed and make my way down the stairs as slowly as if I am made of concrete.

"There you are," Pa says, unsteady on his feet as I come into view. "John-Joe has the car running."

Father Michaels takes my case, and I follow him and Pa outside. I sit in the back seat of the small silver car, which smells of well-worn socks and Guinness. Father Michaels puts my case in the boot and shakes my father's hand before he sits in the passenger seat next to John-Joe.

"You're going to love Ballyvale Convent," he says, twisting his head over his shoulder. "Mother Superior is wonderful. She runs a tight ship. But once you get used to it . . ."

Ma comes skidding into view. She's clutching her chest and waving at the same time. Pa reaches for her but she shoves him away.

The car begins to move, and all too soon my parents, my home, and the life I thought I would have disappear out of view.

12

Margaret

The roads leading to Ballyvale Convent are narrow and winding and seem to stretch on endlessly. Green fields populated with cattle, horses, or sheep line each side of the road, with only the odd thatched cottage or barn to break up the monotony. I am familiar with the route. Joseph and I passed this way often on our trips out of town in search of the next dance hall. I usually love the sounds of mooing, neighing, and bleating that carry across the landscape. But today the animals are hushed, as if even they do not know what to say.

The gates of the convent finally come into view at the end of a laneway lined with neatly kept hedging on both sides.

"Are you asleep?" Father Michaels asks, twisting in his seat as John-

Joe brings the car to a stop outside the commanding gates. "You were very quiet all the way."

I don't open my mouth.

He turns back and shakes his head, and I can tell he would much rather I were my sister.

Two nuns appear, like ghosts. They're dressed head to toe in long white robes and equally clean white veils, hiding every strand of hair. I find myself curious as to how they keep them so bright. Ma uses bread soda and vinegar on Pa's and the boys' smalls, and they still go grubby over time. The nuns also wear chunky mahogany crosses, dangling like necklaces, and they remind me of Pa's rosary beads. Their skin is bright and their smiles are wide. They can't be much older than me. They take a side of the black iron gate each and drag it open. The car rolls forward and the gates close behind us, sealing me inside. I can't breathe. But slowly I find myself inhaling when gardens as beautiful as if Monet himself had painted them come into view. The grass is lush and neatly cut. Flowers are in bloom, pansies and carnations in the colors of the rainbow. There is not a weed in sight. There's a vegetable patch, too, and I'm curious what treats grow beneath the green leafy heads poking aboveground. The convent sits proudly in the center of the gardens. It's made entirely of limestone and its face is turned toward the sun. Starched curtains hang in the windows. It is every bit as inviting as a watercolor painting.

John-Joe stops the car outside the main door, and Father Michaels is first out. He greets a nun on the porch. In contrast to the girls at the gate, she wears all black robes and stands rounded like a question mark, her shoulders hunched, and the sun has stamped the years on her face like splashes of spilt honey. She searches the car for me and beams when she finds me inside the back-seat window.

John-Joe gets out and lights a cigarette, mumbling something about stretching his legs and hoping this doesn't take long because he could use a pint. Father Michaels takes my small case from the boot, then opens the door of the car and waits for me to step out.

"Margaret, this is Mother Superior," he says.

I extend my hand, but the elderly nun doesn't shake it. Instead, she bows her head and says, "Welcome, child."

Father Michaels passes me my case and turns away.

"Wait," I gasp. "What about my parents? Will they come today?"

Father Michaels sighs, exasperated, and then opens the passenger-side door and sits. John-Joe licks his fingertips and quenches his half-smoked cigarette between them. He slides the remaining half above his ear and says, "Good luck, love. Do the Lannigans proud, eh?"

He joins the priest in the car as the gates squeak open once more. Mother Superior and I watch them drive away without a word between us.

It's then that I notice the sleepy building across the road. It stands two stories high, with a porridge-colored exterior and rectangular latticed windows. Tall gates and high walls obscure my view of the gardens.

"Is that another convent?" I ask, pointing.

Mother Superior grimaces but doesn't answer. I repeat myself, a little louder this time, assuming she's hard of hearing.

She ignores me once more and says, "Inside, please." She steps aside so I can enter first. Inside smells of candle wax and the leather of old books. It takes my eyes a moment to adjust from the bright day outside. When they do, I find the hall is large and hexagon shaped, with checkered floor tiles and a multicolored oval rug the likes of which I've never seen before: the pile is as dense as freshly cut grass in summer. In front of me is a sweeping mahogany staircase, and Mother Superior brushes past me to ascend it. She doesn't speak, but she curls a finger and beckons me to follow. The stairs deposit us on the second floor, where a slender corridor leads to a stained-glass window as colorful as the gardens it overlooks. There are several doors on each side, which I assume open onto bedrooms. I wait for Mother Superior to guide me toward one. Instead, she glides her arm through the air, drawing my attention to another staircase. A metal spiral thing. She points a bony finger upward.

"There's another floor?" I ask.

"For the novice sisters. You'll find your room on the left. Second door. It's a simple space, but I trust you'll be very happy there."

I step aside to let her lead the way, but she looks the winding iron staircase up and down and shakes her head. "I'm too old, I'm afraid."

I glance up at what can only be described as dark attic space, and once more I ask, "Are my parents coming?"

"Not today."

I feel tears prick my eyes. "When?"

She doesn't reply.

"Please. It all happened so suddenly. I didn't get to say goodbye. And my mother—"

"Is very proud, I'm sure," she says kindly.

I clamp my back teeth together so my mouth doesn't open and let out the roar I feel brewing inside me. My mother isn't proud. She is broken. Ma buried one daughter and lost another to the convent, all in twenty-four hours. But how can this tiny, frail woman understand? Her title might be Mother Superior. But she is not my mother. I so badly want my ma.

I clear my throat and try to explain. "There's been a bit of a misunderstanding."

She cocks her head, and her expression tells me she's intrigued.

"My pa had been drinking, you see. And Father Michaels . . . ?" I take a pause before I blurt something blasphemous about the local priest. I swallow and try again. "Anyway, my ma thinks that my pa will come to his senses soon and . . ." I'm rambling and I doubt the elderly lady is quite following along, but I don't stop myself. "So, if there is a bicycle I could borrow, I could pedal out to them. I'd be there in a little over an hour. I know some shortcuts."

She takes my hand in hers and her fragility shocks me. Her skin covers her bones like papier-mâché on a balloon.

"I know this is unexpected," she says warmly. "But you will do a wonderful job of filling your sister's shoes, and someday you will see that this is all a blessing."

I snap my hand away. "You know my sister died?"

"I'm very sorry for your loss."

"A week ago, she was fine. She was well. And then her throat started bothering her. A fever followed. And poof . . ." I click my fingers as a lump swells in my throat. "She was gone."

"Aye, diphtheria is a nasty business. But at least she has no pain now."

"Diphtheria," I echo, but scarcely any sound comes out. I'm surprised at how well informed she is about Sheila's passing. Father Michaels must have spared no detail, I decide. "Then you know I shouldn't be here. You know this is not my place."

She looks at me with empathetic eyes that almost unravel me completely.

"So, if I could borrow a bicycle. I will return it, of course. After I talk to my pa. I'll bring it straight back."

She points up the stairs once more, stands a fraction straighter, and softly repeats, "I trust you will find your room to your liking."

"You're not listening to me. I'm not supposed to be—"

Mother Superior raises her hand, and I close my eyes, anticipating the blow. The nuns at school liked to smack for back talk. But when nothing comes, I peel them open again, one at a time.

"That's enough now," she says, retracting her hand and shoving it into her robe pocket. "I can only imagine how much you miss your sister, but tantrums are for children. And you are not a child, Ms. Lannigan. You are a novice nun."

She may not have slapped me, but nonetheless my words are knocked out of me as I stand open-mouthed.

"Sister Bernadette will be up to you shortly to check for contraband and see you get settled in nicely. As I said, you will find your room behind the second door on the left."

She turns, steadying herself with the banister, and makes her way down the stairs. I glance up at the corkscrew staircase and then back down at the old lady, who seems to take an obscenely long time to reach the bottom step. I watch as she disappears behind a door in the hallway. The inside of my head pounds as fury courses through my veins. And a new idea crystallizes inside me. I clutch my suitcase against my chest, count backward from five, and charge down the stairs. I nearly stumble trying to hold my pace. I grab the front door, jerk it open, and keep running, picking up speed as I tear up stones underfoot in the driveway. I never look back and stop only when I reach the gate. It's even taller now than it seemed from the back seat of John-Joe's car, but I don't let the height stop me. I heave my case over the gate, then hitch up my skirt and climb. There's a swirling pattern molded in the heavy iron, and if I hook my foot just right, I can use it to gain some traction. But the swirls are replaced by vertical bars midway up and my feet struggle to keep their grip. I fall three times. On the final tumble I curse loudly. I think of Sheila and Linda and our tree-climbing adventures as kids, and I try again. I pull with my arms, seesaw with my belly, and finally fling a leg over. The other leg follows quickly, and I land in a heap on the other side. A sharp pain shoots up through the sole of my foot and nips at my ankle, but I pick up my case and begin walking. My pace is frustratingly slow as pain bites with each step. At this rate, it will take all day to get home. I don't care. The longer I walk, the more time Pa has to sleep off the booze. We'll talk better when he's sober.

After an hour on the road, my throat is dry with thirst and my ankle is throbbing. I consider resting for a while, when a man about my father's age approaches on a horse and cart.

"Whoa, boy, whoa!" he says, tugging on the reins.

The horse comes to a reluctant stop, and I smile. "Hello, sir."

He reaches for his cap and dips it toward me. "Hello there. Are you hurt? I noticed you limping."

"Yes. Yes. I . . . I slipped. I think I've sprained my ankle."

"Slipped?" He shifts in his seat to gain a better view of our surroundings. It's been a particularly warm summer. The overgrown verge on both sides of the road is dry and brittle, and patches of scorched brown grass stand out brazenly.

"Slipped," I repeat, nonchalant. "Are you going into town?"

"I am. Are you in need of a lift?"

"Yes, please." I am light with relief as I lift my sore ankle and balance on the other foot.

He jumps down from the cart, and I hop back as if this square man needs the lion's share of the road. His strong arms fill his tweed jacket and his brown britches are inches too short and show off stripy socks and work boots. There's a strand of blue twine tied around his waist where most men would wear a leather belt. He bends and clasps his hands to create a makeshift step for me. I pause for a moment, weighing up this stranger so like a scarecrow come to life. Then, with a deep inhale, I place my good foot into his hands, and he hoists me up. "Whoosh. There you are now."

The smell of his horse hits me as I sit down on a tatty red cushion next to his driving spot. He climbs aboard and I repeat, "Thank you. Thank you."

He grabs the reins and sluggishly the horse begins to move again.

"Where are you traveling?" he asks, tilting his head toward the case I'm keeping tucked against my chest.

"Erm—"

"You're one of the Lannigan girls, aren't ya?"

"Oh."

I flinch when he recognizes me. I thought I knew most of the farmers in town, but I can't place his face.

"Terrible business about your sister. I'm awfully sorry. She was so young."

"Not quite twenty-one." I swallow. Almost twenty-one years of Sheila and me. Me and Sheila. Our lives intertwined from the day I was born. "My girls, like chalk and cheese," Ma said often. Sheila had no desire to leave Tipperary. I couldn't wait to explore everywhere and anywhere else. Sheila epitomized quiet, small-town living. I manifested a life of city sights and loud music. Chalk and cheese was putting it mildly. Sheila *was* the countryside. She'd have no trouble sitting behind this stinking horse, but it's making me want to hurl.

"Shame. Awful, awful shame." He whips the reins and the horse begins to trot. I have to hold on to the edge of my seat as we are bounced around the road.

"I'm Margaret," I say, suspecting that my name escapes him.

"Austin Dolan."

I search my brain for the bells his name should ring but my mind is blank. I have never heard mention of an Austin Dolan in Thurles before, and I wonder if he's from farther afield. But I dismiss the idea, remembering that he recognized me.

"How are your folks coping?" he asks, as we turn down a side road.

Tall trees line both sides and their branches meet in the middle to form an arch that blocks out much of the sunlight. I'm unfamiliar with this dark lane, and a sense of discomfort settles in me.

"Is this the way to Thurles?" I ask, knowing full well that it is not.

He ignores my question and says, "Your parents must be very proud. Everyone wants a nun in the family."

I suck in a breath.

"A runaway, on the other hand . . ." He makes a *tut*, *tut*, *tut* noise. "Gosh, the family would be the talk of the town. Could you imagine?"

"Who *are* you?" I ask again.

"Austin Dolan," he repeats with a grin. "I'm the caretaker and groundskeeper at Ballyvale. You have Mother Superior awful worried."

I shrink.

"She gave me your description and sent me looking. You don't see many young girls out walking these roads alone. You weren't hard to spot."

"I wasn't just out for a walk—"

"Don't even think about it," he says, catching me gazing over the edge of the cart, eyeing up the road. "You'll hurt more than your ankle if you're foolish enough to jump."

"Then stop the cart, please, so I may get off."

He grabs the reins tighter and the poor horse struggles to go faster.

"I said, I would like to get off."

"And *I* said, Mother Superior asked me to fetch you. It's my job to obey."

"I'll run away again."

He shrugs. "That's your prerogative. But if I may offer some advice?"

I snort. The last thing I want is advice from this man whom I don't know but have quickly decided I despise.

He raises his voice above the clip-clop of the horse's hooves hitting the road as he goes on. "Make a friend of Mother Superior. The days will be easier then. I promise you that."

I'm psyching myself to leap when he whips the reins mighty hard and the horse takes off. I have no choice but to hold tight as we bounce like kernels popping on a hot pan on the way back to the convent.

13

NOW

Riley

Sam sleeps on the plane. I close my eyes for a long time but I can't doze. A trip to Ireland was his idea. "Screw it, let's just hop on a damn plane," he said one evening when I came back from yet another visit to Loving Care that Grammy slept through. In the past two weeks I've run into every metaphorical wall possible. I chased countless emails to Irish bureaucracy, each one with a deader end than the last. And I lost hours waiting on hold, hoping to speak to someone, anyone, who might be able to help.

"I'm afraid I've nothing to add," a girl with a thick accent in the births registry department told me. "Any information we have in the system is already recorded on the certificate."

"Can you tell me if she was adopted? Do you know who her parents are? Are they Derek and Betty Carmichael?"

"I'm sorry," she said kindly, picking up on my frustration. "But that type of thing is way outside our remit. I hope you find her."

"We'll use the honeymoon money. Think of it like a wedding prequel," Sam said.

I hesitated for all of five seconds before I kissed him and asked if his passport was up to date.

Misty teased me that I would do just about anything to get out of DIYing in the evenings.

"Hell, Misty. Why is your mouth so big?" Sam elbowed her in the ribs. "Shut up for once."

Janelle gave them both a smack with the back of her hand. "Don't mind them, honey," she told me, while scowling at her son and daughter as if they were a pair of naughty children. "We know how much this trip means to you. I'm sure Betty would be excited for you too. Fly safe now, you hear?"

The FASTEN SEAT BELT sign goes off, and I reach for my handbag, unzip it, and peek inside, with an incessant need to check that the copies of Mary-Kate's birth certificate are still there. Sam suggested we make copies and leave the real thing at home. "It's an heirloom," he said. "Keep it somewhere safe."

I'm sure he meant for me to slide it into an envelope and stash in a drawer somewhere. My nightstand perhaps. Or the new desk in the back room that we're converting into a home office. Yet I found myself placing it back in the Dr. Martens shoebox and setting the scratchy baby booties back on top. Our closet is a lot more cramped than Grammy's, but I made room for the box beside some folded jeans.

Dublin Airport isn't dissimilar to Newark. It's expansive, techy, busy, and security-heavy. We're waiting at the baggage carousel when Sam says, "Should we rent a car? I can totally drive stick shift. Trust me."

I laugh so loudly the man in front of us turns around.

We enjoy good coffee and a great breakfast in a small café somewhere in Dublin city center, and the friendly server gives us directions and travel advice. "To be honest, traffic is a nightmare at this time of the day. Your best bet is the train."

Sam doesn't admit it, but I think he's relieved his driving skills aren't put to the test when he looks the wrong way crossing the road to the train station, forgetting they drive on the left over here. Soon, we're staring out the train window, swapping the sights and sounds of a busy city for green fields that cover the landscape like a giant patchwork blanket. Grammy had a quilt just like it when I was growing up, and I'm filled with an urge to find it when we get home.

I close my eyes and, finally, the rattle and shake of the train coaxes me to sleep. I rouse when I feel Sam's hand on my shoulder.

"We're here."

My stomach flips, and I can't tell if I'm nervous or excited. I'm grateful for a gentle mist sprinkling my face as we hop off the train, wheeling our cases alongside us.

"Google says it's eleven minutes this way." Sam points toward a winding road with no sidewalk.

I glance in the other direction, where there is a brick pathway that I assume leads into the town.

"You sure about this?" I ask, glancing back at the narrow road, which gives me the creeps.

"C'mon. If we hurry, we'll make it to our hotel before the downpour."

I look up. The sky is almost cloudless, and yet gentle raindrops dance on the top of my head. It's strange weather, I decide, and I wish we had a car after all. Thankfully, there isn't a lot of traffic as we walk. But the few cars that do pass honk their horns, irritated by our dangerous choice to travel by foot. I can hear the rain become heavier, but we are not getting wet. The branches of the trees on both sides of the road meet in the middle, like a leafy green canopy. My eyes burn with tiredness, and I am concerned that we are walking miles in the wrong direction, and yet I can't stop smiling. I am a little girl again, sitting on my poppy's knee as he tells me stories of a trip he once took to Ireland. A trip that changed his and Grammy's life, he always said. This narrow road, with rain and sun battling for space between the leaves overhead, is perfectly aligned with the quaint and romantic images that Poppy's stories conjured in my mind's eye. It is as if someone has reached into my young imagination and painted what they found. I suspect Ireland hasn't changed at all since 1959. *How lovely.*

Finally, an open gate comes into view. I pick up my pace.

"Oh, so now you trust Google." Sam laughs, hurrying after me.

"Wow," I gasp when I spot a long driveway that leads to a grand Georgian building made of a dozen shades of limestone.

"Is this our hotel?" I turn to look at him, and his eyes are as wide and impressed as mine.

Sam nods. "Ballyvale Abbey Hotel. It's pretty close to the address on the birth certificate. And it has a four-point-eight average on Tripadvisor."

A low stone wall that looks as if each boulder was stacked by hand encompasses the building and pristinely manicured lawn. BALLYVALE ABBEY is engraved above commanding double doors right in the center, and I'm looking forward to a warm shower or maybe a long soak in the bathtub. We're halfway up the driveway when I stop under a tall apple tree and nudge Sam in the ribs. "Do you think it's haunted?"

He laughs.

"I'm serious. I'm getting a vibe. Aren't you getting it?"

"Nope. This place is cool." Sam picks a tiny apple from the tree and rubs it against his sweater before he bites. He squints. "Yuck. Not ripe yet."

"Don't eat that," I say, knocking the apple out of his hand. "You don't know if it's safe." The small fruit rolls along the grass. When it comes to a stop, four black birds with white breasts swoop out of nowhere and begin pecking at it.

"They seem to think it's okay," Sam says.

A shiver runs down my spine, and I can't quite put my finger on why. I'm lost in my thoughts and I jump when I feel Sam's hand on my back.

"You okay?"

"I need the restroom," I blurt.

It's not a lie, but it's not the answer to his question. I'm starting to worry that coming here was a mistake. What if I find out something that changes everything I thought I knew?

"Riley?" Sam says when I zone out again.

Dementia has stolen years from us: birthdays, hugs, conversations. There is rarely time for words anymore. Giving me the birth certificate said everything Grammy couldn't say herself. She wants me to be here. *I* want to be here. *I'll find her, Grammy. I'll find Mary-Kate O'Rourke for us both.*

"Riley?" Sam tries again, sounding worried now.

I look up at him and smile. "I'm okay. Let's get inside."

14

1956

Margaret

The convent gates are open and waiting for us. Mr. Dolan slows the horse to a gentle trot as we pass through. The noise of hooves clip-clopping on the loose stone brings Mother Superior to the door. Her arms are folded and her eyes are dark and oval like the rosary beads hanging around her neck. They glare at me, full of disappointment. The rest of her face is equally as stern, from her slender nose to her high cheekbones and dimpled chin. The years have sharpened her, but I can only imagine that once upon a time she was very beautiful indeed.

"Thank you, Mr. Dolan," she says as he brings the horse and cart to a stop parallel to the door. "If you could tend to the potatoes now, that would be a fine thing."

The middle-aged caretaker nods, and the cart rattles when he jumps down. I brace myself as he makes his way around to me, stopping briefly to pet his tired horse.

"Attaboy, Vixen. Attaboy."

At my side, he offers me his hand. I don't take it and instead jump down independently. Hot, sharp pain shots through my damaged foot and I almost stumble. Mother Superior and Mr. Dolan glance my way, but I will not give them the satisfaction of yelping.

Mr. Dolan tips his cap toward the elderly nun and accepts his marching orders, taking Vixen by the reins. At the side of the large concrete building, they turn out of view, and I can only assume there are more gardens around the back. Then it is just me and Mother Superior, alone in a beautiful garden again. My stomach aches.

"Did you enjoy your walk?" she asks, as breezily as if she were asking how I take my tea.

I don't speak as I dab my sleeve around my eyes, catching tears before they have a chance to fall.

"It is not customary for any of the sisters to leave the grounds, Margaret."

"Not customary or prohibited?" I snap.

Mother Superior exhales long and hard. "Are you going to be trouble, Miss Lannigan?"

"I want to go home."

Mother Superior glides her hand through the air. "This is your home now. And you are so very welcome."

"Please!" Her face tells me she's not used to being interrupted. "I want my ma and pa." I hate myself for letting her see how distressed I am.

"And your parents want you here. What exactly do you think would happen if you turned up on their doorstep?" She doesn't give me time to answer before continuing. "Knowing you're here brings them great comfort. After everything they've been through, that's a small blessing, at least. *You* are a blessing."

The pressure in my chest is hard to bear. I love my ma and pa so very much, and I ache to make them proud. But not like this. Never like this.

"I love someone." The words tumble out as if my heart is spilling right out of my chest. I doubt she'll care or understand, but that's not why I said them. I said them to remind myself that even if I cannot go home because Pa would march me right back here, I have my Joseph's arms to fall into.

"Ah, you had a fellow." Her expression softens, and for a moment I almost believe she feels sorry for me. She steps gingerly down from the porch and makes her way to stand beside me. She has to roll onto her tiptoes to give herself enough height to drape her arm over my shoulder.

"You should write to this fellow of yours," she suggests, guiding us inside with small steps. "Padar Brinkly, the postman from the village, stops by once a week to take our post. Lovely man. I'm sure you know him."

I sniffle and walk alongside her, my case dragging from my arm. Everyone in Thurles knows the singing postman, who whips around the town on his bicycle whistling a tune. Padar the postman will collect my letter in a week and then Joseph will come and we can run away together. *A week.* Ma will have talked to Mrs. Maloney by then, too, and this whole mess will be cleared up. The weight in my chest lifts a fraction as I think about throwing my arms around Joseph's neck and kissing him. I can manage a week, I decide.

Inside, Mother Superior separates from me and closes the door behind us. The bang isn't particularly loud, but it still makes me jump.

"Are you hungry?" she asks, pointing to a nearby door that I imagine leads toward a kitchen or dining area. "I could have Sister Bernadette fix you something. Kippers and toast, perhaps?"

I shake my head and her face falls.

"Really, I'd like to see you eat something. Fasting starts tomorrow, and you don't want to take a dizzy spell."

"Fasting?"

She clasps her hands as if in prayer and smiles. I can see some of her teeth have turned black where the tooth joins the gum, and I wonder if she's ill.

"It's nothing to fear. A fine young thing like yourself will sail through the three days of penance."

My eyes widen. "Three days of fasting?"

"Indeed. All novice sisters undertake the fast when they first arrive. Some find it harder than others, I won't lie, but in the end they all agree that they have a greater appreciation of God's gift of good food when their fast is over. So, shall I have Sister Bernadette fry up those kippers?"

"No, thank you," I say firmly.

I've had little to no appetite since Sheila passed away. Three days without food sounds no different from any other day right now.

"All right." She sighs, defeated. "Let's get you to bed now, eh?"

"The letters," I say, caring far more about making contact with Joseph than about my stomach. "What day does Postman Padar call?"

"Monday."

I'm lightheaded. Today is Wednesday. Monday is a mere five days away. If a fast is what Mother Superior wants, then a fast she shall get. I make a plan to get some water and then I will hide away in my room until I can reach Joseph. He'll be here by Tuesday morning; I don't doubt it.

15

Margaret

With no electricity on the top floor, the long, windowless corridor is spooky. The single candlestick Mother Superior gave me offers little help and instead casts shadows on the wall. I tuck my case under my arm, cup the flame with a shaky palm, and hurry toward the bedroom door to escape the ghosts of sisters past. The smells of damp and dust hit me instantly and I cough, accidentally quenching the candle. Thankfully, a small window offers good lighting, and I open it quickly. A gentle gust flies in, carrying the scent of freshly cut grass. I poke my head out and inhale until my lungs are full of summer. Up here, I have an unobstructed view of the gardens, and they're even more impressive than I first thought. I can see over the tops of trees and the tall gates and into the grounds of the stone building across the road. There are people tending to the garden around the building. I jut my chin, trying to see them more clearly. They're all dressed similarly in pale brown uniforms and crouched like garden gnomes, weeding, I think. I begin to count. There must be at least fifteen of them, and I decide that seems like an unusual number of caretakers, even for a grand old house. I wonder if Mr. Dolan has a team to help him here, or if he does the work of fifteen men alone. I decide he must work alone and that it explains his succinct temperament.

I take my time pulling myself back inside and look around. It comes as quite a surprise that the room is almost twice as big as the room Sheila and I shared. A single bed with a commanding wooden headboard is pushed against the wall on one side. A desk, a chair, and a matching wardrobe are pushed against the other. The wardrobe is tall, and swirling flowers are carved all over it. I've never seen a finer piece of furniture. The simple dresses and shoes Ma and I hurriedly packed certainly don't need a wardrobe of such grandeur. I don't bother to unpack. I decide I won't be staying long enough to make the task worthwhile. I simply open my case, take out *Little Women*, and slide the case under the bed. Tears prick my eyes as I must find out how the story ends without Sheila. I lay the heavy book on the pillow and take some measured breaths.

When I've collected myself, I turn my attention to the desk. I'm grateful to find a pen and paper waiting. I dive into the seat, almost toppling it over, and pick up the pen. I sit with a blank page for a long time. The words to describe the last few hours won't come. I am overwhelmed and numb all at the same time. But I think of my favorite *Little Women* character, Jo March, and how she loved to write, and somehow it gives me the courage to start.

Ballyvale Abbey
Ballyvale Upper
Roscrea
Co. Tipperary
11th July 1956

15 White Water Lawn
New Road
Thurles
Co. Tipperary

My dearest Joseph,

I hope this letter finds you well. Or, in the least, I hope it finds you better than me. My heart is breaking and I've never known pain like it. Part of me wants to lie in bed and never again rise. But what good would that do? Nothing I do will bring Sheila back, and so I know I must be strong and carry on. I know I can do it with you by my side.

I'm sure by the time this letter reaches you that my ma will have explained everything. Did she make tea and offer you the biscuits with the tiny raisins that she saves for special guests? I hope she hasn't wasted them all on Father Michaels.

Please know that none of this was my idea. I did not want to come here. I do not want to be here. I will not stay here. As soon as you arrive, we will be on our way. You'd don't even need to step foot outside your car. There is a small window in my bedroom. I'm sitting next to it right now as I write to you. It has a view of the garden and the driveway. I will watch with my eyes peeled for your car to arrive, and I will greet you at the door. It's with a very heavy heart that I confess that I do not think I can return to Ma and Pa's house. Pa will march me back here quick smart and he'd be furious and embarrassed. With Father Michaels and that damn John-Joe Lynch in his ear, I've come to accept that I don't stand a chance of changing his mind. And Ma won't speak up. You know as well as I do that she hasn't a tongue in her head when it comes to standing up to my pa's rule making. Maybe Sheila would still be alive if she had stood up to him. If I had.

We won't be able to return to your house, either; it's the first place my pa would look. And so, dear Joseph, I am asking you to take me away from this town and this place. I know that we hadn't planned to leave for a life in Dublin for another six months, or a year perhaps. But where is the harm in a head start? I have butterflies just thinking about it. I am going to make you so very happy, Joseph Maloney. That I promise. I am going to be the best wife and, God willing, the best mother any family in Ireland has ever seen.

I doubt there will be time to reply to this letter before your visit, but please know that while I wait, my head is full of thoughts of you and our bright future.

With all my love,
Your Margaret x

I set the pen down just as a knock sounds on my bedroom door. I freeze, startled for a moment as I remember the creepy darkness of the corridor. A second, firmer knock comes, followed by a timid voice.

"Hello. Hello in there."

"Who is it?" I call back.

There's a gentle cough before the voice speaks up. "It's Sister Bernadette. Mother Superior sent me. She said you might be hungry."

I'd been expecting an elderly nun, someone Mother Superior's age, but I can tell from her voice that Sister Bernadette is young.

"Is it all right if I come in? This corridor gives me the willies."

A subtle laugh breaks somewhere inside me. "Yes. Come in. Come in."

The door creaks and a small round woman wearing a veil and long black tunic stands in the gap. She reminds me of Ma and I swallow a lump. Her lips are straight but her eyes are smiling and immediately I think I like her.

"Goodness me, you're a pretty thing," she says, edging inside shyly.

Her feet are hidden beneath her long robe and she seems to float. She pauses and waits for my unsure smile before she closes the door behind her, sealing the two of us away from the rest of the convent. A white garment is folded in her arms.

"This is for you," she says, placing it on the end of my bed. I don't ask what it is. I know it's a habit, pristinely starched like the ones the young sisters at the gate wore when I arrived.

"It's just for now. When you graduate, you'll get one like this." She steps back and runs her hands down her long black garment. She stands statue-like for a moment, and I wonder if she is waiting for me to comment on the clothing. I can't muster a compliment, so I remain quiet.

When the silence becomes awkward, she asks, "You settling in all right?" She flicks her eyes onto the desk, and the paper filled with my handwriting. There's a flash of something on her face, gone too fast for me to catch it. Irritation, maybe. "You got the best room. Father Michaels must be fond of you. No doubt he had a word in Mother's ear. Called in a favor." I pick up on a hint of jealousy, and I hurry to reassure her that's it's wasted on me.

"I'm not staying." I mean for it to come out confident and certain, but there's a wobble in my tone.

She arches an eyebrow. "Hmm. If I had a shilling for every time I heard that . . ."

"Oh. Do a lot of girls leave?"

Her face grows a fraction more serious and she reaches for my hands. Her grip is clammy and I want to pull back.

"The first few weeks are always the hardest. Saying goodbyes to family and friends is never easy. And the fasting. I struggle with a fast, I must admit. I love a slice of good cake." She pokes at her belly and chuckles.

I don't laugh, although I can tell she wishes I would.

"You will grow to like it here. We all do. I couldn't imagine my life any other way now."

"Do you ever leave?" I ask. Her shoulders round and, although I think I have my answer, I ask again. "Do you?"

"What would be my need?"

"Shopping, for a start."

"Not at all. You will soon see that we have everything we need right here." She glides toward the window and points outside. "Fresh fruit and vegetables grow all year round. September is particularly exciting, when the apples and plums are ripe. Plums are my favorite. Just wait until you try my plum tart. It's a treat, I promise."

"I don't like plums," I say, although that's a lie. I like plums quite a lot.

She deflates slightly, and I feel bad for upsetting the nicest person I've met all day.

"Well." She straightens up. "I'm sure you'll find something else outside to delight you. Mother is very proud of the gardens. We all are."

"Yes. It seems everyone around here loves to be outdoors." I gesture outside, but my point is lost when I find the garden across the way empty. "Oh. That's strange. They were there a moment ago."

"Who was where?"

"Groundskeepers, or caretakers maybe?"

"Groundskeepers?" Her eyebrows rise.

"Yes. Fifteen or so. They were tending to the garden. Weeding, I think. I thought it was odd but—"

She reaches across me, accidentally elbowing me in the chest as she closes the window. There is a flash of that something in her eyes again, and I wonder if Sister Bernadette is as nice as I first thought. She takes my hand and leads me to sit on the bed.

"Meat, milk, and bread are delivered once a week," she says matter-of-factly.

"What *is* the building over there?" I ask, my curiosity piqued more than ever.

She puffs out, flustered. "It's a laundry. Now, as I was saying . . . for anything that needs doing in town . . ."

"A laundry? In a building that size, and with such large grounds? What could they possibly be washing?"

She pats her knees and ignores my inquisitiveness. "For anything needed in town, we have Mr. Dolan."

"I thought it was part of the convent. It looks similar. I thought it was owned by the nuns."

"It *is* owned by us."

"Us?" The word tastes odd in my mouth as I accept that Sister Bernadette considers me part of the establishment now. I am as much a piece of the furniture as the headboard or wardrobe.

"Yes. *Us*. The Sisters of Penance mostly reside here, in the convent, but we take care of the laundry also. It is our duty. Now, where was I—" There is a sudden clap of her hands that makes me jump. "Ah yes, Mr. Dolan! He's a gentleman; I must introduce you."

"We've met."

"Oh, good. That's good."

"Is it?" I ask.

"Of course," she says, unstiffening. "He takes care of all the grounds. The convent and the laundry."

"He does all that by himself," I say, wondering what the people I saw earlier could possibly have been doing in that case.

"Yes. He's a treasure."

"So he's been inside the laundry?" I go on.

"Oh, I'm not sure about that."

"Have you?"

She has a tic, I notice. She picks at the skin around her nails when

I make her uncomfortable. I am wasting my breath. Sister Bernadette doesn't want to talk about this. Which makes me all the more curious.

"What do you do in your free time?" I ask, trying a different direction.

She stops picking at once and her sunny smile returns. "You'll find life is quite evenly paced here, Margaret. You won't be short of ways to spend your time."

"I mean for fun. What do you do for fun? If you don't leave, then you must never go to the cinema or dances. Surely you miss dancing?"

She looks horrified, as if I suggested a trip to a brothel and not the local hall.

"It's just, I couldn't live without music and dancing," I explain.

"Oh goodness. Let's not hear talk like that," she says, but there is a longing in her voice, and I suspect she misses her old life sometimes.

I feel sorry for her as I try to imagine a life without dancing. I glance over my shoulder at the letter to Joseph waiting on my desk. Relief is instant, knowing my love will come for me soon. She follows my gaze, and focuses on the paper.

"You have a pen pal," she says, and she sounds excited at the prospect. She stands up and picks up the letter. "You have lovely penmanship."

I snatch the paper rather more aggressively than is necessary. She's startled and begins to pick her nails again.

"Thank you. My ma always said so too," I say, trying to set her at ease.

"Mother takes care of the posting," she tells me, still picking, and I'm concerned she'll draw blood soon. "She keeps a box on her desk and has plenty of envelopes and stamps. You can give it to her."

"That's kind," I say, trying on a breezy tone that is so at odds with everything I'm feeling.

"Mother is wonderful in every way. If you respect her, of course," Sister Bernadette gushes.

I understand. I must be on my absolute best behavior until my letter is safely in Padar's satchel and I watch him cycle into town with my own two eyes.

"Now, shall we get you some grub?" she asks.

As if on cue, my belly groans.

She drapes her arm over my shoulder and says, "Come along. There's tart downstairs. Mother saved you a slice."

16

Margaret

Fasting is harder than I anticipated. My stomach aches and rumbles sporadically, and my mind wanders all too often to thoughts of Ma's roast lamb with gravy. Thankfully, I pass time reading *Little Women*, but it's not the same without my sister's constant interruption to discuss the characters. I find myself pulling my eyes away from the pages to stare at the ceiling, wondering what Sheila might say about Beth's latest tantrum or Jo's recent outburst. I imagine her poking my ribs and telling me to read on. And so I do. The rest of my time is spent trying to peer into the garden of the laundry across the treetops. I bore quickly when there is rarely anyone outdoors, and I can only assume they don't get much business.

By Saturday, hunger has all but taken over. My eyes are tired and I am dizzy if I move too quickly. I haven't left my room since I arrived, except to use the bathroom, and no one has come to check if I am still here. Running away again crosses my mind several times, but my foot still aches and I know I would be no sooner out the gate than Mr. Dolan would be hot on my heels. I know I must wait for Joseph, but I never knew time could move so slowly. There's a small clock on the wall, and the tick of the second hand is amplified by the stillness of the room. Sometimes, at a loss for something to do, I count along with it until I fall asleep.

I distract myself by observing the comings and goings of the convent. I learn quickly that life here is one of strict routine. Bells chime long and loud each morning at 5:30 a.m. and by 5:35 there are footsteps in the corridors as the nuns make their way down the stairs to pray together in the hall. Morning Mass follows, and their hymns and angelic voices carry in the air. Sometimes I sing along, remembering carefree Sundays at Mass with my family, Sheila and me reciting gibberish instead of Latin prayers and waiting for someone to notice. No one ever did. I think of my brothers playing footsie in the pews. My father often spotted that, and it ended with a smack to the back of one of their heads. I see my brothers in my imagination now, standing side by side like steps of stairs, their hair sticking up and standing out as it so stubbornly does most mornings. I ache to reach out and hug each one of them. I imagine their hearts are hurting as much as mine. My darling little Finbar will struggle most. At just ten, how can he understand? I decide to buy him a stick of rock when I reach Dublin. If Pa feels too ashamed to let me visit the house, then I'll post the sugary treat to my littlest brother. And in time, I *know* my parents will see that I make a better wife and mother than I would ever make a nun.

On the whole, the convent is a silent and peaceful place. There is very little chatter, and when I do hear voices, my watch tells me it's lunch or teatime and the nuns are dining and cleaning up afterward. Occasionally I spot a sister walking alone in the garden, her head bowed as she enjoys solitary fresh air.

On Sunday morning Father Michaels arrives in a shiny new car I've never seen him drive before. It's large and silver and looks expensive. I've no doubt my pa oohed and aahed over it, knowing just how to stroke the priest's ego. I can barely control my excitement when Father Michaels opens the back door and a man in a brown suit and a woman with a summer bonnet step out.

"Ma. Pa," I call out, fumbling to open the window as quickly as I can. "I'm up here—" I cut myself off when I realize the couple are not my parents. They are much younger and the woman seems anxious, keeping her head bowed as she follows her husband and Father Michaels inside like a stray puppy. I wait by the window, painfully curious about these guests. They're too young to be one of the novice sisters' parents. Perhaps they're visiting their sister or a beloved aunt. It's more than an hour later before I see them again. They retrace their steps back to the car. The woman holds her head high now, beaming as she cradles a baby swaddled in a knitted cream blanket in her arms. I could swear her arms were empty when she arrived. I saw them dangling by her sides. Or did I? I must be more delirious than I think, I decide, as I watch them get into the car and drive away.

Lightheaded, I reach for the water on my desk and I'm frustrated to find the jug empty. A headache follows rather quickly and I try to ignore it as I kneel at the side of my bed and pray that Father Michaels returns tomorrow, this time with my parents in the back of his car. The longing to hug my ma sits heavy inside me like a boulder as I quietly chant several Hail Marys.

There is little to differentiate the weekend from the weekdays. Sunday is marked only by a longer Mass and louder hymns. It's hard to believe that just two weeks ago I was dancing until my feet blistered in a town hall in Galway. There's a dance in Limerick next week. TIME TO JIVE, the flyer said. I plan to wear the lemon dress folded in my suitcase. It was Sheila's favorite, but she always let me borrow it.

"Sure, where would I have to be wearing it anyway?" she used to say with a sense of melancholy in her eyes. Staring at the four walls of this place, I finally understand her downheartedness. I doubt a pretty dress has ever made it out of a suitcase here.

By dusk on Sunday evening my mind is my enemy. It's becoming increasingly hard to sit still and I find myself with my hands in my hair every so often, tugging until it hurts. Another day is drawing to a close and my parents still haven't visited. The senses of abandonment and anger battle for space inside me. I curse. I string off every swear word I've ever heard, the type that would earn you a wallop of Ma's wooden spoon, and I don't pray after.

When Monday finally dawns, I am awake before the 5:30 a.m. bells. I don't know how long I've been sitting on the edge of my bed with Joseph's letter folded in my clenched fist, waiting to go downstairs. The moment the bells chime, I jump to my feet and open the door. A young woman is leaving the room across the corridor at the same time. She's a head and shoulders taller than me, but roughly the same age. She's dressed in the long white robe, and with her porcelain skin, she's wholly angelic. I freeze for a moment when I realize I haven't seen my robe in days. Perhaps it's tangled up in the sheets at the end of my bed. Or maybe it fell off the bed completely and slid under. I shrug thoughts of it off as I wave and say, "Good morning."

The girl looks at me and places a single finger against her lips.

"Can't you speak?" I ask.

She shakes her head.

"Are you joking? Why not?"

She continues walking in silence.

"But how will we introduce ourselves without speaking? I'm Margaret. What's your name?"

Another young woman in the white robe appears from behind the next door.

"No talking before prayers," she whispers.

I make a face. I can't understand how after days of solitude these girls aren't itching to talk to someone, like I am. I tap the angelic girl on the shoulder. "Will you tell me your name after prayers?" She nods. I accept their silence as we take turns navigating the winding staircase.

On the next floor we are joined by nuns in black habits. Not a single word is spoken. I cough to see if that's allowed. A middle-aged nun glares at me with beady eyes. And so I cough some more. Downstairs, the sisters walk toward a prayer room at the back of the convent and I break away from them and set about finding Mother Superior's chambers. There are five closed doors in the hexagonal hall—all identical. I knock on the door with the distinctive smell of incense wafting from underneath.

There is no answer. I knock once more before I turn the brass knob and enter. No one is here, and yet my breath still falters. Inside appears to be an office. There is a curved desk with a leather armchair tucked behind it, a tall filing cabinet in the corner, and a bookshelf filled with leather-bound books that smell distinctly old—mostly hymnbooks. The desk is messy, with papers and pens strewn haphazardly across the top, and it seems so at odds with the regimental routine and cleanliness of the convent. A stupendous stained-glass window stretches from floor to ceiling behind the desk, boasting beautiful colors and textures—bottle green, sky blue, red, yellow, vivid orange. It is a scene from the Last Supper. The low morning sun shines through the glass and colors splay on the floor like a rainbow collage. I could stare at it all day.

"Margaret." A voice behind me speaks my name like the crack of a whip.

I turn and come face-to-face with Mother Superior.

"You shouldn't be in here." She eyes me up and down. "Prayers are starting. Where is your robe?"

"I have a letter," I say, noticing that interrupting her is becoming a habit and one that doesn't seem to shock her anymore.

"Ah. You took my advice and wrote to your sweetheart?"

"I'm afraid I don't have an envelope or stamp and I was hoping I might—"

"Of course, of course." She cuts me off and brushes past me to fetch an envelope among the mess of papers on her desk.

She passes it to me, along with a pen. I slide the precious letter inside the envelope and I lean on her desk to write Joseph's name and address on the front.

"There's no need for a stamp," she tells me. "We pay for postage in bulk. All the sisters have someone back home they write to. Family and friends." She points to a stack of letters on the left side of her desk.

"Oh," I say, and I can't keep the sadness out of my voice as I take in the height of the stack. I've never thought of a convent as a building full of women missing someone back home before, but I'm not sure I'll think of it any other way from now on.

"What time is Postman Padar coming?" I ask.

"Usually after breakfast."

My heart skips. With Postman Padar arriving so soon, it's possible my letter might be in Joseph's hands by this evening.

"Now run along, Margaret," she tells me. "And for pity's sake, wear your robe from now on. All novice sisters must dress in white at all times outside their rooms. We'll make an exception today, but after that—"

I won't be here long after today, I think. I'm at the door when I hear the squeak of chair legs being pulled across the floor. I turn around to find Mother Superior sitting at her desk.

"Aren't you coming to prayers?" I ask.

"I've work to do, I'm afraid."

I watch her move the stack of envelopes across the desk with her elbow to clear the space in front of her. I can just about make out Joseph's name and address in my neatest handwriting on top of the pile.

"Go," she snaps, pressing the heel of her hand against her forehead.

I leave before she loses her temper, and I feel a strange mix of emotions as I leave my words to Joseph out of my sight.

17

Margaret

Breakfast is not quite the feast I had hoped for. I'm famished, yet a bowl of warm porridge and a glass of milk are all I can manage. I sit at the end of a long table. Girls in white robes line both sides. There isn't much chatter and the few words that are spoken seem to be exchanged in hushed voices. The table behind us is larger, with more nuns dressed all in black. They range in age from not much older than me right up to Mother Superior's age. They chat more freely and there is laughter among them and I can tell they are mostly friends.

The girl from the corridor this morning is sitting beside me. I'm waiting for her to finish eating before I introduce myself again. But as soon as she sets her spoon down, she takes a Bible from the pocket of her robe and begins reading.

I interrupt her. "Hi. I'm Margaret."

She looks up and whispers, "Yes. You said earlier. Hello, Margaret. I'm Joyce."

"Nice to meet you, Joyce. Where you from?"

"Kildare. You?"

I edge closer to better hear her. "Thurles."

"Ah, a local."

"Yes. Just around the corner, really." My heart pangs, thinking about home. "Do you know Tipperary well?"

She shakes her head and I watch an unexpected sadness creep into her eyes. "I thought I might get to know it when I moved here. But I haven't been outside the gate yet. I placed my name in the volunteer book for town, but so far nothing has come up."

"What's the volunteer book?"

"Haven't you signed it? You add your name if you feel you could help in an emergency. Cycle into town to fetch Father Michaels if need be. Or Doctor Henry." Her eyes dance with wanderlust. "Deliver an important letter that can't wait for Postman Padar. That sort of thing. But there have been no emergencies in the last six months—" She cuts herself off and sighs, before shifting her tone. "And we should be thankful. Thank the Lord."

"You've been here six months and you haven't set foot outside the gate?" My voice is shrill.

"Where is your tunic?" she mumbles; her eyes focused on the small print in front of her.

I run my hands over my pleated red skirt, which I've paired with a cream blouse and green cardigan. I must stand out like a Christmas tree in this sea of white and black.

"I'm not sure. Under my bed maybe."

Joyce sucks air in through her teeth as if I have punched her in the gut. I get the impression she has never set a foot out of place in her whole life. She's the type of girl who would walk through fire if someone senior told her to. My pa would love her.

"I'll look for it," I assure her.

She doesn't say anything, but the corners of her lips twitch as if it pleases her that I'll find it, and she turns a page in her Bible and reads on.

"Do you like it here?" I ask, requiring more conversation.

"I am here for my love of our Lord and savior."

"Yes, but do you like it? If you never leave the convent, then isn't it a prison?"

She looks up at last. "I love God. I am truly overjoyed to devote my life to serving Him."

"How old are you?"

"Twenty-one."

I snort. "Don't you want to have fun? Don't you miss it?"

I try to imagine six months of this life and I feel goose bumps line my arms.

"A life of devotion is not for everyone. But for people like us it's a calling." Joyce swirls her finger in the air, gesturing that everyone in this room—sipping tea or spooning porridge into an open mouth—is who she is referring to.

I shrug. "Not for me. I don't belong here."

"Shh!" She places her finger on her lips just as she did upstairs. "Don't say such things."

"I don't care who hears me."

She snaps her Bible shut and clamps her hand over my mouth. Her hand is hot and clammy against my face, and I push it away but my eyes stay locked on her. She can spout all the mumbo jumbo she likes about *a calling*, but I'd put money on her being trapped here too.

"Do you have somewhere you can go?" I ask, lowering my voice. I am so close to her my nose is almost brushing hers. "If your parents won't have you back, is there anywhere you can turn?" I wonder if Joseph and I could help her. Maybe Joseph could drive her to a relative's house. I'm sure he wouldn't mind. Kildare is on our way to Dublin.

"My parents are wonderful," she says, and she sounds sincere. "I told you, the Sisters of Penance is my calling. Father Michaels would not be pleased to hear you speak like this."

Staying in the priest's favor is important to Joyce. As if living up to expectations is the internal metronome that keeps her well-being balanced.

"I would like us to be friends," she says, and there's the slightest crack on her last syllable that tells me, calling or not, Joyce is lonely.

Under any other circumstance I would be happy to get to know her. I hope that when I leave, she can find a companion in one of the other girls. Someone more like her.

"Do you hear that?" Joyce asks.

My attention has also shifted toward delicate singing outside the window. Baritone humming draws closer. It's subtle and I lean on my chair to better hear it over the purr of sisters chatting as they eat.

"The singing postman," I exclaim, so enthused that heads turn and stare at me yet again, and I have to fight the urge to poke my tongue out at them.

"You see, that's the spirit," Joyce says. "I write home often. It helps with the homesickness."

I look at her pretty young face, so much prettier than mine, and her words ring in my ears. *Homesick for six months.* The poor girl.

It's not long before there is a collective sound of spoons clinking against bowls. I'm lost in a daydream about Joseph reading my letter, and it takes a nudge from Joyce before I grasp that we are sending our bowls to the top of the table. I pass my bowl to Joyce and she passes it to the girl next to her and so on and so on. We repeat the process until all the bowls are stacked at the top of the table. There is a single ding of a bell that makes me jump, and as complete silence falls over the large dining room, I understand that our time for chat is now over. The older nuns begin filing out of the dining hall in order of their seat positions. They lower their heads and clutch the rosary beads dangling from their belts. My observations over the weekend tell me it's time for them to retreat to their rooms. Or walk around the garden. Time to be alone, more. So alone.

"Should we offer to clean up?" I whisper in Joyce's ear, desperate to do anything for company.

She doesn't reply.

"I'm happy to wash or dry. But my ma says I'm a speedy drier, so maybe you could wash?"

A redness creeps across her cheeks. "It is reflection time, Margaret. We cannot speak."

"Again?" I huff and step forward, dreading returning to my damn room. Joyce's hand grabs mine and I almost lose my balance when she tugs hard. I whip my head over my shoulder to look at her. Her lips are pursed. I follow her gaze as she flicks her eyes onto the final handful of sisters, age hampering them as they make their way toward the door. Joyce won't say it, but she doesn't have to. I work out that we must wait our turn. No white tunic can budge until every last black tunic is gone. Pecking order, I get it. I adjust the waistband of my skirt, which suddenly feels tight, and decide that, dressed like this, I should wait until last.

I begin to worry that Joyce, a stickler for the rules, might never make a friend here if she rarely opens her mouth. I wait my turn, and I can't help but smile when Joyce waits with me. I want to thank her. But I don't say a word.

Despite the wait, we catch up with two senior sisters in the corridor. Their dark tunics hang from hunched shoulders and drag at the front hem, highlighting how slowly their feet move. And although I am condemned to silence, when I cock my elbows and smile they take my offer of assistance. We take our time making our way up the stairs. At the top I unlink them and the eldest of the two, a tiny lady considerably older than Mother Superior, beckons me to bend to her height. When I do, she kisses my check. We don't exchange a word, and yet it's the nicest thing anyone has done for me since I came through the gate at Ballyvale.

Joyce and I fly up the iron spiral stairs to the third floor. We nod a silent goodbye and part. I slam my bedroom door behind me just to hear the bang of it. The vibration shakes my window, and when I look outside, my frustration melts. I spy Padar the Postman throwing his satchel full of letters over his shoulder and mounting his bicycle. I open the window to catch his sweet tune as he begins to pedal, and I am overcome with relief as I watch two young nuns open the gates just enough for him to cycle through.

"Oh, Joseph," I say aloud, as if my voice will hitch a ride on the back of Padar's bicycle. "I will see you soon, my love. Very, very soon."

18

Margaret

My tunic stares at me, tangled between the sheets at the end of my bed. It has more creases than Mother Superior's face. I shake it vigorously, but that seems to make it worse. I settle for draping it over the back of the chair and crossing my fingers that the creases fall out before the next round of prayers. Then, I root under my pillow for *Little Women*. I get comfortable on the edge of my bed, swinging my feet back and forth like a child as I read the final chapters aloud.

"*'Into each life some rain must fall. Some days must be dark and sad and dreary.'*"

"That's it, Sheila," I say, as if my darling sister can hear. Part of me is certain that she can. That's the end. It feels oddly perfect to finish the final page of our beloved story before starting the very first chapter of my new life with Joseph. "You understand, don't you? You understand why I can't stay here? This was to be your life, not mine. I see now that I was always going to lose you. Lose you to the four walls of the convent or lose you to eternal rest above the clouds, but either way, you never really belonged to me. Or to Ma or Pa or the boys. You were always a thing of God's. You and Joyce would have been great friends."

For the first time since Sheila died, I think of her without tears following. I smile and hope that the rain in my life stops falling soon and it is once again bright. I slide the book back under my pillow and lie down. My eyes are heavy, and after seeing Postman Padar pedal away, for the first time all week I sleep easily. Too easily. When I finally open my eyes, my room is dark. I jump out of bed and hurry to the window. The moon is round in a cloudless sky, bathing the garden below in a silver glow. I press the heel of my hand into my forehead and accept that I've slept the day away. Panic momentarily swells inside me as I worry that Mother Superior will be angry. Or, worse still, that she will tell Father Michaels. But the feeling quickly dissipates when I remember that it doesn't matter. I've no doubt that Joseph will arrive at first light.

I embrace the silence as I wait and wait for the chime of the morning bells. I use the time to put myself together. I hoist my suitcase onto the bed, fiddle with the wonky lock, and pull out Sheila's beautiful lemon dress. I slip into it and it's looser on me than the last time I wore it, I note as I zip up the side. I return to the case and rummage around the bottom for some hair clips, but to my surprise my fingers stumble across a cool metal cylinder. The delight that follows stops me in my tracks. I know before I pull it out that it's Ma's best lipstick. My gleefulness is compounded when I pull my hand back and see that I am right. I pop the lid and run the ruby red lipstick over my lips. "Oh, Ma," I whisper. "Thank you." I brush my hair and pin it into a French roll—Joseph's favorite style. "You look just like Audrey Hepburn with your hair like that," he told me one evening after a dance in Cork. I don't look anything like the famous actress, but Joseph made me feel as special as a movie star. Some kissing in the car after that nearly led us to get carried away.

I slapped his arm playfully. "Ah, stop that. I look nothing like her. She's the most beautiful woman in the world."

He edged closer, leaning over the gear stick to cup my face in his hands, and between breathy kisses he whispered, "No, Margaret. You are."

I'm not foolish enough to let Joseph Maloney's silly compliments convince me that I am any more of a looker than average, but I want so much to see him look at me today the way most men look at posters of Audrey Hepburn.

I give myself the once-over in the full-length mirror that hangs on the side of the wardrobe. My collarbones are more pronounced than I'm used to seeing, and my face is a fraction slenderer. I hate to admit it, but I don't think I've ever looked better, and I think I might burst counting down the hours until Joseph arrives. Finally, I take the crinkly tunic from the back of the chair and pull it on over my head. I shimmy my hips until it falls into place, covering me completely from neck to toe. I check my reflection in the mirror again and snigger. I look like an entirely different person than I did just seconds ago. I certainly look the part of a novice nun even if I don't feel it.

Light as a feather, I make my way into the hall to join the other novice nuns and the rest of the sisters, where I will follow the day's mundane routine before it's time to go. I smile for prayers and Mass. I'm once again ravenous as I eat my porridge. I pass my bowl to the top of the table. I do not ask who will wash up, nor do I offer to help. I take a walk in the garden. There are several of us dotted around the grounds, like newly hatched butterflies, curious and exploring. As per protocol I don't utter a word to a soul. So I'm not the one who calls out, "What was that?" when a scream pierces the air like a knife popping a bubble. But the question is equally on my mind too. *Yes indeed, what* was *that?* The nuns continue to walk but all the novices are still, as if the disquieting shriek has frozen us to the spot.

There's another squeal, and then a wail. I begin to wonder if some poor animal is hurt. A fox caught in a trap, perhaps. Or, worse still, Vixen, Mr. Dolan's horse. A third scream is followed by commotion and raised voices and I know it's not an animal in distress. A person is hurt—over at the laundry. I stretch myself as tall as I can, but it's no good, I cannot see over the top of the stone wall. I find myself wishing I had chosen to spend reflection time in my room, where I have a view. If I hurry, I might make it upstairs in time to see what's going on over there. I'm rushing, practically trotting, when the front of my robe gets caught under my feet and I take a tumble. I bang my knee, and I suspect it's grazed or bleeding, but it's my pride that hurts the most when Joyce appears over me, holding out her hand. I take it and she helps me to my feet.

"Thank you," I mouth silently.

"Are you hurt?" she asks.

I shake my head.

"Good. At least that's something." Her smile is crooked and I suspect she wants to laugh at my humorous tumble now that she knows I'm not hurt. "What has you in such a hurry?"

"You're talking," I say.

She shrugs. "We're allowed to talk in the garden."

"Are we? Then why don't we spend all our time out here?"

Joyce titters. "Oh, Margaret. You are a funny one, aren't you."

The commotion over the wall dies down, and I accept that whatever it was, I have missed it now. Disappointed, I turn my attention to Joyce and the small, leather-bound book tucked under her arm. Her Bible seems to go wherever she does.

"My pa says talking to flowers makes them grow," she says. "I don't have much to talk about. So I read to them instead."

"Do they listen?" I smirk at the notion of flowers with ears.

"I think so, yes." Joyce gestures toward some well-fed and watered red and white roses growing in a semicircle around the base of a large oak tree. I decide I like the idea, that flowers, just like people, enjoy a good story.

"Does it have to be the Bible?" I ask, treading gently for fear of offending her.

"It's the only book I've got. I love reading, you see. My house was mighty busy, what with being the eldest of thirteen girls. Growing up, reading was just about the only peace I got."

I didn't know Joyce had this much chatter in her. I guess the bookworm in her can't resist talking about reading. Conversation continues to flow as we walk around the garden. She tells me how much she loves her family and how she hopes some of her younger sisters will join her here in Ballyvale someday. Her youngest sister was a newborn when she left home six months ago, and her ma's letters confirm that she is pregnant again.

"Gosh, your ma's hands are full," I say, borrowing a phrase I've heard my mother use often when a friend or relative announced an umpteenth pregnancy.

"That's for sure. I'm hoping it's a little boy this time, for my pa's sake. I know he'd love a priest in the family," Joyce says.

She looks at me. I know she's expecting a nod of understanding. My sympathy for a poor sonless family. But it's all I can do to keep the frustration off my face. The poor wee fella isn't even born yet and already his family are deciding his fate. I hope hard that Joyce's family have a fourteenth girl. For that baby's sake.

It starts to rain, and Joyce holds the tiny Bible over her head in a laughable attempt to keep dry.

"Quick," she calls out, but I'm already two steps ahead of her, trying to keep my hair and lipstick dry for Joseph. The rest of the day drags on in the same monotonous pattern, and when bedtime approaches and Joseph has not arrived, I find myself filled with contempt for Padar Brinkly. Doesn't he understand that a delay delivering a letter can quite literally turn a person's life upside down?

The following day plays out in the exact same pattern. Morning bells. I wear my yellow dress again, ready and waiting under my tunic. Then it's prayers, Mass, more darn porridge, a walk in the garden, and a chat with Joyce. Second prayers follow, then dinner, which I struggle to finish, a second walk, a second Mass. Supper. Wash. Bed. Joseph does not come.

After four mornings of dressing in Sheila's lemon dress under my tunic, I know I cannot possibly stretch to a fifth. I take a cardigan and a pleated skirt from my case and make do with them.

The day after that, I miss the dance in Limerick, and the yearning to attend is so great I don't touch my porridge and I don't walk in the garden. I sit by the window in my bedroom, staring out at gates that don't open. Finally, I take pen to paper, and words to Joseph spill out in a frantic scrawl. Pages and pages. I share every waking moment since I've been here, and by the end my wrist is cramping.

It's lights-out and bedtime, but I ignore the rules and scurry downstairs to Mother Superior's chambers. I knock three times, and her sleepy voice tells me to come in.

I'm surprised to find her still behind her desk, signing papers of some sort. She doesn't seem surprised to see me.

"I have another letter," I tell her, waving it like a flag.

"For this lovely young man of yours?"

"Yes. For Joseph."

"You do know it's time for rest right now, Margaret, and Padar won't be here until tomorrow."

In my hurry I've worked up a sweat, and a bead of perspiration trickles down my spine. "I know. But I can't sleep until I've placed this on the top of the pile of outgoing post."

"Don't you want to wait for a reply to your first letter to him before you bother him again?"

"Bother him?" I snap.

Mother Superior's disapproval of my tone is perceptible. She squints and sucks air in through pursed lips. I'm instantly chilly, as I worry that

I've infuriated her and she will refuse to post my letter. I know my ma would. She'd punish me for such cheek.

"Put it there," Mother grumbles, and I suspect she's too tired to scold me.

I want to thank her. I want to promise that I won't disturb her in her chambers ever again. But I'm too afraid to open my mouth and risk saying anything that might get my letter removed from the posting pile. I smile and back out of the room. I close the door with a gentle click and make my way to bed.

19

Margaret

Day after day, I wake with hope, and by night I fall into bed with an aching heart. Each time I pick up my pen to write to Joseph, I find the words increasingly more difficult to summon. It has been almost two weeks since I entered the convent, but it feels much longer. I begin writing to Joseph daily. I keep my pain and sense of abandonment off the page, as I keep my message brief and consistent: *Come get me!* By the time Postman Padar calls next week, I'll have a small stack of envelopes ready for his satchel. Joseph cannot ignore seven letters, surely.

I'm sitting at my desk, ready to pen the next letter before the morning bells, when there is a subtle knock on my door. No one ever comes near the third floor. I am on my feet in an instant. I cross my fingers behind my back and hope that today is the day Joseph comes.

A second, firmer knock follows, and I clear my throat. "Come in. Come in. Do please come in."

The door creaks open and the hinges whine against the otherwise silent convent. Sister Bernadette remains standing in the frame of the open door. Her expression is pensive and narrow and at odds with her round and jolly frame. Her voice cracks when she says my name. "Margaret, you are needed downstairs." Her somberness confuses me. She seems like a lovely woman, but we are not all that well acquainted, certainly not well enough for her to miss me when I go.

"Mother Superior is waiting in her chambers," she goes on, steadier now.

"Do I have a visitor?" I ask, my excitement bubbling.

She blinks, and a reply takes time and finally comes in the form of a nod.

"I'll be as quick as I can," I say, almost breathless with anticipation.

"Take your time, Margaret. There is no rush. Not today."

She disappears with a swish of her robe, and I can't get to my feet fast enough. The first clothes that come to hand are a gray skirt and a bottle-green blouse. It's not quite the breathtaking outfit I hoped to greet my fiancé wearing, but so much time has already been wasted, I won't fritter away another second.

I fetch my suitcase from the bottom of the wardrobe. There's not much to pack; my hairbrush, some hair clips, and yesterday's socks, rolled up at the end of my bed. Some of my other smalls and Sheila's sundress have been sent across the garden to the laundry and haven't come back yet. I'm saddened to leave without my sister's dress, but it feels like a necessary sacrifice—the price to pay to leave this place. Sheila would understand, I tell myself. Everything else is still in my case from when I arrived. I almost forget *Little Women* tucked away under my pillow. I double back and fetch it before I buckle the case and race out the door. The case clatters and bangs against my thigh, and it's sure to give me bruises as I thunder down the stairs, my footsteps no doubt disturbing the peace.

I come to a stop just before I reach Mother Superior's chambers. A mix of exhilaration and excitement has me panting. I wonder if I'm red-faced; I certainly feel sweaty. I should take a moment to gather myself, but my hand is raised and knocking before I have time to think.

"Enter," Mother Superior calls.

I curl my fingers around the knob and notice I'm shaking.

Oh, Joseph. Oh, Joseph.

I push open the door, and the absence of ever-present incense stops me in my tracks. There is a tray with a china teapot, some cups, and a plate of biscuits on Mother's desk. The treats are a jarring sight, especially before prayers. But the smell is divine, and my mouth waters. The second surprise is less pleasant, as I can see that Joseph is not here. Instead, Father Michaels is standing, towering over Mother, even with his head bowed.

"Is he coming?" I blurt, as a foreboding chill runs down my spine.

"Margaret, child, have a seat, please," Mother says. I can't look at her. I'm wary of the glint in her eye. It's the same sheen no adult can hide when they're about to share bad news.

"Please. Please say he's on the way? He wouldn't leave me here. Isn't that why you've called me?"

She glides her arm through the air toward the waiting chair as sitting becomes an order. "You'll have some tea, won't you?"

She doesn't see me shake my head as her eyes burn into the empty chair. I know she won't say another word until I do as I am told.

Sitting down, I am acutely aware that my elders remain on their feet.

"Father Michaels comes with some news this morning," Mother says, her eyes briefly dropping to the case I've set down at my feet.

The priest lowers himself into the chair next to me and takes my hand. His chubby warm fingers curl around mine and my skin crawls, but I don't dare pull my hand back.

"I have some upsetting news," he begins. There's static in his voice, a rare glimpse of emotion.

"News for me?" It comes out mousy, and I hate that this man's presence can unravel me like a ball of twine.

"It's your ma and pa," he goes on, stroking his thumb across the back of my hand as he draws in a shuddering breath.

It is close to impossible to keep a lid on my contempt for this man, and my knees bob with the resentment of it all.

"It's diphtheria." His thumb stills, and I look into his eyes for the first time. They are narrow and pained.

"Your sister must have passed it on. There are quite a few folks in town with it now. The Kellys and the Smiths. Three generations each. Terrible, just terrible."

"The boys?" I pull my hand away and tug at the neck of my tunic, as if it's suddenly too tight, squeezing all the air out of me. "What about Colm, Matthew, and Finbar?"

"Vaccinated, like you. They are well."

I'm dizzy as I get to my feet. "I must go," I tell Mother Superior. "I have to go. Ma won't be able to take care of the boys if she's poorly. She'll need helping. And my pa will need caring for too."

Mother Superior's eyes glisten, and I want to jam my hands on my ears so I don't hear what comes next.

"They didn't make it," Father Michaels says. "Your parents passed last evening."

A screech follows. I clasp my hands over my mouth and try hard to lock the sound back inside me.

"Your ma passed first, and your pa a couple of hours later. I was there to bless them. They are in the arms of our Lord now."

I take my hands away from my mouth and I want to scream in his face. Tell him that I will never forgive him for stealing their last days away from me. Tell him that he is a bad man. But nothing more than a puff comes out.

Mother Superior places her hand on my lower back. "Oh, my child."

My heart sits in my chest in a million pieces as I'm forced to imagine a world without my ma's hugs or my pa telling me about the latest news he's read in the paper. Pa won't walk me down the aisle. And Ma won't have the chance to spoil my babies the way doting grandmothers do. But worse still, they won't see my brothers grow up. The boys' loss feels even more difficult to bear than my own. They are children still, and children need their mas and pas.

"Finbar must be so scared," I say, finally managing words. I ache to scoop my little brother into my arms and kiss the top of his messy hair the way Ma did. I am the nearest he has to a mother now.

"This must be an awful shock, Margaret," Mother says kindly, as she wraps her wafer-like arms around me.

I glance over her shoulder to make eye contact with Father Michaels. "Do they know? The boys. I'm assuming Doctor Henry told them."

"They know."

I wriggle free from Mother as the desire to be with my brothers floods my senses.

"We should go," I say, picking up my case, which feels so much heavier than before, as if just lifting it exhausts me. "The sooner the better. I'm already packed."

"Your brothers are on their way to Mayo," Father Michaels tells me.

I almost drop the case. "Mayo?"

"To your uncle Seamus and aunt Mildred."

"Millie," I correct him. "My pa's brother and his wife."

"Aye, that's them. Lovely couple."

Seamus and Millie *are* lovely, from what I remember. But Pa and Seamus had a falling-out a while back. It must be at least two years since the boys and I last saw them.

"Finbar doesn't really know them," I say. "He won't understand. It makes much more sense for them to stay at home with me. I'm almost twenty-one. Plenty old enough to care for them. Ma was married at my age."

I watch as Father Michaels's nostrils flare. "Millie is a kind woman, and with no children of her own, three strapping young men will be a blessing. She will love them as her own."

I have no doubt that this is true. But they are not her own. They are *my* family. My responsibility.

"The boys need to be in their own home. They've never been to Mayo in their lives—"

"Let's have some tea," Father Michaels says, dropping his eyes to the china pot, and I think he expects me to pour.

My face scrunches. I hate this man.

"A warm cuppa will help with the shock," he adds.

I glance at Mother Superior, confident she will understand my urgency to go home. She nods and agrees, "Tea really will help."

"Jesus Christ!" I clasp my hands and press them down on the top of my head. "Will tea bring my ma and pa back to life? Bring Sheila back, or make sure my brothers are all right?"

"You forget yourself, Margaret," Father Michaels tells me sternly. The sorrow in his voice is replaced with clipped irritation. "Blasphemy has no business here. Now, if you take your tea and some biscuits to your room, I think Mother Superior will understand if you would like to give morning prayers a miss today."

"Indeed," Mother softly says. "And take the rest of the day, too, if you need to. Grief is a hard business, and we understand."

"You're not listening to me." I am bewildered and beginning to sway—lightheaded. "I *have* to go home. If you won't take me, Father Michaels, I will walk. But one way or another, I am leaving here today and going home to my brothers."

"Margaret, even at a time like this you make things harder than they already are." He sighs, then lowers his voice to a mumble before adding, "God took the wrong Lannigan girl, that's for certain."

Mother doesn't flinch, and I know she didn't hear him. I suspect he didn't intend for me to hear him, either; even Father Michaels wouldn't be so openly cruel, I think. But his nasty words strengthen my resolve.

"My ma would want the boys taken care of," I spit out.

"That she would," he agrees, placing his hand on Mother's arm and smiling. "And I'm seeing to it."

"My family is not your business. Especially now, without Pa."

They share a gasp, as if what I just said is so awful neither of them can quite believe their ears.

"Your pa used his last breath to ask me to take care of those boys," Father Michaels tells me. This comes as little wonder. Pa was always so keen to place his children's lives in Father Michaels's hands. "John-Joe Lynch is buying your parents' house," Father Michaels goes on.

"What? No. He can't. That's our home. Me and the boys."

"He is quite insistent, I'm afraid. As a good friend of your pa's, he says it's the least he can do. He means to take care of your brothers. This way, the money from the sale of the house can be put toward their education and whatnot. Schooling is expensive. You know that."

"But . . . but . . ."

"The boys need an education. Unfortunately, I cannot see another way."

The fear that he is right sits with me for a moment before I shake it off. "I'll figure it out. I'll get my old job back. I'll get a second job if I have to. I'll make it work. Ma and Pa did."

Father Michaels pulls his lips to one side, the way he so often does when he's had enough of my talking.

"I know you're worried. But your uncle and aunt will take mighty fine care of your brothers. This is what your parents would want. I hate to say it, but you cannot provide what those boys need, and I think you know that, don't you? I have a responsibility to put the boys first. That's what real love is, Margaret. Sacrifice."

I imagine Finbar wrapped in Millie's loving arms. I imagine her cuddles and stories soothing him.

"But Finbar is only ten." I swallow hard. "He'll forget me."

"I'm sure Millie and Seamus will tell them all about you. And you could write to them. Mother tells me you haven't received any letters yet. Pen pals will cheer you right up."

The dig at Joseph's lack of correspondence doesn't hurt the way Father Michaels no doubt intended it to. There is no room for any more heartache inside me today.

"And Colm will be off to join the priesthood soon. Is it next summer he turns eighteen?" Father Michaels asks, with an overzealous smile. His glee is inappropriately timed and revolting. I wish my pa could see this, see the man Father Michaels really is.

"April," I say. "Colm's birthday is April 27th."

"April 27th, 1939, yes?"

"Yes."

"Almost eighteen indeed. They grow up so fast." He's not talking to me. He's turning to Mother Superior now, and I can tell he's getting ready to leave. Without me.

"And who knows, in no time, he might be here saying Mass. Wouldn't that be nice."

Mother Superior's expression brightens. "Oh, indeed. That would be a true delight."

"A nun and a priest in the family. Donny and Mary would be so proud, Lord rest their souls," Father Michaels says, before blessing himself.

"Lord rest their souls," Mother repeats.

"What about the funeral?" I blurt. Memories of the day we buried Sheila flash in my mind. Finbar was inconsolable. I can't bear to think of his little feet walking the streets of Thurles behind another hearse so soon.

"I'll say Mass, of course." Father Michaels nods. "And Father McCarey from Glenakilly parish will most likely join me. Your father did the collection there sometimes if they were stuck."

I know. I was only too aware that if the church needed helping, my pa would always oblige.

"What day?" I ask.

"Friday. Ten a.m. Mass."

"Friday," I echo, letting it sink in.

Mother Superior reaches for my hand and it's the strangest thing: I can see her knobby fingers curl around mine but I can't feel anything. It is as if I am no longer inside my body. "We are a closed order," she says, as if I didn't already know that we never leave this hellish place. "So you'll need to stay here."

"But they're my parents. Surely—"

"We will make sure the hearses drive by, of course. It's a slight detour, but it can be arranged." She strokes her other hand against the chunky mahogany cross that dangles around her neck. "There will be an opportunity to wait at the gate as they pass, and you can say your goodbyes."

"That's ridiculous. That's not a goodbye. That's, that's . . ." I am lost for words. I feel as if I should be crying, but tears elude me. I grapple with the ridiculousness of it all—so condemned to this place that I cannot even seek release to bury my parents.

"I know it hurts, child," Mother says, and I bristle and pull away from her. "This is how it must be. You have your fellow sisters and the Lord at your side here at Ballyvale. Take some comfort in that."

Her words ring in my ears. *Take comfort?* I doubt I will know comfort ever again. My sister is gone, now my parents too. And soon, the house I grew up in will belong to the local barman. My brothers will grow up miles away because as much as I might want to, I cannot financially provide the life they deserve. Dead or alive, my family are lost to me. And my Joseph has let me go. I have no one and nothing if I do not have this place. I am a nun now. No more and no less. Father Michaels has stolen my world and trapped me like a bird in a cage. But I will not sing. Not for him. Not ever.

20

1958
TWO YEARS LATER

Margaret

Joyce is as giddy as a goat this morning. There's a spring in her step and whimsical wonderment dances in her eyes, like she's a little girl waking up on Christmas morning, bursting to see what gift Santy has left.

"It's wonderful, isn't it?" she whispers, as we descend the winding staircase from the third floor for the last time. "I can't believe it's finally graduation day. Can you? Can you actually believe it?"

Ballyvale is not somewhere time moves quickly, but, not wanting to burst Joyce's happy bubble, I say, "Shh, no talking before prayers, remember?"

Joyce clamps her hand over her mouth, but I still notice her blush.

I give her a gentle poke in the ribs with my finger. "I'm teasing. I'm teasing."

"You're truly as wicked as Beth." She sniggers.

"How many times have you read *Little Women* now? It must be at least six?"

"Nine, and every time I love it even more."

Sister Bernadette meets us at the bottom step of the stairs. "Look at you. Oh, just look at you." She takes me by the hand and twirls me around. "A fine picture. But still as skinny as the day you arrived. I can't seem to put a pick on you, even with plum tart." She points to my robes. I'm dressed head to toe in black, but I couldn't bring myself to look in the mirror this morning as I pulled on my new garments for the first time.

"We're not girls anymore. We're women now," Joyce says, with so much joy in her voice I think today might be the best day of her life.

"Women of the cloth," Sister Bernadette agrees.

"Our Lord has high expectations for us," Joyce goes on, smiling my way.

"Really, he told you so, did he?" I can't help teasing.

"Oh, Margaret." Joyce titters, placing her finger on her lips. "Hush now, no talking before prayers."

I am reminded that even today, the happiest of Joyce's days, nothing makes her happier than conforming.

"Well, ladies, I best get back to the kitchen, I've a crumble in the range. And you know Father Michaels doesn't like to be kept waiting. He's trimmed his ear hair especially for the day."

Joyce giggles. "I thought I was the only one who noticed his hairy ears."

Sister Bernadette leans closer. "Sometimes I'm not listening to the sermon because I'm daydreaming about taking a scissors to them."

"Me too." Laughter folds Joyce in the middle like an envelope.

"Oh, listen to us," Sister Bernadette says, cupping her face in her hands and shaking her head. "We'll have to go to confession later."

Joyce's laughter is abruptly halted as she comes to her senses. "Yes. Indeed."

Sister Bernadette lowers her hands and winks. "Ah, but it was worth it."

I suspect I delight in this moment more than both of them combined—two of my favorite people bad-mouthing that man is the most I've enjoyed myself in weeks—and I certainly won't be going to confession for it.

"Well, go on. Quick, quick," Sister Bernadette says, still chuckling quietly to herself as she makes a shooing motion with her hands. "Before you get us all in trouble."

"Let's get this over with," I mumble, taking Joyce by the hand and speed-walking ahead, but I'm rooted to the spot when we reach the chapel. The altar is adorned with fresh carnations. Fluffy pink heads, slender stems, and wispy green laurel leaves perfume the air. Generous bouquets of snow-white roses are hand-tied to the backs of every dark timber pew with ivory ribbon. It is as if the senior nuns have carried the garden inside for us to enjoy, petal by petal, thorn by thorn, leaf by leaf. I am agape. It is Joyce who finds words as she curls her fingers a fraction tighter around mine.

"See, didn't I tell you it would be wonderful?"

Joyce is casting her net of wonderment wide. I know she speaks broadly and that her reverence is not only for the beautiful sight before us, but for the day itself, the convent, the nuns and our joining them.

Father Michaels arrives and kisses the altar. Dutifully, we all stand and sing. Mass is long but beautiful, and I have never felt closer to God than in this chapel at this time.

At the end, Father Michaels raises his arms and says, "Go now in peace." But nobody gets to their feet like usual. There is silence and veneration. As if we are a congregation of stunned rabbits, shocked by the gravity of this ceremony.

Mother Superior is first to stand. She raises her hands, mirroring Father Michaels, and says, "Congratulations, one and all. I am proud beyond words."

Everyone waits until her hands are firmly back on the pew and she is steady on her feet before clapping and cheering. My fellow graduates are overcome with joy. It sits on their cheeks like round red apples. It sparkles in their eyes like the stars in the night sky. I hear it in their chatter like birds at dawn. I have never experienced the convent fuller of life and merriment. And although I don't wholeheartedly share their ecstasy, I am enjoying the celebration. Joyce hugs me, and her happiness emanates until it fills me with warm joy and I hug her back, tighter than I ever have before. But my happiness quickly cools when Father Michaels leaves the altar to come shake our hands. I try to slip away, but I am wedged in the pew between Joyce and several of the other exhilarated girls. I count backward from fifty, trying not to shiver as he shakes hand after hand, edging closer to me.

Finally, he pauses in front of me with a supercilious grin and extends his hand. My flesh creeps the second his palm touches mine. "Congratulations, Sister Margaret."

Sister Margaret. It doesn't seem to fit. Like a dress that won't quite button up at the back, or a hat that is too large and falls off if you move your head.

"Donny and Mary would be mighty proud of you today. I know I am," he says.

I pull my hand back and shove my clenched fists into my pockets. My nails dig into my palms. I want to make it clear that Father Michaels has no right to be proud of me. He is nothing to me. Less than nothing. But I promised myself I would never speak to this man again. Besides, a look is often worth a thousand words. I know I've said plenty when he moves on to shake the next girl's hand.

Finally, we make our way to the dining room. Chitchat hums in the usually silent halls, and I wish every day could be like this. Nothing shy of a feast awaits us, and suddenly you could hear a pin drop as no one can quite believe their eyes. The long table is set with sparkling silver cutlery and gleaming white delft. Fresh fruit is stacked on oval platters in the center—raspberries, strawberries, apples, and plums, like an oil painting come to life. There is no porridge to be seen. Instead, crispy bacon and eggs sit on every plate, and I smell freshly buttered toast before I see it. There are pots of tea and apple-and-rhubarb crumble for after.

"Sit, sit," Sister Bernadette tells us, brushing crumbs off her apron and flour out of her hair.

I want to thank her and tell her that she has truly outdone herself, but I am momentarily startled when I notice Father Michaels joining us. He sits in Mother Superior's usual spot, and she has shifted a seat over. But even this man's presence cannot dampen my appetite as the delicious aromas make my mouth water.

Soon, my belly is fuller than I've known in years, and my throat is dry from talking and laughing.

"I don't think I've ever been happier in my whole life," Joyce says, with a little gooey egg running down her chin.

I pass her a napkin and smile. When our plates are empty and some of the girls have enjoyed second helpings of apple-and-rhubarb crumble, Father Michaels stands up. Instantly, chair legs squeak as everyone else gets to their feet.

"Sit, sit, please," he says, with a downward gesture of his hand. "Enjoy more tea. More crumble. This is your day."

"Must you dash away so soon?" Mother Superior asks disappointedly.

"Afraid I must. I have a wedding in town. The first of the O'Rourkes. Lovely family. I don't know the other family—the Maloneys—all too well, but he seems like a nice chap. The wedding breakfast is in the Munster Lodge, if you don't mind."

I clutch my chest.

"Oh, how nice. The lodge is a lovely spot for a wedding," Mother says. "But expensive, I daresay."

The other girls have taken their seats again, and some are asking Sister Bernadette for another helping of crumble. I curse their chatter, as it hinders my ability to eavesdrop.

"Aye, and the poor O'Rourkes have had their fair share of money troubles over the years. Farming is a precarious business, bless them," Father Michaels says, bowing his head. "But they've pulled out all the stops for this wedding. Linda is their eldest girl, so I suppose—"

I jump to my feet and knock my chair back; it hits the ground with a crack.

"Linda O'Rourke is getting married?" I blurt. The words shoot out of me like bullets from a gun.

"Margaret," Mother scolds, glancing in my direction. She points a warning finger.

"I'm sorry, I'm sorry." I'm dithering and barely able to speak. "Who is she marrying, Father? Please tell me."

"Margaret," Mother says again, this time sounding more concerned than angry. "What has gotten into you?"

Father Michaels ignores me as he wraps a rasher sandwich in a napkin. But it doesn't matter: I knew the answer even before I asked the question. *Oh, Joseph.*

"I best be off. It is customary for the bride to be late, but not the priest." Father Michaels chuckles, tickled by his own joke, as he shoves the bulky napkin into the pocket of his trousers.

I bend in the middle, the air knocked out of me. My lungs are burning, and I can't seem to inhale deep enough or fast enough.

"What is it, child?" Mother asks with sweetness in her voice now. "Do you know these people?"

I sob. "Yes. Linda was my best friend."

"Ah. I see."

"And . . . and . . ." I drag my sleeve across my eyes. "And *I* was supposed to marry him. Not her."

"Oh."

Mother Superior looks to Father Michaels. He folds his arms, shakes his head, and walks out the door without saying another word. She turns back to me and says, "Hush now. Hush, hush. It's all right. You have your sisters."

Some of the girls have set their teacups down and started to stare. Joyce looks particularly concerned. I try to straighten but the ache inside won't let me.

"I love him. I love him so much."

"This is the boy you write all those letters to," Mother says, knowingly.

"Yes."

"How many is it now? It must be hundreds."

My voice crackles like radio static. "Seven hundred and eighteen letters. One every day for almost two whole years."

"And yet he never writes back."

Her words cut deep. No one writes back. Not Joseph and not my brothers. I am a forgotten thing. A teddy you once loved, but you misplaced it at the park or by the lake, and now you can't quite remember what color it was.

"Maybe it's for the best, Margaret. Life on the outside must go on, we all know that. Now that this young man is taking a wife, you can take your heart back and fully dedicate it to the Lord. He will never break it. I can promise you that."

Mother Superior doesn't understand that my heart is not mine to give to God. It belongs to Joseph. It has been his ever since I was ten years old and we sat side by side in school.

"May I be excused?" I ask, finally managing to straighten up.

Mother Superior takes my hands in hers. "I know it hurts. But pain heals. In years to come, you won't remember his name."

"It should be my name too," I snap. "If I didn't have to come here, it would be."

"Oh, Margaret." She drops my hands and I see a hint of vexation creep into her eyes. "That's not how I see it. I see a young man who could so easily forget you. A man who never once wrote to you. A man who will spend the rest of his life lying next to your best friend."

Sobs shake me.

"The Lord has called you here and spared you so much pain, and yet you keep a guard up. I worry about you, Margaret. I truly, truly do."

"May I be excused?" I ask once more.

She sighs and shakes her head. "Go. Yes. Just go."

I gather my robes so as not to trip and I hurry out the door, leaving the happy chatter of newly ordained nuns behind me. I fling open the heavy main doors and charge into the garden. The loose gravel crunches under my feet as I race across the grounds, kicking up stones. A single small pebble lands in my shoe and nips at the sole of my foot with each step. I keep running. I reach the gate in a jiffy and grab the metal bars with each hand. I place my foot on another bar, take a deep breath, and then—nothing.

I find myself still like a statue. I wait for the urge to climb, the drive to scramble to the top of the gate and fling myself over. But I don't budge. I am hollow inside. Carved out and empty. I am scattered like grains of sand on the shore. I am carried on the wind to the grounds of the cathedral in Thurles. I see Linda. Dressed in white lace and frills, with a garland of pretty flowers in her strawberry-blonde hair and a small bouquet in her hand to match. Her little sister skips behind her in a simple cotton dress of pink, or maybe blue. An adorable flower girl admiring the beautiful bride, no doubt imagining her own wedding day as all little girls do. I did. Many, many times. Always with Joseph by my side. Always. He comes into my mind's eye, more dapper than ever in a suit as gray as the sea after a storm. His pink tie matches the little girl's dress, and they are all so blissfully happy. I drop my face into my hands and try hard to remember how to breathe.

"What are you doing?" a voice behind me calls out.

I whip around to find Mr. Dolan. He has a cloth in his hand and he's polishing something silver.

"I'm leaving," I shout.

"Right so."

His blasé tone irks me.

"I am," I shout louder, although there is no need to as he edges closer. "My pa is dead. There is no one to force me to come back here this time."

He comes close enough to lower his voice, but not close enough for me to see what's in his hand. "I'm sorry for your loss. But the way I hears it, your folks died some years back."

"And what if they did?"

"Well, correct me if I'm wrong, but if your folks were all's that was stopping you, why didn't you leave then?"

His glare is scorching, and I know he won't look away until he gets an answer.

I had nowhere to go. I squash the intrusive thought and settle on, "It's complicated."

"Always is."

I tighten my grip around the gate. "Are you going to snitch on me?"

He shakes his head. "Aren't nothing to say. Mother Superior told me a long time ago not to bring you back again if you tried to leave. You know, when your folks passed."

I wheeze. "Really?"

He smiles. It's both warm and smug, and I'm not sure what to make of this conversation. "Aye. As you said, there was no one to tell you what to do anymore. And yet, you stayed."

"I stayed," I whisper. The emptiness inside me begins to fill. Surprise and disgust creep in. "I stayed because I was waiting for someone to come for me."

"Are they coming now?"

I glance through the gaps in the gate at the inviting countryside waiting to be explored—rolling green fields filled with farm animals, a clear blue sky that disappears behind tall, leafy trees. A narrow road that I know winds on for miles, but I can't remember if it's a left or a right at the crossroads that leads into town. Suddenly, I'm not sure of much at all. I'm not sure if I belong on the far side of this gate anymore, where Linda O'Rourke is now Linda Maloney and soon will cradle Joseph's babies in her arms, no doubt.

"I can open it for you," he says, finally revealing the finely polished key in his hand. "So you don't hurt your ankle this time, eh?"

I lower my foot and snap my hands away from the cool metal. He steps forward as several magpies fly overhead, exploring the skies.

"Beautiful creatures, aren't they?" he says, tilting his head back to marvel at the black birds with plump white breasts as they fly past.

"I suppose."

"You know, they could go anywhere. They can fly for hours. And yet they never stray far. Their nest is in those trees just there." He shifts his gaze onto the tall evergreens at the far side of the vast grounds. "I always think of the sisters here like beautiful magpies."

I look at my new robes. Black all over with a white collar and coif. I see the resemblance.

"One for sorrow, two for joy." He begins reciting the familiar nursery rhyme as he points overhead and counts them. *"Three for a girl, four for a boy. Five for silver, six for gold."*

"There are seven," I say, spotting a smaller magpie that struggles to keep up.

"Well, look at that. Seven. This fella must be new. A baby. *Seven for a secret never to be told.*" He looks toward the sleepy building across the road that mirrors the convent.

I sweep my eyes over the building. There's not much to see, really. The odd car once in a blue moon. I rarely see the driver, but anytime I do, it tends to be a young man behind the wheel. They never pull up at the main doors and always drive around the back. Small trucks—not much bigger than a bread van and almost always white—arrive once a week or so. I can only imagine all the activity that takes place back there: dropping off bags of dirty laundry, loading up freshly washed garments. In contrast, the front is silent and still. The curtains are almost permanently drawn in every room and I imagine it's dark and spooky inside, like a haunted house.

"Have you ever been inside?" I ask, turning to look at Mr. Dolan once more.

His blank stare raises my suspicions.

"Don't you think it's odd that no one ever uses the front door? I mean never. In two years, I've never seen it open. Not once. But I've heard people. Voices. Who works there? I didn't know anyone in town growing up who worked out this way."

His face remains expressionless.

"You should go back inside now, little magpie," he says. "It's not my place to answer your questions."

"Then who *can* I ask? Is it dangerous in there? I've heard screaming. Not often, but I *have* heard it."

He takes off his cap and bows his head. "You're no one's fool. I'm sure you will figure it out. I'll be here when you do."

He places his cap back on his head and fixes it straight, then walks away briskly.

Magpie, I think, mulling the pet name over in my head. *Magpie.* I've never had anyone call me anything other than Margaret before. Sheila tried *Maggie* once, and Pa gave her a clip around the ear and told her to have respect.

"*Magpie, Magpie, Magpie*," I whisper, and I decide I like it. Then I turn away from the gate and the road, back to the place that has become a part of me.

21

Margaret

As ever, the routine of Ballyvale is unfluctuating. I come to learn that life as a nun is not much different from being a novice. My bedroom is on the second floor now, which is wholly inconvenient, not least because my view of the laundry is diminished but also because some of the older nuns snore like motor engines. It has been three days since my conversation with Mr. Dolan, and it irritates me to no end that although I have read every Agatha Christie book written, detective work is nowhere near as exhilarating in real life. In fact, it's slow, boring, and unfruitful.

Silence before prayers or not, I'm preparing to rant about my lack of progress to Joyce this morning when I notice Father Michaels downstairs in the foyer. I groan inwardly and pull Joyce away from the stairs.

I wasn't expecting to see him so soon, and I can't bear to make eye contact with him. And yet I can't pull my eyes away.

The sight downstairs is nothing out of the ordinary. Joyce and I have seen him bring couples to the abbey previously. The routine is always the same. They gather in Mother Superior's chambers with long, somber faces, and leave beaming with joy with a baby in their arms. My curiosity about where the babies come from is like an itch I can't scratch, but I know better than to openly inquire about Father Michaels's business. Couples of mixed ages, shapes, and sizes come. Different in all the ways imaginable, but the one thing they have in common is money. The men arrive in finely tailored suits and woolen trilby hats, and the women carry leather handbags and have silk scarves around their necks, even in summer.

"What do you make of those two?" Joyce whispers, inclining her head toward the couple as Mother Superior leads them and Father Michaels into her chambers and closes the door. "Look rich to me. And American. They're always American, aren't they?"

"I wouldn't know," I whisper back. "I can't get close enough to hear them speak. I'm never called upon to serve them tea, like you. Father Michaels is probably afraid I'd spill it all over them."

She tuts and knocks her shoulder against mine. "Or shoot your mouth off and ask them why they're here."

"I would not!"

Joyce laughs. We both know that given half a chance, I absolutely would.

"Shh," I whisper, pulling her toward the ground so we can bob on our hunkers and spy between the banisters. Joyce's expression protests at first, but I lower my voice even more and go on. "But America. It seems like an awfully long way to come."

"My cousin went to New York once. Nice chap. Never came back. He's married over there now, I hear," Joyce says, as if that explains anything. "Anyway, I can't be sure. I'm no good with accents, but they always speak English and I don't think they're British. What matter where they're from anyway? They're mighty good people giving a wee orphan a home."

I press my hand to my chest as my heart suddenly pangs. I think of my orphan brothers and their new life in Mayo. It was little Finbar's birthday last week. He turned twelve. Almost a teenager. I wrote to him. I included a handmade card that I spent weeks creating. A drawing of him as a baby from memory. But as ever, he didn't write back. I'm certain they blame me for not coming home. I only hope someday they understand. I wonder if he's tall now, like the other two were at that age. I try so hard to imagine him older, but the image of him as a young boy is stamped into my mind.

"Uniting families is the work of God," Joyce says, pulling my attention back to the goings-on downstairs behind a closed door. "And Father Michaels and Mother Superior are angels on earth."

Her adoration of Father Michaels is like a pebble in my shoe, uncomfortable and irritating. But even I have to admit that his dedication to finding a family for the babies is unwavering.

"I hope I'm just like Mother Superior someday," Joyce coos.

We've both grown quite fond of Mother Superior over time. In the absence of mothers of our own, she has come to fill the void, always with a supportive ear to lend and sage advice to offer. "At graduation, you may keep your own names or choose that of a saint you admire. I kept my own, because I have worked tirelessly to ensure that the messenger of the Lord that I admire the most is myself," she told us last week after our final Sunday Mass as novices.

I chuckled. Not because I fail to admire her—I think she's quite wonderful—but because none of us have any idea what her real name is. We've never known her as anything or anyone except Mother Superior.

"Imagine being head of all this one day," Joyce says with hungry eyes.

The thought sends a chill down my spine.

"You will be," I tell her. "You've a heart of gold. Someday it'll be you in those chambers, helping the babies."

"Do you really think so?"

"I do. I do."

Joyce begins to sway, beaming and lost in thought.

"Joyce," I say.

"Um."

"Do you ever wonder where the babies come from?"

My eyes are burning into the door of Mother's chambers. "Surely it's unusual that there are so many."

Joyce steadies herself and her expression pinches. "One every few weeks. It's not all that many."

"Do you think *all* their parents died?" I ask.

Joyce's eyes fill with pity. "You know better than most how cruel illness can be."

I'm about to say something generic about grief and change the subject as I always do, but I don't have to, as the sound of a baby crying cuts us off.

"Listen," Joyce says, her expression softening once more. "A tiny one. Isn't it a beautiful sound."

The distinct cry of a days-old baby carries through the hall, growing louder and nearer as the door of Mother Superior's chambers opens and the glamorous visiting woman steps out cradling a swaddled baby in her arms. She bounces the tiny bundle and says, "Hush, hush, little one. There, there."

She looks in her early to mid-thirties, with sun-kissed skin and freckles dotted across her nose and cheeks like nutmeg on a cream cake. Her black hair is pinned back in a neat bun, and I suspect when she lets it down it's long and wavy like mine. Her lips are cherry-red and her eyes are green-blue like the sea in summer. I wonder if she likes to dance. I wonder if she keeps a beautiful home on a quiet suburban street.

I wonder if she will be an adoring mother to the child in her arms. And most of all I wonder if she will cherish every minute of living the life I so desperately want.

The man, her husband, is older. Closer to fifty, I guess, with a bald spot and a salt-and-pepper mustache that curls toward his nose on each side. He shakes Father Michaels's hand and says, "Thank you. Thank you so much. We have waited so long. We had all but given up hope of ever having a baby. We're married ten years this coming fall."

"Congratulations," Father Michaels says, the long handshake emphasizing their mutual respect. "A decade is a milestone."

"No, no, *this* is a milestone. Our very own baby." The woman looks away from the baby in her arms to smile brightly at the priest. "We owe the abbey everything. We'd have paid every penny we have and more for this little one."

Joyce is whispering something, but I'm not listening to her. My ear is cocked toward the couple. I can't shake the unsettling feeling the woman's words have stirred in me. *Paid every penny.*

Mother Superior smiles and flashes mottled teeth. "Mm-hmm. Well, as I said, your donation for the leaky roof is much appreciated."

The woman is dumbstruck, but she returns the wide smile.

"Now go," Mother Superior says, with an encouraging gesture toward the grand front door. "Get this precious little one home. You're a family now."

"We are. We really, really arc," the man says, leaning to kiss his wife on the cheek. Then he bends and places a kiss on the baby's head.

Father Michaels leads them toward the door. The clip-clop of his heels echoes around the hall and sends a shiver down my spine.

"Remember, this is your baby now," he says, lowering his voice. I push my face between the banister posts, to better hear him. "You must tell people he was born while you were traveling overseas. Maybe you didn't even know you were expecting." His eyes burn into the woman, who is busy cooing at the newborn, and I doubt she is listening. "You took a trip and, to your surprise and delight, your son was born while you were there. And thankfully, mother and baby are doing well."

"Yes. Of course." The man nods, placing his hand on his wife's back as he encourages her to keep walking. "We understand, don't we, darling?"

My mouth is gaping as the front door opens. The gush of fresh air catches my breath and I need to cough. I try hard to hold it in, desperate not to draw attention to Joyce and me watching from above.

If I crane my neck right, I can just about see the driveway through the door. And I spy another new vehicle. Bigger than the last and black this time, with a cream interior. It's a wonder how a priest in a small town like Thurles can afford to buy a new car every six months when most folks struggle to buy a single one in a lifetime.

"Leaky roof?" Joyce whispers when everyone finally steps outside.

I strain to hear the remainder of their conversation, but I can't make out a word above the hum of the car engine that comes to life.

"Where do you reckon it is? The third floor, probably. I always said it's damp up there. I said it, didn't I?"

I roll my eyes. "Father Michaels may well have promised Mother the donation, but I bet he keeps it for himself. Or a good chunk of it, at least. I'm willing to guess every couple who collect a baby make a donation. And you've seen the sort of folk who come here. They're not shy of a penny or two. I haven't seen any repairs to the convent, have you?"

"I really couldn't say."

I sigh. "You mean, you really *won't* say. Oh, Joyce."

I stand up and pull Joyce to her feet. I watch as she hops from foot to foot, shaking off pins and needles. I like Joyce. In the two years I have been at Ballyvale, she has become my closest friend. My only friend, really. But sometimes, I wonder how deep that friendship truly goes. Growing up, Linda O'Rourke and I told each other everything. We knew each other's deepest secrets and we guarded them with our lives.

We shared clothes and coordinated our lies and excuses when a dance ran over and we were late home.

"We had to help a priest from a nearby parish put the chain back on his bicycle."

"The old lady who plays the organ in Mass lost her dog. We helped her find him."

I don't think Joyce has it in her to tell a lie. And if she did, she'd probably lock herself in the confession box for at least a week. I desperately want to discuss what we've just witnessed. I want to mull over body language and clues until Agatha Christie would be proud. But I can't talk to Joyce about it. She'll crack under the pressure, and word would almost certainly make it back to Father Michaels. For now, I will have to keep my burning curiosity to myself.

Fingers click next to my ears, and I know without looking I'll find a senior sister at my side.

"There you are. What's keeping you two?" Sister Bernadette says, rolling her shoulders back. I can smell that she has broken fasting and enjoyed a cup of tea already this morning. "You're late. And chatting before prayers. Really, sisters. This is not the example you should be setting for the novices."

Joyce shrinks. "I'm sorry, Sister Bernadette. We got to talking about the ba—"

"Baked tart," I cut her off. "Something smells delicious."

Joyce snorts and glares at me as if I have lost my mind. Sister Bernadette's expression is equally as confused. The convent smells of dusty rugs and incense, as always.

I grab Joyce's hand and start running down the stairs. "I'm sorry, Sister Bernadette," I call back. "We won't be late again, I promise."

Joyce tugs her hand free when we reach the bottom step. "You need to go to confession. Lying is a sin."

"You're right. You're right. I'll go later."

Joyce nods, satisfied. "I'll join you. I think spying is a sin too."

I bristle like a startled cat. "Are you crazy? You can't tell Father Michaels that we were eavesdropping."

"I have to. I have to ask the Lord's forgiveness."

I jam my hands onto my hips. "Joyce! The Lord might forgive you. Father Michaels will not. He will blow his top."

"Sisters. Prayers," Sister Bernadette says firmly, reaching us at the bottom of the stairs.

Joyce scurries away before I have a chance to say another word.

"Is everything all right?" Sister Bernadette asks.

"Mm-hmm," I say, lying to her for the second time in as many minutes.

22

Margaret

Joyce refuses to look my way all morning. She sits at the far end of the table at breakfast and doesn't stand beside me during prayers. I'm searching for her in the garden when I feel a shovel-like hand on my shoulder. I turn around and find Father Michaels behind me.

"A word please, Sister Margaret," he says, stone-faced.

He doesn't wait for a response, just turns and walks off. I follow with my heart in my throat like the convicted to the gallows. We pass the chapel, the kitchen, and the cloisters. He says nothing. Finally, he opens the door of a room I've never noticed before.

The last time I was this afraid to walk through a door was the day I entered Ballyvale for the first time. Nonetheless, I pick one foot up and place it in front of the other. The room is small, with a slender window overlooking the back garden. A desk, two chairs, and a lamp take up all the space. To my dismay, Mother Superior is not here.

"Sit, please," he says, closing the door behind us with a clunk.

I do as I am told. Bright summer light shines through the rectangular window, warming my face. He pulls out the chair beside me. The spindly legs screech against the tiles, and the seat creaks in protest at his weight when he sits.

"Let's have a quick chat. I'm covering Mass in Clonmel in less than an hour. Father Buckley is sick again, so there's no time for tea, I'm afraid," he says, as nonchalant as if we were discussing the weather, or books we have recently enjoyed.

"You've been reassigned," he says simply.

I blink. "Reassigned?"

"You're not going far. Just across the road, in fact, to Ballyvale Home for Fallen Girls," he says, smoothing his cassock. "You leave today."

My pulse kicks like it wants to bolt. *Fallen Girls*. The words feel sour.

He clasps his hands and leans forward, all mock concern and paternal guidance. "Joyce joined me for confession this morning. She told me you've been . . ." He pauses as if searching for the best word. "Distracted. And dragging her into it with you," he tuts, and my knees bob with a nervous twitch.

"Joyce is diligent. Obedient. Devout. She knows her place. You, Sister Margaret, ask too many questions and offer too few prayers."

I open my mouth, but no sound comes out.

"It's not a punishment," he says, almost cheerfully. "Quite the opposite. It's a calling. You'll be assisting the sisters at Ballyvale. Helping with the babies."

My breath catches. "Babies?"

He nods, as if he's offering me a gift. "I'm sure you've put two and two together by now and know that the girls there have gotten themselves into a spot of bother. But Ballyvale helps them reclaim some dignity. Offers them a second chance. We find wonderful families who can raise their children properly."

I frown. "They . . . give them up?"

"Yes," he says, with firm conviction. "It's a kindness to all. The babies face a bright future and the girls can go home. If their parents are accepting, that is. Which many are, once the burden is . . . resolved."

He says it like it's a mercy. Like it's kind. I sit with that. Let it curdle.

"You like babies, don't you?" he asks.

"Of course. Very much."

"I thought as much." He nods. "It's hard work, but I'm sure you'll rise to the occasion. Changing nappies. Feeding. Singing lullabies, perhaps. A perfect fit for someone with your . . . erm . . . energy."

The idea of rocking a baby to sleep, of holding something small and soft and loved, lights something warm inside me. Something hopeful.

"Let this be a chance for redemption. For you, and for them. You've always had a streak of defiance. Ballyvale will help to smooth that out."

"And if they don't want to give up their children?" I ask, my knees finally steadying as I take it all in.

"Then Lord have mercy on them, because we cannot help them. These girls are sinners, but even sinners want salvation. They're fortunate the church is here to help."

"Someone told me it's a laundry," I say gently, not quite sure if I have the right information.

He rolls his eyes. "Something has to pay for their keep. By day a few laundry duties are penance for their sins. By night they pray for forgiveness. It's a system I'm practically proud of."

He checks his watch and stands up.

"Will I come back?" I ask, standing up slower than he did.

He smiles, broad and wolfish, and leaves without a reply. And there it is—my punishment! Once I leave, I cannot return. The rules of the cloistered order are written in stone, as if engraved into the walls of the convent itself. The only people permitted on the grounds are a priest and his guests. And Mr. Dolan, of course. Not me, not anymore. And as much as my friends care for me, there will be no rule bending. This much I know with certainty. I will be little more than a garden away, and yet this is the last time I will see them. Joyce, Sister Bernadette. Mother Superior. Gone. And still, I cannot deny the bubbles of excitement that continue to fizz inside me.

This is the second time this man has ordered me to pack, and I am certain my life is about to be upended just as much all over again.

23

NOW

Riley

We take a cab from the hotel into Thurles, and I'm pleasantly surprised when we arrive in the town in less than fifteen minutes. Thurles center is a weird shape; squarish, but narrowing in places, as if someone is squeezing the town for no apparent reason. Shops, cafés, and bars line both sides of the square, and I can sense that Sam is itching to explore them all.

A man stands on the street corner with a tin whistle and a baseball cap upturned on the ground. The enchanting tune makes me want to dance, and Sam tosses some euros into the cap. A small group of teenagers zip past on electric scooters, laughing loudly. There's a man in a suit with a cell phone pressed to his ear as he orders coffee from a hatch.

A woman with a bleached-blonde updo and hoop earrings smokes a cigarette outside a small corner store.

"You like it here," Sam says, placing his hand gently on my back.

"I do."

"You ready?" he asks, stepping aside to avoid Updo Lady's line of smoke.

"Hey, don't look at me." I hold my hands up in mock surrender. "This was your idea, remember?"

"Technically, it was Misty's."

Sam's right. Misty was the only one ballsy enough to say what everyone was thinking but was afraid would offend me.

"If your grandmother *is* trying to tell you that your mom was adopted," Misty had said, leaning against the kitchen counter, "then technically you're chasing a ghost. Ghosts don't have LinkedIn profiles or Facebook. But they do have family. And odds are, at least someone in the family is still living in Thurles. We're like the fifth generation of Jeffersons in Hoboken, or something like that."

"Haven't loads of your cousins moved out of state?" I asked, while googling *What percentage of people live in one place all their lives?*

Misty took a sip of her coffee and ignored my poking holes in her plan. "Irish people love their booze, don't they? So chances are someone in the bar knows someone who knows someone. You know how these things work."

Now that I'm here, I'm not so sure I *do* know how these things work. But when Sam points to a light-up TIME FOR GUINNESS sign blinking nearby, I hope I'm about to find out.

"Start with Lynch's bar." Misty grinned. "It hasn't changed its name in seventy years. If anyone is going to know the history of that town, it's probably someone in there."

The *L* has peeled away, and the *y* is more of a weathered *v*, but we're clearly in the right spot. JJ Lynch's. Sam opens the door and my stomach somersaults.

"Jeez," Sam whispers as we step inside and take in a place where time has stood still. It's dark and smells of leather booths and timber floors, tinged with the overwhelming musk of years of alcohol. There's an open fire even in July, and yet it's just the right temperature. Mismatched chairs are dotted around square tables. The windows are small, with floral-patterned curtains drawn across them. Somehow, instead of being dark and dull, it's cozy and quaint. I want to curl up in a fireside armchair with a good book, the way Poppy and I used to when I was a kid.

A tall man with a bald head that shines under the soft indoor lighting approaches from behind the bar. "Afternoon, folks. What can I get you?"

"Hello," Sam says, a little too chipper. His accent seems to stand out. "Two Guinnesses, please?"

"Ah, Americans," the barman says. "Tourists always go for the Guinness. But can I recommend whiskey instead? It's local. Brewed not too far in County Cork."

Sam, a seasoned whiskey lover, and the barman, who introduces himself as Vincy, get into a discussion about good whiskey. Sam endeavors to try them all someday.

"How long are you here for?" Vincy asks.

"Just a week."

"Lovely. Lovely. And what brings you to these parts? Family, is it?"

"Sort of," Sam says, taking the first glass Vincy places on the bar top and passing it to me. "We're actually looking for someone."

Vincy's eyes narrow with curiosity as he pours more whiskey over chunky ice cubes and slides it toward Sam.

Sam cups the glass with both hands. "Do you know a Mary-Kate O'Rourke, by any chance? She was born around here. About sixty years ago."

Vincy nods enthusiastically and I hold my breath, hopeful for a moment.

"Don't know any Mary-Kates, I'm afraid. But there's O'Rourkes out the mall road. And another family out by the water. They're not related, mind." He stops to scratch his head as if he's thinking hard. "I think they even spell *O'Rourke* differently. Although for the life of me, I can never understand why people do that. A name's a name, isn't it?"

Sam shrugs and takes a mouthful of whiskey.

"Good?" Vincy asks.

"Very." Sam places his drink on the counter and sits on one of the high stools.

Vincy picks up a glass and whips a towel off his shoulder to polish it as he continues. "There's Ita, of course, she lives near the church. Not an O'Rourke herself. A Clifford. But her mother was an O'Rourke. Gone now, but a lovely woman. Not much of a drinker, though."

"Are any of them related to a Mary-Kate?" I ask, pulling out a stool to sit beside Sam.

"Ah, love, I wouldn't know a thing like that. But the Cliffords are a big family. There might be a Mary Jane among them."

I don't correct him. "Unfortunately, Mary-Kate Clifford is not who we're looking for."

"Don't you have an email or phone number or something for her?" he says.

I shake my head.

"John Clifford, Ita's other half, will be in later," Vincy says, holding the polished glass up to examine it under the light. "He usually comes in for a few pints around five. Maybe you could ask him about Mary Jane then."

"Mary-Kate," I whisper under my breath. I feel Sam's hand on my knee.

"Does she owe you a few bob?" Vincy asks with a devilish grin.

"A few bob?" I echo, confused.

His grin breaks into a laugh. It's hearty and comes from his belly. "Money. Does she owe you money, love?"

My hand covers my mouth and I almost knock my whiskey over.

"No. Oh gosh, no. Nothing like that. I think she was very important to my grandmother. Or she's someone my grandmother wants me to find out more about, at least."

"Oh." His smile flatlines as he places the spotless glass on the bar top. "Is your nanna . . . erm . . . is she—"

"Alive?" I ask.

"I was going to say, 'Is she American too?'" He blushes, and his white lie makes me smile. "Your accent. New Jersey, is it?"

"Yes," I say, excited he guessed correctly. "Grammy is New Jersey born and bred, too, and she still lives there now."

"Ah, I knew it. I bet everyone guesses New York."

I nod.

"But I was a big fan of *The Nanny* back in the nineties. And she was from New Jersey, wasn't she? Ah, you're probably too young to remember. Good show, though. Very funny." I sip my fiery whiskey as he continues. "Anyway, it's good to hear your nanna is alive and well. Is she visiting with you?"

I feel Sam's hand draw small, supportive circles on my leg. She would love it here, I decide. She would love this unsymmetrical town and this charming bar. She'd enjoy Vincy and his nineties TV references too.

"Unfortunately, Grammy's not all that well," I say, and swallow a large mouthful of whiskey, which burns all of a sudden.

"Ah, I'm sorry to hear that. Is that why you've come all this way? To find your nanna's friend before—" He cuts himself off and clears his throat. "Well, while you still can."

I drink the last of the whiskey and place the empty glass on the bar top. "Something like that. Grammy couldn't tell me much. But she gave me this. . . ."

I open my bag and pull out a copy of the birth certificate. There's a flash of something across Vincy's face. It's gone before I can pinpoint what it is. *Recognition? Sadness? Empathy?*

"Right," he says matter-of-factly, and then ducks his head under the bar. There's some rummaging and clanking of glass. When he reappears, he places two shot glasses and a bottle of amber something on the bar top. The label is yellowing and peeling at the edges. Sam eyes me skeptically as Vincy fills both glasses.

"On the house," he says with a crooked smile. Then he snaps his fingers and shouts, "Oi, John, get over here. You might be able to help this young lady."

"John Clifford?" I whisper as I check my watch. It's shortly after 3 p.m. I catch Sam's eye and wonder if we've adjusted the time difference incorrectly.

Chair legs squeak in the corner, and a man stands up and walks toward us. He's tall, with a bushy salt-and-pepper beard and a fire-engine-red baseball cap.

"This girl is looking for a Mary Jane O'Rourke. There's no money owed," Vincy says with a wink, and I'm not sure if the statement is directed at me or John. "Anyone on Ita's side of the family by that name?"

My heart races. "Oh, goodness. If you did know her, or know *of* her, that would be amazing."

The man takes off his cap, revealing a head of curly hair, and his age seems to come into focus. I guess he's in his mid- to late sixties.

"Can I see that?" he asks, pointing at the paper in my hands.

I stiffen and instinctively clutch the paper tighter for a moment before I relax and pass it to him. His intake of breath is sharp, and the fine hairs on the back of my neck stand on end.

"What is it?" I ask.

"Right," he says, passing it back to me. "You should probably come with me."

I slide the paper back into my handbag and catch Sam shaking his head from the corner of my eye.

John fixes his cap back on his head. "My house is just a couple of miles out that road." He points as if we'll find his home on the tip of his finger. "You're going to want to meet my wife."

"Does Ita know Mary-Kate?" I ask, much too enthusiastically.

He sighs. "It's complicated."

A huge smile bursts across my face. I like the sound of complicated. Complicated means there's a story. And a story means there is something to tell. I look at Sam. He's statue-still, but I can see the sparkle of intrigue in his eyes.

John gestures to the two glasses on the bar top. "You might want to drink that. I'd say you'll need it once my wife gets talking."

Vincy laughs and his deep chuckle fills the air. He nods at me encouragingly, and Sam and I both reach for the glasses, not quite sure what it is. But it feels the least of my concerns as we plan to follow a stranger, in a town we don't know, to his home. I am suddenly glad there's still daylight outside as I tilt my head back and drink.

24

1958

Margaret

I pull my suitcase out from under my bed. I didn't think I'd have a need for it ever again, and I'm shaking as I lay it on the bed and pop it open. I fetch Sheila's dresses from the wardrobe, dresses I haven't worn in years. They smell of damp and lack of wear, but their colors are as vibrant as ever. I reach under my pillow for *Little Women*, satisfied when I remember it lies under Joyce's pillow now. I hope when she reads it anew, she will think of me. In my excitement to leave, I haven't stopped to think of all that I will miss about the convent. Joyce. Mother Superior. Sister Bernadette and her delicious tarts. I have grown from a child to a woman behind these walls, and they are a part of me now—bones and blood and heart.

I begged Father Michaels to let Joyce join me. But he said, "Girls like Joyce are best suited in the convent. And girls like you are best suited over there."

I didn't ask what he meant by that. I was afraid to open my mouth too wide in case he changed his mind and made me stay. I wasn't quite sure what awaited me in that fascinating building. But the idea of traveling outside the walls of the convent and going somewhere babies enter the world was thrilling.

"What would a man know about having a baby?" Ma said once, when she was expecting Finbar. She was talking about my pa, of course. But I can only assume that what little my pa knew, Father Michaels knows less. I'm certainly no fountain of knowledge myself, but I am more than willing to learn. I will study hard and fill my mind to the brim with everything there is to know about caring for mothers and babies. I will have purpose and my days will be of value. It's a dream, really.

I close my suitcase. Then I close my bedroom door one last time behind me. My stomach is full of butterflies.

Downstairs, Sister Bernadette, Joyce, and Mother Superior are waiting in the foyer. Joyce is sobbing, and I hug her.

"I'm sorry. I'm so sorry. If I hadn't confessed, you wouldn't have to go. Please forgive me."

She smells like roses and musty paper, and I will miss her so much I almost have second thoughts. I let her go and promise, "We will always be friends."

Sister Bernadette passes me a tea towel covering something warm, and I can tell from the glorious smell wafting up that it's a tart or crumble.

"For the road," she says, as if the journey will take longer than five minutes. "You will write to us, won't you?"

I nod and dab at my eyes as I look at Mother Superior for reassurance, just as I would have looked at my own mother in years gone by.

"God has called you, my child," she says. "And goodness knows those young women need care. They need to find their way back to God. I have every confidence you are just what they need."

Her faith in me buoys me as we smile at each other. Emotion chokes her, and just when I think she might cry, Joyce takes a tissue from her pocket and passes it to her. Mother Superior blows her nose and crumples the tissue into her pocket.

Joyce watches her the way an adult child might watch an aging parent. She will take care of Mother Superior as the years roll on. I will miss my friend with all my heart, but I finally understand that Joyce is exactly where she belongs.

"You are the best of us, Sister Margaret. You just remember that, won't you?" Mother says.

Joyce is by far the superior nun, but I've always known Mother has a soft spot for me. I like to think I remind her of herself when she was young. I guess now I will never have a chance to ask. But I don't need to. That's the beauty of loving someone. We often say the most in the space between words. She takes my hand in hers one last time and says, "Now go, before the goodbyes become too hard."

I nod. I have said far too many goodbyes in my life already.

25

Margaret

Mr. Dolan is waiting outside. It spits rain as I climb aboard his cart, and he warns me to be careful. I notice new, hand-stitched cushions immediately, and the idea that he might have a wife to go home to after long shifts at the convent is heartwarming. He fluffs them and says welcomingly, "Sit. Sit." As soon as I'm steady, he jumps up beside me and grabs the reins. "Giddyup, boy."

We take off as if there is far to travel. The nuns wave at me from the porch, and I twist in my seat to blow them a kiss. My knees shiver despite the warm summer sun shining above us.

"Nervous?" he asks.

I shake my head. We are out one gate and in another in a matter of minutes. Trotting up the long driveway, I am unsurprised by the similarities to the convent. There are the same gray stone walls, the same latticed windows that I have come to learn let the icy wind creep through in winter. There is the same heavy front door, the same neatly cut grass. Up close, I observe that the similarities stop there. The grounds are vast, but the absence of fruit trees and vegetable patches is notable. The ground-floor windows wear rusted steel bars, and my stomach lurches at the sight of them. The curtains on the floor above are all drawn. It's close to lunchtime—surely no one is still in bed at this hour.

"Whoa, boy. That's it. That's it, ease up now," Mr. Dolan says as he tugs on the reins and brings Vixen to a stop outside the door.

I'm reminded of the day he picked me up and returned me to the convent like a prize parcel. I never imagined two years later I would find myself once again climbing down from his cart and starting fresh.

"What are you waiting for?" he asks when I don't budge.

I'm not quite sure, but it takes counting backward from three in my head to encourage my legs to jump down. I knock on the door and wait for an answer, but no one comes.

"Should we go around the back?" I ask, shrugging as I turn to look at him.

"Try again," he says.

I turn back and roll my eyes. I've never seen this door open, and I've long suspected it is for decoration and not purpose, but nonetheless I raise my fists and pound with enough force to rattle the timber on its hinges. Nothing.

I glance overhead. There are no birds to be found in the cloudy sky. Wind doesn't rustle the trees, and the rain has stopped. The eerie stillness sends a shiver down my spine, and I jump when there's a rattle and creaking, and the door opens slowly.

A small nun with a face as harrowed as the walls appears. Wiry gray curls poke out from underneath her veil and there is a stain on her collar, something red—jam, perhaps. Her huge glasses enlarge her bug-like eyes and she fidgets with her pockets, shoving her hands in and out of them as if she's full of an energy that she doesn't quite know what to do with. It almost feels as if she is apprehensive about meeting me.

Mr. Dolan leans over the side of the cart until I think he might tumble out. "This is Sister Margaret. She's from Thurles. Margaret Lannigan."

"Oh, the Lannigans." The woman's face animates, and she seems pleased by this tidbit of information. "You must be Donny's girl."

"Yes."

"I was in school with Donny. Tell me, how is he?"

I shake my head, and her sadness is sudden and genuine. "Oh dear. I'm sorry. He was a lovely man. I'm sure he would be very proud."

I swallow.

"And sisters? Do you have any? Will any more Lannigan girls be joining us? Your father always said he'd fill the world with more priests and nuns if he could."

"It's only me."

"Ah, well, it's lovely to have you here, I'll say that."

"What is your name?" I ask.

A sudden whimper sounds in the distance. It steals my attention as I try to peer inside and find the source.

Mr. Dolan jumps in to introduce her. "This is Sister Teresa. She's been keeping the home here in tip-top shape since Sister Dymphna fell ill."

Sister Teresa sighs and makes the sign of the cross on her forehead with her thumb. "She passed last week. Eighty-one she was. But she didn't look a day over seventy."

"I'm sorry," I say. "It must be a very hard time for you."

"Thank you. But it has brought you here."

Another wail echoes in the distance—a distinctive sound of distress.

"Do you hear that?" I cup my hand around my ear as I turn my head toward the door.

I wait for another screech, but the only sound is the magpies cawing as they finally fly overhead.

"The girls call me Tee." Sister Teresa strokes the ground with the tip of her shoe as she avoids my question. "You can, too, if you like."

"For Teresa?" I say.

"And because I bring them tea and toast after the hard work of labor is over."

I imagine a new mother tucked up in bed, rocking a precious baby in her arms. A tiny hairless head, a button nose, ruby lips, and round cheeks. I imagine the primal love that no doubt consumes a woman the moment she sets eyes on her baby for the first time, and the pang of jealously tastes bitter and I want to spit it out. "Come, come in," Tee says. She waves her hand above her head and raises her voice. "Thanks, Austin. We'll see you tomorrow, eh?"

"I'll be here. Eight in the morning as the usual."

"We've a few bags less this week," she goes on. "With Sister Dymphna's passing, it's been a difficult few days. The girls are tired. They didn't get as much laundry washed as usual."

"Not a worry," he calls back. "Until eight."

Then he drops his eyes onto my case, and as soon as I retrieve it, he "giddyups" away before I have a chance to say goodbye.

The door behind us closes with a *ka-thunk*, and I note how much duller it is inside compared to the convent. It smells different too. No books or incense. I pick up the scent of damp and water-washed floors, but it doesn't entirely cover the stench of sweat and urine.

I look away and try not to retch.

Tee pulls out a gold pocket watch, checks the time, and says, "The girls will be working at this hour. But it gives us time for a chat."

I stand to attention, ready to discuss my duties and share my eagerness to get started.

Tee slips the watch back into her pocket, and a heaviness consumes her. "What do you know about this place?"

I share everything Father Michaels told me, but I am unraveled when I'm met with disappointment in her eyes.

"Hmm," she says, stroking her chin. "And what do you know about delivering babies?"

I balk. "Delivering them?"

Her facial expression softens. "The babies have to get here somehow."

"But I thought—"

"I'm sure you did," she cuts me off. "But before you can cuddle newborns, you have to bring them into the world safely. That's our job." She taps her chest, then points at me.

Sheila and I were at home when each of the boys was born. We huddled on the top step of the stairs and waited, while Pa paced downstairs in the kitchen. Doctor Henry took care of Ma, and we didn't see a thing until the baby was in her arms.

"I'm a quick learner," I assure her. "And an avid reader. I'll read every book we have on birthing. And I'll do any chore the doctors ask." I smile and try to ignore how alert my stomach is and how it struggles with the stinking air in here.

"There are no books. And certainly no doctors," she mumbles, and for a second I wonder if I heard her correctly. "But don't worry, you will learn on your feet."

"But I'm not a m-midwife," I stutter.

Tee's bottom lip quivers. "None of us are."

"How many of *us* are there?" I ask.

Tee shrugs. "Nuns? Plenty. Enough to keep a close eye on the girls all the time. But it's just me—and now you—delivering the babies."

I may not know much about birth, but I know it's dangerous and that a woman needs professional care. What is this place? What has Father Michaels signed me up for?

26

Margaret

I follow Tee through dull corridors. The cold stone walls are in desperate need of fresh paint, as years of grubby stains and chippings pepper both sides. The damn windows need opening. *When was the last time the air was freshened in here?*

Our steps echo on the tiled floors. This is not the place of my imagination. I envisaged wards filled with beds and young women. I imagined doctors and nurses aiding them. I imagined noise and chaos and my feet run ragged helping—fetching medications, mopping floors, disinfecting bed linens. I never once imagined lifeless corridors and a haunting silence.

Tee comes to a sudden stop outside a set of tall double doors. "Are you ready?"

I suck my lips between my teeth and nod.

She presses her palms against the doors and pushes both open at the same time. Finally, noise! The huff and puff of hard work. I gasp and blink, hating my eyes for what they see. Before me is a cavernous space, lit by a single flickering bulb in the center. I squint to better see. Rows of industrial washing machines line the back wall, their rhythmic rumbles and clatters creating a monotonous symphony. The air is thick with the pungent scent of bleach mingling with the odor of the damp linens. I spy the offending white fabrics drip-drying across countless lines suspended from the ceiling. The walls, which I imagine were once a cheery yellow, now bear the marks of time and the stains of years of labor.

The several young women working diligently around the space are barely more than girls. They stand behind wooden tables piled high with soiled laundry, their faces etched with a weariness far beyond their years. Their skin is pale but their cheeks are rosy as they whisper to one another, not daring to let their hands fall idle. Their uniforms, faded brown and threadbare, cling to their figures as they scrub and wring out fabrics.

I am stunned to observe they almost all have round bellies hiding under their pinafores. I catch the eye of one of the youngest girls as she stops working for a moment to brush her hair, damp with sweat, out of her eyes. I smile tentatively. She jolts, darts her eyes away, and hurries back to work.

"This is the laundry!" I gasp, as I stare at girls working their fingers to the bone. "Some of these girls look about due. Shouldn't they be resting?"

Tee places a single finger against her lips and whispers, "Shh. Not now."

An overseer, a stern-faced nun with a disapproving gaze, patrols the room. She spots us from the corner of her eye and smiles, although the action makes her face appear as if it might crack.

One of the girls notices and whispers to her comrade, and they both dare to giggle. The subtle tittering costs them a smack of the matron's hand across the backs of their heads.

"Hey, stop that," I call out.

Tee's hand is instantly wrapped around mine, squeezing so tightly I'm about to yelp, until I catch her eyes pleading with me to steady myself and close my mouth. I don't quite understand, but I get the feeling that speaking out on the girls' behalf may be much worse for them than if I stay silent. I nod, and Tee lets go.

I turn my attention back to the girls. Talking has stopped and the only sound is the swash-wallop of laundry plunging against steel washing drums.

"Hello there," the matron calls to us, her voice as sharp and ascetic as she appears. She moves slowly toward us, as if her shoes are made of lead. "She's here," she observes to Tee as she points at me. I realize that although I have found out about this place only today, they have been expecting me.

"Indeed," Tee replies. "This is Sister Margaret. Margaret, this is Matron." I wait for Tee to share her name, but it doesn't come. I accept she is called by her title.

Matron takes my hand and shakes it firmly, the way old men do after Mass.

"We run a tight ship here," she says, and I suspect she might plan to use that expression as often as a sailor.

"I see that."

The matron's face glows as if she's misconstrued my observation as a compliment. "A stern hand. It's all it takes. More bags than any other laundry in Ireland." She tilts toward a corner of the room, where a small window allows a feeble stream of daylight to shine onto countless bags slouched against the wall like overstuffed flour sacks.

Two girls fetching clean linens from the table and bagging them in the large sacks continue to whisper despite the silence that has fallen among all the other girls. I cannot hear their words above the hectic chores, but I can tell by their furrowed brows and rapidly moving lips that worry or fear is their discussion.

Matron spies them, and she paces toward them like a greyhound. Tee is hot on her heels.

"Please, let me," Tee says, positioning herself between Matron and the girls, who have lost all the color in their faces.

Matron steps aside and delegates the dishing-out of a scolding to her colleague.

"Oh, girls," Tee puffs out. "What will we do with you?"

"But, Tee . . ." one of the girls begins. Tee raises her hand, and I hold my breath as if she might bring it down across the girl's face.

Thankfully, I am wrong, and her hand remains raised as a signal to stop talking. The girl closes her mouth.

"Outside for five laps of the courtyard," Tee says, and the girls' faces fill with relief.

"A stroll." Matron huffs and folds her arms. "You want these blabbermouths to take a stroll like a couple of gazelles?"

"Fresh air is good for the babies in their bellies," Tee says.

"I think you had best leave the discipline to me from now on." Matron scowls. I clamp my teeth down on my tongue for fear I might stick it out at the old hag.

The girls hurry toward the door, and Tee catches the nearest one by the arm and whispers something to her. The girl nods and mouths, "I promise."

A sharp cry pierces the air.

Matron rolls her eyes. "Not another screamer. I can't listen to that all day. I still have a headache from the last girl. Someone find her and shove a sock in her mouth, won't you."

A flash of disgust ripples across Tee's face, but she's quick to wipe it. "Gosh, I know, I wish they would keep it down. I'll talk to her."

"You'll need to do more than talk. Give her a good kick if need be."

"I will take care of her. That I can promise you," Tee says, clearly choosing her words carefully. This is a dark place, but already I can tell that Tee is a beacon of much-needed light.

27

Margaret

We leave the rattle and bustle of the laundry room behind, and it's silent once again. I can sense Tee's restlessness, and I dread to think where we're headed next.

"Remember what I said about learning on your feet?" she asks as we walk briskly.

My pulse races. "I'll help in any way I can."

"Good. Good. We need high spirits. Have you seen a baby born before?"

Another scream echoes through the halls. It's shrill and laced with urgency.

"I know it's scary, but all hands are useful," Tee says. "How old are you?"

"Twenty-two."

"The same age as some of our girls. We've lots younger, too, mind you." She puffs, our speedy pace testing her fitness.

"They are still children themselves," I tell Tee, trembling with heartache for these girls.

"They are sinners," Matron interjects, appearing behind us, making me jump.

I wonder if Matron has ever been kissed. Ever held hands with a man, or felt his fingers knotted in her hair. Ever felt soft lips dot kisses on her neck after a long stroll. Ever felt a warm chest pressed against hers. Ever had to channel all her strength and willpower not to give in to the desire and lose herself in the person she loves. I lost count of the times Joseph and I fought our burning ache and curiosity. Our desperation to be one. I imagined Joseph's naked body against mine many times, even more so since we were parted. I tried to rid him from my mind once I heard he was married, but he still comes to me in my dreams. I wonder what Matron would say if she knew I sin often in my imagination, if nothing else.

"Sin must not go unpunished." She folds her arms and places them on her stomach, round with years of apple tart.

I look toward the nearby wall, where a large chunk of paint has flecked away and revealed damp, dull plaster underneath. I think of the bars on the windows. The closed curtains. The empty, lonely gardens even on a summer's day. The dark and smelly laundry room. The girls' gaunt faces and sweaty, unkempt hair. This is punishment. This is hell.

Another scream comes. A plea for help that tugs me like the moon pulling waves, but I don't know where to go. I glance at Tee, urgency etched into my face. But she doesn't budge.

Matron reaches into her pocket and pulls out a small ball. She passes it to Tee, who nods, and there is a silent understanding between them. The wind is knocked out of me when I decipher that the ball is in fact a rolled-up old sock.

Matron's words replay in my mind. *Someone shove a sock in her mouth.*

"I am going for a lie-down," Matron announces, rubbing her temples as if they throb.

Tee doesn't waste a second; the moment Matron is out of earshot, she hoists up her long habit.

"Quick, quick. We must hurry."

We round corner after corner. The sun may be splitting the stones outside, but with boarded-up windows and shut doors, it's as cold as a December afternoon in here. But despite the darkness, I can't take my eyes off the sock in Tee's hand.

"She doesn't want you to—"

"Laboring women are noisy," Tee says breathlessly.

28

Margaret

It's Rosie, I'll bet," Tee pants. "I knew by the look of her this morning that her baby was coming."

Tee is completely red-faced by the time we reach a distant end of the building. The smell is worse than ever. The scents of unwashed underarms, sweating feet, and excrement assault my nose. I bend and gag.

"Oh, don't you dare," Tee says, her words commanding but her tone kind. "I need a strapping young girl like you to be a help and not a hindrance. Breathe through your mouth if you must. Now come along."

We meet two stony-faced girls in the corridor, one blonde and one brunette. Their complexions are as gray as the concrete beneath their bare feet. Their quivering lips are chapped and sore. They both have round bellies under their uniforms, one large, one smaller. They wrap their arms around themselves as if they ache all over. They don't look a day older than me.

"It's Rosie," the brunette girl says, panic flickering in her eyes. "It started a couple of hours ago. That's what we were trying to tell you. Back there." She crosses her thumb over her shoulder and points, and I suddenly recognize them as the talking girls from the laundry room.

"Oh, Lucy, you know better than to talk when Matron is on the floor. Making her angry only makes things worse for everyone. Especially Rosie, if she gets her hands on her," Tee says.

"But the screaming is getting bad now," the other girl says. "We tried to keep her calm while you were busy."

"Thank you, Anna. I know you did your best." Tee touches Anna's elbow.

"She's only fifteen," Lucy says. "Same age as my little sister. You can't let her die, Tee. You can't."

I wait for Tee to tell the girls that no one is going to die. But she doesn't. The nervous wobble inside me and the rancid smell suddenly become too much. I lean to the side and vomit. When I gather myself and stand straight, I find the girls staring at my case, which has been attached to me like a body part since I arrived.

"She's new," Tee tells them. "She's here to replace Sister Dymphna."

The girls' mouths gape, and I get the impression Sister Dymphna won't be missed.

"Sister Margaret is here to help. You can trust her," Tee tells them.

The girls' fear is palpable, and I can tell that trusting me is the last thing they are prepared to do.

Tee moves her hands in a shooing motion. "We can all get to know one another later, but we have more important things to attend to right now."

A scream pierces the air like a pin popping a balloon, and I jump.

"The first time is always the scariest," Tee assures me, then turns toward Lucy. "You know what to do."

Lucy nods and scarpers away. Anna stands like a deer in headlights. She grips her large belly with both hands as if afraid to let go in case it drops off.

"Is it really bad, Tee?" she asks, her voice high-pitched like a little girl's. "It hurts bad, doesn't it? I know it does. I'm scared."

Tee cups Anna's elbows with both hands and steadies her. "You've weeks yet, Anna. Don't worry yourself none now. Run along and help Lucy. We'll be needing that hot water and towels before you can turn around twice."

"Lucy and Anna," I whisper to myself, making sure to commit their names to memory.

"She's only fifteen," Anna says, as if Tee needs reminding. "Please, please don't let her die—"

"We won't," I cut in. "I promise."

Tee waits until Anna turns the corner before she lowers her voice and her head and says, "Oh, Margaret. Don't make promises you can't keep."

I swallow hard, and suddenly I feel as terrified and helpless as the day Sheila died.

29

Margaret

I follow Tee into a dimly lit room, where the cries have turned to exhausted moaning. There's just about enough room for a narrow bed to push up beside the wall and leave space to walk alongside it. A pretty teenager with fair skin and features that have yet to change from those of a child to a woman lies on her back. Her nightdress is tangled around her enormous belly, and a thin white sheet tinged with speckles of fresh blood attempts, and fails, to protect her modesty. It takes me a moment to note the absence of a window, as flickering candlelight casts dancing shadows on the stone walls.

"There you are," Tee says, and I can hear her relief to set eyes on Rosie at last. "You're doing great. You really, really are."

Rosie grips the edge of the bed and bends her knees as she twists in pain. Beads of perspiration gather on her forehead like summer rain on a windowpane.

"I can't," Rosie screeches. "I can't do it. It hurts."

Tee hurries to her, drops to her knees at the side of the bed, and takes her hand.

"You can. Oh, I know you can. You are strong and brave and your baby will be in your arms soon."

Rosie squeezes Tee's hand with a desperation that mirrors the tension I feel.

"That's it, just breathe." Tee guides her. "That's it. In and out. In and out."

I'm relieved to see Rosie follow instruction, and for a moment, I am hopeful that her pain has eased. But another scream sets the fine hairs on the back of my neck standing on end. I have longed for children since I was a child myself, but I was naïvely unprepared for the way pain seizes a birthing mother—merciless, all-consuming, and arresting in its power. Tee goes to the door, and Rosie's face is gripped with fear the moment Tee's hand slips away from hers. I start, drop my case, and fill Tee's spot at Rosie's bedside.

"Who are you?" Rosie asks, puffing.

"Margaret. But you can call me Maggie if you like."

"You're a nun."

"I am."

Rosie shuts her eyes and cries out. I take her hand and stroke my thumb over and back against her clammy skin. The pain pushes her to the edge of her endurance, and I will it to stop. I plead with the Lord, silently, in my head, to leave this child be.

She steadies at last, and her eyes open and focus on my face. "But you're young. You look silly dressed like that."

"Young women can be nuns too. Although I look a bit like a magpie, don't I?" I say, hoping Mr. Dolan's observation might make her smile.

Rosie's lips curve as she studies me, and I'm grateful my appearance can provide a distraction for a moment at least. "Sister Maggie-pie." She titters, and her youth is more obvious than ever.

"Sister Maggie-pie," I murmur back, quite liking it.

"Thank you, girls," I hear Tee say, and I turn my attention toward the door. "Now quick, get back to the laundry before Matron wakes from her nap."

I don't see the faces behind the door, but I hear their worried voices and I know it's Lucy and Anna. Tee closes the door with her foot, her hands full with a basin of steaming water and towels. I hurry to assist her. We place the basin on the floor and the towels at the end of the bed.

I want to ask Tee what happens next, but, as if reading my mind, she says, "Now we wait. It's in the Lord's hands."

There is no clock in the room, and yet I seem to hear the ticking of one in my head. Time speeds up and slows down all at once. Hours blur, and without a window it is impossible to tell when day ends and night begins. But my feet ache from standing and my back cracks from leaning over the bed to stroke Rosie's damp hair.

Tiredness drains the volume from her screams. Her throat is raw and her pain is expressed now in low, animalistic hums. Tee has never once touched Matron's sock in her pocket.

"We're almost there, Rosie. You're strong. Stronger than you know," Tee says as her weathered hands wring out a small towel to place against Rosie's forehead.

Tee is ever calm. She rubs Rosie's feet. She sings. She encourages Rosie to lift her head and sip water. And, finally, when time has lost all meaning and I worry that Rosie can't take much more—the pain seems to be at its worst—she screams louder than ever and Tee catches the delicate, shriveled baby. She places the shrieking newborn on the bed between his mother's legs while she dunks an old scissors in the hot water. I watch with fascination as she cuts the cord.

Tee was right, birth is terrifying. It is messy and brutal and loud. The pressure to keep mother and baby safe is suffocating. And I have never witnessed a single more beautiful moment in my entire life.

"Maggie, the towels. Quick, quick, this wee fella is freezing." Tee clicks her fingers, slicing into my thoughts.

"Wee fella?" I hear Rosie exhale. "Is it a boy?"

"It's a beautiful, healthy little boy," Tee says.

Rosie glows as she whispers to herself, "A boy. A little boy. Oh my."

Somehow, she suddenly looks older, her sandy hair dark with perspiration and matted strands clinging to her flushed face. I have never seen anyone look more exhausted, or more proud.

I fetch two towels. Tee wipes the baby's small body with one and then she carefully swaddles him in the other.

"Can I hold him?" Rosie asks, using her elbows to push herself to sit up in the bed.

"Of course." Tee walks around the side of the bed and places the tiny baby into his young mother's arms. Tears stream down Rosie's flushed cheeks.

"Hello there," she says, beaming down at her son. "Hello, my little Daniel."

"Oh, Rosie, no," Tee says, in a rushed whisper. "You know you shouldn't name him. It makes giving him away even harder."

"I'm not giving him away."

Tee shakes her head. "I know it's hard, but—"

"I am not giving him away," Rosie repeats, with more force.

I busy myself cleaning Rosie and the bed. She barely notices me wipe her legs and clean her up as she rocks the baby in her arms.

"How about I fetch you some tea and toast," Tee says. "You must be starving."

Rosie is suddenly energized, and I gasp when I realize she is attempting to stand. Tee places two strong hands on her shoulders to steady her in the bed.

"You can't take him," Rosie cries.

I hear the pain between her words. It's not like before; there is no screaming in agony. This pain is different but no less crippling. This is the pain of a mother's heart breaking.

"That's it, good girl," Tee coos. "Rest up now—"

Rosie's face reddens and fills with anger. "I won't let you take him. No! No!"

"Rosie, please. You have to calm down. You don't want the other nuns to hear you." Tee's distress shakes the ground beneath me.

"I don't care who hears me!" Rosie continues to shout, but the fear etched into her brow tells me she actually cares very much indeed.

"Rosie . . ." Tee places a finger to her lips.

"I'll run away. I'll take Daniel and go. You can't stop me. I'm not pregnant anymore."

"You've just had a baby," Tee tells her. "You have no strength. And besides, you know Father Michaels doesn't tolerate runaways. You know what happened to Julia Brown."

Rosie's fleeting expression tells me that whatever happened to Julia Brown might scare *me.*

"Please help me, Tee." Rosie begins to cry. "Don't let them take Daniel. You're the only one who can help."

Tee doesn't say another word. Instead, she strokes Rosie's hair, just as she did when the girl was in labor.

"Look at him," Rosie says. "Isn't he the most beautiful thing you've ever seen?"

"He's a very sweet boy," Tee says at last. "If you feed him and keep him quiet, you can stay here for a while. But you must keep him quiet, do you understand?"

Rosie nods. "And then will you help me?"

"I'm going to get you some tea and toast now. You need to get your strength back."

"And then will you help me?" Rosie tries again.

Tee places her finger to her lips once more, and she smiles and winks. "Nice and quiet, all right? Nice and quiet."

Rosie pulls her nightgown aside to feed her baby. He wriggles against his mother's skin, wrestling against her best effort. My chest is tight, as I think he is going to cry. But soon he finds his way and Rosie grins with pride when he suckles.

"He's a hungry one," I say. "You'll need extra toast, I think."

"That she will," Tee says, smiling as she begins to gather wet, stained towels.

I help her tidy, and soon the only evidence that a baby was born here is the mother and child cuddled together in a bloodstained bed.

"We'll come back for your suitcase later," Tee whispers to me, glancing at my arms full of soiled linens. "For now, let's give them as much time as we can."

"What happens next?" I ask.

"We make toast."

30

Margaret

Tee moves slowly, and I am grateful for the change of pace, as the weight of my thoughts bogs me down. I've no doubt this place has taken its toll on Tee over the years too.

"Why can't Rosie keep her baby?" I ask.

Tee's brow knits. "You know why. Her parents would die of shame. Why do you think she's here? Why are they all here? No one can know about Rosie's baby."

"But if her parents just meet the wee fella. He's precious."

Tee lowers her head and mumbles something I can't make out.

"Only, well, I wouldn't have liked to come home to my parents pregnant before I was married. They'd have hit the roof. But given time, they'd want to meet their grandchild, I'm sure."

Tee stops and turns to look at me. "Are you so sure? Knowing your pa—"

"No way," I snap. "My parents would never send me here."

"And yet here you are." Tee's words cut deep. "As far as the people of Tipperary are concerned, there is nothing worse than falling from grace. Not even this place."

"Father Michaels said we take care of the girls. But this isn't caring. This is . . . this is . . ." Words fail me as I grapple with all I have learned in just a few short hours. "It's stealing. We're stealing their babies."

Father Michaels's flashy cars come to mind. And the leaky convent roof. The rich Americans who arrive at Ballyvale as a couple and leave as a family, their donations lining church pockets.

Tee clutches the bloodied towels to her chest, and I notice she's trembling.

We walk on in silence.

I follow her into the kitchen, and I'm shocked by how small it is. Sister Bernadette's kitchen at the convent was a fine space laden with modern appliances and plenty of shiny worktop space for baking. I doubt a cake has ever been made in this tiny kitchen with grubby green walls and matching floor tiles. There is a poky larder made from uneven timber planks nailed together. It tilts to the left. It's sparsely stocked with a couple of bags of oats and a loaf of bread. There are no fruits or vegetables to be seen. I search for eggs and butter, but I cannot seem to find any of those, either.

Tee opens an empty cupboard and stuffs the dirty towels from her arms inside. She takes the linens from me and adds them on top, then closes the cupboard and marches to the sink, where she scrubs her hands with a bar of chalky soap.

"Are we leaving them there?" I ask, confused. "Won't they smell?"

"We'll come back for them later and take them to the laundry room. But for now, I don't want Matron to know it's all over. She'd expect Rosie to get straight back to work."

"She barely has the strength to stand," I say.

"Matron would not care."

"Should we talk to Father Michaels?" I ask.

Tee sighs as she fetches a pot, fills it with water, and places it on the stove.

"You have known Father Michaels all your life, am I right?"

I nod.

"And have you come to find him a particularly sympathetic man in that time?"

"He would never physically harm someone," I say, surprised to find myself defending him.

A flicker of dissent crosses her face before she says, "I can buy her some time. Until tomorrow morning, maybe. But after that, Matron will come looking."

"Then we tell her where to go."

The pot begins to boil, and Tee raises her voice to speak over it. "Are you mad? Speaking up makes it all so much worse for the girls."

"What could possibly be worse than this?" I outstretch my arms in reference to all the abbey encompasses.

Tee points at the pot, and I don't understand.

"As I said, we must do our best to keep the girls safe. And often, Maggie, that means keeping our mouths closed. Silence is a small price to pay to save another poor girl from a scalding."

My eyes flick to the boiling water. Steam swirls into the air and bubbles pop at the surface. "Julia Brown?" I gasp, remembering the fear on Rosie's face when Tee mentioned her name.

Tee's expression fills with the memory, and I can't bring myself to imagine it. She cuts some bread and spears it with a fork. She passes it my way and tells me to open the rusty old stove and toast it over the flame. I do as I am told, all the while with my eyes on her, curious and learning. She opens another cupboard and pulls out a battered silver biscuit tin. The lid squeaks as she opens it and retrieves a tea bag.

"I'm down to the last three." She sighs. "I hope Austin is going into town soon. I hate asking him to spend his own money, but without him there would be no tea for the new mothers."

"He buys the tea from his own pocket?"

"And biscuits, too, on his payday. Garibaldis are the girls' favorites, but they like rich tea too. He's a good man."

I find it hard to equate the reserved man who brought me back to the convent two years ago with the kind soul in Tee's story.

"Will Mr. Dolan take Rosie into town?" I ask, thinking of the lovely cushions on his cart. I wonder if he has them to keep the girls comfortable on their way back home after their babies are born.

"She will have to wait until someone comes for her. A male relative over eighteen must sign for her."

"When will they come?"

Tee shrugs. "There's no telling, really."

I twirl the fork and brown the bread all over as evenly as I can. It smells good and my stomach rumbles. Tee makes a face at the sound of my hunger, but she doesn't comment. She is busy fetching a small cup to drop the tea bag inside. Then she takes the pan from the stove and pours the boiling water into the cup.

"There is no milk," she announces, with such despondency that I think she might cry.

She stares into the cup without blinking for a long time. I watch the steam swirl around her face and I wait for her to snap out of her trance. I pull my arm back from the stove and set the toast down on the narrow countertop.

"What is it? It's not milk, is it?"

"It is." Tee slouches. "Rosie should have milk in her tea. She's just brought a baby into this world. I can't help her much, but the least I can do is bring her a nice cup of tea."

Tee wears her namesake like a badge of honor. The tea she brings the new mothers clearly means a great deal to her. But I'm not convinced that milk, or a lack of it, will really make a whole lot of difference today.

"Tomorrow, when Rosie is back on her feet, I will have to tell Matron that her baby boy is here," Tee says. Her eyes glisten. "And Matron will tell Father Michaels."

I push past the lump in my throat. "How long will Rosie have with the baby, once they know?"

"It varies. If the adopting couple travels from England, they could be here in a day or two. Americans seem to take longer. A week, maybe."

"I hope they're American," I say cheerfully. "It will give Rosie some time with him."

Tee shakes her head. "It gives Rosie time to fall even more in love with her son. The longer it takes, the greater the bond and the worse the heartbreak is when they take the baby away. I've seen it all too often before."

The realization is heavy. Little more than a child herself, Rosie will carry the secret of her lost son with her for the rest of her life.

"Will she stay here until they take Daniel? What if her family comes for her before that? She won't leave the baby."

Tee takes my hands, and a shiver runs the length of my spine with trepidation about what she will tell me next.

"Father Michaels will inform her parents once the baby is adopted, and then, in time, hopefully someone will come for her. Rosie is the eldest child, but she does have a brother. Once he is eighteen, he can come."

"What about her pa?"

Tee shakes her head. "I've never seen a father come. Ever."

"But Rosie is only fifteen herself. If her brother is younger, it will be years before he is old enough."

"Rosie will be here for a few years, yes," Tee explains.

"She's not pregnant anymore. There is nothing to hide. That's not fair." Reeling, I catch the countertop to steady myself.

"No one ever said it was fair."

I cannot bear this. I want Tee to take it all back. I want to rewind and go back to being a naïve nun staring over the convent walls at a place I once believed was a sanctuary. But Ballyvale Home for Fallen Girls isn't a home at all. It is the farthest place from a haven or safe place that I can imagine. It is a workhouse at best and a prison in truth. The girls' only crime is unwed motherhood. I watch Tee warm her hands around the mug. Her fingers twitch and tremble in an unspoken acknowledgment of the burden and heartache that each young girl who walks through the doors of Ballyvale Abbey carries and the cruel weight of not being able to change a thing.

"I hate it here," I hiss through a tight jaw.

"I suspect that's why he sent you," Tee says.

He is of course Father Michaels, and I think Tee is right.

Tee looks up, worried. "But you won't leave?"

"No," I say, shaking my head. "I won't leave."

"We are going to be good friends," she tells me, her voice breaking like a weak signal.

"The best," I say, equally choked up. "Now. Let's get this tea and toast to Rosie while it's still hot."

31

Margaret

Daniel is a hungry little chap, content only when feeding at his mother's breast. Rosie doesn't seem to mind. She holds him close and sniffs his head. Despite her young years, she has taken to motherhood like a duck to water, and Tee says, "It's a beautiful thing. All the pain a mother goes through to bring life into the world is almost instantly forgotten the moment that baby is placed in her arms."

"Did you ever wish for a baby of your own?" I ask her, when Rosie finally drops off to sleep and I take Daniel and rub his back to bring up wind.

"Oh, my time is long past." She waves her hand dismissively.

"But before, when you were younger?"

"We all want things we cannot have when we are young. But I'm the eldest daughter in my family and so my place is here."

The baby burps and we both smile.

"Good boy," Tee says. "What a good boy."

I'm about to ask her some more questions about when she first came to Ballyvale, but footsteps in the corridor startle us both.

"Matron," I mouth silently.

Tee nods and pulls a watch from her pocket. "Half past six. She'll be looking for supper, no doubt. We must go."

I hold my breath as the doorknob twists and the door creaks open. Matron enters without an invite.

"There you are," Tee says, smiling at the pinch-faced nun. "I was just coming to look for you. Tea? I could murder a cup myself."

Matron brushes past Tee as if she is invisible. "What do we have here?"

"Rosie had her baby," Tee says.

"When?"

"Oh, not long ago." Tee is effortlessly casual, and I suspect she tells similar time-shortening white lies all the time.

Matron steps deeper into the room. She pushes onto her tiptoes to inspect the baby bundled in my arms.

"And you helped?" she asks.

I nod, proud.

She flops back onto her heels, and the snap of her patent shoes against the tiled floor echoes around the room. Rosie wakes with a jolt, and the baby in my arms begins to cry.

"Shh, shh," I whisper, instinctively bouncing him.

Rosie rubs her eyes and stretches out her arms. I step forward to pass Daniel to her, but Matron raises her hand and I stop in my tracks.

"And what, tell me, is this?"

I follow her gaze as her eyes sweep the dim room.

"A feast?" She points at the tray on the low table beside Rosie's bed. There is a plate with toast crumbs and a cup of cooled tea that Rosie could only manage to sip half of. She edges close to the bed, and Rosie draws her feet back and tucks her knees into her chest.

Matron picks up the cup and swirls the tea around.

"Stone-cold," she hisses. "This isn't freshly brewed. It's hours old. As, I suspect, that baby in your arms is, Sister Margaret."

I dare not reply, but my silence seems to enrage her further.

"When was it born?"

"It's a boy," Tee says in a gentle whisper, as if hopeful that hushed tones will bring calmness. But even in the poor lighting I can tell Matron's face is growing red around the temples.

"When was *it* born?" Matron glares at me.

My insides shake. I am acutely aware that one wrong word may cost Rosie precious moments with her baby.

"The screaming stopped hours ago," she says. "Do you think I'm stupid?"

"No, Matron. Of course not. It was a difficult birth. We just needed some time to make sure mother and baby are all right."

"And is he? Is the boy healthy?"

I smile. "Yes. He is. He is a perfectly healthy baby boy."

"Good," she says with a firm nod. And then she opens her arms to receive him.

I step back and clutch him closer to me.

She shakes her arms impatiently, and Tee's face fills with worry as she nods. I know I must hand him over. Reluctantly, I step forward, but before I can pass him into Matron's arms, Rosie cries out.

"You can't have Daniel. I won't give him up."

Matron spins with unexpected speed. The smack from the back of her hand against Rosie's jaw happens so suddenly that neither Tee nor I could have predicted it.

"Matron, no, please," Tee says, hurrying to place her body between

Rosie and the angry nun. "She's tired. Exhausted from birth. She's young and doesn't understand what she's saying."

"I know what I'm saying," Rosie snaps as she rubs her jaw. "I know you sell the babies. We all do. But you're not taking mine."

Matron grabs a fistful of Rosie's hair and tugs her to her feet. Rosie jerks and twists, shouting, "You can't have him! He's mine! He's my baby!"

Tee hurries to help, trying to free Rosie's hair, which is tangled around Matron's chubby fingers.

"Matron, please. She's weak. She can barely stand. Don't you see?"

"She's not too weak to talk back."

"I'm not weak." Rosie pushes Matron. She stumbles, taking a chunk of hair in her fist. Rosie doesn't flinch. "I can fight."

"Hush, hush," I say, pleading with Rosie as much as with the baby I bounce in my arms, but Daniel can't be comforted. His newborn cries fill the room.

"Shut that thing up," Matron snarls. "And you." She points a finger toward Rosie, and I notice how unsightly her grubby fingernails are. "How *dare* you scream the place down like a banshee?"

Tee stares at Rosie with beseeching eyes, but Rosie can't be tamed. She tries to push past Matron, but Matron grabs her nightie and begins to beat her about the head with her other hand.

"Let me go. Let me go, you old witch." Rosie wails louder.

"Stop it. Please stop," I call out, loudest of all as I pull Daniel closer to my chest.

"All right," Matron says, her voice suddenly as gentle as a summer breeze. She lets Rosie go and backs away. "Father Michaels will deal with this insubordination from here on."

"Oh, Matron, no." Tee's hands cover her face. "He's such a busy man. Let's not trouble him, eh?"

"I'm sure he'll agree it's no trouble at all," Matron says.

Rosie rubs her head as Matron picks strands of long sandy hair out from between her fingers and discards them on the floor.

"We should go," Tee says, and there's a desperation in her that she can't mask even though I suspect she tries. "It's teatime. We all have holes in our bellies."

I can't take my eyes off Rosie's flushed, innocent face. I don't want to leave her alone.

"Right. You," Matron says, with a click of her fingers. "Back to work."

Tee's bottom lip quivers. "I'm sorry," she mouths silently to Rosie.

"She's just had a baby," I say, ignoring everything Tee has warned me about keeping quiet.

"I can see that," Matron snorts. "But chores are chores. And hers need doing. Of course she can take some time. Ten or fifteen minutes to get dressed."

"She could faint or fall," I go on.

Matron shrugs.

"She's bleeding."

Matron scrunches her nose, disgusted by the mechanics of birth.

"It's heavy," I lie. "What if she gets blood on the linens? I can't see Father Michaels being best pleased about that."

Matron rolls her eyes and sighs. "Fine. She can go straight to the dormitory. But if I do not see her in the laundry first thing in the morning—"

"You will see her," Tee cuts in. "In the morning. But for now, she needs rest. And we need supper. Margaret brought apple tart from the convent," she announces, as if she is inviting her friend to a dinner party."

Her obsequious pandering to Matron is hard to watch, but I remind myself it's all for Rosie's sake.

"Oh, lovely." Matron smiles widely. It startles me. Up close I notice her two front teeth are as black as her habit and look as if they could come loose and tumble to the floor at any moment.

"Can you escort Rosie back to her usual bed?" Tee asks me. "Get her settled with the baby and whatnot."

I have very little idea where anything is located, least of all the sleeping quarters. But I read between the lines of Tee's words. I know she will keep Matron distracted while I help Rosie. Maybe I could get her washed up and watch the baby while she sleeps.

Tee links Matron's arm, and as they walk away, she says, "I hope we have some ice cream. It would go nicely with the tart."

I hope Matron chokes on her first bite.

32

Margaret

Rosie guides me toward the girls' dormitory. She seems to grow stronger with each step. By the time we reach the dorms, she is as full of energy as any girl her age. I'm surprised to find the other girls kneeling and praying by their bedsides, instead of in the laundry. Matron knew the workday is over. She had no intention of sending Rosie to the laundry. She just wanted to scare Tee. My head pounds as if someone is beating an imaginary drum against my brain. I am familiar with hatred—I will forever hate Father Michaels for stealing my life away—but it pales in comparison to my contempt for Matron. I have known the woman less than a day, and with each passing minute I abhor her more.

"Are you all right, Maggie-pie?" Rosie asks me, and I realize I've stopped moving.

I glance at the baby, once again sleeping in my arms, and it's hard to comprehend that just hours ago, this fresh-faced girl was screaming in agony as she pushed him into the world.

"Oh, don't worry about me. Come on, let's get you settled," I say.

The dormitory is a large, open space stuffed with narrow, metal-framed beds lining the walls. Wafer-thin mattresses lie on top with neatly tucked-in off-white sheets. The timber floor, perhaps once a finely polished oak, is dull, like everything else in this place.

The girls with small bellies—or none at all, yet—jump to their feet and hurry toward Rosie the moment they set eyes on their friend.

"Well?" the hazel-eyed girl from earlier asks. *Lucy.*

"A boy," Rosie says, beaming.

It takes Anna, the other girl I met this morning, longer to stand up. She tries several positions—her leg to the side, her arms grabbing the edge of the bed, and both legs bent underneath her—but she's struggling under the weight of her ready-to-burst belly. Finally, one of the girls with no belly at all comes to her aid. She slides her arms under Anna's and counts.

"One. Two. Three. Whoosh."

Anna's smile is meek but full of gratitude.

"What's your name?" I ask, smiling at the helpful girl.

"I'm sorry, Sister. I'm so sorry. I just . . ." Her face clouds over until there is no color left in her cheeks. "I only meant to help. I know we're not supposed to . . ." She trails off and cowers, as if she is waiting for something awful to happen.

"You're not supposed to what?" I try to keep my voice low because I can tell she is afraid of me—afraid of the robes that I wear and what they might mean for her if she has broken a rule. "Are you not allowed to help each other?"

"We're not supposed to touch each other," Anna explains, waddling closer.

"Not even when you can't get out of bed?"

"Not ever."

"Oh." I shake my head, but I dare not share my thoughts and upset them further. "Well, you don't need to be afraid of me, I promise."

No one utters a word. Eyes blink in pale, achingly thin faces.

"Sister Maggie-pie is nice. Honest," Rosie says, full of animation, and I wonder how she could so easily dismiss what happened just now with the other nuns. I suspect her age and her innocence. "She's like Tee. Just not old."

I smile cautiously. Young girls gather around me like delicate butterflies. I'm afraid to move in case I spook them and send them scattering. Slowly they soften, one by one. Lucy is first to relax.

"Hi, Sister Maggie-pie," she says.

"Hello again, Lucy." I study her middle and guess that she's not yet halfway through her pregnancy.

She catches the side of her nightgown to fidget with it. "How old are you?" she asks, and the other girls gasp in unison as if her simple question was too bold to dare ask.

"Twenty-two," I say. My answer hangs in the air for a moment, with everyone too afraid to speak, until finally Lucy says, "It's my birthday tomorrow. I'll be twenty-two too."

Lucy could be mistaken for being years older than me. Her cheekbones are chiseled and high. Her skin is gray-washed like all the others, but a rosy hue clings to her cheeks.

"Happy birthday," I say, and I hope the crack in my voice isn't noticeable. I hate to think of any young woman spending her birthday like this.

"When is your birthday, Sister Maggie-pie?" she asks.

I don't have time to answer before Anna jumps in with a question. "Why are you a nun?"

This one startles me, and, noticing, the girls freeze once more.

"My father thought it was best," I say, at last.

"My father thought this place was best too." Someone joins the conversation from the shadowy corner. A girl with no belly and bare feet pads across the floor. "But what he meant was, this place is best for him. Couldn't have the whole town talking about poor pregnant Bridie. Imagine the shame when he goes to the pub on a Friday. Probably couldn't enjoy his pint if the neighbors knew his daughter was knocked up."

She catches me scanning her flat stomach, and her hands instinctively go to it.

"I had a girl. If that's what you're wondering. Almost a year ago now."

I look at this thin young woman, still here a year after giving birth. I think of Rosie, in the bubble of excitement and happiness that new motherhood has brought. With only a younger brother, she, too, will still be here in a year. And a year after that. Rosie will grow from child to woman in this place. The thought of it bends me in the middle.

Aware of countless sets of eyes on me, I straighten. "Where is your baby girl now?"

"No idea. It's not like they tell us where they're shipping them." Bridie shrugs. "Well, all the ones who survive."

I cradle Daniel's delicate sleeping body closer to me, so grateful that he made it through birth.

"Tee knows what to do," I say hurriedly.

"No, she doesn't. She's not a doctor or a nurse. If anything goes wrong, either mother or baby or both snuff it." Bridie drags her finger across her neck and makes a choking sound.

Anna clutches her huge belly. "I don't want to do this. I can't do this. I don't want to die."

I hurry to her and tilt my arms so she can see Daniel's beautiful face sleeping soundly.

"Look at him," I encourage her. "He's healthy. And Rosie is well. Tee kept them safe. She will keep you safe too."

I bite my lip, remembering Tee's instructions. *Don't make promises you can't keep.* But when Anna smiles, I am glad I said it.

Bridie tuts. "And then Father Michaels will snatch your baby away and you will be stuck here like me. Washing towels and bed linens for fancy hotels that the likes of us will never be a guest in." Bridie is bitter and full of hate, and I cannot blame her. But her words carry a weight greater than she knows. She is scaring the girls who have yet to give birth.

I help Rosie into bed. I fluff her limp pillow as best I can and place it between her back and the wall, where a headboard is noticeably absent. I tuck the light blankets over her slightly swollen legs and pass the baby to her.

"Do your best to keep him calm," I say, repeating Tee's advice, my understanding of it so much greater now.

The other girls return to their knees and resume praying. I tap Bridie on the shoulder and we step aside. Despite my gentle tone and slow and careful movements, I can tell she isn't prepared to trust me, or even particularly like me.

"Why are you still here?" I whisper, trying to keep out of earshot of the other girls.

She folds her arms. "May I return to praying now?"

"Wait," I say, desperate to soften her hostility. "Do you have family? A brother or a cousin? Does anyone know you're here?"

She remains stiff but trembles slightly, and if I had to guess, I would bet she has spent the twelve months since her daughter was taken away hardening her shell.

"Does anyone know I'm here?" she echoes with a snort as she jams a hand on her waist and juts a hip out. "I'm an only child and my ma is dead. So, what do you think?"

"I'm so sorry to hear that. Is she long gone?"

Bridie shrugs as if she doesn't hurt, but I can tell she aches all over inside. "She died when I was two. I don't remember her. It was just me and Pa. But then I got pregnant and he handed me over to that damn priest as if I was a sack of spuds. He doesn't even go to Mass. Doesn't believe in all that heaven and hell stuff. He just did it because he'd be too ashamed to face the town. Too ashamed to know he had raised a harlot."

"Don't say that. Don't call yourself that."

"Why? He did. And Father Michaels too. And Matron shouts it in our faces if we don't stuff enough bags full of clean linens. So why wouldn't I say it? You tell me that."

"Because it's not true. You just fell for a boy, I bet. Was he nice? Did you love him?"

She rolls her eyes. "What does that matter now? He's long gone. Lucky fucker."

"Does he know? About the baby, I mean."

"Oh, he knows. He was the first I told. But he had no interest in a wedding or nothing. He took himself off to the pictures with his friends the very night I told him. Next morning there he was on my doorstep telling me he wasn't ready to be a pa. He said he was sorry." She stops to exhale. "*Sorry!* Can you imagine hearing that from the man who put a baby in your belly? Off he took to Dublin or London or somewheres, but I didn't hear tell of him again. And as for my pa . . ." She takes a step back and stretches her arms as wide as they can go, as if she is hugging the room. "Well, I'm here, aren't I, so you can see how that went."

"Is he going to come for you?"

"Why would he do that? Haven't you ever heard that out of sight is out of mind?"

"There must be someone else. Someone you could write to. You could tell them your baby was born almost a year ago. You're free to go home."

Bridie laughs. But it isn't a happy sound; it's reckless and fueled by madness. It's wild and disconcerting. And noisy. I shake my head and will her to stop.

"Shh. Shh. The nuns will be finished with supper soon. They'll hear you."

I don't have to say more. Bridie closes her mouth. When she lowers her arms, her expression is solemn and she seems even older, suddenly, as if hardship will show her no mercy until she is old and gray.

"You don't think they actually post anything we write, do you?" She frowns, and I cross my fingers that she will not start laughing again.

I rush to reassure her. "Postman Padar comes on Mondays, and if you leave your letter with me, I'll see he gets it."

Bridie is prickly as a hedgehog, and isn't the type of person I usually care for. In years past, she might have even frightened me. But the days and weeks and months have shaped me anew. I know now that people build walls when it's all too much. Bridie's walls are sky-high, but I am determined to scale them.

"You get me a pen and paper and I'll write you a letter, Sister," she says, with a troubling smile. "Let's see you get it posted, because nice as pie doesn't get you far around here. But you'll learn that soon enough. Even that cape of yours won't keep you safe from Matron's tempers. You'll see."

There's a sudden shriek and I look across the large hall to find Anna bent and clutching the edge of her bed. A puddle is gathering on the timber floor around her ankles.

"Now?" I say, not quite able to believe that another baby may be joining us today.

Anna looks up at me with fearful eyes.

"Right," I say, shaking off exhaustion to snap into action. "Lucy, you know what to do. Fresh towels and hot water, please."

"Yes. Yes," Lucy says.

"Bridie, I need you to fetch Tee. She's having supper with the other nuns."

Bridie shakes her head. "We can't disturb them at mealtimes."

"But there's a baby on the way," I protest.

Countless girls look at me, wide-eyed, their silent refusal clear.

"Okay, fine." My palms begin to sweat. "How long does supper usually take?"

"There's prayer too, after," Lucy explains. "We can't interrupt."

"Tee won't mind," I tell them. "She'll want to know."

"And if we tell her now, while she's with the other nuns, Matron will know too," Bridie says, quick as a flash.

My heart races.

"You're right. Of course you're right."

"Babies take ages to come, Anna," Rosie pipes in. "You'll be just fine. Tee will be long finished with supper and prayers by the times you'll be needing her. You'll see."

"Yes, yes," I say. Panic gathers in the form of tiny, sweaty beads on the back of my neck, and I wish so badly I could take my collar off, as it feels chokingly tight all of a sudden.

"You need to get her to the birthing room," Lucy tells me.

My face questions, and Rosie is quick to fill in the blanks. "That poky room with no windows where I was. It's where all the babies are born."

"It's the farthest room from the rest of the abbey. The nuns don't hear the screaming so much from there," Bridie explains.

"But we haven't changed the bedsheets," I say. I want to add that the tiny, dark room is musty and stinking and the bed is damp and spattered in blood, but as I look around at the bleak condition of the dormitory, I realize it is unlikely there is any room in this place where a birthing mother might be comfortable.

A loud growl much too big even for the large space of the dormitory bursts out of Anna.

Bridie looks at her friend with pitying eyes. "Clean sheets are the least of our problems, wouldn't you say?"

Anna is panting like a thirsty dog. "It's coming. Oh God, it's coming. I can feel it."

The other girls back away, as if labor is contagious and they might catch it.

"It's all right," I say, trying to channel some of Tee's composure, but inside I am shaking like a leaf.

The puddle between Anna's legs turns pink, then red, growing darker and gaining in size.

"Is that normal?" Rosie asks. "That didn't happen to me."

The perspiration trickles down my spine. I catch my veil and tug it off, feeling instant relief from the building heat. The girls retreat to the far corners of the dorm, making themselves all but disappear as they cower together, unable to believe their eyes and unable to help.

"We need to get her to the birthing room," Lucy repeats.

I bend and check Anna. Blood is coming thick and fast, as is the baby. "We won't make it. Help me get her onto the bed."

Bridie nods and hurries to take Anna by one hand. I take the other and we turn her around. Her grip on my hand is tight like a vise and I yelp, but I don't dare let go.

"That's it," I say. "You'll be more comfortable up here."

Anna exhales as we help her to lie down. Her nightgown is bright red from the waist down. Seeing it, fear ripples across the girls, and some of them begin to cry.

"I'm dying. I'm dying," Anna chants.

"Is she?" Bridie whispers.

"I don't know," I whisper back. "But I don't think this is right."

"Haven't you done this before?"

My silence gives her my answer.

"Get Tee," I shout. I'm not speaking to any girl in particular. "Get Tee now. I don't care where she is or what she's doing. Get her."

Several of the girls muster the bravery to begin running.

"Teeee!" I hear them shout as they scurry down the halls.

Lucy returns with a basin of water and towels draped over her shoulder, but as soon as she sees Anna, she drops the basin. Water splashes across the floor, washing the bloody puddle away.

"She's very quiet," Bridie says, and it's only then that I grasp that Anna should be screaming, or moaning at the very least.

Lucy brushes past me and Bridie to take pride of place at Anna's bedside. I don't move her. She clutches her friend's hand and begins to cry. "You can do this. You're brave, Anna. I'm the scaredy-cat, not you."

A deep whine sounds from inside Anna like the wings of a hummingbird. I stare at her still body and will her to wriggle and squirm the way Rosie did. But she doesn't budge.

"Can she hear us?" Lucy cries.

Anna's skin is whiter than before, and although her eyes are closed, they twitch.

"Yes, I think so," I say, hopeful. I fetch the towels from Lucy's shoulder and position myself at the end of the bed.

"I can see the baby," I say. "Oh, Tee, where are you?"

A door swings open behind us, hitting the wall with a bang, and Tee appears, flushed and sweating.

"Oh, Anna." Tee's voice catches.

She hurries to the end of the bed and I step aside, relieved to let her take control.

"Will she be okay?" I ask, my pulse pounding in my ears.

Tee doesn't waste time answering me. She clicks her fingers and Lucy steps forward. "Hurry outside and fetch Mr. Dolan. You must tell him that it's Anna, and that she's in a bad way. Tell him to hurry into town as fast as he can and to come back with Doctor Henry."

"Yes, Tee," Lucy says like an obedient soldier.

But before she reaches the door, Matron arrives with a cup of tea in one hand and the other hand raised. "Stop right there," she tells Lucy.

Lucy glances over her shoulder at Tee, waiting for orders to leave or stay.

"She's in a bad way," Tee says. "We need Doctor Henry."

"And have the whole town talking? I don't think so," Matron says. "She'll be fine. It's just a baby."

"And how many have you birthed?" Bridie snipes, but thankfully for all our sakes, Matron doesn't hear her.

"She's hemorrhaging," Tee explains, and her effervescent calmness falters.

"And the baby?"

"I can't see. There's too much blood."

"Well, wipe it away and let's get on with this. You know Father Michaels is hoping for a girl for that nice couple from Chicago."

"We need Doctor Henry!" Tee is shouting. Her lips are close to my ears and her words ring inside my head, and yet I still feel she is not nearly loud enough.

Lucy begins to run, to fetch Mr. Dolan, but she doesn't get far when Matron pushes her onto the floor. Lucy grabs her belly, and I hurry to help her.

"Don't touch her," Matron warns me with a wagging finger.

I ignore her and reach my hand out to Lucy. "Are you all right?" I ask as she takes my hand and I help her to her feet.

Lucy doesn't have time to answer before heat explodes across my face and I am dizzy from the back of Matron's hand clocking my jaw. I'm startled and my ears are ringing, but above it all I can hear someone announce, "A girl. It's a girl."

Matron claps her hands joyously as she says, "Oh, how wonderful. Father Michaels will be pleased."

Tee is shaking her head, and it takes me a moment to follow along. I glance at the space at the end of the bed between Anna's legs. A tiny baby lies covered in her mother's blood just as Rosie's Daniel did earlier. I wait for the baby's first breath and the cry that comes with full lungs. I wait. And wait. And then I understand. This baby will not cry. Not ever.

Noise finally comes in the shape of Lucy's voice. "No. No. You can't go, Anna. Please no."

I am numb, but somehow my feet still manage to run. Lucy and I are at Anna's bed in seconds. Her lips are colorless.

I shake my head. "She can't," I say, helpless.

"She's gone," Tee says, and she wipes the tears from under her eyes with a bloodied hand. "We lost them both."

Lucy drops to her knees and wails. The girls in the corners cry too. There is so much sorrow in the room I think it might swallow us all up.

"How could you let this happen?" Matron grumbles.

Tee peels herself away from the end of Anna's bed. There's an audible crack as her spine straightens and she turns to face Matron. "How could *I* let this happen?"

"Yes. You. I don't see anyone else in charge."

Tee opens her mouth, but no more words come out. Instead, words tumble out of me. Even as I clamp my hand over my mouth, I cannot stop them.

"Do you see a doctor here? Or a nurse? Or anyone who could help? No, and that's exactly the problem. No one here can help, because no one cares if these girls live or die."

My eyes whip to the girls in the corner, and I wait for my words to register on their already traumatized faces, but they don't budge. I haven't shocked them. They've known since the first day they walked through Ballyvale's doors that no one cares about them. But they are wrong, because Tee and I care. And watching their hearts shatter for Anna and her still baby, I know how deeply they care for each other.

"Clean this up." Matron clicks her fingers.

"And for pity's sake, fetch Mr. Dolan," she adds, glaring at me. "Tell him to find a patch in the back this time. The last baby he buried in the front disturbed that grass, and it took weeks for it to look right again."

"We must inform her parents," I say. "They'll want to bring her home, surely. And the baby."

"Haven't you said enough?" Matron's eyes narrow, and she looks away from me and into her teacup. "Just find Mr. Dolan."

She leaves, grumbling something about her tea getting cold. As soon as her footsteps fade out of earshot, everyone begins to sob as loudly as they need to.

"Don't call Mr. Dolan yet," Lucy begs me. "Can we have some time with her?"

I want to tell the girls they can have as long as they need, but I am past words as I rub my throbbing jaw. I nod, and they know. Girls line up to touch Anna. They kiss her forehead, stroke her hair, touch her hand, whisper to her.

"She was so scared," I tell Tee, my voice finally returning. "She was so afraid of dying, right from the moment I met her. It's all she talked about."

"She's at peace now," Tee says with tears glistening in her eyes. "She will be together with her baby forever."

"That's all she wanted," Lucy sobs. "Just her and her baby."

I drape my arms over Lucy's shoulders and let her cry into my neck. "She was my best friend. I hate this place. I hate it so much it makes me sick."

"Me too," I say, blinking back tears. "My God, me too."

33

Margaret

Time is a funny old thing. We spend so much of our life taking it for granted. Growing up, old age is almost too distant to comprehend. Aging is something, somewhere, that happens to someone else. But the old lady with a comma-shaped spine who can't walk without her stick was once a sprightly child running around carefree. An overworked and exhausted parent with a noisy house might ache for days of quiet, never considering that every night when they close their weary eyes, an empty, silent house creeps a little bit closer. Time is not shared evenly, and some of us aren't given nearly enough. I doubt any of us give time much thought, until there is none of it left.

A week ago, I was a reluctant graduate of the Sisters of Penance convent. I held my hand to my chest and pledged my heart to our Lord.

I drank tea and ate crumble. I laughed. Days later I undertook a new adventure, out one gate and in another. I learned the truths behind secrets I had long been curious about. I helped as a baby boy entered the world. And I watched, helpless, as a tiny girl and her mother left it. Just twenty-four hours in Ballyvale Home for Fallen Girls has given me knowledge and shown me sights that will be etched into my soul for the rest of my days. I will never again be able to close my eyes and not think about the beautiful wee baby that never got a chance to open hers.

I ask Tee if I can stay with the girls in the dormitory tonight, but with hollow eyes, she shakes her head.

"It wouldn't be good for you, and it would be worse for them, if Matron found out."

"But under the circumstances—"

"Surely by now you understand, Maggie," Tee says, dabbing around her eyes. "Doing our best by the girls often means going against our hearts."

I hear her words, but the girls are inconsolable, and I am desperate to comfort them. They cry for their lost friend and they cry for themselves.

Lucy fetches more water. There's no more need for it. Tee has washed all signs of Anna's pain away. She lies still in the slender bed, youthful and calm, and I could almost believe she is simply sleeping. Her precious baby is washed and wrapped in a small white towel. She lies tucked at her mother's side.

I watch Lucy struggle with the weight of the basin as she carries it to Anna's bedside. She is a shell of a girl now. She lifts the bottom of the sheet and gently folds it back, revealing Anna's feet. The soles are grubby, I can guess from padding barefoot on the laundry floor just this morning. Lucy soaks a small cloth and wrings it out. She takes her time with her friend as gentle sobs rock her. Finally, she re-covers Anna's feet and smiles through her tears.

"There," she says. "Now she will look her best when she knocks on heaven's door."

Tee exhales. "Aye. That she will." She takes Lucy's wet hand and guides her toward her bed. "Come now. Get some sleep if you can. Mr. Dolan will be here for Anna soon, and you'll want all your energy to say a proper goodbye then."

Tee and I work together to settle the girls into bed. There are plenty more tears and questions, and I wish I had better answers. Or any answers at all. Finally, when Tee quenches the last bedside candle and the girls are plunged into darkness, she says, "I'll show you to your room."

"When will the funeral be?" I ask once we are in the corridor and out of earshot.

Tee lowers her head and stares at her feet. A yellow bulb flickers overhead, muted and meek, as if offering its respects.

"Mr. Dolan will come for them tonight."

"Will Father Michaels say the Mass?"

Tee sighs. "Mr. Dolan will bury them in the garden. Tonight. Once it's dark."

I am winded. "No. No, he can't. The girls have to say goodbye. Lucy has to—"

"Hear me now, Maggie. Anna is not the first and, Lord rest her soul and forgive me mine, she won't be the last. These girls are having babies without so much as a Disprin or any trained professional. Lord knows I've no formal training besides what I've learned about birthing babies over the years. And I know there's not much you know neither. Matron would deny these girls a doctor to save their lives—do you think she's going to offer a funeral after all that?"

"Everyone deserves a funeral," I say meekly.

I don't think Tee has ever been able to verbalize my sentiment, but I have no doubt her feelings match mine.

She sighs, broken and exhausted. "Let's get some sleep. There is nothing more we can do for lovely Anna now, and who knows if one of the other girls might need us before dawn."

"Will you miss her?" I ask, suddenly aware that I have known Anna less than a day and Tee has probably known her since the day she arrived.

"I miss them all," she says as she looks up and begins walking.

Tee and I walk up a carpeted staircase. My feet sink into the thick pile. The second floor smells entirely different. Clean and fresh, like the summer's night outside. She opens a door, and, weary, I step inside. A huge bed with room enough for two awaits. There's a floral bedspread, fluffed pillows, and matching curtains. A small chandelier shines in the center of the ceiling. There's a large writing desk and a leather armchair with a cushion and a footstool. Fancy furniture to match the oak headboard—a tall chest of drawers, a wardrobe, even a dressing table with a mirror.

"Oh, Tee." I gasp at the fineness of it all. It is like a grand hotel in Dublin, I imagine. I spin around, taking it all in. "It's beautiful."

"And it's all yours."

"Thank you." I smile. But I cannot shake the sadness in me. The contrast between the huge, luxurious room with a thick mattress and warm bedsheets is shocking compared to the girls' cramped dormitory. "I can't stay here."

Tee's expression changes. "You have to. And you will do it gratefully, accepting it as the gift that it is. You will never let your guilt show. Not to Matron, and not even to the girls."

"But it seems so wrong."

"My room is across the hall. It is a little larger, but in all other ways it is the same."

"How do you do it, Tee? How do you stay so strong?"

"You see those fluffy pillows?" she says, pointing toward the bed that, if I am wholly truthful, my exhausted body aches to flop onto. "When you cry into them, no one really hears you."

"Oh."

"Good night, Maggie." Tee leans toward me and kisses my forehead the way my mother used to. "Tomorrow is a new day."

My breath catches for a moment. "Good night, Tee."

34

Margaret

I climb into bed to find the pillows are just as soft, the bedspread just as cozy, and my body and mind just as tired as I thought. I'm in a deep sleep when the commotion starts. Shouting and crying. I'm on my feet before my eyes are open, and my first thought is that another of the girls has gone into labor. I worry that I might never sleep a night through again. But as I fish around in the darkness for my robes, I notice how different the racket is. There is no low, animalistic hum of pain. Instead, the sound of raised voices jolts me mid-step. I freeze with my ear cocked toward the door. But I cannot make out words. I dress quickly—foggy with sleep, nerves buzzing with alarm—and I leave my room. I meet Tee in the corridor. She's still in her nightwear, and she's holding a candle with the wax burned down to a near stub.

"What is it? What's happening?"

"Father Michaels is here," she says, as the light of the candle shines under her chin, highlighting her troubled face against the darkness.

"In the middle of the night?"

Tee nods. "It's always bad when he comes at night."

"Is he here for Anna?"

"Unfortunately not," Tee says, as she takes me by the hand and leads me down the stairs. "Stay calm," she warns me. "It'll be worse if he knows you don't approve."

There is no time for explanations as Tee and I breathlessly retrace our steps from earlier, rewinding our way back to the dormitory. The commotion grows louder with each step.

Tee opens the dormitory door and I hook my hip close to hers. I almost crumple when I see Rosie sitting on a kitchen chair in the middle of the floor. Blue ribbon is bound around her ankles, tying her to the chair legs. Her shoeless feet are bluish white with the cold. Her wrists are equally secured, as more ribbon ties her hands behind her back. Matron and Father Michaels stand shoulder to shoulder in front of the young girl. They're asking her questions in hushed tones, and when an answer doesn't come, Matron strikes Rosie across the face with the back of her hand. The chair rocks and I don't breathe until it steadies again.

"What are you doing?" I call out, my voice screechy like a needle stuck on a record.

Matron turns. "Good. You're here."

"Stop this. Please?" I catch Father Michaels's eye and shake my head, horrified. He grunts and looks away.

"Tell Father Michaels how badly this young slip of a thing behaved today," Matron directs me.

I try to seek out Rosie's eyes, but her head is bowed and she is shaking. The rest of the girls remain in their beds, most of them with the sheets pulled over their heads. I'm confused until I notice the black iron kettle in Matron's hand, with steam swirling out the top.

"This one screamed the place down," Matron continues, tapping an accusatory finger on Rosie's shoulder.

"She was in pain," I say, stepping warily forward. Tee's hand grabs the back of my robe and tugs. I lower my voice. "She was disoriented and scared."

Matron nods, acknowledging that birth is a painful business. "But she had her wits about her when she called me a witch. I was terribly upset, I must say. Witchcraft is a sin."

"I'm saddened to hear you say that, Matron. Because you are no sinner. Isn't that right, Rosie?" Father Michaels says.

Rosie doesn't lift her head, and when Father Michaels draws his foot back, I can't hold my tongue.

"She was scared," I murmur, like I'm reasoning with something feral. One wrong move and Matron's kettle might tip. Father Michaels lowers his foot, and I breathe a sigh of relief. I'm trembling as I try to reason with a man my pa once considered a friend. "She had just given birth and she wasn't ready to part with her baby. It was a little misunderstanding in the heat of the moment. That's all. Now, can you please let her go?"

No one speaks. And worse still, no one sets about freeing Rosie.

I clear my throat and try again. "Let her go, please. She's exhausted. She gave birth and lost her friend all in one day. I think any of us would be reeling. I know I am."

"Yes. I heard of the Gaynor girl's passing," Father Michaels says. I wait for regret to register on his face, but his deadpan expression betrays no feelings. "What was her name again . . . ?"

"Anna."

"Ah yes, like her mother. Pretty thing."

I cannot bring myself to look left to the bed where Anna took her last breath just hours ago.

"I know her father well," he continues, painting a family picture as if they are still whole and not missing the brightest color in the shape of their daughter. "A lovely man. Always sits in the second row at Mass on a Sunday. I think they could dig into their pockets a bit deeper, mind you. Only twenty pence from him most collections, and they have a big farm and all. I think I'll be needing to have a word."

"Best you do, Father," Matron says. "But be kind. I'm sure the poor man will be mortified by his shortcomings."

"His daughter just passed," I interrupt, sickened by these people.

Tee tugs so hard on the back of my robe, I almost lose my footing and tumble back on top of her. I will Rosie to look up, to meet my gaze and know that I am here for her.

"They have been informed of the girl's death," Father Michaels says, growing weary as he looks away from me and toward Matron. "Her ma was very upset, as you'd expect, and the little sisters too."

"Time will help with that. And I'm sure it'll be a lesson to the younger ones," Matron says, as she passes him something silver that catches under the light. I squint and wait for the light to reveal what it is. I draw back, horrified, when I discover a small, sharp thing with silver blades and a navy-blue handle. I recognize it as the scissors Tee used earlier to cut baby Daniel's cord.

Father Michaels steps forward and grabs Rosie's hair. Rosie yelps as her head draws back.

"Can't we do something?" I plead with Tee, her grip still firm on my clothes.

Tee's eyes are cloudy with tears, but she holds them back as she shakes her head. I can hear the whimpers of terrified girls hiding under their bedsheets. I can see Matron's grip on the kettle tighten, ready to pour. Hoping for the slightest twitch to give her an excuse.

"Please," I beg, desperate. "She's just a child herself."

"Get her out of here," Matron bellows in Tee's direction.

"Yes. Of course." Tee places her hands on my shoulders and tries to turn me toward the door. I dig my heels into the ground.

Father Michaels shakes his head. "Let her stay. I think our young sister might need a lesson as much as this girl. It's time Margaret Lannigan grew up."

Tee nods obediently.

Without another word, Father Michaels raises his hand.

"No!" I scream.

But no one flinches. No one even looks. Father Michaels just smiles—a sick, twisted grin—as shiny lengths of Rosie's hair fall like ribbons to the floor.

The feeling that rushes through me is unexpected. Relief. Relief that it's her hair he's cutting, not her skin. And then, just as quickly—disgust. He has no right. No right to lay a hand on her. I want to tear across the room and rip the scissors from his grip. But I'm learning from Tee. So I stay still. Heavyhearted. Silent. Useless.

He cuts and cuts until Rosie's scalp is visible and all that remains are stray tufts.

"There," he says, lowering his arms. "That'll teach you to have some respect."

Rosie is as silent as a church mouse as fat tears stream down her cheeks. A small bloodstain is growing on the back of her nightie, evidence that she gave birth just hours ago.

Father Michaels drops the scissors on the floor and turns toward Matron. "How's about a cup of tea?"

"Certainly, Father. I could use a cup myself. Helps me sleep."

Father Michaels and Matron are side by side as they leave the dormitory.

As soon as their footsteps fade away, Tee hurries to Rosie.

"Pick them up," she tells me with her eyes on the scissors. I do, and without further instruction I use them to cut Rosie's hands and feet free.

Rosie flops forward, and Tee just about catches her before she comes clean off the chair. We help her to stand on shaky legs. Tee bends and tucks herself under Rosie's arm. I do the same on the other side, and slowly, we guide her into bed.

"Is it bad?" she asks, running a hand over her head.

"Oh, Rosie," Tee sighs.

Rosie sobs, and it's a relief to hear her make noise at last.

"It will grow," Tee promises. "And with a pretty face like yours, I think short suits you."

"It does. It really does," Lucy says, finally appearing from under her sheets.

"It's pretty," Bridie adds.

Soon, there is a swarm of girls gathered around Rosie's bed, telling her how beautiful she is. Lucy runs a hand over Rosie's scalp and says, "It'll be so much better in the laundry now. Less sweaty."

Watching Rosie's spark return lifts me. I'm tucking the sheets around her tired body when I feel a tap on my shoulder. I turn around to find Bridie with a letter in her hand.

"You wrote to someone," I blurt, caught off guard in the moment.

"Writing was the easy part." I watch her swallow and I know she's fibbing. I know it took all her courage to put pen to paper, and I cannot hide my happiness.

"I don't have an envelope nor nothing," she says, passing me a small piece of paper with some smudged ink on the front.

"Not to worry. I'll see to that. Do you have an address?"

"S'on the back," she says in a whisper.

I nod and smile.

"No one will come, you know." She shrugs.

"You won't know unless you try. I'll get this posted."

"We'll see," she says.

Her lack of hope saddens me, but I hide it as best I can.

I fold the paper in half, taking care not to mess the ink any further, and I slide it into my pocket for safekeeping. I edge forward and open my arms to hug her, but Bridie steps back.

"I'll get it posted," I repeat, and she nods and returns to her bed.

With all the girls back in bed, and dawn not far around the corner, Tee and I leave them to find our own beds once more.

"Will they be all right?" I ask her, as we tiptoe toward our rooms.

"I hope so. Most girls survive the birth, Maggie. Our Lord doesn't take many of them, I promise."

I swallow with relief, and then I say, "That's good, I suppose. But I mean their minds. Will their minds be all right? When someone comes for them and they go home. How will they ever forget this place and all that has happened here?"

Tee takes a deep breath and stops walking to meet my gaze. "They won't. None of us will."

Suddenly, I am more tired than ever.

35

Margaret

Three days after Anna's death, Mr. Dolan takes me by the hand and leads me to the patch of freshly turned earth that cradles a mother and her child six feet below. I can't look at him, or at the damp brown clay contrasting against lush green grass. Earth, dark and dirty like the hearts of the nuns who run Ballyvale Home for Fallen Girls. I drop to the ground and pummel the soil with my fists until my hands are numb.

"Why didn't you warn me?" I spit between thumps. "You knew how awful this place was and you never said a word."

Mr. Dolan pulls me to my feet, and I feel as if the wind could carry me away like a whisper. He slides two fingers under my chin and tilts my head, forcing my gaze to meet his. "The home needed someone like you. I hoped Father Michaels would send you."

His eyes are red-rimmed and swollen, and the knees of his trousers are mucky. It's only then that I notice a freshly planted apple tree, a timid, twiggy thing in need of compost and sunshine. A headstone will not mark the spot where Anna and her unnamed baby girl rest, but a tree will grow in their memory, and I will nurture it until it is the finest tree in all of Tipperary.

"Why didn't you tell me the moment we met? I'd have come sooner if I'd known," I say.

Mr. Dolan dusts his knees and shakes his head. "Do you think Father Michaels would have sent you if you requested it—if he thought you wanted to be here, wanted to help? He's punishing you, Maggie-pie. The home is your punishment for spying on him, and I was banking that it would be."

"You set me up."

"Aye. That I did."

A magpie swoops and lands on a skinny branch close to the top. The branch bounces under the weight of the beautiful black-and-white bird with a bellyful of worms. I glance overhead to look for his friends. But he is alone.

"One for sorrow," Mr. Dolan says, and at the sound of his voice, the bird spreads his wings and flies away. "You should talk to the tree. Someone told me it makes them grow." He winks and walks away.

I run my finger along a twiggy branch that seems so frail without leaves and wait for words to come, but they don't.

"Psst, psst," I hear nearby. I duck behind the scrawny tree, which offers no cover at all. "Psst. Psst." The wild hedge between the home and the convent is sparser than I remember. If I squint and peer through just right, I expect to spot some magpies scratching for worms.

"It's me," a voice says.

Joyce!

"Mr. Dolan cut the hedge back," she tells me. "He says he thinks you'll be out here a lot from now on."

"I never thought I'd see you again," I gasp, as if it has been months instead of days since we last spoke. "What else has he told you?" I ask, peering through the gappy brambles and ivy. I can almost see her face.

"He's not a talker."

I snort. "No, he's not. But I'm learning he finds other ways to make his point."

"He's sort of the opposite of you, really, isn't he?" Joyce giggles, and it's beyond wonderful to hear the sound of laughter.

"Oh, I'm learning to keep my mouth shut."

Joyce doesn't reply, and if I could better see her face, I'm sure her expression would say she doesn't believe me. *Sweet, kind, naïve Joyce.*

"I have something for you." She pulls something out from behind her back.

"*Little Women*," I gasp as she holds the book up and I can just about make out the cover.

"You left in such a hurry, you forgot it."

I don't tell Joyce that I didn't forget, because suddenly I would desperately like to read about the March sisters again. Read about Jo and her courage to stand against the patriarchy. Although I am fast learning it is much easier in fiction than in real life.

"I've read it ten times now," Joyce tells me. "I'm certain I could recite it by heart if I needed to."

"Eleven times is possibly a time too far," I say, giggling the way we used to when we first started walking the convent grounds together.

"I could read it a hundred times," she says hurriedly. "But I thought you might like to read it out here, under that new tree. It's mighty scrawny and could do with someone reading to it to help it grow."

My heart pangs. I like that idea very much. Joyce and I take care passing the weathered book through the foliage. Thorns prick and scratch us, but they leave the cover intact, and once it's safely in my hands, I tuck it against my chest and sway. It feels like hugging an old friend. Like hugging Joyce.

"So tell me. What's it like over there?" she asks excitedly.

My heart sits in my chest in countless pieces. I've seen the horrors of Ballyvale with my own two eyes, and I struggle to believe it. Joyce is delicate, like the roses that grow in the convent gardens. She insists on confessing the smallest of fibs—I can't imagine how much a secret as great as unmarried mothers hidden away to have their babies would burden her. But I need a friend more than ever, and so I start with a half-truth. "It's not all that different. Lots of praying. It can be boring."

"Oh, Margaret. Praying is never boring. It's—"

A bell chimes, and Joyce's attention is summoned by the ever-pristine convent.

"I better go," she says, looking over her shoulder.

"Wait. Wait. Can I see you again?"

"Of course. All the time."

"Great. Can you bring me something?"

The convent bells grow louder as the morning birds sing and the symphony carries over the gate and across the gardens. I turn to look at the abbey, where the sound of the bells instructs the girls to drag themselves out of bed, weary with the hard work of the day before, to start again.

"Food?" I say, racing against the damn bells calling her away from me.

"Food?"

"Yes. Please. Bread, maybe. Or cheese. And milk especially."

"Are you fasting?"

"No. No, it's not for me. . . ."

"Oh, Margaret, what are you up to?"

"Please." I race my words. "Just help me. I'll explain everything, but tomorrow, bring what you can?"

There is a final loud dong, and Joyce nods, turns away, and begins running toward the convent. I turn toward the home and go inside for prayers. Praying that Joyce can help.

36

DECEMBER 1958
FIVE MONTHS LATER

Margaret

It's so close to Christmas I can smell it in the air. Morning dew glistens on the grass like countless fallen stars, and ice clings to the branches of trees, hugging tight. I like to get up before dawn and walk. Joyce and I have fallen into a routine of stolen minutes to chat at the hedge. I never miss a morning—unless of course one of the girls is in labor. But that hasn't happened for almost a month now. Tee says they're like dominoes and we'll have several babies arrive all at once soon. I do hope so. I can see how desperate the girls are to go home to their families. Especially the younger ones.

"Good morning, Anna," I say, touching a twiggy branch. "It's nearly

Christmas," I tell the tree, which has become my favorite spot. "We'll have lots of Christmas babies soon. It's such a lovely time of year for a birthday, isn't it?"

"Psst."

I hurry to the hedge.

"Morning," Joyce whispers.

I notice a loaf of brown bread and a ball of purple wool in her hand.

"I brought you some more," she whispers. "One of Mother's cushions. She has so many, she won't notice."

"She'll notice soon enough if you keep unraveling them." I laugh, thinking of the yellow ball of twine she brought last week, and the red ball and the green ball before that.

Over the months Joyce has passed me enough wool to knit a pair of booties for every baby born in Ballyvale.

"If they have their booties, they have a piece of you," I tell the girls.

I suspect most of the adoptive parents will discard the tiny shoes in favor of something more expensive the moment they pass through the gates, but nonetheless, sending their babies away with a keepsake lifts the girls' spirits just a fraction. Joyce and I ran out of balls of wool a few weeks back, and Joyce has been getting creative in her desire to help.

Over the months, stolen moments with Joyce begin to feel like old times, and conversation flows. Although no matter how much we talk, I can never quite bring myself to tell Joyce why I love this apple tree dearly.

"How is Mother?" I asked, inhaling the smell of the wool, which reminds me of her chambers.

Joyce sighs, and my heart twists before she replies, "Still no sign of improvement. I've never seen her so poorly. I'm worried."

"Me too. But I'm praying for her every day."

I can just about make out Joyce's half smile between the brambles.

"How are the girls?"

"Good," I say, trying to be cheerier. "No babies for a while now."

"Oh," Joyce puffs. "Soon. Hopefully."

"Yes, hopefully. It's getting colder by the day, and some of the girls are falling ill."

The bells chime, and as ever, we part.

"Tomorrow?" Joyce says.

"Tomorrow," I say, blowing a kiss through the hedge.

Life at the laundry isn't all that different to life in the convent. The girls start their day kneeling barefoot at their bedsides, and chant several Hail Marys and Our Fathers. Any girl who dares lean on the bed, yielding to the weight of a growing belly, receives a firm poke from Matron's stick. I often see her watching the roundest of bellies with a gleeful smirk, waiting for the weight of the large bump to become too much, like a hawk ready to swoop in.

Routine is upheld with the strictest of rigor. Dormitory duties must be carried out before breakfast. Beds dressed. Smocks pulled on over nightgowns. Floors swept. And all without a word spoken.

Breakfast, a single slice of bread and water, is served in a small room with a considerable number of tables. Sometimes there are so many girls in the abbey that there is not enough room for everyone to sit. And sometimes after those girls go home, there are so few left that even the poky space seems too big for their lonely souls.

This morning, the room is quiet, and I can offer the girls a much-needed extra slice of bread each.

"Your hair is really growing," I tell Rosie as she sits at the long table.

She runs her hand over her head, where jagged strands are longer on one side than the other, and smiles. Her smock is bulky, and I know she's wearing a bottle-green cardigan underneath it that brings out the emerald flecks in her otherwise hazel eyes. It was Sheila's. When cold weather showed signs of creeping in, I began giving away Sheila's clothes to the girls. A dress here and a jumper or blouse there. Anything that can keep them warm—under their smocks—out of Matron's sight. It's worked a treat so far, and I only wish I'd packed more.

"Daniel is five months old today." Rosie holds up five fingers. "Can you believe it?"

"Eat up," I say, dropping my eyes onto the plate in front of her. Two slices of the buttery brown bread that Joyce gave me are barely touched. "I hear the laundry is busy today, and you'll need all your strength."

"I think about him all the time. I wonder what the woman who took him is like."

"Oh, Rosie."

"It's the not knowing that's the hardest, Maggie-pie. I think if I just knew he was safe. Loved. Well looked after. Then I would be all right, you know."

"He is. He is," I rush in. "The people who take the babies love them. They are good and kind and so desperate to be a family."

"They are thieves," she snaps. "Our Lord says thieves are bad. My poor Daniel."

I hear the clip-clop of Matron's shoes as she enters the room and place my finger to my lips. Rosie nods.

"What is this?" Matron asks, coming to a stop behind me. She points over my shoulder at Rosie's plate. She counts the measly couple of slices of bread. "One. Two." Matron presses her hands onto my shoulders and her nails bite into my skin.

"I wasn't hungry this morning," I lie, hoping Rosie has the sense to stuff herself on Joyce's bread before Matron snatches it. "And rather than have it go to waste, I thought—"

"Gluttony." She snatches one slice off the plate to throw it on the floor. "Now," she declares, "we have a new girl joining us today."

I glance at the wasted bread and try to squash my rage. The last thing I want is to scare whatever poor creature is about to walk through the doors.

"This is Delia," Matron says, clicking her fingers to summon the girl in the corridor.

I can't believe my eyes. She's so familiar and so pretty. Her copper hair sits cropped just below her ears, warm and shining like a summer sunset. Her powder-blue eyes and fair skin are youthful and glowing. If I squint, I can make out the faint freckles dotted across her cheeks. Her dainty shoulders and long, slender legs. She is every inch a replica of her older sister and my childhood best friend, Linda O'Rourke.

"Delia," I gasp, edging closer, as if she is a precious thing that will crumble to dust if I dare touch her. The joy of seeing little Delia O'Rourke all grown up and standing right in front of me is quickly crushed by the realization of why she is here.

My eyes sting. "A baby?"

Delia palms her face and shakes her head before running to me and wrapping her arms so tight around my neck I can scarcely breathe.

"Margaret. Is it really you?" She lets go so she can stand back and take me in with a sweeping gaze. "It is. My God, it is. We thought you'd run away."

"Run away?" I choke. "What? No. Why would you think that?"

She shakes her head. "Father Michaels told us. He said you couldn't cope when Sheila died. And well, when you didn't come home for your ma and pa's funeral, well . . . erm . . . Joseph was a broken man. He didn't eat for weeks."

"Who else did he tell?"

Delia stares at me as if she is seeing a ghost. "Everyone. No one knew where you were."

"My God," I say, as horror but not quite surprise sinks in. Colm, Matthew, and Finbar never wrote. Not once. I always knew Father Michaels must have told them something. I just never thought it would be this.

"I hear Joseph and Linda are married," I go on, daring to hope that Father Michaels may have lied about that too.

"Yes, they are. Almost six months now." Delia stiffens, a little uneasy. "But they talk about you all the time. They miss you. Just wait until they hear I've found you. . . . Ouch." She rubs the back of her head, and I realize Matron has given her a clout.

"That's enough. You'll get out of this." Matron points to Delia's pretty pink-and-red knitted dress and leather ankle boots. "And into work clothes. Fallen girls earn their keep around here. And you're no different. Don't think because you knew Sister Margaret in another life that you're special. If anything, it's reason enough to work twice as hard. You hear me?"

Delia clings to me as if I can protect her, and I immediately fear for her. I can see in Matron's eyes that Delia's affection for me has made her an enemy of the old nun.

I peel her off me and say, "Come. Let's get you changed and down to the laundry."

"I want to see blisters on her hands by the end of the day," Matron demands.

"Blisters?" Delia asks.

"From wringing out laundry. Now, come on."

Delia follows me like a shadow. She falls a couple of paces behind, and I sense her glancing around. At the end of the corridor, I take pause as I always do before introducing a girl to the dormitory for the first time. I place my hand around the rusting knob and ask, "Are you ready?"

I cannot look at the face she shares with her sister as I introduce her to what lies in store.

"I just want to go home," she says, the way they all do, and the innocence in her voice reminds me of a time gone by.

I open the door and give her a moment. She holds herself like a lost lamb, unsure how she has strayed away from the pack.

"Choose a bed." I point out the several empty beds that previous girls left behind when a brother or a male cousin claimed them.

"I'll not be stopping," she says, clutching a small case I didn't notice before now against her chest.

I swallow the pain of a past I thought I had long buried as I fetch clean bedsheets and clothing from the linen cupboard at the back of the dorm.

"Choose a bed," I repeat as I return, and it scares me that I sound just like Matron.

Delia begins to shake.

"Choose."

"This one." She stands beside Anna's bed, and I balk. This bed has remained empty for five months, but I knew it was only a matter of time before another girl would lay her head there. I had no idea it was to be *this* girl. A child I remember with pigtails in her hair as she played hopscotch with her friends, now all grown up and with a baby growing inside her and no husband.

"How old are you now?" I ask, doing the maths I should know in my head. "Eighteen? Nineteen?"

"I'm twenty."

The answer shocks me, although it shouldn't. The two-year age gap between Linda and Delia seemed huge when we were thirteen and she was eleven, but as we stand face-to-face at twenty-two and twenty, I don't think anyone could say for certain which of us is older.

"You won't be needing this." I take her case and slide it under her bed. Then I pass her a nightgown and smock. "Put these on. You need to be in the laundry before Matron gets there. Trust me, you don't want to make her angry."

"And you? Have I made you angry?"

I want to snap that, yes, seeing her here has made me furious. For more reasons than I can bear. I hate that her life will never be the same now. I hate that she will be shaped and scarred by Ballyvale just as the other girls are. I hate that she was foolish enough to let some boy put a baby in her belly and then fill her head with promises that he won't keep. I hate that seeing her reminds me of Linda, and in turn of Joseph. And most of all, I hate that none of it is her fault and yet I can't help but blame her, simply because she is here.

"Hurry up. Get dressed," I snap as she stands staring at me.

I turn away to give her some privacy, but I still catch a glimpse of a belly that has a long way to grow before her baby is ready to be born. She will be here for many months. I set about dressing the bed where Anna died. I pray with all my might that Delia's future is different.

37

SPRING 1959

Margaret

Delia is a Trojan worker, and it stands her in good stead. Matron got the blisters she desired. When Delia dares to rest, yielding to the weight of her growing belly, Matron clips her around the ear, barking instructions. "Get back to work, you lazy girl. These towels won't dry themselves."

I never intervene. Not when Delia's hands bleed from wringing out wet cloth, or when the color drains from her lips and she looks as if she might faint.

"You can talk to Maggie-pie, you know," I hear Rosie tell her as they pin dripping white nurses' uniforms on the line overhead.

Delia shakes her head.

"No. Really. She's not like the other nuns. She's like a friend. She takes care of us all. She took such good care of me when my little boy was born. She let me hold him for hours. They're the memories I have of him now. She gave them to me."

"I don't think she wants to be my friend. Not anymore," Delia says, pinning the shoulders of a starched doctor's coat on the line. "She's ashamed of me."

Delia's words wound me. But I must keep my distance from her. Matron cannot learn I care about her as deeply as I do.

"Lucy Cunningham," Tee's voice calls out, and I look toward the laundry doors to find her standing with her hand above her eyes like a visor, seeking Lucy among the machines and steam and drying clothes. "Lucy Cunningham, where are you?"

I spy Lucy next to the row of clunky washing machines that rattle and shake as they work just as hard as the girls.

"Psst," I call to her.

She looks my way, and I point toward Tee standing in the doorway.

Panic flashes across Lucy's face. "Am I in trouble?"

"Lucy," a male voice calls out. It is raspy and breaking, a young voice on the cusp of manhood.

"Joe," Lucy calls back, dropping to her knees. "Joe, is that you?"

The other girls dare to lower their busy hands and let them fall by their sides as everyone turns toward the door. Even Matron offers her attention that way.

A skinny young man with dark, wiry hair like a scrubbing brush steps out from behind Tee. He's wearing a brown pin-striped suit that is at least two sizes too big for him, and I suspect it has been fetched from his father's closet.

"You can't go in there," Tee tells him.

"Lucy," he calls again, brushing past her.

Rosie and Delia help Lucy to her feet. I've never seen her smile so brightly. I didn't know she had such straight teeth.

"Joe," she repeats, squinting in the steam as she takes a tentative step forward. "Are you real? Have you really come for me?"

"I was eighteen yesterday," he says with a wobbly voice crack. "Ma says I can bring you home now."

Lucy runs. She flies past Matron and the other girls. She whips between the hanging clothes, pushing them out of her way as she hurries. She doesn't slow even as she gets closer to him. Her body collides with his and he teeters but stays on his feet as she wraps her arms around his neck.

"Look at you," she says. "You're taller than me now. And all grown up."

"What is this place?" There is much disgust in his voice as he looks around the laundry that has been Lucy's home and prison for almost a year.

"Don't you worry yourself about that. My little brother is all grown up and we're going home." She untangles herself from him and steps back so she can take in his face. "I've missed you. I've missed you so much."

"Right, that's enough," Matron says, with a firm clap of her hands. "Back to work, girls."

I catch Delia roll her eyes as she gets back to work, and I hope for her sake she doesn't make a habit of it. Matron would hit the roof if she spotted her.

"Well, go on. Get!" Matron says, poking Lucy in the back.

Lucy's voice cracks. "I need to say goodbye."

My heart sinks as her eyes seek out mine. I know she won't miss the abbey, but she will miss the other girls. When she goes home, no one there will understand. Her family and friends will be looking for the Lucy they know to return. But that girl is long gone. This place has taken her.

"You may leave now," Matron tells Joe.

Bridie attempts to walk toward Lucy, but Matron steps in her path, her hands on her hips as she stares a much-too-thin Bridie down.

"Please, Matron. I just want to say goodbye."

"Back to work."

Lucy bends forward, shouting, "I'll write to you." Her lip quivers. "I will. I promise. I'll write every day if you want me to. And soon you'll be going home, too, and we'll go dancing and to the pictures, like we talked about."

Matron places a firm hand on Joe's shoulder. "Take this girl home. Or so help me—"

"Come on, Luce. Let's go." Joe links his sister's arm and guides her like a lost puppy toward the door.

I follow them into the hall.

"You really will write to her, won't you?" I ask. "Her family never wrote back," I whisper, feeling guilty that I ever suggested that she write to them in the first place. I know how soul-destroying it is to wait for a reply that never comes. Lucy turns at my voice. Her bright smile fills me with joy. I will miss her, of that I have no doubt, but I am so grateful that her little brother grew up and came for her. I wish the same for all the girls. Especially Bridie.

"I will come visit," Lucy promises.

I sigh. "You know you can't do that."

"But I can try."

"The gates are locked. No one will let you in. Once you leave, you cannot ever come back."

Lucy nods. She drags a shaky arm under her nose and sniffles.

"Try to forget this place. Now, come on. Let's get you dressed. You have a big, beautiful life waiting for you."

Lucy and Joe follow me like two sheep to the dormitory. I can see Joe fill with discomfort and questions, but he remains button-lipped. Ballyvale scares him, as it does any girl when she first arrives. But Joe is lucky. He doesn't have to stay.

I fetch Lucy's case from under her bed and blow away the dust that has gathered on the top over time. Lucy takes out a bronze pleated skirt and matching jumper and boots.

"I almost forgot what this looked like," she says.

Joe turns away as I help Lucy into the outfit that I know she must have worn the day she arrived.

"There," I say, when she's dressed.

Everything is much too big. The jumper tries to swallow her, but I roll it at the waist and hope it stays. I take a safety pin from my pocket and do my best to clip the waistband of her skirt to stop it from slipping down over her tiny hips.

"You get plenty of your ma's Sunday roasts into you, now," I tell her, horrified to see that she is half the girl she was when she arrived.

She hugs me, and I hold her tight in return.

"Thank you, Maggie-pie," she says, teary. "Thank you for everything."

"I wish I could have done more."

"You did your best. This place is horrible. But you make it better. Take care of Bridie and Rosie and all the other girls like you did me. And don't forget Anna. I never will."

I swallow hard. "Never. I promise."

As I watch her and Joe walk through the doors and back to a life she should never have had to leave, I smile wider than I have in a long time.

38

SUMMER 1959

Margaret

Summer is my favorite time at the abbey. The bright leaves crowding the branches of tall trees remind me of a watercolor painting that hung in my parents' hall. I wonder where it is now. I hope one of my brothers has it hanging in his room, wherever that may be these days. Summer mornings feel kinder; the girls can enjoy the fresh air without picking up a chill, and even working their fingers to the bone doesn't feel so bad when their hands aren't freezing too. Today they are weeding the garden when a shiny white van I've never seen before arrives at the gates. Delia is first to notice. Then Rosie and Bridie and the rest.

"What do you suppose that's about?" Delia says as she pulls up a thistle. "Dammit." She drops the spiky weed and shoves her pricked finger into her mouth.

"Maybe it's a delivery of fresh bread," Bridie says, hungry as always. "Wouldn't that be wonderful."

There is a collective agreement among the girls that fresh food would be glorious.

I make my way to the back of the garden and pick an apple from Anna's tree, which is doing its best to yield some fruit. Mr. Dolan says it'll be another year or two before it really takes off. It saddens me that the girls might have to wait so long for fresh fruit. I pop the single small red-and-green apple into my pocket. I will pass it to Bridie later when she is alone. I'm worried about her weight, as she seems to be fading away right before my eyes.

The gate creaks open and the van tires rumble over the stones. It comes to a stop beside the girls, and I'm startled to discover that Mr. Dolan is the driver. He opens the door and climbs out. I hoist up my robes and run toward him, almost taking a tumble on the soft grass.

The girls are filled with questions for him, and it's noisy. I'm worried they will draw Matron's attention and will be herded back inside like cattle when they so desperately need the sun on their pale skin.

"Hello," I say, reaching him at last.

"Hello." He shoves his hands in his pockets and pulls out some jelly sweets. The girls squeal like tiny birds in a nest with their beaks open. He passes them one each.

"Come on, girls, back to work," I say, encouraging them to stay focused.

They quieten and return to gardening, but there is excitement as the taste of sugar sits on their tongues.

"You'll get them in trouble," I warn Mr. Dolan. "If Matron finds out—"

"We best make sure she doesn't then, eh?"

"Hmm."

"You still don't like me all that much," he says.

"That's not true."

"Ah. Maybe not entirely true. But you haven't forgiven me, have you?"

"What for?" I ask. "For bringing me back to the convent that day, or for tricking me into coming here?"

"Ah," he says, and I could swear his feelings are hurt. "I'm not all bad."

I know. I see his kindness to the girls. The gap he created in the hedge for me and Joyce. His fondness for Mother Superior. The way he looks at Father Michaels with narrowed eyes the minute the priest's back is turned. The way the sight of Matron makes him look as if he wants to hurl.

"I'm not a man for confession, Maggie-pie," he tells me, in a tone that ironically feels much like confessing. "I haven't been since I was a young boy, in fact. But if you ever feel like listening, I have a few things I'd like to get off my chest."

I inhale slowly, hold my breath for some time, and let it back out even slower. The years have whittled my impetuous nature and offered me patience in return. There was a time I would have run a mile from this conversation and this man, but today my bones ache and my legs are tired. I don't quite have the energy to walk away.

He lowers his head and, in a voice that has grown huskier with age, says, "I was sent to fetch you."

"I am aware, Mr. Dolan, I was there," I snap. Clearly, I have not developed as much patience as I thought.

He casts his eyes onto the nearby grass verge.

"Sit if you want to," I say.

He lowers himself slowly, and I can tell that his fall from a ladder last month while cleaning the gutters is taking longer to heal than it should. He reaches for my hand and I balk. His skin is calloused and hardened from years with a shovel or an axe in his hand.

"She only wanted to protect you, you know."

"Mother Superior," I say, assuming that's the "she" he is referring to.

He nods. "If Father Michaels found you before I did, he'd have beaten you senseless. And dragged you back to the convent anyway. Your parents none the wiser."

I shiver, as a sudden breeze whips by. Mr. Dolan speaks the truth. I wouldn't have believed him back then. Regrettably, I have no doubt now.

"Mother Superior told me to put the fear of God in you. Enough to keep you here and to keep you safe."

"Well, you succeeded. I'm still here, aren't I?" I say, and then I lower my voice to whisper, "And I am still scared. Most days."

"Aren't we all." He sighs.

I look into his round eyes. I see the same weary glisten in my own every time I look in the mirror. It's in the eyes of all the girls, and Tee too.

"You *are* a good man in many ways," I tell him at last.

His expression softens, and I wonder if he has waited patiently all these years to hear me say it.

"I have a van now," he tells me abruptly.

"Yes." I shift my gaze to the white van. "Is Vixen all right?" I am suddenly filled with a fear that the beautiful tan horse I have grown fond of over the years is ill or worse.

"Ah, Vixen is grand. Getting old like the rest of us. But not a bother on him, really."

"Then why do you have this?" I point at the van as if it offends me.

"Father Michaels's idea."

"Oh."

"He's sick of forking out for the hire of trucks. He thinks this will save him a fortune."

I snort. "No surprise there. It's always about money with that man."

"He says we can collect and deliver laundry every day now."

I jam my hands on my hips. "Are you mad? The girls are already exhausted and now that awful, awful priest wants to work them twice as hard? He won't be happy until every last one of them is in the ground."

The girls overhear me and their attention turns my way.

"It's all right," I tell them, trying to sound cheery. "Don't mind me. Keep up the good work."

"It's not my idea," Mr. Dolan reiterates.

"But you drove it here."

"What choice did I have? Father Michaels bought it in Dublin yesterday—"

"Do you always do everything that man says?"

Mr. Dolan sighs. "I'm afraid I do. Yes. The money he pays puts food on my family's table."

I know I'm being unfair. Mr. Dolan couldn't have argued with the priest. He'd lose his job, and then who knows who Father Michaels would send?

"It's too much." My voice breaks.

"I thought maybe now that I have a vehicle I could fetch a few bits in town for the girls." He sways awkwardly on the spot.

"Oh."

"A hot-water bottle or two. Some toothbrushes, maybe? It'll be easy for me to shop a few towns over now that I have an engine. No one in Thurles will know a thing. . . ." He shakes his head as he picks a blade of grass. "It's the best I can offer without losing my job."

"That is so kind of you. But neither the girls nor I have any money, so—"

"I have a little extra. Not much. But enough for the odd thing. If you and the girls can keep the secret—"

I don't answer the rhetorical question. We already share a secret in my interactions with Joyce. Although I won't tell her about this. Talking with Joyce is like baking a cake—you must stir the flour in slowly so it will rise. If you add all the flour at once, the cake will sink.

Mr. Dolan offers me his hand, but before I shake it, I have a secret request of my own.

"How well do you know Doctor Henry?" I ask.

His forehead furrows at the change of direction. "As well as anyone in town, I suppose. I haven't need of him much, I'm healthy for my age. But we've had many a chat in passing over the years. Why?"

"Does he know what goes on here?"

"On some level, everyone knows."

I didn't. But before I beat myself up, as I have done many times over the years, I allow myself to forgive the naïveté of any child.

"I need to do better by the girls. When they're in labor, I mean. I need antibiotics. And gloves. Needles, surgical thread, and disinfectant. The very basics—"

"Needles and thread," he cuts in, his mouth agape.

Mr. Dolan may have opened my eyes to this place, but I'm the one educating him now.

"Birth is a turbulent business. And we're not a fraction as prepared as the girls need us to be."

"Say no more. I'll get what you need."

"And most importantly," I say, my voice commanding, like that of a stern schoolteacher, "I need books. Medical journals—with diagrams and such." Maybe I could have saved Anna if I'd had the right information.

Without another word, Mr. Dolan glances toward the apple tree—leafy and green and thriving. When he looks back, I offer him my hand, and it takes him a moment to realize I'm suggesting he shake it.

"Do we have a deal?"

His grip is warm and firm. "We'll make good of this van, eh?"

39

Margaret

The van is both a blessing and a curse. The increased workload pushes the girls to the breaking point, and Matron cracks her metaphorical whip harder than ever. But the girls have clean teeth, brushed hair, and packets of biscuits hidden under their pillows. Best of all are the medical journals that are tucked away in a drawer in my room. I study them night after night until I can see the labeled diagrams with my eyes closed.

Mr. Dolan is as good as his word, and after long, sometimes endless days on the laundry floor, the girls sit up in bed and pass three wobbly and warm hot-water bottles around between them.

"My toes are so toasty," Delia says, with bare feet placed on top of a dark green hot-water bottle that Mr. Dolan snuck in this morning when he picked up a record-breaking load of snowy tablecloths and napkins for some fancy hotel in Cork.

"All of me is toasty." Rosie giggles, curled like a vine around a maroon bottle.

"Quick, quick, Matron is coming," Bridie whisper-shouts from her position standing guard at the dormitory door.

The girls hide the hot-water bottles under their pillows and pretend to be asleep. Bridie makes a dash for her bed and makes it just as the clip-clop of Matron's shoes reaches the door.

"A word," Matron says, eyeballing me.

I place my finger against my lips as if I am asking her not to wake the girls. She huffs and raises her voice to repeat herself.

I step into the corridor and close the door behind me. I begin to walk, attempting to guide her away from the dormitory, but she folds her arms, tilts her head, and does not follow. When I turn back, I find irritation scribbled into the lines around her eyes.

"What is it, Matron?" I sigh.

"There hasn't been a new baby born in almost five weeks."

"Yes. It has been quiet," I say.

"Father Michaels is not best pleased. We have several couples waiting. They're prepared to donate generously. If we keep them waiting much longer, they may go to another home. I hear the Sisters of the Savior have thirty-four girls heavily pregnant in Cork. Thirty-four."

"None of the girls are ready yet, Sister," I say softly. "Some aren't even halfway."

"I saw some today with enormous bellies. Either their babies are ready or we're feeding them too well."

"There are two girls who are close, but they have at least another couple of weeks to wait. There's no rushing babies; they come when they are ready."

She stands straighter, unimpressed. "Who are they? What are their names?"

I'm afraid to shine a spotlight on any girl. But I know for the girls' sake it would be even worse to deny Matron their names.

"Delia O'Rourke and Catherine Murphy." I sigh.

"Catherine Murphy." Her eyes narrow as she tries to remember a face.

"She's new, Matron. Only here a week."

"Ah yes, the foolish girl. She thought she could hide her pregnancy," she says, rolling her eyes. "It's a blessing that her father found out. What a good man."

I swallow. I haven't had a chance to get to know Catherine well yet, but I've held her a couple of nights as she cried herself to sleep. Matron and I have very different ideas of what makes a good man.

She clicks her fingers. "Bring them here."

"They're sleeping."

"Then wake them."

"But—"

Matron exhales, and her sour tea-and-apple-tart breath hits me.

"I want them outside in five minutes."

I don't need to pull my pocket watch out to know it's close to midnight. The sun has long set and I hear the drumming of heavy rain against the roof and windows.

"Delia and Catherine have been working since eight this morning," I say matter-of-factly. "They need to sleep."

She glares.

"They need rest to keep their babies healthy," I add.

"And we need a baby." She juts her jaw forward, and instinctively I pull back from her clammy breath. "I want them up and dressed in five minutes. Laps of the grounds should get labor started for at least one of them."

"Running?" I recoil. "They can't. If labor *does* start, they won't have the energy to push a baby out."

Matron raises her voice, as if I am struggling to comprehend her. "Either *you* take them outside or I will."

"All right," I concede. My chest tightens at the thought of Matron outside with the girls. "I'll get them up."

She walks away without another word, and I note how much weight she has put on recently.

Back in the dormitory, Delia and Catherine are up and standing beside their beds. "We're ready," they say, having heard every word.

I try not to stare at the violet bags under their eyes.

"It's raining," I warn them, pointing toward the folded shawls at the ends of their beds, which I knitted recently from Joyce's wool. "Boots, too. No bare feet outside, eh? And hurry if you can. We don't want her to come back if we can help it."

Unfortunately, I didn't consider the cold, and wind bites my cheeks. I fold my arms across my chest as I hop from one foot to the other, trying to keep warm.

"A lap or two should do it," I tell them, hating the words as they come out of my mouth. I point to the old abbey, which stands proud against a cloudy night sky. To my surprise, Delia and Catherine take off with a burst of energy. They lap the grand building in record time. Their cheeks are flushed and the tips of their noses are red, but they are smiling and giggling.

"Another?" Delia suggests, pushing wet hair off her face.

I nod.

"Come with us?" Catherine reaches her hand out for me.

"Oh, I couldn't."

"It's fun," Delia says. "Just like when we were kids."

"And it'll keep you warm," Catherine adds.

I glance around the sleeping gardens. The moon casts shadows across the grass as trees blow in the wind. At this time, the abbey is silent and unassuming—a place of beauty. At this time, you would never guess the secrets it has to tell.

"Come on. No one will see us." Delia winks, and I am reminded of her rebellious streak, which saw her get a slap of the wooden spoon plenty from her ma when she was just a little girl.

I suck in a breath and take Catherine's hand.

"One . . . two . . . three," I count, and we charge.

We run and run. Our legs don't hurt and the girls' backs don't ache. We laugh and pick up pace as rain dances on our heads. For a moment I am not a nun and they are not fallen girls. We are simply three young women, carefree and laughing. I am not Maggie-pie or Sister Margaret. I am Margaret Lannigan and it is wonderful.

Our fun comes to an abrupt halt when Matron's voice cuts through the calm night air. "What are you doing?"

Thankfully, I know the question is for me and not the girls. I free my hands from theirs and drop them by my sides. The girls step back, as if standing in my shadow can keep them safe.

"The girls are running."

"I heard laughing."

"Oh . . . that was me," I say quickly. "I'm sorry. Did I wake you?"

Matron's expression is as stony as the abbey behind her. She folds her arms and marches down the steps toward us. She's almost at the bottom step when her legs fly clean out from under her and she lands sprawled on her back like a fat black beetle.

"Is she dead?" Catherine asks.

"We're not that lucky," Delia replies.

"Matron," I call out, hurrying to her.

I crouch over her and check that she is breathing.

"Well, is she?" Delia asks, arriving behind me.

"She's alive," I say.

Delia lets out a disappointed sigh.

"Help me get her up." I bend and make attempts to raise her. "We need to get her inside."

The girls are reluctant, and although I can't blame them, I still find myself sternly saying, "Help me."

They bend as best they can, and between the three of us we drag her unconscious body up the steps. I don't say a word when Delia lets

Matron's head knock on the top step, and I pretend I don't notice Catherine's satisfied smirk.

"We need to get her into her chambers. She's wet and cold."

"Outside was her idea," Delia reminds me.

"I'll make sure she knows you two were very helpful getting her back inside. I'm sure she'll be grateful."

Delia's face scrunches. "No, she won't."

"She would get pneumonia if we left her out there, and I know neither of you wants that on your conscience. I know I don't."

"I could live with that." Delia snorts.

"I doubt Father Michaels would let you," I say, as I open the door of her chambers. "Now, help me get her into her chair."

Catherine pulls the chair out from under the table and although it's awkward and Matron is painfully heavy, we manage to flop her limp body into the leather armchair.

"Fetch some blankets," I suggest, pointing toward the large oak dresser against the wall.

Delia opens doors and drawers and rummages until she finds some knitted blankets. She pulls out a gray and red patched one and shakes it out. Envelopes scatter to the floor like confetti.

"What's this?" I say, though I know the girls are as stunned as me.

I leave Matron and hurry to the pile of envelopes littering the floor. I pick one up and read the front aloud.

"Mr. Shaw. Willow Lawns House. Cashel. County Tipperary." The envelope trembles in my hand. "Mr. Shaw. Bridie Shaw. This is a letter to Bridie's pa."

"Why is it here?" Catherine asks.

I pick up another. "Mr. and Mrs. Martin. Rosie's parents." I pick up several more and read the addresses aloud. "Mr. and Mrs. Dunne. And Burke and Lynch." I shake my head and I can hardly push the words out as I look at Delia and say, "Mr. and Mrs. O'Rourke. Oh, Delia. It's the letter to your parents. She didn't post it."

Delia's eyes burn. "Are you still so glad we brought her back inside?"

I glance at Matron slouched unconscious in the chair, and I wonder, had Delia or Catherine slipped in the garden, if she would have left them there. The answer chills me.

"I told you Joseph never got any letters from you. Now you know why. She . . ." Delia points a shaking finger at Matron, and her face is puce and full of the same hatred that festers inside me for that woman. "She never posted them."

"I wrote to Joseph while I was at the convent," I correct her. "I didn't know Matron then."

"Sounds like whoever was in charge of the post over there wasn't posting them either," Delia huffs.

I contemplate taking offense. Delia doesn't know Mother Superior. If she did, she'd never make such an accusation. Mother took exceptional care of the post, and she delighted in passing letters from loved ones to the sisters. Joyce's ma wrote to her every week. I was the only one who never received a letter. Never from Joseph. And not even from my brothers. A spark ignites and I feel fire inside. *Father Michaels.*

Delia steps back from me as if I might explode. "What is it? What's wrong?"

"Runaways don't write letters," I hiss.

Her shoulders round and sadness creeps into her eyes.

"Postman Padar plays the organ at Mass," I say, dots joining in my head. "A whisper in his ear from Father Michaels and my letters were tossed into a ditch somewhere between here and Thurles. Father Michaels knew Joseph would come for me. He knew how much he loved me. That's why he told everyone I ran away. He knew Joseph wouldn't waste a second."

I am so full of rage and so full of relief that they seem to cancel each other out until I fold in on myself and crumple like paper to the ground. Delia crouches beside me, wrapping her arms around me.

"Joseph loved you," she whispers.

Loved. I know she doesn't mean for it to, but Delia's choice of tense pierces my heart. He loves Linda now, and although I know he never betrayed me, it still hurts as if he did.

"They are good people," Delia tells me, as if I need reminding after all this time. "They didn't want me to come here, you know. Neither of them. They said they'd give me and the baby a home. Linda said she'd pretend it was hers. She'd walk around with a cushion under her dress for nine months if she had to. And Joseph said it was a good idea. But my pa wouldn't hear of it. He was ranting and raving about the deceit of it all. He said if Linda fell pregnant for real, the O'Rourkes would be the laughingstock of the town. Like I care what anyone in Thurles thinks about anything."

It's a while before I can stand, and when I do, Catherine already has the letters gathered and placed in the makeshift bag she has created with the blanket.

"Is it too late to post them now?" she asks with an uncertain shrug. "Most of these girls have probably gone home. But maybe it would be a good thing if their parents finally found out how hard things were for them while they were here."

Delia sighs. "Padar is the only postman. And if Father Michaels—"

"Father damn Michaels," I bark, and Catherine almost drops the blanket. "To hell with him. We will find a way. We will see that every last one of these letters makes it home."

It breaks my heart that I will have to tell the girls that their letters never made it out the gate. I wish them all a Joseph of their own, who could come for them if only he knew where to look. "Come, girls," I add, gathering myself. "There must be some apple tart in here somewhere. Let's have a feast before we get to bed."

"What about her?" Catherine flicks her gaze to Matron.

I march over to the sleeping nun and push her off the chair.

Delia and Catherine gasp when she lands in a heap.

"There," I say, satisfied. "That's better."

40

Margaret

The follow morning, the nuns' breakfast finds Matron with a limp and complaining of a headache. It's difficult not to sneer. Especially when I ask if I can help and wish her well.

"What happened?" she asks, holding her head as if it might fall off if she lets go.

"You slipped. On the ice. Remember?"

"What were you doing outside at that hour?" Tee asks.

Matron lowers herself slowly to sit at the round table, pain etched into her face as she pushes the bowl of porridge in front of her away. She tells the story of the girls running laps.

Tee glances at me, horrified.

"I can't remember much after that. I woke up on the floor in my chambers. . . ." Matron trails off.

"On the floor?" Tee echoes with her eyebrows raised as she looks at me.

"Did it work?" Matron asks. "Were there any babies born last night?"

Tee shakes her head. "No babies."

Matron slams her hand on the table and her bowl of porridge jumps. "Well, more laps tonight it is. I want a baby. And one of those girls is going to give me one if I have to run the legs clean off her."

The heat of Tee's rage warms me like a furnace. I reach under the table and take her hand. When my eyes meet hers, I hope she can tell that everything will be all right. I will be there for the girls, and we will enjoy playacting in the garden every night until their babies come. Maybe Tee might join us. I'd like that.

Breakfast is followed by prayers and supervising the girls' chores. Tee escorts them to the laundry and I slip into the garden for a few stolen moments with Joyce.

"Good morning, Anna," I whisper as I graze past the branches of the apple tree to navigate the thinnest part of the hedge. The leaves rustle in the wind and my heart soars, as it always does when I feel Anna nearby.

"Morning," a voice calls back, and I'm delighted to find Joyce waiting.

"Sorry I'm late," I puff out.

"It's okay." Joyce gestures with open palms toward me, and I'm quietly disappointed to see she hasn't brought bread or milk for a third morning in a row. I squash the feeling, knowing Mother Superior's health is on her mind. I'm confident I know just how to lift her spirits.

"You're not going to believe what happened now," I whisper, and we both edge closer until there is just some twiggy bark and a few stray leaves between us. The words tumble out of me like cascading raindrops. She nods and listens to my tale of last night, but when I confess to pushing Matron off the chair, she steps back as if I've splashed her.

"Oh, Sister Margaret. How could you?"

I scoff. "Believe me, I wanted to give her more than a shove."

She takes another step back. There is distance between us now, and if we want to continue talking, we will have to raise our voices above a comfortable whisper.

"You can't hurt people," she says.

"They do it all the time. They hurt the girls. Every. Single. Day."

"You can't hurt nuns." The clarification reeks of superiority.

"She didn't post their letters," I say, with rage bubbling up inside me.

"What will Father Michaels say?" Joyce says, wrapping her arms around herself.

"How will he find out? Only Delia, Catherine, and I know. I didn't even tell Tee."

Joyce doesn't say a word, but her knitted brow sets my teeth on edge.

"Joyce?" I edge closer—thorns pricking me.

Nothing.

"Joyce!"

It pains me to ask my next question for fear of the answer. But still I say, "Do you talk to Father Michaels? Outside of confession, I mean. Have you become friends?"

Joyce stands firm and her silence tells me everything. *Oh God.*

"Does he know we talk out here?" I inhale.

She is frozen. It is as if Father Michaels's shadow is behind her with his hand clamped over her mouth. I should be scared. I should worry that my dearest confidante has rehashed our conversations with *him*. But I am not. Ballyvale is already ugly and at its worst. I should be hurt, deeply wounded that Joyce has betrayed me. But I am not. Father Michaels is a magician and his promises of a blessed afterlife are his spells, so effortlessly cast on those eager to listen. My pa. John-Joe Lynch. Postman Padar. And now my dear, dear friend. *Oh, Joyce.*

Joyce begins talking at last, and hearing her feels as if I am pulling myself up from underwater.

"If I'm going to be head of the convent after Mother Superior—"

"Is she worse?" My heart begins to beat again.

Joyce swallows a lump, and I finally see her become emotional. "It's her cough. Father Michaels doesn't think she'll see this winter out."

Air escapes me like popping a balloon. "Maybe I could visit?"

Joyce's eyes glisten. "You know we're a closed order. I'm sorry."

"But if she passes?"

"I could give her a message from you."

"Please, Joyce. I miss her."

"Oh, Margaret. Can't you ever accept there is a certain way of doing things here?"

"Do you remember when Amy March was your favorite character in *Little Women*?" I ask, swallowing the lump wedged in my throat.

Joyce pats around the side of her eyes with the sleeve of her robe and she nods. I know she's remembering our wonderful friendship over the years. I drag my sleeve under my nose, remembering too.

"You're just like her, you know. Amy March," I say.

Joyce tilts her head. "How so?"

"Starting out one way, then growing up and becoming another. Amy March started out shy and playful and grew into someone determined to get what she wants."

"Thank you," Joyce says, misinterpreting me.

I roll my shoulders and stand tall. "Amy is my least favorite character."

Joyce calls my name several times as I walk away. It breaks my heart not to turn around. I am in search of Mr. Dolan. I need to ask him to let the hedge grow back.

41

Margaret

If I had to guess, I would say that Jo March is most people's favorite *Little Women* character. Strong, feisty, and prepared to fight for what she wants, I used to think I was a Jo. In fact, I molded myself in her image. But I see now I'm Marmee, Jo and Amy's mother. I am a mother. Not to children of my own, of course. But in a home full of young girls about to become mothers themselves, my place is to put their needs above my own. I am here for them when their own mothers are not. I am here to love them when they feel that no one else does. I am here to make sure this place doesn't change them as it has changed Joyce. And as much as I don't want to admit it, it has changed me. I am stronger than I ever thought I could be. And I must use that strength to make sure that the girls have a lifeline, a way out of here. It starts with their letters.

My first attempt is conversation with Postman Padar. I watch like a hawk from an upstairs window as Matron and the elderly postman chat in the driveway. He stands with one foot to each side of his bicycle. A large, worn leather satchel, draped over his shoulder, dangles by his side. She passes him several letters—from whom, I'm not sure, but I know there's not a single letter in the mix from any of the girls. He laughs at something Matron says and places them into his bag. Next, she produces something wrapped in a checkered tea towel—a baked tart of some sort. She places it carefully in the wicker basket attached to his handlebars. Finally, they finish up their chatter and she comes back inside, and Padar turns his bicycle, to cycle away.

I race down the stairs, out the back door, across the lawn, and over to the back wall as fast as my legs can carry me. I'm leaning over the wall with my head stuck in the bushes when he rounds the corner and cycles down the narrow road that runs parallel to the back of the convent.

"Psst," I call out as he draws near. "Psst. Postman Padar. Over here."

His handlebars twist and he almost loses his balance. He steadies himself just in time.

"Who is it? Who's there?"

"It's Sister Margaret," I whisper, spitting out leaves that catch in my mouth. "Can you stop for a moment, please?"

Padar hops off his bicycle and peers through the bushes, trying to find me.

"Are you on your way to town?" I ask a question that needs no answer. "Can you post a letter for me, please?" I tap my pocket, where I keep a single letter to my aunt in Mayo. I addressed the letter using her maiden name, in case the sight of *Lannigan* on paper rings a bell for the postman.

I thought it best to test the approach with a letter of my own first—that way if I fail and Matron finds out, it will be my head on the chopping block and not one of the girls'.

"I have the letters, Sister," he says, confused. "Matron passed them to me, just moments ago."

"Oh, eh, she forgot one."

"Oh. Not to worry. Pass it here now."

I sigh, surprised by how easy it is to shove my arm through the hedge and hand him the small envelope. He opens his satchel and places my letter next to the others.

"There now. All sorted out."

"Well, erm," I say, my heart racing as I choose my next words carefully. "Do you think I could give you some more letters next week?"

"More?"

"Yes. Letters from me."

His head tilts toward his bicycle as if he's getting ready to cycle away. "Letters from you and not from Matron."

I gulp. "Yes."

He tuts and opens the satchel once more. He rummages for a moment before he pulls out my envelope and reads the address. "Mayo. Oh, I see." He stretches his arm out toward me. He wants to give me my letter back. "I think it's best you hold on to this."

"Please," I try one last time. "Please, won't you help?"

He flexes his arm as straight as he can, and, reluctantly, I take my letter back.

"I won't tell nobody about this," he says. "But that's about the best I can do."

"Thank you," I say, defeated.

"Bye now, Sister."

"Goodbye."

I remain by the wall for some time. I watch as the odd horse and cart, car, or fella on a bicycle passes by. Finally, a small group of children skip my way.

"Hello there," I call out.

"Hi," they chirp back, obviously excited by the voice in the bushes.

"Can you help me?"

"Depends," one of the tallest among the boys says. "Whatcha want?"

"Can you post a letter for me?"

I reach my arm through the bush and wave the letter his way. He points back.

"There's no stamp."

"Oh."

My heart sinks. Of course a letter needs a stamp. My face reddens as I feel foolish.

"Could you get a stamp for me?"

"Sure. You got money?"

The young boy's question is wholly reasonable, and I find myself embarrassed when I must say, "No. I'm sorry. But if you could help—"

"Sorry. We've only got tuppence between us and that's for sweets."

"What if I made you a cake? Do you like apple tart?"

His face scrunches. "My ma makes apple tart every Sunday. I'm sick of the sight of it."

I search my brain for something else I can offer these boys. But all my possessions amount to rosary beads, a battered copy of *Little Women*, and some hymn sheets, none of which will interest young boys.

"We gotta go," a smaller boy says. "The shop closes for lunch and it's still a long ways yet."

I hear them laughing and giggling as they walk away talking about me.

"Imagine trying to post a letter without a stamp. Silly nun."

"Shh. You can't say that about nuns. God will hear you and smite you."

"Will not."

"Will too."

They turn the corner and are out of sight. Once again I am alone with a letter in my hand. I shove it into my pocket and make my way across the gardens to face another day supervising in the laundry. It will be busy today, with a whole van to fill this evening when Mr. Dolan comes.

42

Margaret

The girls are reeling with the workload. There are three accidents before noon. Rosie is racing with a basket of wet towels on her hip when she trips over her own feet. She reaches out to steady herself and knocks a basin of boiling water off the worktop. Her scream is sharp and shrill, but she closes her mouth before the panic distracts Matron.

Tee is first to reach her.

"There now. There now," she whispers, lifting Rosie's nightie and smock to reveal a fiery red thigh.

I dunk a small towel in cool water and hurry over. Rosie flinches as I press it against her scalded skin. The other girls notice the commotion, but they continue to work, taking care not to pique Matron's interest.

Tee waits until Rosie stops shaking before she says, "You'll be all right, love. Your smock caught the most of it. But best to get yourself off to bed. Rest this leg for today."

"What's wrong with her?" Matron shouts, unfortunately observing us from across the laundry.

"A burn," Tee calls back. "Nasty enough. I think a lie-down—"

"Clumsy oaf." Matron checks her watch. "Back to work. We're already behind."

Rosie nods, and I watch as she lifts her basket and limps toward the washing line.

"She can scarcely walk, Matron," I say. I feel Tee's elbow in my ribs, but I can't hold my tongue. "The floor is wet. It was an accident."

"Then who didn't mop it?" Matron says.

"It's the clothes drip-drying," I explain, pointing overhead. "They're dripping onto the floor."

"I can see that. What I asked is who didn't mop."

Catherine tries to step out of view. Matron grabs her hair and shouts in her ear to fetch a mop.

I notice the panic in Catherine's eyes.

"Mops are in the cupboard near the washing machines. Down the back," I direct quietly, and she nods gratefully as she hurries away to find one.

Matron watches her for a moment before she turns toward me and asks in a sickly sweet tone, "When did she join us?"

"Erm, last week. She's one of the girls who helped you in the garden when you had that fall, remember?"

"A week and she's not picked up a mop. Well, well."

Matron walks after Catherine. I'm about to call out when I feel Rosie's hand on my back. Her eyes say what words don't. *Shh. Please. You'll make her even madder.*

I stop in my tracks and smile at Rosie, who seems to grow an extra inch every time I look at her. She's head and shoulders taller than most of the other girls now, but she always stands hunched over. I hate how the months at Ballyvale have reshaped her. The abbey has carved out her youth and vibrancy and left her a skittish, submissive shell.

Delia is next to succumb to the pressure and pace, and she catches her finger under the roller of the huge metal linen press. She yelps and sucks it and insists she is fine. But she struggles with loading the clothes onto the machines after that, and I am worried that she might have broken it. I will check later when Matron's eyes are no longer on us.

One of the other girls trips over a full bag of laundry, and Matron thumps her hard on the shoulder for being so foolish. Then she seeks out the girl who filled the bag and gives her a thumping too. The day is long and hot. Steam swirls, and the girls sweat. I bring them bread and water.

"Can't have them passing out if we want a full van," I tell Matron when she glares at the girls pausing for a moment to stuff dry bread into their hungry mouths.

Thankfully, she understands that the girls need food. And she allows them regular toilet breaks, after one of the girls wet the floor last week.

"Five minutes and counting," she says, when any girl leaves the laundry floor for the toilet. I see her check her watch each time.

Despite the injuries, punishments, steam, and heat, the work pace is staggering and the girls pack enough laundry sacks to fill the majority of Mr. Dolan's van. He arrives at 5:50 p.m., as always, and there is a rustle of excitement when the sound of his tires rolling over the driveway stone crunches outside the poky window.

"He's here, Matron," Rosie says.

Matron pulls a key from her pocket and saunters toward the rusty metal door at the back of the laundry near the wall of washing machines. She unlocks the door and the daylight rushes in.

"Evening, all." Mr. Dolan smiles at the girls and tips his cap as usual.

"Mr. Dolan."

"How many stops am I making today?" he asks.

"Three," Matron answers with a firm nod. "Three bags of nurses' uniforms for the hospital in Nenagh. Four bags of tablecloths and bedsheets for that new hotel just outside Limerick. The Mount Clare. I hear the apple tart is very good."

"Not as good as here," he says, buttering her up, and when she smiles, I shudder.

"Finally, there's a bag of habits for the novice sisters arriving next door tomorrow. Six of them, I hear. How nice."

Mr. Dolan's eyes peer over Matron's shoulder, but as soon as they meet mine, I shift my gaze to the floor. When I first pulled on my white novice robe, it had most likely been laundered here too. A shiver runs down my spine.

Matron checks her watch once more and says, "Six p.m. Time for the Angelus. I trust I can leave you to ensure all is well here, Mr. Dolan?"

"Of course, Matron."

She passes the key to Mr. Dolan and says, "Lock up when the van is loaded, won't you? Return the key to me afterward." She glances at me and huffs. "Only me. You hear?"

"I hear," he says.

The girls grab a sack each and waddle toward the small door at the back of the laundry. They toss the bags one by one into the back of the van, and the suspension rattles and squeaks with each load.

When the van is full and the girls look as if they might crumple with exhaustion, Mr. Dolan reaches into his pocket, pulls out a small brown bag, and offers it to me. "For the girls. The best I could do. Money is tight this week."

I open the bag and glance inside to find plenty of colorful bonbons. Enough for the girls to enjoy a couple each.

"Thank you," I whisper, and I find myself on my tiptoes, kissing his cheek gratefully before I have time to think. His skin is rough, like gritty sand against my lips, and he blushes as he says, "Ah shucks, Maggie-pie. 'Tis just something small."

The girls gather around and create a semicircle, watching as Mr. Dolan counts the bags and closes the back door of the van with a firm bang. They cup their hands and hold them out, and I pass bonbons into each of their palms.

"For you and you and Catherine. And Rosie and— Oh no." I drop a bonbon. I bend to retrieve it, furious that I have deprived the girls of a single sweet, when I feel Mr. Dolan kneel beside me.

"What's this?" He holds up a letter that has slipped out of my pocket and onto the drenched floor.

I blush and quickly scrunch the top of the paper bag, trapping the remaining bonbons inside. The girls close their hands around the measly few sweets I've dispersed and retreat to hiding places around the laundry to share them. They duck behind the washing machines or under large sheets hanging on the washing lines, and the sound of their happiness titters in the air like songbirds.

"That's mine," I say, ready to snatch my letter back, but Mr. Dolan holds it above his head, waving it to shake tiny droplets of water off.

"Millie Connolly," he begins, reading my handwriting on the front of the envelope out loud. "Are you planning on posting it?"

"Excuse me?"

"Well, there's no stamp, so—"

"I am aware there is no stamp, Mr. Dolan. You'll see that is why it's in my pocket and not in a postbox."

"Because you'll be needing a stamp if it's going to Mayo."

"Yes. I realize as much."

"Do you need one?" he says, lowering the envelope, but I surprise myself when I don't take it back.

I stare at the empty corner where a stamp belongs, and with a glimmer of hope, I ask, "Do you have one?"

"No. Not right now. But I can bring one."

My heart soars for a moment before I remember that Postman Padar is under Father Michaels's thumb.

"Next time, when I come for the washing. If you're planning on posting it, that is," Mr. Dolan continues.

I wince and wish he would stop looking at me the way he is. As if he pities me, or wishes he could save me, or at the very least bring me comfort.

"Or . . ." He takes a breath and fidgets with his cap. "I could post it for you, if that would help?"

I look up.

"I could be way out of line here, and I do apologize if I am, but I'm thinking you'd rather the other nuns didn't know about this letter."

I wonder when he learned to read me so well. I get the feeling it was the day we met, when I nearly broke my ankle trying to escape this life.

He recenters his cap and coughs. "I could . . . eh . . . pop it in the letter box in town."

"Could you put it in a letter box somewhere else?" I say, my stomach knotting. "Maybe somewhere in Limerick, when you're delivering the laundry. It would be good if no one local at all knew about this."

He blinks slowly, and I can tell he understands that Postman Padar is unequivocally loyal to Father Michaels and our efforts would be pointless if he came across the letter. Or worse still, he might share my words with the priest.

"What about letters coming back to you?" Mr. Dolan's face falls, and I can feel he's losing faith in this plan. "Will Postman Padar deliver them here?"

My heart sinks. I'd been so focused on getting an envelope to leave the abbey, I hadn't stopped to think about return post. We both know his question was rhetorical, but I answer anyway. "It's hopeless. Father Michaels has it all sewn up. I can't win."

"What about my house?" he whispers, so softly I almost don't hear him above the gentle chatter of the girls enjoying their sweets.

"Your house?"

"It's simple, really," he says, glancing at the name and address on the envelope once more. "Tell this Millie Connolly not to reply to you here. Tell her to send her letter to my address. Then I can bring it to you. No one ever has to know."

"You would do that for me?"

He shrugs. "Sure. It's no skin off my nose."

We both know it will cost him his job if he gets caught. When my lips part to thank him, the words "She's my aunt. My brothers live with her and my uncle" tumble out in a throaty rattle instead.

"Ah." He sighs, and we share a look that expresses my gratitude more than words ever could.

"Grab a pen and write a note to explain," he tells me. "Then I'll pop my address on the back. Hopefully you'll hear from those brothers of yours soon."

I lunge forward and fling my arms around him. He smells of freshly cut grass, and he's warm and a little sticky, but I hug him tighter than I have hugged anyone in a long time.

With a kind smile, Mr. Dolan leaves and locks the door behind him. Soon the van engine sounds. I dare to toss a bonbon into my mouth. The taste of sugary strawberry explodes against my tongue, and for a moment I am lost in thoughts of my childhood. Walking with my sister and brothers after Sunday Mass and buying sweets in the corner shop. I find the girls and share the remaining bonbons among them, and I hope the taste brings them equally happy memories.

43

Margaret

Sure enough, a few days later when Mr. Dolan arrives to collect freshly washed, dried, pressed, and folded laundry, he comes with more than just bonbons. This time, when the chime of the Angelus bells summons Matron's punctual exit from the laundry, he produces a couple of packets of custard cream biscuits and pulls an envelope from his pocket.

"They wrote back?" I gasp, not quite able to believe it worked.

His face is full of color as he offers the slightly bent envelope to me. "It arrived this morning."

I take it, and my eyes blur when I try to focus on the familiar handwriting on the front. Matthew's handwriting. I instantly recognize his practice of writing his *M*'s much taller and rounder than his other letters, even after all these years. I drag the sleeve of my habit under my eyes as I blink away tears and read to myself.

Care of Mr. Austin Dolan
25 The Waterlands
Cashel
Co. Tipperary

When the machines are switched off and the steam clears, I hate the laundry the most. I detest the mold that spreads like scattered raisins in the corners where the walls meet the ceiling. I loathe the mottled green tiles that heavily pregnant young women slip on when they're wet. I despise the lines that hang overhead, vacant and unassuming as they wait patiently to be put to use tomorrow. But mostly, I abhor the silence that comes with a resting laundry. When the girls are working hard and the laundry is loud and busy, there is little time to think about anything besides keeping them and their babies safe and without injury. In the evening, when the work is done, all there is to do is think. Think about the day that has passed, the days that are to come. Think about the girls who have gone home, whom I miss, and the poor unfortunates yet to arrive. I rarely think about my family. I have grown up away from them. Thinking about them growing, too, getting a little older and a little taller, brings me pain. Now, standing in a sleeping laundry with a letter from my middle brother in my hand, I am that innocent girl ripped away from her family all over again.

I scarcely notice Mr. Dolan doling out custard creams to the girls as I seek out a corner of my own to hide in. I slip behind a large wicker basket and an industrial-sized box of detergent. I take care opening the envelope, and it's only when I slide the paper out that I realize I've been holding my breath.

Hello Margaret,

I hear Matthew's voice in my head as my eyes sweep the first line, and I have to lower the paper for a moment to grip my chest, as if I can somehow hold my heart together from the outside. I take some deep breaths and read on.

Thank you for your letter. It comes as quite the surprise for reasons Uncle Seamus says I must not get into for fear of upsetting you, but I cannot stress how much joy I feel to know that you are safe and well.

Did you know that I have been living with Uncle Seamus and Aunty Millie? They have a beautiful home and they made me and Colm and little Finbar feel very welcome. Although Finbar is not so little anymore. He's taller than Uncle Seamus these days. Aunty Millie's roast lamb is delicious. Although not quite as good as I remember Ma's. I like Mayo too.

I attend the local school and I go fishing at the weekend with the other boys. I used to fish with Colm, but he moved away soon after we arrived here. He's a priest in Kerry now, and Aunty Millie loves to tell people in town all about him.

Uncle Seamus says I will leave and join the priesthood, too, once I finish school. But I have to say, I would rather not. I haven't met a nice girl or nothing, but I think I'd like to. I'd like to get married someday and have a regular job. Like a car salesman or a carpenter. I know how terrible it is to wish for this life. I know I am letting people down and setting a bad example for Finbar. For this reason, I haven't told Uncle Seamus or Aunty Millie yet. I know how disappointed Pa would be. But I am not like Colm and you. I do not want to devote my life to God. It will not make me happy. You might wonder why I am confessing this. After receiving your letter I learned some things about Father Michaels that disgust me. But I can't open my mouth around here. Uncle Seamus won't have a bad word said about that man, and tells me his heart was in the right place and it's what Pa would have wanted. But dare I say it, I wonder if that man has a heart at all. And now I fear I have said too much, but I am desperate to talk to someone. I think it is easier to put my thoughts in a letter than to say them to your face. Please do not be too disappointed in me, Maggie. I couldn't bear it.

I love and miss you.

Yours with all my heart,
Matthew x

I lower the letter, and I can't get to my feet fast enough. I stumble and knock the wicker basket. Mr. Dolan catches me just before I hit the ground.

"What is it?" he asks, cupping my elbow until I steady myself. "You look as if you've seen a ghost."

"Can you post another letter for me?" I splutter.

"Yes, of course."

"Thank you. I'll just be a minute. Please don't leave."

He glances over his shoulder at several bags of laundry yet to be loaded onto the back of the van. "I'm not going anywhere."

I race back to my room and fetch a pen and paper. I write so quickly the ink smudges, but I don't stop.

Matthew,

Finish school and get yourself out of Mayo. Go to Dublin, or London would be even better. And from there, tell the world about Father Michaels. Find that nice girl and get yourself married someday. And if you are lucky enough to be blessed with children, please, please be nothing like Pa.

Yours always,
Margaret x

P.S. Please write to me again soon, my little brother. Tell me more about fishing and your school friends.

I don't have an envelope, but I don't let that deter me as I hurry back to the laundry room and give the folded paper to Mr. Dolan. He takes it, smiles, and slides it into his pocket. Neither of us needs to say more. I know he will find an envelope and provide a stamp and he will post it to the same address as last time. I trust he will not read it, nor will he ask questions about it or my haste to reply.

"Thank you," I say as we load the final bag of laundry onto the van and he closes the doors.

"Are we friends at last?" he asks. He doesn't give me time to answer before he goes on. "You'll miss her."

I know he's speaking about Joyce. I wait for him to ask me what happened, but he doesn't.

Instead he says, "Joyce was born to wear a habit. The Catholic Church is in her bones. She will never see the flaws of Ballyvale, because she doesn't want to."

"I *will* miss her," I confess to myself as much as to him.

"She is a good person," he insists. "Loyal to a fault."

"Yes." I sigh. "She is."

I've always known that the differences between Joyce and me are as vast as the ocean, but a tiny part of me hoped someday we would find our way to shore together. I used to think Ballyvale changed people—sink or swim—but now I contemplate whether it simply brings out everything that was in your bones all along.

"Friends?" he asks once more.

Tee has a heart of gold, but her willingness to conform and keep quiet frustrates and upsets me in equal measure. While I am fond of the girls, at the end of the day, there are degrees of separation between us. I will never know what it is like to grow life inside me like they do. I sleep upstairs in a comfortable large bed with soft pillows. They sleep in lumpy beds with flimsy sheets. They are grateful for me, that much I can see in their eyes. But I can also see that their guard is never fully down. At the end of the day, I am a nun and they are fallen girls.

It's different with Mr. Dolan. Although he is closer in age to my pa than to me, we share a mutual desire to make the girls' lives better in any small way we can, even if that means taking risks, breaking rules, and keeping secrets. We may have started out on the wrong foot, but now, at last, I have warmed to him. More than that.

"Friends," I declare, with a resolute nod.

"Can I send a letter?" Bridie steps out from behind a washing machine. There are biscuit crumbs on her tunic, and she brushes them off, noticing.

Mr. Dolan winks. "I think I have room for one more."

Bridie reaches under her tunic and nightie and pulls out a crumpled paper that I wonder how long she's been keeping up there.

"It's for Lucy. I didn't have nothing interesting to say, but I miss her, that's all."

"We all miss her," I say. "But she'll be so happy to hear from you."

Bridie shrugs, and her uncertainty drags me back down quickly.

"We can get letters out now," I tell her quickly. "It works. I promise. My brother got my letter and he even wrote back."

"The letters come to my house," Mr. Dolan explains. "As soon as they arrive, I'll bring them here. It should only take a few days."

"You can send one to your pa too," I say.

Bridie shakes her head. "Just Lucy."

"Can I write a letter?" Delia approaches from the shadows.

"And me," Rosie asks, with a mouthful of custard creams.

"You can all write," Mr. Dolan says, with a confident nod.

"We'll need to find a way to pay you for the stamps." I blush. I know without counting that there are currently thirty-one girls at the laundry—the most there have been in a while. That is money for thirty-one stamps out of Mr. Dolan's paycheck each week if the girls receive replies.

"Don't worry about the money. I collect a pretty penny for this clean laundry." He points his thumb over his shoulder, toward his van. "Who's to stop me dipping into it for a few stamps?"

I shake my head—not in disapproval, but in disbelief and delight. Mr. Dolan understands.

"Right. Well. I best be off. This laundry ain't going to deliver itself."

As always, he exits through the heavy metal door, locks it from the outside behind him, and drives away.

"Come on, girls," I say encouragingly. "Let's get some supper. I've managed to sneak some ham for sandwiches from the nuns' kitchen."

The girls come alive at the thought of meat for the first time in weeks.

Rosie is the only girl to flinch.

"What is it?" I ask. "Aren't you hungry?"

"What if Matron finds out? About the letters." She shifts her hand to stroke her hair, which has grown out to reach her chin at last. "It's only just come back. I can't lose it again."

I take her icy hands and squeeze them gently. I've long stopped being shocked that the girls' extremities are usually like frost to the touch. "I know it's scary," I begin. "But think how excited your brother will be to hear from you. My brother said my letter filled him with joy. I bet your brother will feel the same."

"He's a lovely boy," she tells me as her stomach rumbles.

"If he's anything like you, I'm sure he's wonderful."

Rosie knits her spindly arms around my neck, and it startles me. In all my time in Ballyvale, none of the girls has ever hugged me. Not even after I place their babies safely in their arms. We usually share a look that says a thousand words, but we never embrace. I hold Rosie tight for a long time. And I do the very thing Tee has often warned me against—I promise Rosie that everything will be all right. For the first time in years, I believe it just might.

Later, when I finally blow out the candles on the dormitory, instead of the exhausted silence that usually follows, I am delighted to hear whispers of letter writing. The girls share my anticipation of a brighter future, and I have a hunch we will all sleep like babies tonight.

I'm enjoying a sweet dream about Matron almost breaking her neck on the slippery laundry floor when there is a gentle knock on my door. I rub my eyes and get up.

"Rosie," I say, when I open the door.

"I know it's late, Maggie-pie, but Delia's baby is coming."

44

Margaret

Although I have delivered many healthy babies in my time at Ballyvale, the birthing room is still a place I detest. Windowless, damp, and hidden in the farthest darkest end of the abbey, this cramped space can't even be cheered up by the cushions I have knitted and scattered on the bed, or the wild flowers from the garden that I keep on the windowsill.

Tee and I work together like gears on a well-oiled machine. Tee soothes and comforts the laboring girl, stroking her hair, holding her hand, and whispering encouragement, while I put everything I have learned from Doctor Henry's books to good use: methods to shift a baby in an unfavorable position. Ways to minimize bleeding. Tricks to prevent or lessen tears. With each birth my knowledge and capabilities grow.

It is afterward that is out of my hands. The time when mother and baby are separated and the girls cry harder than they ever do in labor. I have never hated this room more than when my best friend's little sister lies on the bed, gripped by pain and begging me to make it stop.

Delia O'Rourke goes into labor on the last night of July, in filthy weather. Even without a window, Tee and I can tell that a lightning storm is battering the world outside. Thunder rumbles, booming through any nook or cranny it can find in the walls, and heavy rain batters the roof until it feels as if it might come crashing down on top of us.

The thunder cries all night, Delia cries all night, and at times Tee and I want to cry along too.

Tee fetches some water and returns saying, "It's daybreak."

"She can't take much more," I whisper to Tee, counting up the hours on my fingers. Delia is exhausted, and we are no closer to baby's arrival than when we started.

"She has no choice," she whispers back.

I close my eyes and mentally flick through the pages and pages of medical journals I have stored in my mind. I see detailed diagrams of anatomy and jargon that I'm not sure how to pronounce correctly but that I fully understand how to practice. But no matter what I try, nothing seems to move this labor along. My eyes are heavy, and each time I close them, I drift to sleep. And each time, minutes later, I am woken again by Delia's cries.

"Help me, Margaret," she begs, squeezing my hand so tightly it pinches. "I'm scared. I don't want to die."

"You're not going to die," I say, shaking off my tiredness. "We're going to do this together. You are going to be brave and strong and soon you will have a baby safely in your arms."

The storm outside abates, but inside is wilder than ever. Delia is hysterical. She calls out for her mother. And Linda. Her eyes glaze over, like a wild animal caught in a trap. She stands and begins pulling at the bedsheet, pulling her hair, tugging at me.

"I can't. I can't. I can't," she repeats, as if the words are stuck in her mouth and there is nothing else she can say.

"She's delirious," Tee says. "Help me get her back to bed."

I do as Tee requests and we try to guide Delia to lie down. She thrashes her arms and wails. Her elbow collides with Tee's jaw, and Tee stumbles and clutches her face. "She's lost her mind." Tee steps back, eyeing up the door behind her. "We need Matron's help. We need to pin her down."

"We never need Matron," I growl.

Suddenly, I spot the drip-drip-drip of blood on the floor. The flashback is instant—Anna's pale face as she lay on her bed, crimson blood pooling around her limp body as her life slipped away.

"Noooo," I cry. "Delia, no."

Tee reaches for me, pulling me back from Delia, who is pacing and flailing her limbs about as if she is trying to escape her body.

"Careful, Maggie. Be careful."

I shake Tee off and get close to Delia. "Lie down on the bed now. Lie down."

I am always softly spoken when a girl is in labor. No matter how tired or overworked I am, I am conscious that she is scared and I must be comforting. There is nothing soft about me now. I am barking instructions at Delia. I am forcing her to lie on the bed, no doubt bruising her arms as I pin her down. I am, I imagine, as scary as Matron when she is mad. And I am wholly determined to do absolutely anything it takes to make sure Delia survives this birth, even if it means she might never speak to me again.

"We have to stop the bleeding." I state the obvious.

Tee's face is gripped with fear. She is little help to me now.

"We need a doctor." I keep my hands firmly on Delia's shoulders. She bucks and kicks, but I don't budge.

"Now," I shout.

Tee winces. "I know. But—"

"No buts this time. It cannot happen again. Delia cannot be the next Anna. We need a doctor."

Delia's glassy eyes meet mine, and when I look back, I see the little girl who played hopscotch on the street.

"I don't want to die," she whispers.

I bend and kiss her sticky forehead. "You can do this."

Her eyes roll and my heart all but stops. "Nooooooo." I don't breathe until she opens her eyes again and twists and screams once more.

"It's the pain," Tee says. "She's passing out. Fetch me a cool cloth. I'll place it on her forehead."

Tee's request angers me. It shouldn't, because she is trying to help, but I know there is little a damp towel can do for Delia. I cock my ear toward the door, hearing the sound of collective footsteps getting closer.

"Breakfast," I say, without checking my watch. "Stay with her."

Tee turns my way and opens her mouth to say something, but I race out the door without a second thought. I hurry around the corner, where, just as I expected, I find the girls walking single file with their hands clasped as if in prayer and their heads bowed on the way to the dining room.

I grab the girl at the back of the line and spin her around. She squeaks with fright and I place my hand over her mouth. "Rosie. It's me," I say firmly. "Shh."

Rosie's face relaxes for a moment when she realizes who is holding her, but fear quickly trickles into her eyes.

"Delia? The baby?"

I shake my head.

Rosie's shoulders round, and I think if I wasn't holding her, she would hit the ground.

"No. No. No," I'm quick to add, sensing where her mind has gone. "She's still with us. But there is no sign of the baby and she is in a lot of pain."

"But it's been hours."

"Yes. Too long, I think. She can't take much more."

Rosie wears the concerned expression of girls much older than her seventeen. Some of the other girls turn, curious.

"Keep going, girls," I say, with an air of authority I don't often exude. "Make your way to breakfast, please. Everything is all right."

The girls turn back and walk on as requested, but I can tell they suspect I am lying.

"I need your help, Rosie," I whisper, guiding her aside.

She straightens like a soldier ready to take up arms.

"I need you to fetch Mr. Dolan."

She nods. "Where will I find him?"

"I'm not sure. Outside somewhere, or in the sheds at the back. Search everywhere. Tell him it's Delia. Tell him to take the van to town and get Doctor Henry. Tell him not to come back without him."

"Oh, Maggie-pie." Rosie's eyes narrow at the gravity of my request. "What about Matron? What if—"

"Delia cannot die, Rosie. Tell me you understand."

Rosie swallows hard, and I know I can count on her.

"Go. Now. And please hurry."

45

Margaret

The minutes tick by in exaggerated slow motion. Delia's throat is dry from screaming, and although I try to get her to drink water, she's disoriented and pushes me away. It's a relief when she loses consciousness for a few seconds and is peaceful. As the sounds of the machines in the laundry coming to life trickle down the hallway, I begin to lose hope that Rosie has found Mr. Dolan.

"It's getting worse," Tee says, checking Delia's bleeding. "And she's waking less and less."

I don't reply. I know from my books that without forceps we don't have much longer.

Finally, after a pain so great my ears ring from poor Delia's screaming, there is a knock on the door and I hear male voices outside.

"Come in, come in."

The door creaks open and daylight cuts into the room like a slice from a chocolate cake.

I begin to cry when I see Mr. Dolan, and my composure slips completely out the window when I spot Doctor Henry next to him. My knees buckle and I grip the edge of the bed just before I tumble.

"Oh, thank you, thank you so much," I babble.

"All right," Doctor Henry says, marching into the room and placing his large leather bag at the end of Delia's bed. "We're not out of the woods yet. Tell me everything. What time did it start?"

I compose myself and answer his string of questions about the events so far. I watch as he pulls medical equipment I recognize from pictures out of his bag. He injects something into Delia's upper thigh that I hope is oxytocin. Then he dabs a small, clean cloth over a bottle before holding it under her nose until she passes out once more.

"Why wasn't I called sooner?" he asks. "This poor girl has lost a lot of blood."

His anger is well placed and fair. He should have been called sooner. If only he knew all the other times he should have been called as well.

"Can you stop the blood?" I pant, panicked.

"Sister, please. Hysteria will not help. I thought you were a midwife. I was under the impression my journals would be put to good use here."

"They are," I say quickly. "I'm not a midwife, but the information you shared has saved lives."

His brow furrows. "Dammit, I can't see a damn thing. Why is there no light in here?"

He looks at me as if I am the problem, but I brush off his cold shoulder and ask, "How can I help?"

Without further instruction, I know my position will be to assist him. I fetch spotless steel scissors from his bag. He pushes his sleeves up his arms, pulls on gloves, positions himself between Delia's legs, and cuts. Tee winces and looks away.

He extends an open hand. "Forceps."

I clip the pieces of the cold equipment together until it resembles a large salad tongs, just as the diagram in my books advises.

"Good, thank you," he says.

The tugging is forceful and efficient. Tee covers her eyes and mumbles prayers. I cannot look away, although my heart is in my mouth. The bed creaks. Tee shrieks and a baby's cry finally fills the air.

"A girl," I say when Doctor Henry passes the baby to Tee. The relief on her face is immense, but I know our work is not done.

"The bleeding," I say.

Doctor Henry nods and injects Delia's other leg. He watches for the placenta and I wait with bated breath.

"There," he says, relieved. "Now stitch."

"Me?" I gasp, tapping my fingers against my chest.

"Yes. You. You may not be a midwife, but I'm guessing you're the one around here delivering these babies. You need to learn. Stitch."

He passes me a C-shaped needle and the finest thread.

"She'll wake soon; you need to act fast."

Without hesitation I take his position at the end of the bed and await instruction.

"Yes, just like that. Now loop and back over. Careful, you don't want to catch any of the muscle at the back. Good, yes. That's it."

After, he checks my work and nods. "As good as any midwife I've ever seen."

"Seven pounds and six ounces and healthy as they come," I hear Tee call out.

I glance at the baby in Tee's arms—a tiny pink thing in a white towel, nestled against Tee's black robes. I drop my eyes back to Delia and pull her nightie back over her knees as she begins to rouse. Then I burst out of the room, desperate for fresh air and light. Mr. Dolan is pacing the corridor. His head is down and he's staring at his feet. He looks up when he sees me, and his expression asks countless questions that need only one answer.

"She's alive. They both are."

"Oh, thank God," Mr. Dolan says as he leans against the wall when his legs need help holding him up.

I burst out crying. Loud, grateful sobs shake my whole body.

"It's all right, Maggie-pie," he tells me. "She's all right now. You were brave. You did the right thing sending Rosie to fetch me."

"I wasn't brave," I confess. "I was terrified."

Footsteps clip-clop behind me and I turn to face Doctor Henry. His usually dapper appearance is knocked off-kilter. His jacket is off and his white shirt, rolled to the elbows, is blood-spattered and stained. His hair is slick with sweat and there is exhaustion in his eyes. And yet all I see is a hero. A man who saved Delia O'Rourke's life. I will go to my grave grateful every day for his service.

"Thank you. Thank you so much." I extend my hand to shake his, but he doesn't take it.

"We nearly lost her, Sister," he says, brimming with disappointment. "Why didn't you call me sooner?"

"Matron didn't want us to bother you." I swallow. "But I will call you in future. If any girl needs you, I will—"

"See that you do! Now, she needs rest. I do not want to hear of her out of bed for a week."

I nod.

"I'll come back to see her then. And it might be wise if I were to check on some of the other girls then too."

"Yes. Yes. That would be fantastic. Thank you so much, Doctor."

"I'll drive you back to town, Doc," Mr. Dolan says, breaking away from the wall to take Doctor Henry's bag.

Tee and I watch them walk away before she says, "Oh, Maggie. What have you done? Matron will hit the roof. You've made everything worse."

"Delia almost died. Anna did. I did what needed to be done, to hell with Matron."

I don't say another word to Tee as I turn on my heel and walk back into the birthing room. It smells acutely different in here now. Antiseptic and sterile, like a hospital. Delia is sitting in the bed, poorly propped by a couple of colorful cushions. Her face is the color of snowdrops in spring, but her smile is bright as she holds her baby girl in her arms.

"You did it," I tell her, hurrying closer to take a peek. "Oh my, if she isn't just the spitting image of your pa."

Delia's smile widens. "Her name is Mary-Kate."

I stroke the tiny peach cheek of a newborn girl. "Hello there, Mary-Kate O'Rourke. It's your birthday."

46

NOW

Thurles

Riley

Are we mad?" Sam whispers as we follow the man we met in the bar out of town and onto yet another country lane with no sidewalk. "Who even is this guy? He could be a serial killer, for all we know."

"He introduced himself. He's John Clifford," I say.

Sam lowers his voice more. "Oh my God, this is like the stuff you hear about on true crime podcasts. 'Two Americans killed in Ireland while searching for long-lost relative.'" I hear the air quotes in his tone. "They'll make memes of our faces."

I roll my eyes. "No, they won't. Now shh. He'll hear you."

I glance around at the calm open space. Greener than anything

I've seen before. Field after field with cottage-like farmhouses dotted sporadically about, like in some giant game of Monopoly. It's silent except for the noises of the outdoors—wind rustling in the trees, birds chirping, a horse galloping in the nearest field, a sheep bleating, too far away to be seen but determined to be heard. This is the Ireland of my imagination. The Ireland of Poppy's stories. Lush and untouched by time. I take a deep breath of countryside air and I am revived. And, once again, I am confident that following John Clifford *is* a good idea.

"This is us up here," John says, coming to a sudden stop.

I glance over his shoulder at a gap in the roadside foliage. A heavily rusting white gate hangs on ivy-covered pillars. Beyond it, a long pebble driveway winds toward a cream cottage.

"Is this your house?"

"Me and the missus. 'Tis indeed. The kids are all grown up. Scattered across the world, they are. Two in Australia. One in Canada and the youngest is in France. Lord, her French is terrible, but she'll get there. We see them on special occasions and whatnot."

I can hear the longing in his voice, and I get it.

"Family is everything," I say.

"Ah, we see them at Christmas. The noise of them would lift the roof. Lovely to see them coming. Lovely to see them going, I say."

Sam laughs.

"Right. Let's get you inside."

I hold my breath as we walk through the gate and up to the house. I step in a puddle along the way, and mucky rainwater floods my sneakers.

"Shoot!" I shake my foot.

John looks at my shoes, which started the day white and shiny and are now brown and wet. Thankfully, he also notices me blushing and doesn't say another word until we are inside.

"Hello, love," he calls out. "I've brought some people to see you."

A woman's voice calls back, "Ah, John, I'll kill ya. Who is it, the place is a tip!"

"Just some Americans, Ita love. I found them in town."

"What?"

I glance at Sam, who is grinning widely at the exchange between John and his invisible wife. Soon she comes into view. She's petite and fair-skinned, with wild amber hair pulled back and tied up. She's graying at the temples, but she's fresh-faced and seems younger than her husband. There's a splash of flour on her cheek and plenty on her apron too, and she's holding a wooden spatula in her hand. She points the flat end at Sam and me and says, "Well, hello there. Excuse the cut of me. I wasn't expecting anyone."

"I'm sorry. We didn't mean to disturb you," I say, fidgeting as I stand in the hallway of their house, which is much larger inside than it appears from the roadside.

"Ah, 'tis grand," she says with a look thrown in her husband's direction that says she might kill him later.

"There's good reason I didn't call, love," he explains. "I didn't call because I didn't want to get your hopes up or send you into a tizzy. But these two have something I think you're going to want to see."

"Oh?" She lowers the wooden spatula.

"I'll stick the kettle on," John says as he brushes past his wife.

Ita stands open-mouthed for a moment before she gathers herself and says, "Right. Well, do come in. Will you have a cup of tea?"

"Sure." I leave my mucky shoes by the door.

We follow her through the house and into an unexpectedly large kitchen, with a back wall made entirely of glass that overlooks a garden full of colorful flowers and old trees. A field of horses frolic behind, and I'm frozen for a moment, taking in the beauty of it.

An oven timer dings, and the smell of freshly baked bread makes my mouth water.

"Scone?" Ita asks, plating up the home-baked goodness.

Not sure what I'm signing myself up for, I say, "Yes, please."

John guides us to sit at the round table next to the window. He passes us cups of tea, and Ita places plates of scones and jam and cream in front of us. The food is delicious and the conversation flows, but finally, when Ita can't hold it in any longer, she blurts, "So why are you here?"

My mouth is full of sweet fluffy pastry, but I'm desperate to answer. Sam has finished his scone but remains silent.

"Sorry. That was rude," Ita says. "What I mean is, what has brought you to Ireland? And, well, to be honest, I'd like to know why my husband here has brought you to my house today."

John jolts, and I get the feeling Ita has given his leg a kick under the table.

I try not to smirk. I swallow my mouthful of dessert, take a deep breath, and say, "I'm looking for someone, and John thought you might be able to help."

"Oh, did he now?" Ita says, chasing the crumbs on her plate with her finger and guiding them into her mouth.

I open my bag and take out the birth certificate.

"Do you know a Mary-Kate O'Rourke?" I ask as I pass her the paper.

Her jaw drops and her eyes dart to John. He nods. She swallows and wipes her hands on her apron before she takes the delicate piece of paper from me.

"Oh, John," she says, as tears gather in the corners of her eyes. "Oh, John."

"Do you see now why I didn't call?"

"Oh, Jesus, I do. I do. I'd have had a heart attack, wouldn't I?"

"That's what I was afraid of."

"Oh, John, is this true? Is it really her?"

"I think so, love. I really think so."

John stands up and wraps his arms around his seated wife, who has started to cry. Sam looks at me with concern, and I shake my head. I am just as confused as my fiancé.

"I'm sorry," I say. "We didn't mean to upset you. It's just we're looking for information about Mary-Kate, and if you know anything, anything at all—"

"Where did you get this?"

"My grandma."

"Oh. Let me look at you," Ita says, pushing her chair back. The legs squeak on the tiled floor as she stands. She leans over me and holds my face in her hands. I don't budge. There's something oddly comforting about the way she touches me.

"Yes. I see it. The O'Rourke eyes. The very same as Delia's, aren't they, John? Your grandmother had beautiful eyes."

John nods.

"My grammy's eyes are brown," I tell her, blinking my blue eyes.

"No. I mean your biological grandmother. If you are who I think you are . . ." She looks over her shoulder at John, who is nodding and encouraging her to continue. "And you are, or how else would you have this?" Her eyes drop to the birth certificate. She inhales deeply.

I can't move. I'm not entirely sure I can breathe.

"Riley's not adopted." Sam speaks for me. "That's her mom Stacey's date of birth." He points.

"Yes. Yes, I see," Ita says. "It's a date we know well. You might know Riley's mam as Stacey. But ever before that, she was Mary-Kate O'Rourke, and she was born in a home for fallen girls here in Tipperary. She was adopted as a newborn baby by an American couple in New Jersey."

My eyes whip to John. Vincy and John didn't recognize my accent from some nineties sitcom. They knew who I was the moment I said the words *Mary-Kate O'Rourke.*

I shake my head. Ita's words rock the foundation of my entire life. Suddenly I'm not sure I want to hear this. Not sure I want to be here. I glance at Sam and he stands, ready to take me home.

"You came here because you want to find out who you are?" Ita says.

"No. I came here because my grammy loves me and she wanted me to know who Mary-Kate is. I'm doing this for her."

"And I am telling you Mary-Kate is your mother. You are an O'Rourke. Delia's granddaughter. You may never have stepped foot in Ireland before, but Tipperary blood runs in your veins."

I stand beside Sam, and feeling his hand on my shoulder gives me the confidence to ask, "How do you know all this?"

"Because Delia was my aunt. My mother, Linda, and Delia are sisters."

"It's just . . . it's just . . ."

"Sit down," John suggests. "It's a shock."

I nod. And sit back down. Sam does too.

"I am excited," Ita says. "So, so excited. We hoped this day would come. The day our family is united again. I've listened to stories about Ballyvale and your mam since I was a little girl myself. Mary-Kate is only a few months older than me. My mam always wished we had grown up together."

She places her hand on her heart and looks at John, who smiles back lovingly, and I wonder how often they've talked about my mom over the years.

Ita chews on a nail. "I can't wait to meet her. Oh, John, what'll I wear?"

I swallow. "My mom passed away when I was a kid. It's just me and Grammy now."

Ita drops her hand and looks at John as if news of my mother's passing has wounded her. "I'm so sorry," she says. "Delia hoped that Mary-Kate had a wonderful life in America."

"My mom *had* a wonderful life. Grammy and Poppy loved her so much."

Memories of growing up in a happy family flood my mind. Baseball games with my poppy. Dance recitals with Mom and Grammy. Summers at our family lake house. Thanksgiving dinners with plump turkeys and all the sides.

"That makes me very happy to hear," Ita says, but I sense regret in her tone. "Delia told me herself of the day she wrapped her baby girl in a hand-knitted blanket and green booties and held her for the last time before they took her away. She kissed her baby's head and wished her a better life on the other side of the Atlantic."

"The booties," I whisper, catching Sam's eye.

"Delia passed away three years ago, but she never forgot her first-born," Ita says.

"She died."

"She did. I'm sorry you didn't get to meet her. She was wonderful. Just like your mother, I'll bet."

"I don't know what to say," I admit, overwhelmed.

"You don't have to say anything. We are family. And sometimes families don't need to talk. They just need a hug. Can I hug you?"

"Yes," I say, surprising myself that the answer slips out so easily before I have time to even think. "Yes. I'd like that."

47

1959

Thurles

Margaret

It comes as no surprise that three days after Delia gives birth I am called into Matron's chambers. I'm also unsurprised to find Father Michaels waiting for me. They sit behind Matron's desk like judges on the bench. Their beady eyes are narrow and attempting to burn into me. I am not scalded. I am, however, singed to discover Tee joining them behind the desk. Her eyes are on her hands clasped in her lap.

"Tee," I say timidly.

She doesn't look up.

"Sister Teresa has nothing to say to you," Matron tells me.

I focus on Tee, but her eyes don't shift.

"I assume you know why you are here?" Matron continues.

I shrug, and Matron's face reddens.

Father Michaels brings his hand down on the table with a loud smack that must hurt. "How dare you," he hisses through a clenched jaw. "Trouble from day one, you were. Calling a doctor was not your business."

"She was dying," I say. I'm speaking to Father Michaels, but I am looking at Tee. I am so disappointed when she refuses to look up. "We had no choice."

"Do not try to drag anyone else into this, young lady. The decision to breach protocol was yours and yours alone," he says.

I inhale sharply as I shift my gaze toward a man I abhor more each time I set eyes on him. "Is it protocol to let young boys believe their sister ran away and abandoned them?"

Father Michaels stands up abruptly, knocking his chair to the ground behind him. The bang makes Tee jump. No one else flinches. Including me.

"Your father was my friend. His wish was for his daughter to devote her life to God. I did everything in my power to see that through."

"And is it within your power to decide which young mother lives or dies?"

"They are not mothers," he snarls, revealing his teeth. "They are cheap, worthless degenerates. They are nothing."

I don't argue with him. I know my energy would be wasted. I focus my efforts where I know he is weak: the babies and their monetary value.

"I waited as long as I could. If I left it any longer to call Doctor Henry, both mother and baby would surely be dead. She had a healthy baby girl. The first baby in weeks. I thought you would be pleased."

"I've been in touch with that nice family in New Jersey," Matron leans toward him and whispers. "With their generous donation, it's enough to paint the abbey from head to toe, twice."

Father Michaels smiles, and it turns my stomach.

"Derek Carmichael arrives tomorrow. The baby is a gift for his wife after losing three of their own," Matron explains.

"How nice," Father Michaels says.

"You're taking the baby tomorrow?" I gulp. "But she's so tiny. She needs her mother longer."

"Her mother is a woman in New Jersey," Matron says. "What a lucky wee baby."

Delia is still so weak. The color is yet to return to her cheeks and she can scarcely lift her head from the pillow. But when she holds Mary-Kate in her arms, I see her determination to be strong. I am so worried that taking Mary-Kate away so soon will hamper her recovery.

"I trust you'll have the paperwork ready, Matron," Father Michaels says, sitting back down.

"Of course."

"Good. Good. I'll meet the father at the airport. Poor man will be exhausted from traveling, no doubt, so if we could have a bite to eat for him. Roast lamb should do it."

"Certainly. I'll have one of the girls whip something up."

"The girl who gave birth, I think," Father Michaels says. "Yes. Have her cook."

"Delia?" I squeak. "She's too poorly. She lost so much blood. Tell him, Tee."

Father Michaels's face sours, as if discussing the machines of birth upsets his stomach.

"Tee," I repeat louder.

"She . . . she . . . it was a hard birth," Tee says, finding her voice at last.

"Fine. You can help her." He points to me. "And best make a tart for Doctor Henry, too. I can only assume you didn't pay the man."

I falter. It had never come into my head that Doctor Henry would need paying for his service.

"I'll arrange payment, Father. Don't worry. The abbey are no scroungers," Matron says, glaring at me.

"Good. See that it's swift, won't you? Send it with the tart. And you." Father Michaels points a chubby finger in my direction. "Get any notions of bothering Doctor Henry again out of your head. We won't be troubling the man under any circumstances, you hear?"

"But he knows now—"

"If something like this ever happens again, there will be consequences for all. Do you hear me?"

"But it's life and death."

He inhales slowly and I watch his chest rise. "Don't be so dramatic. Women have birthed babies for hundreds of years without doctors interfering. But we all make mistakes. This was yours. I trust it will not happen again."

"I—"

"You are Donny's daughter," he says, clearing his throat with a phlegmy cough, and my skin crawls. "Your pa did more for the church than any man in Tipperary, and for that reason I will say no more about this business, nor will I send you away. But I will not discuss this again, Sister Margaret. Do you understand?"

I am silenced. Anything I can think of to say will most likely add fuel to his fire. But as I stand before a room of people who treat young girls' lives with casual disregard, I make a promise to myself: no other girl will die in childbirth while I'm in Ballyvale.

"Now," he says, with a joyful clapping of his hands. "Let's see this wee baby girl. I hope she has chubby cheeks. The last few were scrawny things, and it almost put the new parents off. Her birth mother is quite the looker, so I'll dare assume this baby is worth every penny. Tell me, Sister Teresa. Is she a bonny babe?"

"Aye," Tee whispers, as if she is too broken to speak another word.

48

Margaret

The day the American arrives, Father Michaels wears his best suit, and his shoes are so highly polished they catch his reflection. I guess he is dressed to impress, and I want to scream that his efforts are wasted. People who buy babies don't care about suits and shoe polish. They don't even care about people. They certainly don't care about the girls whose babies they're stealing. A prospective parent has never visited the home before. The babies are always taken to the convent and given to the parents there. I gather this deviation is Father Michaels's way of teaching me a lesson—forcing me to watch Delia lose her baby.

When a man arrives in a small red car he drives himself, wearing casual gray trousers and a knitted green jumper, I am rattled. I've never seen any prospective parent dressed in anything other than their Sunday best. And when he enters the home without a wife on his arm, I must protest.

"Surely we are not giving baby girls to solitary men now, are we?" I whisper to Tee as we stand side by side in the foyer, tasked with offering the American gentleman a cup of welcoming tea.

"Hush." She elbows my ribs.

"But look at him," I whisper. "He doesn't look anything like the other fathers."

"Tea, sir?" Tee asks as he gets close.

"Thanking you, ma'am. It's been a long day."

"Oh, I'm sure."

We make small talk for a while, and he seems like a perfectly pleasant man.

"Will your wife be joining you?" I ask coyly.

"Afraid not," he says.

Tee nudges me so hard I jerk, and my cup almost flies off my saucer. I manage to balance it just in time.

He flicks a disapproving gaze onto her for a split second before turning back to me. "Airfare from New Jersey is very expensive, unfortunately."

I study this man who sips tea from a china cup. His hands remind me of Mr. Dolan's hands, rough and calloused from years of manual labor.

"I don't know anyone who has ever been on an airplane," I say.

"Me neither." He smiles, and it's warm and genuine. "Not until I got on one myself."

"You've never flown before?"

"Never. It took a few years of savings to be up there among the clouds. I'm not looking forward to repeating the experience tomorrow, I don't mind telling you. But I would fly across a thousand oceans for this baby."

My eyes narrow as I try to read him.

"You see, my wife doesn't know I'm here. I didn't want to get her hopes up in case the birth mother changes her mind."

I twitch. I can't tell if he genuinely believes the girls have any choice about the adoption or if he is just trying to be polite.

"My wife is a wonderful woman and she wants nothing more than to be a mother. But we've been married almost ten years and we're without a family still."

"So you've come to Ireland to buy one?"

The third and final time Tee nudges me, my cup hits the floor, and the American man crouches beside me and helps me pick up the pieces. Father Michaels's attention is pulled away from a brief discussion with Matron and onto me. His jaw stiffens as he observes the small puddle of tea and scattered fragments of china around me.

"Oh, Mr. Carmichael, don't bother yourself with that. Sister Margaret will clean up. If you'd like to come this way, we have some papers for you to sign and then the baby is all yours."

The man offers me an apologetic look as he stands up and says, "Derek. Please call me Derek."

My chest tightens. Soon, Derek will take Delia's baby and her heart will shatter into as many pieces as the cup on the floor.

"Sister Teresa, if you would fetch the child, please," Father Michaels requests, guiding Derek into Matron's chambers.

"I'll go," I say.

Father Michaels's bubbly facade slips. "You'll tidy this up."

"But—"

He glares at me with venomous eyes, and I continue picking up broken china. Father Michaels closes the door of the chambers behind him and Derek as I prick my finger on a sharp shard, and suck it. I take my time after that, but I'm almost done when I hear a commotion.

"You can't take her. I won't let you."

I recognize Delia's voice, and I stand and toss the china I've gathered back onto the floor as I race down the corridor, following the sound of her voice. I wish her into silence, knowing how badly she will pay later if Father Michaels or Derek hears her. I round a corner and find Tee walking toward me with baby Mary-Kate in her arms. Delia is trying to chase her. There is a splash of gravy on her tunic, evidence of our morning spent cooking for the man who will take her child. Delia is right behind Tee when Matron latches her arms around her waist and holds tight. Delia bucks, but she is no match for Matron's size and strength.

"She's my baby. You can't steal her. I love her. Give her back."

Tee reaches me and I glance into her arms, where the baby girl is wrapped in a yellow blanket and wearing the green booties that Delia spent most of her pregnancy knitting. The baby looks up at me with precious blue eyes. I shake my head, and Tee lowers her own and whispers, "I'm sorry, Maggie. But you know I have to."

"Please." Delia drops to her knees, her energy flagging from the slightest exertion.

Matron holds Delia so tightly, I'm afraid soon she won't be able to breathe. But she still manages to whisper, "Mary-Kate. I love you. Mammy loves you."

It's all over in a matter of moments. Matron pins Delia to the spot. She never makes it to the foyer to watch Tee pass the baby into Derek's arms. She never gets to see the man who will become her little girl's father. She never gets to kiss the baby's head before he places her into the car and drives away for the airport. She never gets to say goodbye.

And of course, it's not really over. Delia is still crying on the spot where Matron dropped her, when Father Michaels appears and takes her by the hair, pulls her to her feet, and drags her screaming toward the birthing room. He opens the door and tosses her inside as if she is a rag doll. Then he opens his hand and Matron rummages in her pocket for a key. He locks the door with a sadistic grin.

"She stays there for a week."

"There is no window," I tell him. "She has no candle. It'll be pitch-dark in there."

"A week." He slides the key into his pocket and nods. "I'll be back then to let her out."

"But food?" Tee asks, shaking.

He shrugs. "Bread will fit under the door, and I saw a jug of water in there. I'm sure you won't let her starve."

"She's still poorly," I plead, horrified that even he could be so cruel.

"She was well enough to scream the place down. Any more of that carry-on and I'll make it two weeks. You hear me?"

"Father!"

"This is your fault," he tells me, and his burning glare confirms that bringing Derek Carmichael here was done purposely to hurt me. To hurt Delia. To reiterate that he is in charge and we will pay if we rebel.

"Poor Mr. Carmichael didn't know where to look. I had to tell him one of the girls was in labor. And you know I don't like lying. Now that poor girl will spend a week alone in the dark because of your actions, Sister Margaret." He tuts and shakes his head. "Whenever will you learn?"

49

Margaret

I try my best, but for the next week there is no getting a word out of Delia. Mr. Dolan offered to take the door down at the hinges, but Tee was quick to shoot the notion down.

"If Matron—"

She didn't have to finish her sentence before Mr. Dolan nodded and took himself back to work in the garden. We all know the best we can do is simply get through.

"What if one of the girls goes into labor?" I ask Tee.

"Well, she'll have to give birth in the dormitory, I suppose."

"But the other girls—"

"Let's take this week one day at a time," Tee says, and it's frustrating that she never lets her disdain for Father Michaels or the other nuns bubble to the surface, even when she is alone with me.

Every evening for the entire week, I sit outside Delia's door. I creep down the stairs once the whole home is sleeping. I bring a blanket and a cup of tea and sit on the floor to talk. I talk and talk. I whisper about our childhood growing up in Thurles, sharing memories and stories that still make me laugh to this day. But I am laughing alone. I slide bread and butter on a plate under the door, but she doesn't say a word and I can't see what she does with it. I can only hope she nibbles on it, but I am doubtful. I even snatched a slice of apple tart for her, but there was no reaction. Sometimes, when I'm drifting in and out of sleep, I hear her crying. There is not a word I can say to comfort her, and even if there was, I doubt she'd want to hear it. I hope in time she will learn to live with the pain, but it saddens me right down to my bones that she has to.

Father Michaels returns one day shy of a week, and I am grateful for the small mercy of twenty-four hours less punishment. He opens the door and walks away without looking inside. The smell is the first thing I notice.

"Oh, Delia," I say, hurrying to her side and trying not to gag as I ignore that when she needed the toilet, she had to make do with the corner.

As I suspected, most of her food remains untouched. Tee enters to clean it up, retching also.

"Come on," I encourage her, helping Delia to her feet. Her smock is filthy with bloodstains old and new. "Let's get you cleaned up."

Standing, she's as fragile as an autumn leaf, and I am worried that the walk to the dormitory will be too much for her. She squints and draws back as we step into the corridor and she is hit by light for the first time in days.

"Are you hungry?" I ask redundantly.

She doesn't speak.

"Or tired? We could get you into bed first and wash up later."

Still she is silent.

"Or maybe a cup of tea and some toast would be nice. Warm you up from the inside out."

Suddenly, she stops walking, and I worry that we've used up all her energy already. I decide that between us, Tee and I could carry her if we really needed to.

"Do you think she's nice?" Delia asks, cryptically.

There's a crackle in her voice that wasn't there before. As if she has aged sixty years in that room.

"Is who nice?"

"The American man's wife."

"Oh."

"I think she's nice," Delia says.

My face scrunches as I glance into her glistening eyes. "Do you?"

"Yes. I do. I think she has red hair like me and blue eyes, and I think when Mary-Kate grows up, people will tell her she looks just like her mother and they will hug and be happy. The way family should be."

"Is that what you want?"

"No."

"Oh, Delia."

"But I hope it is what happens. Because I want my baby to grow up the happiest girl in the world."

I turn toward her and wrap my arms around her much-too-thin body and hug her. I barely notice the smell anymore as she nuzzles her face into my shoulder and exhales long and hard. I wait for her to cry, but to my surprise, she lifts her head and says, "Is there washing?"

"Excuse me?"

"Who is doing my share of the laundry?"

"Oh, don't worry. The other girls have shared it among themselves. It's only a couple of extra sheets or towels each."

"No. It's not their place to do my work. I'd like to get back to work, please."

"I don't think . . . You're very weak. . . . You're not thinking straight."

"I'll freshen up. And I'll eat," she says, trying to be assertive. But the crackle remains. "But then I would like to go back to work."

"You know you can go home now," I say, hating myself for echoing a choice of phrase that comes out of Matron's mouth once a girl has her baby taken. "You can write to your ma and pa and they will come for you."

I know now that the only letters Matron posts are from girls who are of no more use. The girls who have served their purpose and provided the abbey with a baby. Matron reads the letters first, I assume, and if the girl is informing her parents that her belly is flat and the shame is over, then she passes their request to go home to Postman Padar. Usually, a parent or a brother arrives within the week. Usually.

"I can't go home," Delia says.

"Why not? I'm sure your parents will have you back. I'll bet your ma has been counting down the days."

Delia shakes her head. "If I go back, I'm pretending that it's over."

"But it is over," I say, softly encouraging her to realize that there is an end to this nightmare.

"It's only starting," she says. "I thought getting pregnant and being sent here was the worst thing that could ever happen. But I was wrong. At least when I was pregnant, I had Mary-Kate. I had her safe inside me. Now she is gone. Nothing will ever be worse than that."

"Time will help. Trust me."

She looks at me with so much pain in her eyes it makes me want to look away.

"I would like to get back to work now, please," she reiterates statically.

"Okay." I nod. "Okay."

I feed and wash her and stay by her side as we catch the final hours of the working day in the laundry. Matron is pleased to see her, and she praises me, as if Delia's premature return to work is my doing. Later, when the abbey sleeps, I creep out of bed and wander down the stairs, a habit I've picked up over the past week. I walk past the empty birthing room that Tee has cleaned and freshened and on to the dormitory, where I find every weary girl sleeping except Delia.

She sits up when she sees me and rubs her red-rimmed eyes.

"I brought you something," I whisper.

I produce the slightly tatty copy of *Little Women*, and she taps her chest. "For me?"

"Yes. If you would like it."

"I'm not a good reader. The teachers in school said I was slow."

"Why don't you take all the time you need? At night, like now, when you're finding it hard to sleep, why don't you try reading a page or two?"

"I've never read a whole book before."

"Well, I think there's some characters in here that might help. They helped me when I needed them."

"I don't think anything can help me." A single fat tear rolls down her cheek and lands on the cover.

"Try it. For me. It might remind you that there are worse places you can go than home."

Delia exhales and offers a meek smile. "All right. I'll read it. For you."

I hope the words on the page can lift her spirits, even if just a fraction, and help her see that, as much as I will miss her, it is time to go home.

50

Margaret

The next day, Mr. Dolan arrives earlier than usual to collect the laundry, and Matron makes it clear that she is not at all pleased. He takes off his cap and comes inside despite her icy glares.

"What are you doing here?" he asks, horrified to see Delia next to me as we fold sheets.

Delia doesn't reply.

"Maggie," he says, directing solid disappointment my way.

"She wants to keep busy, and I'm keeping close to her."

He nods, understanding it's the best I can do to protect us both.

"Let me help." He takes the large bedsheet out of Delia's hands and folds it with me. "You sit yourself down before you fall down," he tells her.

"Go on," I encourage her. "You can stand if you see Matron coming."

After we have folded and packed several snow-white bedsheets into laundry bags clearly marked for a hotel in Dublin, Mr. Dolan reaches into his pocket and pulls out some letters. He passes one each to me, Rosie, Bridie, and many of the other girls.

I pop mine into my pocket—saving it for later. Finbar has begun writing to me as well as Matthew, and I cannot wait to read my brothers' news as I lie in bed later with a cup of warm tea.

Bridie is barely able to contain herself as she hops on the spot, waiting for the Angelus bell. Sure enough, on the dot of six o'clock the bells chime, Matron leaves, and there is a collective giddiness and ripping of envelopes before everyone is lost in the words on their individual pages.

"Lucy wrote to me," Bridie says, passing me her letter. "She kept her word and wrote. You were right."

I smile. I never doubted Lucy for a moment.

"Look, look." Bridie taps the paper with a trembling finger. "Says here she's moving. She's going to London."

"London?" I'm wide-eyed, scanning the page for the word.

"Her folks aren't being kind. Her pa won't let her forget having a baby with no husband, and her ma hasn't spoken a word to her since she got home."

I read on, picking out words about *a walloping, icy silence, no dinner.* My heart sinks.

"She wants me to go with her, Maggie-pie," Bridie says.

I read the last couple of lines. "Yes. I see that. But—"

"She says her brother will come for me. He'll sign me out."

I lower the paper and sigh. I know Lucy and Joe mean well, but all their kind offer means for Bridie is false hope.

"They won't have papers." I place my hand on her shoulder as I tell her softly, "Joe is Lucy's relative. Not yours. He can't help you without papers."

"What papers?" Bridie's eyes glisten.

"Proof of kinship."

"Can't we pretend? Joe has blue eyes, just like mine." There's a desperate wobble in her voice now, and I curse Lucy's letter. But I curse myself more for pushing correspondence on Bridie when she was so reluctant to write. This is all my fault.

"There's no fooling Father Michaels," I say sadly. "If it were that simple, every girl here would be gone home long ago."

"Fine, then. I'll run away."

"I wish you could. I mean that with all my heart. I'd help you climb the walls if I thought it would work, but you wouldn't make it halfway into town before they'd find you. Father Michaels would set the *gardai* after you."

"But I can try—"

"No. You can't. Can you imagine the punishment when they bring you back?"

Horror flashes across her face. She sinks to the floor and pulls her feet into her chest. "I wish I was dead. I wish I had died giving birth like Anna. At least she's free."

"You can't say such a thing," Delia says, joining us. "You don't really mean that."

"I do. What life is this? My hands are raw from washing." She turns her hands over to reveal sore, red, and cracked palms. "At least when you're six feet under there's no more damn laundry."

Delia lowers herself to the floor to sit beside her. Bridie flops her head onto Delia's shoulder, and they rock side to side until Bridie is slowly soothed.

"When did you get so grown up?" I ask Delia proudly.

"Right about the time I pushed a baby into the world."

"Ballyvale Abbey has a way of making us all grow up too quickly—" I cut myself off and nearly choke on my words when I spot the corner of an envelope poking out of Delia's pocket.

"You wrote to your family," I say, elated. "Oh, Delia. This is such good news. I knew you'd come around."

She looks at me without a word.

My heart races. "They were happy to receive your letter, weren't they?"

"They were."

"You're leaving," Bridie says, dropping her face between her knees.

Delia reaches for Bridie's hand. "I'm not going anywhere."

"What?" I fold my arms, confused. "But surely your family wants to come for you?"

"They do," she says candidly. "But that's their business."

"Oh, Delia. Not this nonsense again. It's time."

"If I leave, I'll never see you again."

Delia's obstinance dumbfounds me. I'm vexed. Befuddled. Secretly elated. And of course, guilty. How dare I wish to keep her here with me, but I do.

"My ma and pa sent me here, knowing they would take my baby away. I will never forgive them." Delia sighs.

"Then don't go home," Bridie says, her head shooting up. "Let them free you from this place and go wherever the wind takes you."

"You could go to Linda and Joseph," I tell her.

Delia shakes her head. "I told you. I'm not leaving you."

"Are you mad?" Bridie says. "I wouldn't stay in this place a second longer than I had to. No one would."

"Margaret does," Delia says, slowly getting to her feet so she can stand next to me. She takes my hand. "You stay."

"I have to."

"Do you? I'm not so sure that's true. You refuse to write to my sister even though you know she would come for you just as quickly as she would come for me. She would give you a roof over your head for as long as you need."

I'm reminded that although Delia's body is all grown up, she is still young and immature. I couldn't rest in Linda's house knowing she shares a bed with my Joseph under the same roof.

"I told them you're here, you know. In my letter."

I am not surprised, but she looks at me as if she is expecting me to be.

"If you want me to go home, then I'll go. But only if you come with me. I told them I won't leave without you."

"Delia—"

"It's up to you now."

"I can't."

"I know it's difficult for you because he's married to my sister now, but—"

"It's n-not that," I stutter, although it is in part very much that. I take a deep breath as I try to find words. The thought of seeing Joseph, married to Linda or not, fills me with butterflies.

"I know you won't leave because you don't want to leave all of us behind." Delia draws an invisible circle around the laundry, as if encompassing all the girls together in a bubble. "You won't leave us here with Matron and Father Michaels. Or even Tee."

I step back as if distancing myself from the temptation.

"So, it's settled," she says, jamming her hands on her hips the way women much older than her do when they're about to make a firm point. "We're staying. I'll write back to Linda and Joseph and let them know. They will understand. After all, they know you."

My chest is heavy. Linda and Joseph are good people. And good people cannot comprehend Ballyvale. It's a place of horrors greater than anywhere their imagination could take them. No one can truly understand Ballyvale until they themselves step foot inside. I didn't.

Delia extends her hand. It takes me a second or two to realize she wants me to shake it. And although I feel foolish, I do, as if we're a couple of businessmen agreeing to the terms of tender. Her face lights up. "There. Now. That wasn't so hard, was it?"

I will discuss this in more detail with Delia later, out of everyone else's earshot. As much as I will miss her, and my God I will, I have to make her see sense. She cannot waste another second of her life in this place. And if I cannot convince her, I will have to pick up pen and paper, and as hard as it might be, I will have to write to Joseph myself.

"Can I take your place? Can I go live with your sister? You know, so I don't gots to off myself when Maggie-pie's not looking?" Bridie says. She giggles as if she's making a joke, but her delicate laughter does nothing to hide her desperation, and I am fearful, someday soon, that the next time I turn my back might be the last time I see Bridie.

"Right," I say, eager to change the subject. "Let's get this van loaded. Matron will have a coronary if it's not driving out of here by the time the rosary is said."

Bridie and Delia stand up, and the other girls scattered in hiding spots around the laundry emerge and begin lifting the heavy laundry bags and bringing them toward the door, where Mr. Dolan's van waits outside.

He takes a bag from Catherine, whose round belly looks as if it might pop at any moment. "Jesus, love. What have you got in here, a body?"

She blushes and, missing the joke, says, "Towels for Slaven's hotel in Meath."

"Aye," he says. "Well, you best let me lift the rest. We don't want you having that wee baby here on the laundry floor."

The girls pass bag after bag to Mr. Dolan and he stacks them into his van. I can tell by his expression that some are heavier than others, and by the time he receives the last bag, he is perspiring.

He slams the door of the van shut with a loud bang just as Catherine faints from exhaustion. Delia and Bridie hurry to help her, lifting her feet and checking she hasn't hurt her head against the floor tiles. I use the distraction as an opportunity to catch Mr. Dolan out of the girls' earshot.

I lean close and cup his ear. "Your joke. About a body in the bag—"

"Inappropriate, I'm sorry. I was trying to lighten the mood. Poor Bridie is having it rough."

"Yes. Yes, she is. But . . . do you think we could sneak a body out in a bag? One of the girls, I mean. Could we manage it?"

"Oh, Maggie-pie . . ."

"I know it sounds crazy. But we've gotten so good at sneaking things in and out—"

"Ah now." He pulls his ear away from my lips so he can look at me. "There's a difference between sneaking a few bickies in and trying to . . . well, trying to . . . trying to kidnap someone."

"Reverse kidnap," I say, grabbing onto the term and becoming more attached to the idea than I should dare.

"We could easily fit a girl in one of those big bags, but that's not going to be the problem," he says.

"But you're driving all over Ireland now, delivering laundry in Dublin and Cork and whatnot. No one is going to be looking for any of the girls that far away."

"What's this?" Delia asks, as light on her feet as a pixie as she skips toward us and I finally see a spark of her old self returning.

"Nothing." Mr. Dolan slices his hand through the air as if cutting my idea out.

Delia scrunches her nose. "It's not nothing," she says. "Whatever it is, I want to help."

"Now you've got the kids all riled up," Mr. Dolan says. His tone is blunt, but his eyes are dancing with devilment and I know he is on my side.

I turn back and notice Catherine is sitting up once more. "Good," I mumble under my breath. "That's good." Then I pull myself to my full height, which is still decidedly average, and say, "Thank you all for your hard work, girls. Best get yourselves to the dining room for a bite to eat. I'll be along shortly. And whatever you do, hide your letters first. Let's not give Matron any reason to grumble tonight, eh?"

The girls tuck their letters away under their smocks and gowns, and uninstructed, they form an orderly line and leave the laundry in single file. Delia makes a move to join them, but I grab her wrist and tuck her next to me. I wait until the last girl's back is long gone before I open my mouth.

"I have an idea."

"I knew it!"

"It's dangerous."

"What around here isn't?"

I can't argue with that. "If I let you help me, you have to promise you will go home."

She makes a face as she mulls my offer over, and I know I will have to tell her more before she agrees to anything.

"We need to get Bridie out of here. I'm worried she might harm herself if she has to stay much longer."

"She wants to smuggle young women out of here in laundry bags." Mr. Dolan exhales, taking off his cap to rub his head, where a headache is no doubt coming on.

"It sounds wonderful," Delia says.

"Matron leaves us to it while she's saying the Angelus. It's enough time to get someone into a bag and onto the van."

"And what if she comes back?" Mr. Dolan panics. "You know she spot-checks. She counts the bags, for goodness' sake."

"But she doesn't open them." Delia winks, and her observation makes Mr. Dolan smile.

"You're a clever one, aren't you?" he says. Then he points from me to her and adds, "No wonder you are friends. Lick-alike, the pair of ya."

Mr. Dolan would lose his job for certain if anyone discovered he was so much as discussing this, and Father Michaels would make sure he was blacklisted from working anywhere in Tipperary. Maybe anywhere in Ireland. I am asking more of him than I have any right to, and yet I must ask more.

"We'll make sure the girl in the bag is packed in the middle, with plenty of bags of laundry around her. By the time Matron discovers there's someone gone, you'll be miles out the road," I tell him. My heart is pounding so fiercely I wonder if it can be heard outside my chest.

"Deliver the laundry as per usual and leave the girl off somewhere far from here. A town. Somewhere safe that no one will know her."

He's nodding.

"She'll need money," I say, almost afraid to say it in case he backs out. "Much more than we needed for stamps. She'll need bus fare, and money for a hotel or a B and B—somewhere she can hide until the dust settles."

"Oh." He puts his cap back on, straightens it, and immediately takes it off again. "Oh."

"We just need to take a few bob before it reaches Matron's ledger," I say.

"You're going to steal?" Delia is taken aback.

It should sit funny inside me, but it does not. I think of all the poor families who can't pay their weekly dues at Mass. Father Michaels reads their shortcomings from the pulpit as if their hardships are sins.

"I'd call it more intercepting." I shrug. "'Stealing' is a harsh word."

"They stole Mary-Kate," Delia reminds me in a gentle whisper.

"Yes, they did," I say, knowing how desperately she needs to hear me say it.

"People are always crabbing about the price of the laundry," Mr. Dolan says. "The hospitals are the worst. They think because they care for the sick, they should get a discount. I never give them one, of course; it's not my place. Maybe I could now?"

The plan starts to solidify in my mind, and I begin to believe we might actually be able to do this.

"Matron would rather offer a discount than lose a client. Ten percent seems reasonable," I suggest.

"Five," Delia cuts in. "We don't want to make the old witch suspicious."

"Five," Mr. Dolan repeats.

"How much is that?" Delia asks, and I realize she has absolutely no idea of the mammoth amount of money the abbey makes from the girls' hard labor.

"Enough," I say. "A ferry ticket and a month's rent, at least."

"A ferry?" Delia says, her eyes wild with wanderlust.

"Yes. If we do this, the girls cannot stay here. Ireland is too small a place. Someone will know someone only too willing to get word back to the abbey. The girls will have to travel. To Wales, most likely."

"Or America," Mr. Dolan says.

I inhale sharply. The idea of any of the girls so far away on the other side of the Atlantic muddles my feelings.

"Are we really doing this?" Delia asks, trembling.

"Yes," Mr. Dolan says firmly.

I have to offer one final warning. "If we get caught, you have to let me confess it was all my idea. Father Michaels is a powerful man, and he will make it his business to see you never work again."

Mr. Dolan sighs. "If *we* get caught, you must agree here and now to leave Ballyvale. I stopped you once. If this doesn't work, you must let me put that right and finally set you free."

I hesitate. "It has to work. If it doesn't . . ."

I trail off and a silence falls over us all. None of us can bring ourselves to think about what will happen if we fail.

"When?" Delia asks at last.

"Tonight." A voice comes from the shadows, and Bridie slowly appears.

My hand covers my mouth. Already we haven't been careful enough.

"It's too soon." I seek out her eyes and find them burning with determination. "Matron could come back any minute—"

"Take me out of here right now or so help me, I will run down to Matron's chambers and tell her everything."

"You wouldn't dare," Delia exclaims, stomping her foot.

"Shh," Mr. Dolan and I hiss in fearful unison.

Bridie lowers her tone, but no less fiercely she says, "I'll do it. I'll tell."

I can feel the metaphorical gun Bridie holds to our heads as vividly as if the cool metal barrel is pressed against my temple, and I can see she is at a breaking point. I am not afraid Bridie will betray us. She won't. But I am confident that she cannot stay in this place a moment longer. If we deny her this opportunity, she will put herself in the ground, next to Anna.

"Okay, Bridie," I say, quivering as the words come out of my mouth. "Okay."

Delia is a step ahead of me, and when I glance her way, she has already fetched an empty laundry sack and is holding it open for Bridie to climb inside. There is no time for emotional goodbyes. But I pull Bridie close to me as she holds the bag around her knees.

"I wouldn't have done it," she whispers. "I wouldn't have hurt myself. But I think I might have hurt *him*."

I know Bridie is referring to Father Michaels, and I believe her.

"Godspeed," I whisper, kissing her on the cheek. I let her go with my heart in my mouth, and Mr. Dolan ties a loose knot at the top of the sack in mere seconds.

"Can she breathe?" I panic.

"It's fabric. She can breathe," he assures me.

Then he lifts the sack, which looks just like all the others, over his shoulder.

"Omph," Bridie mumbles from inside.

"Shh," he says, rolling his shoulder to give the bag a jolt. "Laundry doesn't speak."

"Take me to Lucy, and you won't hear another word," she mumbles through the thick cotton sack.

Just as Mr. Dolan takes his first step toward the van, the laundry door creaks open.

"Spot-check," Matron announces.

The color drains from Mr. Dolan's and Delia's faces, and I can only imagine mine is no different.

"Oh, Matron, you're back," I say extra loudly, in my best attempt to make Bridie aware of this development. I cross my fingers that she can curb her excitement and remain still while the nun counts the sacks.

"What's this?" Matron asks, pointing at Mr. Dolan.

The confidence Delia had just moments ago fades, and once again I am reminded of the young girl she still is. I pray Matron doesn't glance her way.

Matron folds her arms and tilts her head toward the van with its back doors still open, waiting for Bridie. "How are you not loaded up yet?"

"One of the girls fainted, Matron," I say, taking care to sound normal.

"And that delayed you all." Matron rolls her eyes. "Goodness. Well, come on, then, haven't you taken long enough already?"

Mr. Dolan nods and walk toward the van, lifting the bag with Bridie inside carefully off his shoulder.

"Oh, for pity's sake, man, hurry this up. My apple tart will be getting cold."

He nods, places Bridie's bag on top of the others, and quickly closes the van doors. Then he tips his cap. "Sisters." He hops in behind the wheel. The engine splutters to life, and I can feel the pound of my blood in my veins. I watch with bated breath as the van drives toward the abbey gates.

Delia flashes a gummy smile and I shake my head, warning her to wipe it before Matron turns around. She resets her face just in time.

"What are you still doing here?" Matron says, finally clapping eyes on her.

"Eh . . . she's the girl who fainted," I blurt, barely able to think fast enough as I make it my business to close the laundry door and cut Mr. Dolan's van out of sight. "She missed her chores, so I made her stay back and load the van alone."

Matron claps my back. "Good idea, Sister Margaret. You're learning. Discipline is key with these sinners."

I swallow my hatred for her and fake a smile. "Thank you, Matron. I have everything under control here. Why don't you get back to that apple tart?"

Matron's eyes pinch, and I am trembling inside, but a deep inhale steadies me as I say, "Save me a slice, won't you? I'm hungry."

She smiles as if we are friends. "Of course. Hurry. It's best while it's hot."

Matron walks away, shuffling sluggishly.

Delia and I wait until the sound of her heavy footsteps has faded into the distance before we finally embrace each other.

"Oh God, what have we done?" I pant.

"Something wonderful," she whispers, wrapping her skinny arms around my neck.

51

Margaret

It's less than an hour before pandemonium breaks out in Ballyvale.

"Where is the short girl? The one with the big nose," Matron asks as the girls climb into bed, exhausted after another long day. Most of them are asleep as soon as their heads hit the pillow.

"Who, Sister?" I ask.

"Oh, you know," she says, clicking her fingers over and over, as if the beat will bring a name to the surface of her mind. "The one who's always so sad and mopey, like she needs a good shaking."

"Hmm . . . a sad girl." I speak slowly and exaggerate my vowels as if I, too, am searching for a name. "But aren't all the girls here sad?"

She rolls her eyes. My facetiousness is driving her batty, and I'm quite enjoying it.

"The Shaw girl. Biddie or Bridget or something like that."

I don't correct her. "What of her, Sister?"

"Where is she?"

"In bed, surely."

Matron charges toward Bridie's bed, where a sleeping body lies tucked away. She pulls back the sheets and screeches when instead of Bridie Shaw, she finds a mound of cleverly positioned pillows.

"Where is she?" she repeats, her eyes smoldering with rage as she glares at me.

I remain as cool as if she's asking me for the time. I know by now Mr. Dolan's van must be close to Limerick.

"You." She points to one of the girls whom her screaming has woken. "Get up."

Catherine rubs her eyes and slides her feet over the edge of the bed.

"Hurry up. Hurry."

Getting out of bed takes some maneuvering for Catherine and her large belly. Matron marches toward her and grabs a fistful of her long, curly hair. "I said, get up."

"She *is* up," I say. "Look."

Catherine is standing, albeit shakily, and with sleep-heavy eyes.

"She's up. She's up. Now let go."

Matron lowers her hand.

Catherine's face is worryingly dull—even her usually blue eyes. She's past due and could go into labor at any moment, and without rest, she will have no energy to push her baby out.

"You." Matron shoves her finger in Catherine's face. "You know something. I've seen you talking to that Shaw girl."

"Bridie is my friend." Catherine trembles.

"All the girls are friends, Sister," I say, looking around at the dormitory. "Surely, we're not going to drag them all out of bed. They'll be wall-falling tomorrow and no use to us in the laundry."

"I'll march each and every one of them from here to Cork if it means getting the truth out of them. Someone knows where that girl is and I want telling."

"She might have needed a wee, Sister," Catherine suggests meekly.

Matron casts her gaze onto the single chamber pot in the corner of the dormitory. It's little more than an old china bowl, there for the girls to use if they need going during the night. It's always empty in the mornings, but there's often a wet patch on the ground outside the dormitory window, and Matron complains about the smell in summer.

"The toilets should be locked at this hour," she tells Catherine. "Check them anyway."

Catherine pulls on a tatty cardigan, but Matron gives her no time to slip into boots before she's poking her in the back, insisting that she go outside into the cold night to search for Bridie.

"It's okay, Catherine," I tell her. "Just do your best to find her. No one will blame you if you don't."

Matron pulls several more girls from their beds and sends them to various corners of the home and the grounds to search for Bridie. "No one sleeps until she's found."

Hours later, as the sun begins to rise, Matron hasn't given up the search. The whole home is awake. Every nun and every girl are out of bed. Some of the girls have collapsed with tiredness, and I have helped them into nooks and crannies around the abbey to steal some sleep while Matron's back is turned. Two girls are sleeping under the bed in the labor room, two more in a cupboard in the kitchen. I've squeezed the majority into my room and made sure the girls with the roundest bellies got the bed while the others make do with the floor.

My eyes are just about ready to fall out of my head when I hear the familiar crunch of tires rolling over gravel. Matron makes her way outside with a vigor I didn't know she had in her. She flags Mr. Dolan down as if he's a stranger to Ballyvale, one who will whip by if not for her waving her arms over her head. I hold my breath as he brings the van to a stop and hops out.

"Holy moly, Matron, I nearly ran you over. What is it?"

"We've a problem."

"Oh."

"One of the girls is missing."

"A runaway?" he says, managing to look believably shocked.

I wince and curse his choice of words. No one has dared suggest that Bridie might have left the grounds before now, although it was obvious everyone thought it.

"Yes, a runaway. Bridie Shaw. Do you know the one?"

"Can't say I do."

"Short. Big nose. Sad."

"Right. No. Sorry."

Matron huffs. "Well, how are you going to find her, then?"

"I'm sure a heavily pregnant runaway can't be too hard to spot. I'll search the usual roads. It's a long walk into town."

Matron groans, and I can see the sleepless night beginning to take its toll on her. "She had her baby years ago. She's not going to be as easy to spot as you think."

She's not going to be as easy to spot. I replay her words over and over, and each time I feel lighter and lighter. Bridie is just a regular girl out in the world now. She doesn't stand out from the girl next to her, or the girl after that.

Matron jams her hands on her hips and stares into the distance. Magpies fly overhead, waking and singing. Mr. Dolan catches my eye and winks. I turn my face to the sky, already excited to free the next girl.

52

Margaret

Over the following months, Mr. Dolan, Delia, and I form a strange alliance. We learn to speak in a code that develops organically. We never tell the girls in advance; the excitement may get the better of them, and Matron can sniff out happiness at a hundred paces. We choose each girl carefully, one who is healthy and recovered after giving birth, but whose family are showing no sign of coming for her. We have had only one girl so far refuse to leave—Rosie. Her pa intercepted the letter to her brother and warned her not to write again. She is not welcome at home, and the fear of the unknown is too much for her. She promised to keep our secret, of course, but I worry every day that she might break. Still, we do not let that stop us. We've learned which routes are the safest for the girls. Deliveries to Dublin and Rosslare are the most straightforward. There are ports with ferries to Wales and France, respectively, and Mr. Dolan waits for the girls to board the ferry and for it to set sail before he turns around and drives back to the laundry. It is a frustratingly slow process. We can't rescue more than one girl every couple of months without pointing a finger at ourselves. Matron is losing her mind searching for escape hatches, and she's offered a bath in the nuns' chambers to anyone with information. It's hard to keep a straight face when she asks me if I've noticed any funny business. Father Michaels is like a bear with a sore paw, and sometimes Mr. Dolan offers to drive around for hours searching for a missing girl.

"As soon as I'm out of Tipperary, I pull into a field and have a nap," he confided in me recently. "Getting paid to sleep. I never thought I'd see the day."

It entertains me to no end to think of cows or sheep curiously peeking through the van window to find a middle-aged man with his cap tipped forward, snoring behind the wheel.

Most of the girls write within a couple of weeks of arriving at their new life. Delia and I read their letters with a bubble of excitement in our bellies. Usually we allow ourselves enough time to read each correspondence twice, absorbing as much happiness as possible through the page before we take a match to it and burn it. Setting fire to them was Mr. Dolan's idea, and I didn't argue. I know as well as he that we cannot risk the letters being found.

It is not all plain sailing. There are arguments among us too. Which girl to choose next. Delia's consistent refusal to go home despite taking several beatings from Matron for folding bedsheets too slowly. Scalds and slips in the laundry. Losing babies in labor. Hearing word that Mother Superior has passed away and not being permitted to walk out one gate and in the other to say goodbye is a particularly low point that sets me reeling for days. But by far the most difficult challenge is squashing the girls' dangerous notions that running away alone is achievable.

Father Michaels has Mr. Dolan adding a layer of blocks to the already high walls, and there are instructions to let the hedges grow taller and thicker than ever. Tension is at an all-time high, and life at Ballyvale has never been more exhausting. Or rewarding. And there is not a day that goes by that I am not tempted to write to Joseph and ask him to rescue Delia. But the truth is, we've grown so close, I'm not sure I am strong enough to stay without her. And so I deliver more and more babies and try not to break when each one is snatched away.

By the time Mary-Kate is five months old, we have helped four girls escape the laundry. Tee and I have delivered eleven babies, nine of whom survived. And Delia has finished reading *Little Women*.

"It was all right," she tells me one day, while hanging starched doctors' coats on the line.

"Just all right?"

"Just all right."

"Huh. Well, you think I could take it back now? I haven't read it in years."

Delia peeks around a dripping coat to smile at me. "Actually, I thought maybe I could pass it on to Rosie."

My heart soars at the suggestion.

"It might cheer her up. She's really struggling. By her maths, her brother turned eighteen a few weeks ago and there's still no sign of him or anyone else coming."

I think it will take more than a beautiful story to help Rosie. But I paste on a smile and say, "Sure. Pass it on to her when you're ready. But just make sure she knows to keep it a secret."

"She'll be careful."

I nod. I know. All the girls here always are.

53

JANUARY 1960

Margaret

Some days seem to drag on endlessly, and none more so than today. A January chill hangs in the air, and the walls of the old abbey creak as if they're shivering. One of the girls experienced a particularly long and exhausting labor. I was on my feet for fourteen hours at her bedside, and twice I was tempted to call Doctor Henry no matter what Father Michaels says. But it was all worth it when a baby boy came out healthy, with a head full of hair and a fine set of lungs ready to screech the place down. I have never looked forward to a good night's rest more. But as soon as I turn the knob on my bedroom door and glance at my bed, I'm almost knocked off my feet by the sight before me.

Countless pages have been torn from a book. They are shredded and scattered across my bed like confetti. Without taking a single step, I know which book has been butchered and left as Matron's calling card.

"Rosie," I shriek, clutching my chest. "Oh. No. No. No."

I turn on my heel and hurry downstairs, almost slipping on the bottom step. I don't let that slow me as I race into the dormitory, desperate to reach her before the nuns do but all the while terrified that I am already too late.

"Where is she?" I shout, bursting through the door. The girls sit up in their beds, not a single one of them sleeping. My breath catches when, as I feared, I find Rosie's bed empty. "What happened?"

"Matron found a book," one of the girls tells me, shivering, as her skimpy blankets are little help for an icy January.

"It's my fault." Delia clutches the bedsheets around her, wide-eyed. "I shouldn't have given it to her. But I thought it would help her. Cheer her up."

"I thought she knew to hide it."

"I told her. But her head . . ." Delia sucks in air. "It's all over the place."

"Yes. Yes," I say, painfully familiar with Rosie's deteriorating mental state. "Where is she now? Where?"

There is collective shrugging.

"The nuns took her," someone whispers.

"Why did no one come to get me? Or Tee?"

"You were in the birthing room," someone else says.

"I'm sorry," Valerie—the newest mother among the girls—says, as if somehow any of this is her fault. She bounces her newborn son in her arms. Just hours ago my greatest concern was keeping Valerie strong through the safe delivery of her baby. That concern pales in comparison to the worry I feel now.

I don't waste time on another word. I hurry out the door, calling Rosie's name at the top of my lungs.

"Rosie! Rosie! Where are you, Rosie?"

The noise brings Tee, in her floral nightgown, to the top of the stairs, and she looks over the banister with an expression that seems to ask if I have lost my mind. I think the answer might be that I have. Finally, Ballyvale has cost me the ability to think straight.

"What's the matter?" she asks quietly.

"Where is Rosie?"

She shakes her head. I'm unsurprised that she has no idea what's going on.

"She's in trouble," I tell her.

Tee's expression changes. I know she worries for Rosie's fragile mental state as much as I do.

"The nuns found a book. Fiction. There's some romance in it."

"Oh dear." Tee's face loses color. "There'll be a punishment."

"I know that," I snap. "I'm scared, Tee."

"Wait there. I'll fetch my coat."

54

Margaret

Outside, the wind nips at my face like a hungry dog. A generous smattering of ice covers the entire garden, sparkling like diamonds as the moon shines stubbornly in a cloudless sky. Under other circumstances, I'd take a moment to enjoy the beauty of it.

"Jesus Christ," Tee screams, and drops to her knees, and the fine hairs on the back of my neck stand on end.

I follow the sound of her terror and cast my gaze toward the end of the garden. Rosie comes into view, pale and limp and bound to an old oak tree.

"Get up. Get up," I command. "Help me. For the love of God, get up and help me."

Tee hoists up her nightgown, but her legs refuse to budge. I grip the sides of my head and try to steady myself as I take off running.

"Is she breathing?" Tee calls out as I near Rosie, frozen grass crunching under me with each frantic step.

"Yes. Yes. Help me untie her."

A thick blue rope is wrapped around Rosie's waist like a vine. Her arms dangle limply by her side, and her bare feet are as blue as the rope trapping her. Her wafer-thin nightgown is murky with weeks of unwashed wear and cannot possibly keep her warm in the freezing conditions.

"How long has she been out here?" The words tumble out of me as if Tee could possibly have an answer.

We tug and tug at the rope but are unable to loosen or untie it. I notice the red stains on Rosie's nightdress where the rope has cut into her skin and she is bleeding. "Stop. Stop." I panic. "It's slicing her in two. Rosie?" I say, touching her face and lifting her floppy head. "Can you stand?"

She's unresponsive, and her skin is as cold to the touch as the frosty grass. Her labored breathing grows slower and shallower. I glance around the garden for something that could help. Anything. I spy the door to Mr. Dolan's shed left slightly ajar, and his tools are visible inside.

I run.

"Maggie," Tee calls out.

I don't waste time or energy explaining. I fling the door of the shed open, sending it crashing against the back wall. I search in the dim light for anything sharp and am elated when I set my eyes on the blades of Mr. Dolan's shears. I pick up the rusty old things and hurry.

"Oh, you clever girl. You clever, clever girl." Tee pants. "Cut. Cut. Cut."

It's difficult to slide the blade between Rosie's flaccid body and the rope.

"Don't cut her. Be careful," Tee warns, as I bring the handles of the shears together and try to cut through the thick rope.

"Hold it steady," I beg. Tee does her best to keep her grip on the rope, holding it as far out from Rosie's skin as the tight knot will allow.

It's exhausting and my arms burn as I bring the handles together over and over, fighting what feels like a losing battle. But at last the rope begins to fray.

"That's it. Oh, that's it, Maggie. Keep going."

The rope snaps and Rosie falls to the ground. I drop the shears and I'm on my knees beside her in an instant. Tee follows quickly.

"Can you carry her?" Tee asks.

I shake my head. "Not on my own."

"I'm no use." Tee begins to cry, pointing at her leg. "My bad hip."

I stand up and try to lift Rosie, but she is too heavy. I rush toward the abbey, grab a handful of loose stones from the driveway, and toss them toward the upstairs window. It takes me quite a few tries before I manage to get stones to knock on the glass. Soon, I see faces peeking between the bars. I beckon to them. Then I turn back to Rosie, slip off my cardigan, and wrap it around her while I pray the girls understand and come to help.

Thankfully, in minutes, several of them come creeping down the abbey steps.

"Hurry," I shout, no longer caring if I wake Matron. I'm so enraged, I think I could stab her with the garden shears if she tried to hinder saving Rosie.

Delia is first to reach me, and as long as I live, I won't ever forget the terror in her eyes when she sees her friend.

"We need to get her inside," Tee says, and I've never seen her so assertive, not even in the labor room.

The girls and I bend and take an arm or leg each.

"Three, two, one," I count, and with a heave-ho, we lift Rosie and shuffle awkwardly all the way back inside.

"Upstairs," I direct the girls. "Put her in my bed. It's warm."

The stairs are difficult to maneuver, but as we make it to the top step, Rosie begins to moan, and her simple whimpers bring euphoria to us all.

"You're all right, Rosie," I say. "We have you. You're inside now."

We tuck Rosie into my bed, and her eyelids flutter before she falls back to sleep.

"Go. Quickly, girls," Tee says, pointing toward the door. "Get yourself back to the dormitory before you're caught."

"I don't care," Delia says, fury buried into the fine lines of her forehead.

"They'll make you care," Tee reminds her.

"Look at her." Delia can scarcely catch her breath as she looks at Rosie. "She could have died. They tied her to a fucking tree and left her."

Tee gapes at Delia's language.

In this moment, I don't think there is a single word ugly enough to describe the evilness of Matron.

"She could have died, all because she read a book? It's madness. This whole place is madness. We have to tell everyone in town what really goes on here."

Tee reaches for Delia's hand. "People know."

Delia inhales. "No. No, they don't. They don't know it's like this. Like a horror house."

"Ballyvale isn't a secret," Tee says, stroking her thumb across the back of Delia's hand. "It's not talked about because it's where you send a problem when you want it to go away. You, sweet child, were a problem."

"But they don't know how cruel the nuns are."

"Maybe." Tee shrugs. "Maybe not. But I don't see any parents coming to check up on their daughters or their babies. Do you? So long as the problems go away, they don't care what happens inside these four walls."

"No." Delia jams her hands on her hips. "Mary-Kate was not a problem. She was beautiful and special and I loved her. I love her. I'm going to tell everyone in town. I'll stand in the town square, I'll shout it from every rooftop if I have to, but I am going to make sure every man, woman, and child in Thurles knows the nuns and Father Michaels steal babies and torture their mothers."

"You can't," I say calmly.

"Watch me."

The fire in Delia's belly reminds me of my own when I first came to Ballyvale.

"Father Michaels will destroy your family if you go home and start shooting your mouth off."

"I'm not afraid of him."

"I wish you didn't have to be. But you should be. Your pa works in John-Joe Lynch's pub pulling pints, right?"

"Right."

"One word from Father Michaels and your pa's job is gone." I click my fingers. "And don't think he'd work in any other pub. If Father Michaels so desired, John-Joe would spread word all over Tipperary that your pa is trouble. How's your ma going to feed your little brothers and sister with no money? They'd lose the roof over their head."

Delia's fists are clenched by her sides, her temper flared. She is raring to fight. "What about the girls who disappeared? The ones whose families abandoned them? What if they start talking? They don't have families to protect. They can tell everyone what Ballyvale is like without nothing to lose."

"Oh, Delia." Tee sighs as if Delia's head is in the clouds.

I catch Delia's eye and smile, and I hope we are sharing a thought about the girls we sneak out in the back of Mr. Dolan's van. Giving the girls their lives back is more powerful than screaming in the streets to the people who sent them here in the first place. But the cruelty inflicted on Rosie tonight brings new trepidation. Matron is out of control. Maybe it's the shift in the tone of the abbey. The girls are less fearful, now that they know escape, and Matron is desperate to stay in control. The next girl might not be so lucky. Given Matron's vehement disdain for Delia since the day she arrived, I am afraid my young friend is more unsafe than ever. I must send her home and I must send Rosie with her.

55

Margaret

Ballyvale Abbey
Ballyvale Upper
Roscrea
Co. Tipperary
17th January 1960

15 White Water Lawn
Thurles
New Road
Co. Tipperary

Dear Mr. and Mrs. Maloney,

I hope this letter finds you well. I realize it has been a long time since we spoke, and I can only hope that you hold memories of me as fondly as I cherish memories of you both.

To my shame, I must confess that my writing today is not without a request, and I apologize for contacting you after so long and immediately asking for a favor, but I hope when I explain the nature of my correspondence, you will understand and you will pass this letter to Joseph as soon as you can.

As I am sure you are aware by now, I am a nun at Ballyvale Abbey, a home for unwed mothers and a working laundry. My role is to protect young women and girls and deliver their babies safely. I do my best, but there have been losses, and my heart bleeds for the girls and their babies.

As I push my pen across this paper, I am burdened by the sorrow and anguish that have befallen the innocent souls in my care. The conditions at the abbey are beyond what I can bear, and I feel compelled to share the truth with you, and, in turn, Joseph.

The living conditions are deplorable, and the lack of proper care and compassion is appalling. The girls are treated as if they are unworthy of love and respect, and it pains me to witness their despair. They are subjected to harsh labor, inadequate nutrition, and emotional abuse, leaving them broken in both body and spirit.

As you are most likely unaware, one of the young girls in my recent care is your darling daughter-in-law's younger sister, Delia O'Rourke. Delia birthed a beautiful baby girl last year, and Father Michaels took that baby and sold her to an American couple against Delia's will. He sells all the babies born at the abbey, but maybe you already knew that.

Delia is a beautiful young woman, inside and out, just like her sister. But her kindness and compassion for others are costing her her youth, a youth spent hiding behind the abbey walls. You see, Delia refuses to write to her parents and ask to come home. And so, I implore you to share this letter with Joseph so he and Linda can come to the abbey and take Delia home where she belongs. I realize this is a huge request and that I have put you in an awkward position by sharing the secrets of your in-laws with you, but unfortunately, I do not know Joseph's address in Dublin and I am so very desperate to reach him.

I pray you will help me, my friends. Please know I miss you every day and I think of you fondly and often.

Yours always,
Margaret x

P.S. If you choose to reply to this letter, I beg that you do not address your correspondence to me directly. Please, instead send your reply to my trusted friend Mr. Dolan, whose address I have written on the reverse of this page. He will see that your letter reaches me safely. I thank you for your understanding in this grave matter.

I do not tell Delia of my letter. Nor do I share details with Mr. Dolan when he notices the local address on the front of the envelope. I simply pass him two letters. One for Joseph's parents. One for my brothers. And as always, I thank him sincerely for posting in secret. Days pass without a reply, although I cannot say how many exactly as my focus is elsewhere. Rosie has not opened her eyes since we brought her inside. She lies still in my bed like a beautiful china doll. Sometimes her eyes flicker and we all hold our breath, but they never fully open. It's been days without food, and already so thin, I worry she will fade away completely. Delia risks stolen time and a teaspoon to pour drops of water between her lips. It's messy and I'm not sure how much water Rosie's actually getting. Matron has not mentioned her name since that fateful night. She's noticed her absence on the laundry room floor, her vacant spot at the table, and her empty bed, of course, and I wonder if she assumes she escaped. Or died. I'm sure she hopes for the latter. Tee and I can only imagine what Father Michaels might say if he discovered we have a fallen girl resting in a nun's chambers. I can tell the panic of it all grips Tee every once in a while, but she thinks she's hiding it from me, and I'm happy to let her believe that.

Slowly the ice melts and makes way for softer days, when rain clouds hang overhead but never bother to spill and a wind is too lazy to blow. It's still cold, but certainly more bearable. I can feel my feet again at night as I sleep curled up in a bedside chair next to Rosie. On a mundane weekday in early February, two of the girls go into labor at almost the exact same time. It's unprecedented, and at first there is great excitement as they coach each other through early mild contractions. But quickly things intensify, and Tee and I work in the birthing room shared by two young mothers-to-be and not enough medical equipment for one mother, let alone two. Somehow, the years of experience keep us calm and soldiering on. The girls power through the toughest parts, panting and encouraging each other, and it isn't long before the first baby is safely with us—a boy with broad shoulders and a scrunched red face. "A wee dote," Tee says. The second girl is succumbing to the pain and losing herself when the door swings open without a knock and Delia stands flushed and panicked in the doorway.

"It's Rosie. Something is wrong."

"Go," Tee tells me, looking my way. "Go. I will manage here."

I don't waste a second, and soon I am charging up the stairs two at a time. I fling open my bedroom door and run to Rosie's bedside. Her once-icy skin is burning up. Her cheeks are the color of roses in spring and her hair is wet with perspiration.

"How long has she been like this?" I ask. Delia balks and I find myself shouting at her, "How long?"

"I . . . I . . . I'm not sure. I came up to give her water and she was so hot and—"

"Okay. Okay," I say, not sure if I'm trying to calm Delia or myself. "Stay with her. I'll find Mr. Dolan. We need the doctor."

I turn toward the door and I'm about to start running when Delia's voice cracks. "Maggie."

I know before I turn around that it's too late. Rosie is gone.

The next time I hear Delia's voice I find myself in Matron's bedroom with no idea how I got there. I am standing at the side of her bed with a boiling kettle in my hand. I don't remember putting it on the stove.

"Maggie! Don't do it!" Delia cries out when I raise the kettle, ready to tip it out over a sleeping nun.

Matron wakes. Groggy at first. She sees me, then the kettle. Her eyes bulge and she scrambles in the bed.

"Maggie. You're better than this," Delia says.

The bedsheets change color and I realize Matron has wet herself.

"Maggie." Delia tries again.

I drop the kettle, and hot water splashes the floor, almost scalding me. Without a word, I take Delia's hand and walk away.

56

Margaret

Every girl in the abbey joins Tee and me in the garden for Rosie's service. Mr. Dolan desperately wanted to be here, but I pleaded with him not to lose the trust of the nuns. "If they see you . . . if you lose your job, we can't get any more girls out."

"I'll leave some flowers when it's dark," he suggested, choking up.

"That would be nice."

"She was seventeen. Just seventeen." He cries like I've never seen a grown man cry before—certainly not my pa when Sheila passed. I hug him then and he hugs me back. I can tell we both wish our first embrace of friendship was under different circumstances.

We bury Rosie next to Anna. Mr. Dolan opens the ground next to the thriving apple tree, which has quadrupled in size since it was planted.

There is no money for a coffin, so instead, Tee and I wrap Rosie's body in colorful blankets donated by the girls.

"You'll freeze," I said, when they insisted.

"We want her to have a piece of us."

Neither Tee nor I could argue with that. *And there is plenty of fabric around the abbey*, I decided. *I'll tear down curtains if needed to make blankets. Let's see Matron protest now.*

The girls read handwritten poems, sing songs, and cry, and no one dares protest about the noise. All too soon hunger rumbles in bellies and we are reminded that there are growing babies inside the girls, and much as we might want the world to stop and grieve for Rosie, life will go on. But there will never be a day where Ballyvale won't have stolen lives, and for that, I intend to make it pay.

57

Margaret

In the weeks following Rosie's death, we manage to sneak only a single girl out. The work ethic is at an all-time low, and there have been complaints about the quality of the laundry.

The hotel in Limerick whined that their sheets weren't white enough, and they took their business to a mother and baby home in Kerry. A hospital in Dublin followed suit. And a restaurant in Cork. The demand for clean laundry was halved. Although it meant a lighter workload for the girls, it also meant a half-loaded van. It is riskier to stow away in a half-loaded van.

For a while, Matron was timid. She even baked an apple tart for the girls and suggested they sit when their feet hurt. But slowly, with no one outside the walls of Ballyvale aware of Rosie's death, the nuns learn there is no consequence for their brutality. I worry that we have inadvertently armed them with the freedom to be even crueler. Matron has taken to carrying a kettle everywhere, although I get the impression it's for her protection as much as anything.

Delia is ravaged by guilt, blaming herself. Even when a rare slice of apple tart is on offer, I never see her put a morsel into her mouth. I am terrified that if I don't do something, soon she will be lying next to Anna and Rosie. I do the only thing I can think of, the only thing I can ever think of. I write. When the girls are in the laundry, I search Delia's bed with a fine-tooth comb for letters or a scrap of paper where I might find Joseph and Linda's new address in Dublin. But alas, there is nothing. Delia has no doubt burned every last bit of evidence, just as Mr. Dolan told her to. Joseph's parents are still my only lifeline.

"The Maloneys are a strange lot," my pa told my mam when Joseph and I first started dating. "That Joseph is an only child. He should be joining the priesthood, not off gallivanting with our Margaret."

"Maybe the Maloneys want Joseph to choose his own path," Ma said. Pa didn't speak to her for the rest of the day.

I can only hope my pa was right about them, as I fall on my sword now.

Ballyvale Abbey
Ballyvale Upper
Roscrea
Co. Tipperary
4th March 1960

15 White Water Lawn
Thurles
New Road
Co. Tipperary

Dear Mr. and Mrs. Maloney,

Hello again. I trust you received my last letter and that it found you in good health. I apologize for pestering you again so soon, but

I really have little choice. I know Joseph has moved on with his life, and I have no right to ask favors of him, or of you. But I fear that if I do not, Delia will not live to see her next birthday.

Life at the abbey is fast becoming no life at all. I have seen things here that have broken my heart, even more than losing Joseph did. The nuns are capable of both physical and mental cruelty toward the girls, but I never dreamed they were capable of taking a life. How wrong I was. Just recently they dragged a young girl from her bed, barefoot and in a flimsy nightgown. They took her outside into the bitter cold and tied her to a big, strong oak tree at the farthest end of the garden, where no one would hear her scream. And they left her there to freeze. I do not know how long she remained tied there. It tortures me to think of the hours that may have passed with no one hearing her cries for help. We freed her as soon as we could, but we were too late. The cold was deep within her, and slowly, over the coming days, a fever developed and she left us. She was seventeen years old.

So please, if you did not give my previous letter to Joseph, I implore you to share this one with him. Delia will most certainly die if she stays here, and my conscience cannot bear it. Can yours?

With my best wishes as always,
Margaret

58

THREE DAYS LATER

Margaret

The nights are long and sleep eludes me, knowing I've entrusted so much information about the abbey to Joseph's parents. My fear that they might place the letter into Father Michaels's hands is outweighed by my fear that they might turn a blind eye.

As the bells of the convent signal morning and I am dragging my weary body from bed, I hear the familiar sound of car tires rolling over stone. I hurry to the window with my fingers crossed behind my back that I will not find Father Michaels outside. There is no new baby to come for. If he is here, and at such an hour, I hate to think why. I nearly topple clean over with surprise when I recognize the car pulling up to the main door. I could never forget Joseph's pale blue Morris Minor, in which he drove us to and from dances all over Ireland. The memories flood back. The band onstage, the dresses, the smell of the old timber floors and leather shoes tapping to the beat. His beautiful face.

I watch as the car comes to a stop and Joseph steps out. He's notably older now—almost four years have added weight to his frame. Linda's cooking is obviously to his liking. His dark brown hair still curls on top, but he's wearing glasses that he didn't before. He is still as handsome as ever, and my heart flutters setting eyes on him again after so long. He walks around the car and opens the door for Linda. She is just as I remembered—fair-skinned and delicate, just like her sister. Her belly is large and round and I gasp. He takes her hand and they walk side by side to the door. Jealousy pangs. *A baby. Joseph is going to be a father. If he isn't one already.*

I can't hear the knocking on the front door from my room, but nonetheless, I take a deep breath to steady myself and hurry downstairs to greet them. Matron gets there before me. For a moment it is just the two of us in the foyer, and seeing me, she flinches. But soon, other nuns pass by and her confidence returns.

"In a rush, Sister Margaret?" she asks. "Expecting someone?"

"Yes, actually," I snap.

"Who? I haven't posted a letter for you requesting anyone's presence."

"Really?" I shrug. "Well, you must have missed it. I gave it to you last week."

"I did not read a letter from you," she says.

My eyes widen as I feign surprise. "You read the letters?"

She scoffs, and rather than confess, she changes the subject. "Well, who is it, then? Who is here?"

"Delia O'Rourke's sister. Linda."

Matron snorts. "Why? You know a woman cannot sign a girl out. And we're not about to start taking visitors."

"Mr. and Mrs. Maloney are here," I clarify. "Delia's sister and her husband. Delia *is* going home today."

That wipes the smirk off her face, and it's my turn to smile. I march across the foyer and open the door, coming face-to-face with them. We're still for a moment. The only sounds are the magpies overhead and the rustle of a morning breeze in the trees. My heart is thumping furiously and my mouth is suddenly dry.

It's Linda who speaks first. "It's you. It really is you. I have missed you so much."

She lunges forward and knots her arms around my neck, and we almost topple over. I feel her round belly press against me. It takes all my strength to hug her back, and her chest heaves as she begins to cry. I glance over her shoulder at Joseph. He looks as if he's been punched by a memory.

"Hello, Joseph," I manage to say, at last.

He swallows. "Hello, Maggie."

Linda and I untangle ourselves, and I'm about to ask them inside when Matron cuts in. "If you're taking the girl, you'll need to come into my chambers and sign her out. You." She points to Joseph to make clear whose signature she is demanding.

"Where is she?" Linda asks, her face full of revulsion for this place.

Matron shrugs as if she doesn't know.

"She'll be doing morning chores in the dormitory," I say, and I shock myself with how cold and official I sound. "I'll fetch her while you sign."

Linda curls her fingers around my arm. "Is she all right? Healthy?"

"She's ready to go home," is all I can manage.

59

Margaret

Delia is furious.

"How dare you write to them! You had no right."

I sigh. I'd expected a tantrum. "You asked me to, remember? When you first came here, you begged me to write to Joseph."

"About *you*," she shouts as she continues to dress her bed, as if her chores still matter now. "I didn't want them to come. I told you that."

"I have a duty of care. I have to keep you safe if I can. This is the only way I know how."

"But I'll miss you so much," she says, beginning to crumple.

I tell the other girls to leave their chores and fetch breakfast. They are delighted and hurry away, leaving Delia and me alone. Empty and silent, the dorm seems to multiply in size, and I ignore the eerie chill it gives me. I guide Delia to sit on the bed, and she doesn't have it in her to fight against me. We sit side by side with our hips touching, and I place my hand on her knee.

I swallow my emotion. "She's pregnant. Linda."

"Oh."

"I didn't know," I say. "I'm sorry."

"A baby."

"Yes."

Delia smiles. "Mary-Kate will have a cousin. Wow."

"Yes. Indeed. Wherever she is, wherever she goes, back in Ireland she will always have a cousin."

"A family." Delia whimpers softly.

"A family."

We hug for a long time, and finally, when Delia is ready, we make our way out of the dormitory together for the last time.

There are tears the moment Delia and Linda embrace. I finally cry, too, of course. And Joseph wipes his eyes.

"Have you got everything?" Linda asks gently, as if Delia is packing up after a long holiday.

"There's nothing to bring."

"Oh."

"Take care of her," I say. "See that she gets a good feeding."

I seek out Delia's tear-soaked eyes. "You'll write to me, won't you?" I regret my words instantly when I feel Matron's eyes burning into me. Now she will be expecting to read our correspondence. I hope Delia knows to write through Mr. Dolan. Her subtle wink assures me.

"You're coming, surely?" Joseph says firmly. "You can't stay here. Not after everything you said in your letters."

I hear Matron's sharp inhale.

I stare at Joseph and silently plead with him to hush. But he's full of anger and the pain of stolen years.

"My parents gave the letters to the papers," he says proudly.

Matron and I gasp in unison.

"What did you tell them?" She turns toward me, and panic swirls in her eyes.

I exhale slowly. "Everything."

60

Margaret

Sure enough, MOTHER AND BABY HOME CRUELTY is splashed across the front page of Sunday's *Independent*, accompanied by a blurry photo of the abbey taken from outside the gate. Mr. Dolan bought a copy, and we sit on some logs outside his shed with cups of tea and slices of tart as we read it.

Mr. Dolan sets his tea down on his toolbox, clears his throat, and begins reading aloud.

In the small town of Ballyvale, Co. Tipperary, a mother and baby home has come under intense scrutiny following allegations of misconduct and neglect. The home, which also func-

tions as a laundry, was established to provide care for unmarried mothers and their babies, and has been the subject of growing concern among local residents for some time now.

A source has recently come forward and confirmed that the home has been plagued by a series of troubling incidents, including the deaths of young mothers and their infants. Concerns have also been raised about the living conditions, with claims of cold and damp rife and insufficient nutrients for both mothers and babies.

The allegations have prompted a thorough investigation by the local church, which is working to uncover the truth behind the disturbing reports.

In response to the allegations, management at the Ballyvale Mother and Baby was unavailable for comment. However, a local doctor, who wishes to remain anonymous, can confirm he attended a birth at the home and that conditions at Ballyvale are not fit for purpose.

As the allegations continue, the people of Tipperary are left to grapple with the troubling reality that their town has become the center of a scandal—one which local parish priest Father Michaels says he will "see put right."

When we've read the article countless times, we both come to the same conclusion: that we are unsure if everything is about to get better or worse. Thankfully, the article didn't print my letter. And it never mentioned me by name.

"You know they asked me for a comment?" Mr. Dolan says, picking up his tea again.

I don't speak.

"The journalists. They came here a few days ago."

"I didn't see them."

"It was the day Delia went home," he says.

That explains it. I spent most of that day in bed with the sheets pulled over my head.

"They asked me if I could shed any light on the allegations."

"And did you?"

He shakes his head, and I can sense he is crippled by shame.

"I was afraid they'd print my name and I'd never work again."

"Father Michaels is looking into it." I snort, paraphrasing a line from the article. "He's the biggest problem of all."

Mr. Dolan nods. "But he'll have to be seen to do something now. Send the nuns away. Feed the girls. Paint the bloomin' place."

"He needs to shut this place down," I snarl.

Mr. Dolan sighs. "That's not what people want. Sure, the article makes out that people are shocked. But do you believe that?"

"Yes," I say, willing myself to, but in truth I am doubtful.

"Families want somewhere to send their unmarried pregnant daughters. Mark my words, article or not, girls will still be sent here."

I flop my head onto his shoulder and absorb the truth he speaks. "And as long as they do, we'll keep setting them free."

I feel his warm breath dance across the top of my head as he whispers, "That we will."

61

Margaret

I wish I could say everything was wonderful in Ballyvale after that. I wish I could say we sent every girl home and closed the doors for good. But of course Mr. Dolan was right: more young girls still came. People were quick to forget the article. The news the following week of foot-and-mouth disease spreading in cattle worried people far more.

However, Mr. Dolan was also right in asserting that Father Michaels had to visibly take action. He sent Matron to an open convent in west Cork. The nuns there run a small farm, and I like to imagine Matron is worked to the bone and goes to bed stinking of cow dung most nights.

Sister Joyce has joined us in her place. Ever a stickler for the rules, Joyce makes it clear that the girls' engagement in sex before marriage upsets her. Thankfully, her similarities to Matron end there. She knits blankets to keep the girls warm, and she encourages them to read—the Bible only, but it's a start. I see her in the garden talking to the flowers and Anna's apple tree. With time, even the light she once saw in Father Michaels begins to fade. She'd never say it—doing so would betray something deep within her—but with her eyes open now, I think he fills her with quiet sorrow. Maybe even a kind of shame. I hope that someday we might be friends again.

Tee and I run the place mostly now. Once we get the laundry humming again, the other nuns leave us to our own devices. It remains hard work for the girls, and I worry about them still, but when someone is tired, we encourage them to sit. When someone is hungry, we feed them hearty meals. And when someone is ready to go home but no one comes for them, we pack them into Mr. Dolan's van and wave goodbye. If a girl is in trouble in labor, we call the doctor. And Father Michaels forks out a fee. I remind him that adopting families want healthy babies and it's money well spent. He doesn't argue. He never accuses me of being the whistleblower of Ballyvale, but we both know he knows. I sometimes wonder if it keeps him awake at night wondering what letter I might write to the papers next. I do hope it does.

Days turn to months, and soon to years. My once slender young body is rounder now, and gray hair dares to poke out from under my veil. Over time, the home grows quieter, with fewer and fewer girls arriving. I wonder if fewer girls make mistakes, or if fewer parents condemn their daughters if they do. I tell Tee I suspect it's the latter, but after nearly fifty years at Ballyvale, she has trouble grappling with change.

Delia writes still, albeit less often than at the start. I hear from her now only when there is news to share. She loves to tell me about her husband and children. Four girls and two boys. They are great buddies with Joseph and Linda's youngsters. I imagine them playing together in the garden, or enjoying a family picnic. Joseph wrote, too, in the beginning. But he stopped when I never wrote back. Or, rather, when I never posted the replies I did write. It was too painful to be in touch again, knowing he was living the life I had dreamed of with someone else. Linda never wrote. I think out of respect for me, she left me be. I am grateful for that.

And so, when Delia writes to tell me of Linda's passing from cancer at just forty years old, I am inconsolable.

"Go to the funeral," Tee tells me when I share the terrible news.

"I can't. You know that."

Tee rolls her eyes, and her voice cracks with age. "We're a closed order, sure. But if anyone is good at breaking the rules, it's you, Margaret Lannigan. Don't miss a chance to say goodbye for a second time."

"Margaret Lannigan," I echo softly. "No one has called me that in a long time."

"Well, I'm saying it now. And I'm telling you, you have somewhere to be."

It doesn't take any more convincing. "Maybe Mr. Dolan could give me a lift into town?" I suggest boldly.

"I'm sure he'd be delighted."

"And you tell the girls, no one is to go into labor while I'm gone."

She laughs. "I can't make any promises."

I hug my friend and hurry into the garden to find Mr. Dolan.

62

1976

Margaret

I stand on the footpath outside the church and press my hand against the stone wall to steady myself as mourners brush by. The sky is blue, the trees are green, and the air is fresh. But that is all I recognize of a world outside the gates of Ballyvale. Everyone seems to have a car now, and they are parked end to end alongside the footpath, as far as my eyes can see. Women wear trousers that flare from the knee, or boots that come all the way up to their knees, and skirts so short I can see halfway up their thighs. I could never imagine dressing so boldly—I like it. It gives me hope that while life in the home may have stood still for twenty years, everywhere else was moving on.

The church is filled with mourners and there is no more room to sit.

People are spilling into the aisle and out the side doors. The crowd is a testament to how much Linda was loved. Linda and I made our first Holy Communion in this very church more than thirty years ago. We sat side by side, full of excitement in our snow-white dresses, certain we would be friends for life. I am so glad neither of us knew then what lay ahead.

The air is heavy with grief, its palpable presence pressing down on us all. I stand at the back of the church, my hands clasped tightly in front of me, desperate to blend in as just another mourner but failing miserably in my habit and veil. I stand out as a single, lonely magpie. *One for sorrow.*

I see Joseph standing at the top of the church, shaking countless hands as the community tells him they are sorry for his troubles. Teenagers who I assume are his children stand beside him. Two girls and a boy. Dressed in their Sunday best and turned out like shiny pennies, they copy their father and shake hands. I wish people would notice their pale faces and red-rimmed eyes and leave them be. A little girl not much more than five or six is in Joseph's arms. I don't see her face as it nuzzles into the comfort of his neck. Long ringlets, the color of a sunset, hang down her back. My heart aches for the child, who will grow up without her mother.

As Father Michaels takes to the altar, he sees me standing out in the crowd. His pointed glare tells me I shouldn't be here. But I stare back, undeterred. His words are kind, and he paints a beautiful picture of the woman Linda was. He tells the congregation about her happy life with Joseph and their children in Dublin, and he welcomes her back to Thurles one last time to be laid to rest.

A choir sings as several men hoist the coffin onto their shoulders and walk Linda's body out of the church. I watch as Joseph stands with his children, his face drawn, his eyes distant. I want to go to him, to offer him comfort. But I know that would be inappropriate, that I have no right to intrude on his grief, that I have to respect his boundaries. My heart soars when I recognize a woman who approaches him. Delia. The years have been kind to her, and her beauty is untouched by time. She wraps her arms around her brother-in-law and they cry.

As the mourners begin to disperse, I feel a hand on my shoulder. I turn and see Joseph standing beside me, his eyes filled with tears. "You came," he whispers softly. "She wondered if you would. She would be so happy. She never stopped speaking of you. Never stopped missing you. Neither of us did."

I nod, unable to speak. The rush of gratitude and sadness and longing is all-consuming. I want to hug him, to tell him that I never stopped caring either. About both of them. But of course, the well-trained nun in me knows that I must keep my distance and not hurt us all even more. I hate myself when all I say is, "I will pray for you."

I watch as Joseph walks away, but before he is swallowed up by the crowd, he glances over his shoulder at me, and, as ever, his gaze wraps around my heart. I will pray for him. I will pray that his heart heals, because, for a second time, Joseph has lost the woman he loves.

63

NOW

Riley

More letters than I can count are scattered on Ita's kitchen table.

"That's everything," she says. "That's Maggie and Delia's story right there. Even though Maggie couldn't post her letters to Joseph, she never stopped writing."

I'm not sure what to say. I pick one up and notice the envelope is still sealed.

"It's okay, you can open it," Ita says, before turning her head over her shoulder to say, "John, love. Stick the kettle on. I'd love another cup of tea." Then she turns back to me. "You?"

"Oh no, thank you." My stomach is full of liquid, and I can't believe just how much tea this woman can hold.

"Are you okay?" Sam asks, placing his hand on my shoulder. "You're pretty quiet."

"It's a lot, you know. I think I just found out I have a huge family here."

Ita chuckles. "You do. And we're as mad as a box of frogs, most of us, so you'd best get used to that."

"You're Joseph's daughter," I say, and it sounds all accusatory and weird. I backpedal. "I mean, was Joseph Maloney your father?"

She smiles. "He was. And still is. Eighty-seven and with two dodgy knees and I still can't keep him off the dance floor. I'm his youngest. I was just five when Mammy passed away."

We share a look that says we both understand what it's like to lose your mother at a young age.

"I have so many questions."

"I'll bet you do," she says, grinning as John places a fresh cup of tea in front of her. "But all you have to do is read those." She taps a manicured nail on the front of the envelope still in her hand. "Your grandmother was a hero. She saved so many young girls' lives. She risked her life to send the girls off in the laundry van."

"My grandmother," I whisper, but my mouth instantly feels dirty, as if I'm chewing on something terrible, and my heart pangs for Grammy.

It's hard to bring myself to think of Delia O'Rourke as my grandmother. Or of her baby girl, Mary-Kate, as my mother. And yet, as I sit in this lovely kitchen, overlooking a beautiful countryside, I cannot deny the sense of *home* that I feel.

The stairs creaks and I hear slow, gentle footsteps.

"Oh. They're up," Ita says.

"About time, too," John adds. "Well, for some dancing all night and napping all day like a pair of lovesick teenagers."

Ita giggles. "Ah, leave 'em to it, John. Sure haven't they years of dancing to catch up on still."

The door creaks open and an elderly man walks slowly into the kitchen.

"Cup of tea, Dad?" Ita asks, standing up.

"Lovely, darling. That would be lovely."

John grabs a walking stick from the corner and offers it to the old man, but he shakes his head. "I don't need that thing."

"Stubborn as ever," a woman's voice comes from behind him.

Everyone laughs except Sam and me, who feel very much out of our depth intruding on this family.

"Riley. Sam. I would like you to meet my father, Joseph Maloney, and his lovely wife, Dr. Margaret Maloney," Ita says as she pops tea bags into two cups on the countertop and pours in some boiling water.

"They're married?" My eyes widen with delight, daring to assume it's the right Margaret.

"Yes. Maggie and Daddy have been married over forty years. Ever since Ballyvale Abbey closed its doors and Maggie came home. My mother always said that my father loved the bones of her, but that he loved Margaret Lannigan first."

"Who have we here?" Margaret asks as she takes two cups from the cupboard.

Ita points to the tea she has already made, and without the need to say a word between them, Margaret puts her cups back.

"This is Riley Carmichael and her fiancé, Sam," Ita introduces us. "They've come all the way from New Jersey."

"Hello," I say nervously.

Sam reaches for my hand.

"Oh. Hello." Margaret picks up the cups with shaky hands. She carries them to the table and places one in front of Joseph, who seems relieved to sit down. He thanks her with a devoted smile. Then she sits, curls her hands around her own cup, and smiles at me. "And what brings you to Ireland?"

"You do," Ita answers for me, rejoining us all at the table.

Margaret's brow furrows, and Joseph appears equally as curious.

"Riley is Mary-Kate's granddaughter," Ita says, beaming.

"Oh," Margaret gasps, and knocks her cup. Tea splashes on her hand. "I'm all right. I'm all right," she whispers, and I can tell she's embarrassed. "I'm just a silly old fool. Let me look at you. Oh, let me see."

I let her take my hands and stare into my eyes.

"Your grandmother was my friend. My dear, dear friend," she tells me as her voice cracks. "And your mother was a beautiful baby."

Joseph drapes his arm over her shoulder and smiles with glistening eyes, and I get the feeling these people have been waiting for me for a long time.

64

EIGHT MONTHS LATER

Riley

Sam's family has a beautiful garden, but I have never seen it radiate more so than today. The sun sits high in a cloudless sky, proudly casting a warm glow over everything. The air is filled with the scent of summer flowers: lilacs and roses, my favorites, and ones Sam asked his father to plant last year so they would be ready in time for the wedding. The gentle rustling of leaves adds to the enchanting atmosphere, and although I am a ball of nerves, nothing could possibly be more perfect.

Despite Grammy originally loving the photo of the wedding dress I showed her, after my trip to Ireland, I had a better idea: my mom's wedding dress. The big, puffy eighties sleeves had to go, but in a wonderful, lucid moment, Grammy assured me Mom would understand. The silk swishes when I walk, and the lace train behind me is long and elegant. Sam's mom cried when she saw it. She said, "Oh, honey, if only my dress was half as nice, then there might be some chance of Misty wearing it on her wedding day." Then she belly-laughed and added, "Well, if she ever finds a man to put up with her."

My hair is styled in soft waves and pinned to one side with delicate flowers that match my bouquet. I feel pretty and cherished. White chairs placed side by side are filled with our friends and family. The aisle is lined with tiny candles that keep blowing out in the wind. Misty pops up every so often to relight them. She doesn't know I've watched her from the upstairs window, working tirelessly to make sure everything is perfect for Sam and me today. I will thank her later and make sure she knows how happy I am to have a sister.

Music starts and it's finally time.

"Are you ready?" a raspy voice asks as we stand at the back of the Jeffersons' house, overlooking the garden.

"I'm ready, Joseph," I say, smiling up at the old man and linking my arm with his.

Sam waits at the end of the aisle, nervously twitching.

Joseph's pace is slow and steady, and I'm not sure exactly who is leading who up the aisle. When we finally reach Sam, Joseph pulls himself up straight and shakes his hand, saying, "You take good care of her now. She's precious."

"Yes, sir." Sam nods. "She sure is."

Sam is dashing in his tailored suit, seeming even taller than usual and more handsome. His gaze is filled with love, and I think if I don't look away, I might cry and ruin my makeup.

I watch as Joseph joins Margaret, Ita, John, and the rest of my Irish family in the front row. Grammy is tucked next to them in her wheelchair. She's wearing a new lemon-colored trouser suit, and a pretty patchwork blanket is tucked around her knees. It's so similar to the one from Poppy and Grammy's home, but this blanket is newer—

hand-knitted with love by Ita, who insisted she must bring a gift from Tipperary for the woman who raised my mother and, in turn, me.

The pastor begins to speak. I listen intently, hanging on his every word as he leads us through the ceremony. I feel a sense of peace settle over me, knowing that this is where I am meant to be, with the man I love, surrounded by the people who matter most. Family.

The pastor pronounces Sam and me husband and wife. As Sam kisses me, the world falls away and all I can feel is his lips on mine. The garden erupts in applause and cheers, and I have never been happier.

As we walk back down the aisle, hand in hand, we are greeted by our families and friends. My grandmother reaches out for me.

"Grammy?" I say, pausing to crouch beside her.

"You're a very pretty bride. What is your name?"

My heart sinks until Sam squeezes my hand and says, "This is Riley Jefferson. My wife."

"What a lovely dress," she says.

I swallow hard. "Thank you. It was my mother's."

She drifts to sleep, and I let go of Sam's hand to fix her blanket around her. Misty is beside me in an instant, a vision in a lilac dress and matching shoes.

"I'll take her inside, out of the sun."

"Thank you," I mouth, choking up.

Janelle hugs me tightly, her eyes shining with pride. "Welcome to the family, honey," she says softly. "We are so happy to have you." I hug my mother-in-law back, feeling a powerful sense of belonging.

"So, it appears our family just got a whole lot bigger today, didn't it?" she says, smiling over her shoulder at the group of people looking a little jet-lagged but with wide, bright smiles on their fair faces. "Who knew there were so many of you? I should have ordered more shrimp."

I giggle.

"I'm so happy you found your family, Riley. Roots are important, honey. And besides, I love the Irish. They can really tell a story."

"Yes, they really can."

"Go. Join them. I'll chat with all these other boring guests."

I know Janelle is kidding. She loves Sam and my friends and coworkers, and she will talk and talk today until she loses her voice, enjoying every moment of hosting.

"Thank you so much for coming," I say softly as I reach Ita and John.

They stand up and throw their arms around me. Then Margaret and Joseph hug me, followed by Ita's brothers and sisters and cousins—Delia's grown children, who were overjoyed to finally be in touch with their American niece. They have plenty of children each. When I counted, it turned out I have nineteen first cousins, many of whom are also here today.

Sam says, "You know, Mom is right. We definitely need more shrimp. Your crazy family is even bigger than mine."

As the sun begins to set, the garden is transformed into a magical wonderland with twinkling lights and candles casting a warm glow. Sam and I dance our first dance surrounded by our families and friends, and I wonder if someday we will have children of our own. I hope so. I hope we summer in Ireland, complaining about the weather and enjoying every moment of a place that is now such a part of us.

Epilogue

1980

Margaret

The last baby born at Ballyvale is a girl. She arrives shortly after midnight on the twenty-second of August, 1980. Twenty-one years and twenty-one days after Mary-Kate O'Rourke was born. Ten days later, her mother leaves in Mr. Dolan's van. She sits in the front seat next to him and cradles her newborn daughter in her arms. She looks over her shoulder and waves as my dear friend escorts the last fallen girl out of the gates.

Tee, Joyce, and I stand shoulder to shoulder at the door of the home and wave back. The sun shines in our eyes, but we stay put, none of us quite ready to move yet. Father Michaels's sudden passing from a heart attack last year came as a shock to most people, but not to those of us who knew him best. Tee said he hadn't been himself since the article about Ballyvale in the papers all those years ago, and I like to think she's right. That finally his conscience got the better of him.

Within a month, his replacement, Father Edgeworth—a tall, thin thirtysomething from Mayo—sold the abbey to a fancy property developer. They're turning the place into a hotel, last I heard. Father Edgeworth agreed to stall the sale until every last girl was safely out of Ballyvale—either reunited with her family or set up with a new life somewhere far from here.

"Your brother Colm would be fierce disappointed in me if I didn't do right by these young ladies," he said, shaking my hand the day we met. "We were in the seminary together. Before he left to get married. Lovely couple."

I can't wait to visit my brothers and meet their wives. I have a week before I start my midwifery training. The course has already started, but because of my experience, they made an exception and allowed me to join midterm. Who knows, maybe someday I'll go on and study medicine just like Doctor Henry. *Doctor Margaret*, I think, and already it fits much better than Sister Margaret ever did. The possibilities ahead feel endless, and excitement fills me up as I finally turn around to face the closed doors, place a key in a small white envelope, and slide it under the doormat.

"That's it?" Tee asks, staring at the mat, worn-out from countless feet arriving at Ballyvale over the years.

"That's it," I say. "Father Edgeworth said to leave the key under the mat. He'll come by with the estate agent later and, well . . ."

"Well, now we leave," Joyce says.

Joyce and Tee are joining a small convent in Wexford in need of a Mother Superior. Joyce was elated when she was offered the role, and I am happy she is fulfilling a lifelong dream.

"It's an open order, so I can visit my sisters," she says. "They're all grown up now and married with children."

Joyce never said, but I know it disappointed her that none of her sisters followed in her footsteps and joined the nuns.

"My family are long passed," Tee says, "but it'll be nice to take a stroll around town and whatnot. I might even try my hand at bingo." She chuckles at the thought of it.

"And with Mr. Dolan retired, he can visit plenty," I add.

"Aye." Tee smiles. "He'll be back for us soon. Are you sure you won't change your mind about a lift?"

I shake my head. After more than twenty years I am finally going to pick up my suitcase, the same tatty thing that I arrived with, walk out the gates of Ballyvale, and never look back. Tee and I hug for a long time. Joyce favors mutual nodding. And none of us say the word *goodbye*. Instead, I promise to visit them once they're settled. I leave before Mr. Dolan returns and I change my mind about a lift.

My feet hurt by the time I reach town. And when I finally stop outside a small farmhouse at the end of a country lane, I have blisters, but I feel a sudden burst of energy when I see him.

Joseph is on his knees in the garden, weeding. A young girl skips next to him with a colorful rope; she counts out loud, but I can't hear her above the music, a song I don't recognize with a deep drumbeat, coming from an upstairs window. I assume one of his older children is the culprit. It is a picture of mundane family life, and it is beautiful. Delia told me in her letters that Joseph moved back to Thurles after Linda's passing; she even included a hand-drawn map so someday I could find his house. Today is someday, and I haven't told any of them I am coming.

The girl is first to spot me. She drops her skipping rope, smiles at me, and says, "Daddy, someone is here."

Joseph glances over his shoulder, and his expression when he sees me tells me it's a good thing he's already on his knees or he might have dropped to the ground. His face falls into his hands and his shoulders shudder. It takes him some time to finally look up and stand, and all the while, I don't budge.

"Who is it?" the girl asks, tugging on his jumper.

"Someone I didn't think I'd ever see again," he says, his voice cracking.

Satisfied with his answer, she goes back to skipping. Closer to her, I notice she wasn't counting but chanting—a nursery rhyme. "One for sorrow, two for joy," she chants to the beat of her jumps. "Three for a girl, four for a boy." She doesn't know the rest and repeats the start.

"I was hoping you'd come," he says. "I heard they sold that horrible place. But Delia said the nuns are moving. To Wexford."

"They are." I nod. "They need a new home."

"And you?"

A lump forms in my throat and presses against my voice. Joseph's hair is thinning on top, and his sky-blue eyes are cloudier now. He smells of summer grass instead of the woody cologne I remember, and yet, as we stand face-to-face, he is just a boy throwing stones against my bedroom window and promising to marry me.

Tentatively he steps forward, his eyes burning into mine, and I nod. He scoops me into his mucky, grassy arms and whispers softly, "Welcome home, my Margaret."

Author's Note

In many ways, writing this author's note has been more difficult than writing the novel itself. I hope, by the time you reach the end, you'll understand why.

While this is only my second attempt at historical fiction, I've been writing published novels for almost a decade now. Each one begins in the same way: a spark. A throwaway comment from a friend. Something I overheard in a café. A news headline. A podcast discussion. A small flicker of something that lights a fire.

This novel, though, marks a slight deviation from that pattern. The spark this time didn't come from eavesdropping or scrolling through Wikipedia. It came from my own words—shared on X (though I do miss when it was simply called Twitter. Can we rewind?).

I posted a tweet: a little bird singing into the void. It read, verbatim:

It's my birthday! It's also my daughter's 21st birthday today. I was a teen mam and people said my life was ruined. Today, I'm a published author (with big news coming soon). She's a law student at her dream uni. I think people were wrong, eh?

The post included a photo of a bottle of champagne and a first edition of *The Hunchback of Notre Dame*—three volumes, one story. A birthday gift from my husband. Do I speak or read French? Absolutely not. Do I treasure those books? The answer is obvious.

And the BIG news?

A publishing contract with a dream publisher (*cough cough*, they're publishing this book too).

The tweet blew up. Thousands of likes, hundreds of kind and beautiful comments. But, as always online, there were a few that weren't so kind. One in particular stood out:

The Magdalene Laundries would have put manners on you.

Three things happened: 1) I blocked them. End of; 2) I found myself trying to defend something I wasn't promoting—teen pregnancy. Don't come at me. My daughter is the best of me; and 3) I felt something spark. A story. Sort of.

(And if you're reading this before you've read the book—warning! There are spoilers ahead.)

I was already familiar with the Magdalene laundries—every adult in Ireland is, to some degree. But a quick google while sipping my champagne taught me even more. Forgive me if my memory paraphrases.

The Magdalene laundries were a network of institutions, run by Catholic religious orders, that operated in Ireland for decades. Though their purpose was supposed to be the rehabilitation of "fallen women" (a term as offensive as it is degrading), they became places of forced labor and suffering.

The women—and I use that term loosely, as many were teenagers or in their early twenties—were made to work in grueling laundry services, often for hospitals, businesses, and the state. Their lives were governed by silence, censorship, and religious rule. Many never left.

These places operated like prisons, yet those within had committed no crime. Families, priests, even the courts could have a girl interned—no trial, no due process.

It wasn't lost on me, the irony of sipping champagne beside my husband—my daughter's father—while reading how differently our lives could have played out had I been born just a few decades earlier. Still, I hesitated. This story had been told, and told powerfully, by some of Ireland's finest writers. Who was I to try?

So I shelved the idea and focused on a contemporary novel instead.

Until months later, during brunch with my mam, a new comment popped up on my X thread. I can't remember what it said, but it sparked a conversation I'll never forget.

"Horrible places," Mam said, the pain in her expression unmistakable. "But I feel sorry for the nuns, too."

I was ready to argue, armed with everything the internet had told me. But she continued:

"Shipped off to the convent on their parents' vocation."

"Hold on," I said. "What do you mean?"

"It wasn't just pregnant girls who were prisoners. Young women were forced to become nuns, no matter how much they protested."

And there it was. The spark. And no amount of googling would help me now.

My mother became my most valuable research tool. She remembers everything—sadly.

She told me how, in the 1950s, she loved nothing more than playing hopscotch with her sister. A neighbor, a woman in her twenties, often joined them. She'd read stories, give hugs, gossip . . . until one day, she vanished. No one ever spoke of her again.

Years later, long after my mam had married and moved away, she learned the girl had reappeared, for her father's funeral. She'd spent over thirty-five years in a closed-order convent just a few miles up the road.

While the Magdalene orders weren't cloistered—the nuns could come and go as they pleased—I made the creative decision to blend these stories together. Ballyvale Convent and the Sisters of Penance are fictional, but based on real cloistered orders. The Ballyvale Home for Fallen Girls was inspired by two real institutions: Sean Ross Abbey in Roscrea, Co. Tipperary, and the Bon Secours Mother and Baby Home in Tuam, Co. Galway.

My research into Tuam was at times unbearable. If parts of this book are harrowing to read, know that much of what I uncovered was too distressing to even include.

As a writer, I try to balance light with dark. And amid the darkness, I found stories of immense courage.

One such story came from Galway: Ena McEntee, a laywoman working at the local Magdalene laundry, was horrified by what she saw. She shared the stories with her husband and teenage sons. Together, they devised a plan. Ena and her sons would smuggle girls into the back of a van driven by her husband. They rescued fifteen. Ena lost her job, but she and her family changed lives.

This became the seed for Margaret, Mr. Dolan, and Delia's act of defiance in the novel. I reimagined it to suit the narrative, but the heart of Ena's story—the bravery—remains unchanged.

Though the novel opens in Riley's timeline, I always knew this was Margaret's story. I chose her name with conviction. Of Greek origin, it means *pearl*. Margaret Lannigan—a gem. But that's not the reason I selected it. I chose it for its common diminutive: *Maggie*. Girls and young women confined to the laundries were often called "Maggies"—a derogatory nickname that marked them as outcasts. You may have noticed that no one refers to Margaret as Maggie in the novel until she enters the laundry. "Sheila tried *Maggie* once, and Pa gave her a clip around the ear and told her to have respect." If you missed it, that's okay. It's not a plot device and it doesn't serve to move the story forward. It's simply a gentle thread of meaning, my personal acknowledgment that pearls shine even in darkness. Though Margaret wasn't one of the expectant mothers in the laundries, she was no less a victim of an abusive system. She couldn't single-handedly dismantle a corrupt culture, but I wanted to create a woman who took every opportunity to resist, in her own quiet, steadfast way.

And finally—the magpies.

This was born from nothing more than my obsession with the nursery rhyme. A single magpie can ruin my whole day unless I see his mate. "One for sorrow, two for joy . . ." And always, in my imagination, there were seven magpies in the laundry gardens. They flew away only in 1996, when the last laundry closed its doors.

On February 19, 2013, Irish Taoiseach Enda Kenny issued a historic and deeply moving apology to the women who suffered in these institutions. He said, "We forgot you. Or if we thought of you at all, we did so in untrue and offensive stereotypes."

A fund was established to support survivors. It still exists today.

I want to be very clear: this novel is not intended as an attack on the Catholic Church or the faith of those who follow it. Rather, it is a reckoning with the culture of silence, complicity, and unchecked power that allowed cruelty and abuse to hide behind a sacred curtain. The church, in this case, became the stage—but the real villains were both those who inflicted the abuse and those who turned a blind eye when they had the opportunity and privilege to speak up.

So, to revisit my opening sentences of this author's note, why was writing it so difficult? Well, I think because it is always difficult to hold a mirror up to oneself and really, truly examine the reflection. This novel feels deeply personal for me. Becoming a mother while I was little more than a child myself was hard. But I wouldn't change it for the world. In the coming months, I look forward to my darling daughter's university graduation, and by the time this book hits the shelves, I will most likely have written another. Maybe two. And none of this would have happened were it not for the love and support of my husband and my family. If only the "Maggies" had had a similar support network then, how different history would have been.

Acknowledgments

This book took nine months to research. Ironic? Absolutely. But I knew by then I had to stop. Truthfully, I could have kept going much, much longer, but I'm not sure my heart could have borne it.

As ever, my wonderful agent was there, encouraging me every step of the way. From links to inspirational podcasts and newspaper articles to brainstorming calls that inevitably ended in laughter and complaints about the weather—we're Irish and English, respectively; it's what we do. ☺ Dearest Hannah, thank you for it all.

To my brilliant editor, Hannah—thank you for reminding me to breathe when it's not quite perfect, and for reassuring me that we'd get there. I always look forward to our next Zoom (mostly for the Disney chat, although the book talk's fun, too. **wink, wink**). *Thank you for loving this story as much as I do.*

To Sarah Schlick—thank you for keeping me informed, updated, and steady throughout every step of the publishing journey.

To Polly Watson—thank you for your ever kind and considered copyedit. I'm beyond grateful that you're far better at maths than I am. I solemnly swear I will never write another pregnancy into a novel again . . . never mind several #time #whatwasithinking.

To Nancy Tonik for taking such care with this manuscript—I am so grateful.

To Heather Waters, Jessica Roth, Lucy Nalen, and the wider team at Gallery—thank you for your passion, your energy, and your determination to champion my books. I am so lucky to have you in my corner.

To my dear friend and fellow writer Caroline Finnerty—at this point, I feel I owe you more of an apology than a thank-you. For listening to me go on (and on, and on) about this book, and for somehow still not blocking my number . . . thank you!

Mam—your stories of growing up in a conservative and very different Ireland to the one I know and love have always amazed and inspired me. Your knowledge was invaluable. Any missteps or misrepresentations are entirely my doing.

To my friends and family—thank you for being you.

Sophie, Ciarán, Aaron, Conor, and Chloe—being your mam is the greatest joy of my life. Your happiness is my happiness. The rest is just icing (although I *do love cake*).

And to Brian—for everything, and for always ♥.